THE FAR LANDS

D0807283

JAMES NORMAN HALL

The Far Lands

Mutual Publishing

Reprinted by Mutual Publishing in mass market format 2001
ISBN 1-56647-513-9

Cover illustration by Herb Kāne
Cover design by Sistenda Yim

Mutual Publishing
1215 Center Street, Suite 210
Honolulu, Hawaii 96816
Ph: (808) 732-1709
Fax: (808) 734-4094
email: mutual@lava.net
www.mutualpublishing.com

Printed in Australia

To my wife
SARAH TERAIRÉIA WINCHESTER
whose maternal ancestors of centuries ago
sailed the Great Sea of Kiwa

Contents

Te-Moana-Nui-a-Kiwa

Mother of Oceans! Changeless, timeless Sea . . .
(Until our time. Who knows if that will be
Henceforth? If modern madmen with the power
Of demon gods may not, in one brief hour
Bring death and desolation to all being
Within Thy realm?): grant me a way of seeing
Men of another Age, upon the quest
Never ended, never despaired of; guessed,
Dreamed of, hoped for, ages long ago;
Dreamed of, hoped for, in the days we know.
Tavi-the-Jester's phantom lands still rise
And fade to empty sea before men's eyes.
Lest we grow sick at heart from hope deferred
May we, too, hear the call that Maui heard.

PROLOGUE

In the austral summer of the year 1921, I was voyaging in a sixty-ton trading schooner amongst "The Cloud of Islands," more commonly known as the Tuamotu Archipelago: seventy-four lagoon islands scattered over a thousand miles of the eastern Pacific below the equator; the most distant from any continent of all the islands on the globe.

I was then a newcomer in the Pacific and fell under an island enchantment that remains to this day. Unknowingly, I had, it seems, been preparing from the days of a far-inland childhood on the prairies of Iowa for just this result. My first view of any ocean — the north Atlantic — came as a young man. That was a memorable experience but not to be compared with the later one when, shortly after the end of World War I, traveling through the solitudes of that Mother of Oceans, the Pacific, I saw my first lagoon island. The sight of any remote island in whatever latitude, though it be no more than a bare rock, still gives me something of a boy's feeling of wonder and delight, tropical islands above all others. Their attraction never wanes, nor, I imagine, is it likely to after this distance of time.

On the occasion mentioned it was my good fortune to be traveling with Captain Winnie Brander, whose father's establishment, the House of Brander, had once been the only important commercial and trading company in the eastern Pacific, with interests extending as far as Rapa-Nui, the Easter Island of the mysterious stone images. In one of his letters, dated February 6th, 1891, Mr. Henry Adams — who, with his friend, John La Farge, the artist, was then sojourning on the island of Tahiti — has this to say of the Brander family:

The nine Brander children are now grown; five of them are handsome young men. Their father was the great merchant in these seas. His plantations produced millions of coconuts; his pearl fisheries sent tons of shell to Europe and his income was very great. . . . He sent all of his sons to Europe to be educated as royalties, and the boys duly coronetted their handkerchiefs and their gladstone bags and bore themselves so as to do credit to their uncle-cousin, the King of Tahiti. They were English subjects and Scotch gentlemen. Then their father died and his estate, when settled, shrank to the modest amount of a million dollars. The widow took half, leaving half-a-million to be divided equally among nine children. The boys who were educated on the scale of a million apiece, were reduced to practically nothing.

When I first came to Tahiti, in 1920, two of the Brander sons, Norman and Winnie, were still living there, and a few years later they were joined by their older brother, Arthur, who had long been absent in the United States, Europe and elsewhere. They were, as Mr. Adams had said, English subjects and Scotch gentlemen, but "Captain Winnie," as everyone called him, was a true Polynesian in character. He must have received a greater share of his mother's island blood: that of the old *ariki,* the class of chiefs and kings. The remnants of the Brander fortune had long since vanished and he earned a modest living as an independent trader whose home was the broad-beamed, weather-beaten little vessel in which I was traveling.

Captain Winnie had the dignity, courtesy and graciousness of manner of the ancient Polynesian aristocracy, although in appearance he looked more like a European than an islander. Seeing him at night, stretched out in his deck chair, his florid face with its finely modeled, high-beaked nose revealed by the light of a lantern hanging nearby, I could imagine that a white-haired Roman senator of the days of the Republic was sitting beside me, dressed in a Polynesian waistcloth instead of a toga, his brown feet bare of the sandals he should have worn. He was the perfection of hosts and companions, the kind I cherish above all others: one to enjoy long silences with, no shadow of embarrassment felt on either side. We would sit without speaking for half-hours at a time, but I always felt in complete wordless rapport with him. He had inherited nothing of his father's commercial abilities or interests. One would have said that his voyages throughout eastern Polynesia were purely for his own pleasure and that of any guest who chanced to be with him.

On this particular afternoon we were beating up against a fresh southeast wind toward a lagoon island, the tops of its coconut palms barely visible above the horizon. The schooner was equipped with an ancient Fairbanks-Morse engine, but Captain Winnie was compelled to be frugal with gasoline and the engine was used only for entering or leaving the lagoons of those islands that had a passage to the sea, or for standing off and on beyond the reefs of those which had not. The island we were approaching had such a pass, but Winnie told me that because of several coral shoals above the surface of the water it was a difficult one to enter at night. "But they will have seen us coming," he added. "The chief will have men alongshore to light us in."

The breeze died away after sunset when we were still some distance out, and it was deep night before the native engineer got the Fairbanks-Morse to running. The quiet *katuck-katuck-katuck* of the exhaust seemed only to deepen the silence of mid-ocean. As we closed with the land, the passage could be clearly seen — a wide strip of starlit water. A moment later came bursts of flame from either side, revealing men, naked save for their loincloths, holding flares of dry palm fronds above their heads. The ruddy light was reflected with spectacular effect from the surf piling over the reefs, the quiet water of the passage, and from their brown bodies which stood out in clear relief against the dark background of the land. No hail was given either from the schooner or the men on shore as we entered the passage, and as soon as we were safely through, the torches were extinguished and the men holding them vanished, as though they had been given reality for the moment only, and for that particular service.

Except for the passage the lagoon was completely enclosed by the reef, threaded at intervals with dark ribbons of land, some of them miles in extent. This was one of the larger atolls with a lagoon thirty miles long by twenty broad in the widest part, and the islet-dotted reef stretched away on either side as far as the eye could reach. We anchored a short distance from the beach of one of these islets where a few dim lights revealed the site of the village. The thunder of the surf along the outer reefs seemed only to deepen the silence which the land enclosed; it could not disturb the peace within them, as flawless as the surface of the lagoon, bright with the reflections of the stars. The anchor — at the end of a rope, not a chain — splashed into the lagoon and the ripples moved outward in circles of white fire. A moment later the deck chair alongside my own creaked faintly as Captain Winnie lowered himself into it with a sigh of content. Barefoot, he moved as silently as a shadow about the decks of his little ship; often the slight creaking of his chair gave me the first intimation of his near presence.

"All snug, now," he remarked. "I love this place. I don't care how long we lie here."

As the schooner swung gently to the anchor, the village was lost to view momentarily and we were looking down the full length of the lagoon.

Presently the stillness of the night was broken by a clear lonely call that seemed to come from horizons beyond horizons. The peace and beauty of mid-ocean had been given a human voice . . . But no; it seemed rather to be that of some wandering spirit of the sea itself, giving a listener, if there should be one, a means to measure infinite silence by. It sent little shivers running up and down my spine.

I turned to the captain. "What in the world was that?" I asked.

"Some fisherman out there," he replied. "He's made a good catch, very likely."

"What was it?"

"The fish?" said Winnie. "How should I know?"

"Not that," I replied. "The call. What's the meaning of it?"

Winnie sat up in his chair, turned to peer briefly at me, and leaned back once more without replying. His silence seemed to be a kind of reproof as though he were thinking, "What an absurd question!" I felt a little foolish, having been so strangely moved, and said nothing more, waiting for him to speak. A moment later we saw a small outrigger canoe, shadowy in the starlight, approaching the ship. "That'll be Paraita," Winnie remarked. "He's the chief here."

The canoe came alongside and a white-haired native of seventy or thereabout climbed over the rail, followed by a sturdy lad of ten years. He greeted the captain with a silent shake of the hand; then they spoke briefly together in the island tongue. Graciously Winnie introduced me to the chief. "And this is Maui, his grandson," he added. "There's a Maui or two on islands scattered all over this part of the Pacific; and a proud name it is, eh, Maui?" The boy, not understanding English, gave him a quick smile and resumed his sober scrutinizing appraisal of myself. After a little further conversation the chief and his grandson stepped down into the canoe and paddled back to the village. Captain Winnie returned to his chair beside me.

Presently he said: "Hall, many thanks."

"For what?" I asked.

"For having been stirred by the call we heard just now. For giving me a whiff of the emotion I used to feel upon hearing it years ago. It's . . . well, out of this world. You must have felt that, judging by the way you spoke?"

"I did, very strongly," I replied.

"I've lost the faculty of hearing it as I once did," said Winnie. "It's curious, your asking about its meaning. I am convinced that it did have meaning centuries ago."

"It's an ancient one, then?" I asked.

"I shouldn't wonder if it's as old as the Polynesian race," he replied. "One still hears it in some of the songs handed down from the times of their remote ancestors. It may have been heard all of a thousand years ago when they were making their great voyages eastward, pushing farther and farther out into the Pacific in the search for new lands."

"Where did the Polynesians come from in the first place?" I asked.

Winnie was silent for some time. At last he said:

"There has always been a difference of opinion as to the land of their origin. There are men even today who cling to the belief that they came from South America, basing the belief on the fact that the prevailing winds in this part of the Pacific are easterly; that the equatorial current would have carried them westward, and that the *kumura,* the sweet potato, which undoubtedly came from South America, was found on some of the islands when they were discovered by Europeans. It is possible, though far from probable, that a few South American aborigines, carried by chance far out to sea, may have drifted four thousand miles with the equatorial current, a survivor or two reaching one of the outlying islands of eastern Polynesia. But the great mass of evidence shows convincingly that the race came from the west. There is strong reason to believe that their original homeland was somewhere within the India of today."

"Is anything known of their early history?" I asked.

"It had better be called pre-history," Winnie replied. "They had no written language until a century and a quarter ago, when they were given one by the early missionaries. This was long after the period of their great voyages. Just where they came from in the first place; how long they remained in their legendary homeland; why they left it — some believe as early as 500 B.C.; what their fortunes were before they appeared upon the western borders of the Pacific, or when that may have been . . . in these matters even the most painstaking students of the problem can hazard little more than a guess."

"How could they have managed to cover so vast an area of

the Pacific?" I asked. "What is your opinion, Captain? When did they come and how did they come?"

"I've spent many a day on many an island," he replied, "dreaming out for myself the history, in its barest outlines, of the Polynesians of centuries ago. Imagination is of little help to begin with. One sees only the faintest of shadows moving through the mists of time past. Then I begin to see them, to my own satisfaction, at least: a hardy, intelligent, adventurous folk who, having been landsmen, eventually become seamen. I picture them as they first venture out from the Asiatic mainland, and hear the slow ticking of the centuries as they pass through and beyond the archipelagos and island continents of the western Pacific — the crude little craft of their ancestors are in the process of becoming the great outrigger and double-hulled sailing ships, miscalled 'canoes,' in which they push farther and farther eastward into the unknown sea. I see them in clans and fragments of clans — men, women and children crowded into the ships together, with their pigs and fowls and dogs, with food-bearing plants and young trees carefully preserved to be set out in lands they hope to find. I hear them singing their ancient songs to give them heart and hope as they 'lift up the sky' horizon beyond horizon. Some find the empty sea before them . . . until the last one has perished. Others reach lands where they remain, for greater or lesser periods — building up their numbers once more, leaving scattered colonies of their blood behind them, but the more hardy and adventurous still sailing on in the direction of the rising sun. Guided by the sun by day, the moon and the stars at night — sailing close-hauled when needs must, or running free before the westerly winds that blow during the Austral summer — they pass far beyond the limits of the world known to men of their time; until, centuries before Magellan was born, they had discovered and peopled the remotest islands and archipelagos of the eastern Pacific."

Captain Winnie was deeply stirred while telling me this. He

was proud, and with reason, of the Polynesian blood that flowed in his veins.

"What men they must have been!" I said. "What splendid seamen!"

"And the women, too, and the children — don't forget them," he replied. "Whenever, before or since in human history, have men, women and children set out together in families to explore an unknown sea, hoping to find lands but with no assurance that they would be found, and with no expectation of return?"

"They were heroic people, no doubt of that," I remarked.

"Perhaps I should not say this, being half Polynesian myself," Winnie replied; "but in my opinion they were the greatest race of seafaring folk known in the long annals of the sea. If given their due, Pacific would be called by one of their own ancient names for it: *Te-Moana-Nui-a-Kiwa,* perhaps — the Great Sea of Kiwa. It was their sea long before it was ours."

"What could have impelled them to make such voyages," I asked, "in the mere hope of finding lands? Did war have something to do with it?"

"Undoubtedly," said Winnie. "The ancient Polynesians were akin to other races in their love of war, although they did not make it the universal practice that men do in the modern world. But powerful clans amongst them worshiped the god of war in one form or another. Among these was Koro, or Oro, so powerful throughout eastern Polynesia when the islands were discovered by Europeans. And then, aside from war but often the cause of it, was the smallness of many of the lands found and the resultant scarcity of food for increasing populations. Some were compelled to go elsewhere in a search for new lands, and it was not always or necessarily the weaker. As I have said, they were a great seafaring folk; the love of exploration was in their bones and blood."

Captain Winnie fell silent for a time. Presently he said:

"Once, while trying to piece together some shards, so to speak, of our ancient history, I caught a glimpse through the mists that stirred me profoundly. It was a saying, or proverb; it might well have been a fragment of ancient belief. I found it in one of those legendary tales written down so many centuries after the events in them had happened. This is what I read: 'Sacred to Tangaroa is Man. He shall not be killed.' Later I found a variant of this: 'Life is sacred to Tané. Men shall not kill.' "

"I don't wonder that you were stirred," I said. "Do you think it possible that some of the ancient Polynesians were lovers of peace?"

"Why not?" Winnie replied. "In every age there have been men who loathed war. The Polynesians could not have been exceptional in this respect. I believe that some of their great voyages eastward over the Sea of Kiwa were led by men who, with their followers, were lovers of peace, searching for lands where they and their descendants might live, forever beyond the reach of Koro and of those who worshiped him. Unlike the search for peace in our day in a world completely known and exploited, their quest would have been one in terms of space, for the Great Sea of Kiwa was supposed to be measureless."

"That is a fascinating possibility," I said. "If there were such lovers of peace do you think it possible that some of them could have reached lands where they were able to enjoy it in complete security, and their descendants after them?"

"I could tell you the story of such a clan," Winnie replied. "But if I do you are not to question me too closely as to how I succeeded in piecing together the fragments of legend and folklore to make a connected tale of them. Would you like to hear it?"

"Very much," I said.

"Then I'll tell you the story before we leave here. I'm in no hurry to push on. Are you?"

"Far from it," I replied.

"Good!" said Winnie. "As I've told you I love this place and I'm sure that you will when you've had a chance to look around a bit."

During the week that followed Captain Winnie said nothing more about the story and I did not press him for it. As for the island, I felt as he did about it: I didn't care how long we might lie there.

There are periods in everyone's life, I imagine, when one can say with truth: "This is happiness too deep for words — perfect, unalloyed, with nothing to mar its purity." So I thought and felt during the fortnight that Captain Winnie's schooner lay at anchor in the great peaceful lagoon we had entered in such memorable fashion. It was hard to believe that we were still in the world of reality. Even in these days, Polynesians living on remote islands strike one as being the fortunate descendants of those who, a thousand years ago, may have sought for lands where they could live in peace, beyond the threat or even the thought of war. The simplicity of life on such islands appeals to one's deepest instincts; at least it does to mine. As I wandered over this particular island I caught glimpses of family life, communal life that had altered little through the centuries. The people living there seemed no more than a few steps distant from their Stone Age ancestors.

One evening, fifty or more of them, men and women together, gathered on the beach to sing some of their ancient songs. The night was profoundly still and Captain Winnie and I could hear them plainly from the ship. In one song the call I had heard from the lone fisherman on the night of our arrival floated high and clear above the voices of the others, and again I was deeply stirred as though listening to a voice not of Earth, coming from an immeasurable distance. Winnie told me they were singing some of the old *Pari-Pari-Fenua,* songs handed down generation after generation across the centuries.

"Some of them are so ancient," he said, "that most of the meaning has been lost. I can close my eyes and imagine that I am being carried backward in time and westward through space to the days when our people were making their great voyages."

"What of the story you promised?" I asked. "Wouldn't this be a good time to begin it?"

"As good a time as any — if you really want to hear it?"

I assured him that I was not just being polite.

He reflected for some time; then he said: "I would like to give you the illusion, at least, of reality. Can you perform an act of faith?"

"I can try," I replied.

"Imagine, then, that you are hearing the tale from some present-day descendant of the clan concerned in it. For anything I know to the contrary I may be one. I belong to the Teva Clan, but I will call these folk the Tongans. . . . The story begins at the time when they reach the Land of Kurapo."

I

Kurapo

I TELL THE STORY of our ancestors of the Tongan Clan from the time when they reached the Land of Kurapo. The Tongans were only a small part of the great race that lived ages ago in a land far to the west of the Sea of Kiwa. No memory of that time remains except the names of the land. By some it was called Hawaiki; by others, Irihia. Why our people left it and when, even the earliest of the legends do not say, but it is believed that, fifty generations ago, they had come to the western borders of the Sea of Kiwa and were moving out upon it. And so they became a scattered people, tribe lost to tribe and clan to clan. Some vanished in one direction, some in another, but as far back as memory goes the Tongans had sailed in the direction of the rising sun, searching for the Far Lands of Maui; for they were lovers of peace and those lands had been promised them by Tané, the god whom they worshiped. At the time of this story the search had brought them to the Land of Kurapo.

Of the voyage which ended there nothing is known except that they sailed from a land far to the west, in nine ships carrying more than eight hundred persons. Three of these ships were lost on the voyage. Two others, whether lost or not, became separated from the fleet and were seen no more. In the four ships that reached Kurapo were four hundred and twenty persons, counting an infant born at sea on the day the land was sighted, but this child, with its mother, died on the evening of that day.

These few in the four ships approached the land but could

not reach it because their last strength was gone. Not a score of them could stand and they, half crazed by thirst, doubted that land was there. It is told how Téaro, high chief of the Tongans,[1] clung to the mast of his ship to view the faint blue outlines against the eastern horizon; then, even as he looked, the land blurred and faded before his eyes and he believed that only the empty sea lay before them.

Téaro remembered nothing more until it was deep night. The land heaved and rocked beneath him, but it was land, not the sea. He lay on a mat and his people near him, many at the point of death, and some of the weakest did not live through the night. By the light of fires on the beach and torches that seemed to be moving of themselves from place to place, Téaro saw his ships riding at anchor in the lagoon. A great crowd was gathered there; he heard the murmur of many voices and felt cool sweet water poured between his lips and spilling over his bare chest; but he did not know if this were water in very truth or the dream of it that comes to mock the last moments of a dying man. Then came sleep, and when once more he opened his eyes it was the afternoon of the following day.

So it was that these Tongans reached Kurapo, as their ancestors, sailing eastward over the Sea of Kiwa, had found other lands; and here, as had happened before, they were not the first to reach it. The people of Kurapo were a clan called the Koros because they worshiped Koro, the god of war. Their numbers were above three thousand; they had lived long in this land, and their villages were in two valleys that opened upon the lagoons of the western side. Vaitangi was their high chief, and the priest of Koro was named Puaka.

The Tongan chiefs who lived to reach Kurapo were Téaro, the high chief; Rata, his brother; Métua, the priest of Tané; and three others, Tavaké, Tuahu, and Paoto. Maéva, wife of Téaro, survived, but they had lost two of their children; there remained Tauhéré, a daughter of eight years, and their small

[1] For characters in the story, see Glossary.

son, Maui, whose story is to be told here. At this time Maui was an infant of two years, and, with his mother, was near to death when the ships were brought to land by the Koros. His life was saved by the daughter-in-law of Vaitangi, high chief of the Koros: she suckled Maui with an infant daughter of her own, then three months old. This child was named Hina.

Ten days passed while the Tongans recovered their strength. They were lodged in the House of Strangers, and Vaitangi showed them nothing but kindness. Thanks to the care of Hina's mother, who had fed him at her breast, Maui was soon strong and full of health; but his own mother recovered slowly. The Tongans were deeply grateful, but their hearts were troubled, not knowing how matters would go with them when the time came for telling who they were.

Now came the meeting of ceremony between Vaitangi and Téaro, when the first questions are asked of strangers and the answers given. Téaro knew what he would say, for never did the Tongans fail to speak boldly of the god they worshiped, let come what might.

The assembly ground of the Koros lay by the river. It was three hundred paces long by one hundred wide. The council house of the *ariki* was there, but this meeting was held in the open. Vaitangi, with Puaka, priest of Koro, and all the lesser chiefs of the Koros, awaited the coming of Téaro. Vaitangi was sixty years old at this time. He was a man of great dignity, courteous in manner and slow to anger. Puaka, priest of Koro, was forty-five; huge in stature, with an evil face, and the arrogance common to priests of Koro whose power is great by reason of their office, sometimes exceeding that of the high chief himself. The older chiefs of the Koros were loyal to Vaitangi, but the younger ones, the warriors, looked to Puaka for leadership. Around three sides of the assembly ground thronged the people of the Koro Clan. At the far end stood the Tongans, so small a group in that great company.

Now came Téaro with Métua, priest of Tané, and the four

lesser chiefs of the Tongans. They walked the full length of
the assembly ground, while the Koros enclosing it looked on
in silence. They halted before the Koro chiefs, and when the
greetings were ended Vaitangi rose from his seat and stood
facing Téaro.

He said: "Whence do you come? What is your lineage, and
where is the *marae* of your ancestors?"

Then Téaro spoke. Step by step, generation by generation,
he followed the road back to the far source of his blood. Long
was the telling, but Vaitangi and his chiefs listened with deep
attention; for when clans of our race chanced to meet after
long separation from the time when we became a scattered
people, it was a matter of great importance to know from
what ancestors their chiefs were descended.

At last Téaro said: "And now I come to the sacred founder
of my line, whose blood flows in my veins: Maui-Ataranga."

Nothing could have favored the Tongans more than their
high chief's recital of so proud a lineage, for few could claim
descent from nobler ancestors. Maui-Ataranga was among the
earliest of the *ariki* who came after the age of the demigods.
What favored them even more was that Vaitangi himself was
descended from a collateral branch of that same family. His
clan, like the Tongans, had once been lovers of peace and worshipers of Tané, but many generations earlier they had renounced their allegiance and had become followers of Koro,
god of war.

Then Vaitangi said: "Long has it been since any word has
come of the Tongans. It was believed that the last of your clan
had perished."

Téaro said: "We Tongans shall never perish."

"And you still seek the Far Lands of Maui?"

"We do," said Téaro.

Vaitangi let his glance rest upon Métua. "This chief and no
other must be your priest of Tané." Métua inclined his head,
without speaking. He was even then an old man, but with
undiminished vigor of body and mind. He was tall and spare

of frame, and in the sunlight his white hair seemed to radiate a faint light. His father, grandfather and great-grandfather had been priests of Tané, leaders and teachers of the Tongans — men of serene courage and unshakable faith.

"You seem to me a brave but foolish people who learn nothing by experience," said Vaitangi. "What would you do now?"

"If there is room for us we would gladly stay in this land," Téaro replied. "We would build up our strength and our numbers before proceeding once more on our quest."

"We have land here and to spare," said Vaitangi.

Puaka, priest of Koro, now spoke. "We have land in good measure, but none for the worshipers of Tané."

Vaitangi glanced quietly at his priest. "Do you think Koro so weak that he need fear Tané and these few who worship him? They shall stay here as I have said."

"Then they shall first acknowledge that the power of Tané is nothing, compared with that of Koro," said Puaka.

Rata and Paoto turned toward their chief as though they would counsel him to make this acknowledgment, but Téaro was looking at the priest.

"That we cannot do," he said, and now was the moment he feared, for this was a bold and trouble-stirring thing to have said. A murmur of anger was heard among the younger of the Koro chiefs; but as no one spoke, Téaro added: "If you tell us that we must go, we ask only that we may be allowed to go peaceably, with time given us to repair and provision our ships."

"You would sail on eastward?" Vaitangi asked.

"If we must go — yes."

"There are no lands eastward," said Vaitangi. "We ourselves have sailed six days in that direction and found only the empty sea."

"A short way was that to the distance we shall go," said Téaro.

Puaka now sprang to his feet, grasping the haft of his great war club. "Then go you shall, and quickly!" he thundered, harshly. "For food you shall have such shellfish as you find for yourselves on the reefs! If more is needed beg Tané for it! You shall have none from us!"

As though Puaka had not spoken, Vaitangi rose and with great courtesy dismissed the Tongan chiefs, thus quietly shaming the priest of Koro before them all for his breach of the sacred law of hospitality. He then went with his *ariki* to the council house, where they spoke further of this matter. The younger *ariki* sided with Puaka because Téaro had refused to acknowledge the greater power of Koro, but the older ones agreed with the high chief.

Vaitangi said: "To us who know Koro's greater power what does it matter that this handful of wanderers hold fast to their own belief? They would be less than men if they did not. Furthermore, we can make use of them. You have seen their ships; they are the work of master craftsmen. We have no such shipwrights among ourselves. Though lovers of peace, they shall build our war canoes in payment for the land we shall give for their use." It was then decided that the Tongans should stay. Puaka held out against this for a time, but at last he too agreed, though sullenly. He was bitter because the others followed the counsel of the high chief rather than his own.

Vaitangi went to the House of Strangers where the Tongans waited to learn their fate.

"You shall stay here on these terms," he said to Téaro. "First, the ships in which you came here shall be converted to war canoes for our use, and as long as you remain on Kurapo your shipwrights shall build and keep in repair the vessels of our war fleet."

This was a hard condition for the Tongans but they were forced to accept it.

"There are few of us left," said Téaro, "but we will do what we can. You have enemies hereabout?"

Vaitangi then told him that at a distance of five days' sail to the north were two islands whose people worshiped a god of war that was opposed to Koro and his followers. The Koros were the stronger but they had not been able to conquer those people, though they raided them often, bringing home prisoners who were used for sacrifice.

"The second term is this," said Vaitangi. "Our valleys on the western side of Kurapo shall be *tabu* to your people. I make this condition for your own sakes, lest some small trouble grow to a great one and you suffer heavily for it."

"To this I gladly agree," said Téaro.

They waited for the third condition which they feared was now to be told. The worship of Koro required many human sacrifices throughout the year. In other lands where they had lived the Tongans were forced to pay this endless tribute of blood and they expected no less a condition on Kurapo. But Vaitangi told them that, as a return for building the war canoes, no Tongan man would be taken for sacrifice as long as the Koros were able to secure victims from their enemies on the islands to the north. "This promise I shall hold fast to," said Vaitangi; "but if any of your people break the *tabu* spoken of, then it shall fall."

Great was the relief and joy of the Tongan *ariki* at having so generous a concession made them by the high chief of a Koro-worshiping clan, for it was one they could not have hoped for. That it was made was due in part to the fact that Vaitangi and Téaro were distantly allied in blood. The Tongans were certain that the promise had been given without the consent of Puaka, and they believed that Vaitangi wished to test in this manner the weight of his authority against that of his priest. Their doubts as to what might come of this the Tongan *ariki* kept to themselves, not wishing to cloud the happiness of their people; for, with the memory of the dangers and bitter losses at sea freshly in their minds they had a great longing for rest in this fair Land of Kurapo, and now they could live without the shadow of death darkening their spirits from day to day.

With their ships they sailed around to the eastern side of

the land still unpeopled, which the Koros had set aside for
their own use when the growth of population should require
it. Here Vaitangi gave them a deep wide valley untouched by
men's hands. It was filled with dense jungle divided by a river
that flowed quietly beneath great trees and into the lagoon,
a mile wide at this place. Across the lagoon was a fine passage through the reef with a small islet on either side. At that
time of year the rising sun was in a direct line with the passage
and the mouth of the river and they first saw their valley, the
green hills enclosing it and the mountains beyond in the
golden light of early dawn.

As he stepped from his ship Téaro stood facing the passage,
the land at his back. "Surely, it is the will of Tané that we
rest here," he said. "We are an eastward-faring people, and
when the time comes for us to leave this land, there lies our
gateway to the sea." But his people, so weary of voyaging, had
eyes only for the land itself. They hoped that the day was far
distant when they would be compelled to resume the quest
for the Far Lands of Maui.

Then followed a time of deep content for the Tongans.
They cleared the jungle, planting as they cleared and leaving
many of the trees cherished for their fruits and fragrant blossoms, and those most ancient ones that dappled the river with
their shade. Through the lower part of the valley, one third
of the distance from the lagoon to the head wall, the river
flowed quietly; canoes could ascend it to the place where
Téaro's dwelling and the council house of the *ariki* were built.
Here too was the assembly ground, like that of the Koros
though not so large. Some of the houses bordered the river;
others lay up the slopes and paths led down from them to the
main path, which followed the river for the most part, from
the lagoon beach inland.

The *marae* for the worship of Tané was built at the eastern
extremity of the high land enclosing the valley on the south;
it looked across lagoon and sea to the far horizon. Never
before had the Tongans found so high and pleasant a place

for the building of their temple. There, within a casket black
with age, were kept the four small sacred stones from their
ancestral *marae,* carried from land to land all the long way
over the Sea of Kiwa since first the quest began for the homeland promised them by Tané. Although many ships had been
lost on their voyages, the casket containing the stones from
their first temple had always reached land, and the Tongans
believed that as long as they kept them safe, the finding of
the promised homeland was sure.

When the valley had been cleared and the people settled in
their dwellings, they were required to widen and improve the
path leading to the valleys of the Koros. In loops and turns it
climbed the head wall of the Tongan valley to the open lands
above. It followed fern-covered ridges, crossed grassy plateaus
and entered the forests farther inland. In some places it skirted
deep shadow-filled gorges where tree ferns of great beauty
throve in the cool moist air; at others it lay along the brink
of towering cliffs that fell sheer to the sea along the northern
coast of the land. From there it turned inland once more,
descending the long slopes that led to the main valley of the
Koros. To speak of the distance from the east coast to the
west, a sturdy man, taking no rest, could leave the valley of
the Tongans at dawn and reach that of the Koros by mid-
afternoon.

When the Tongans had finished work on the path the *tabu*
was established. A great tree bordering the path was marked
by the *tabu* sign. The Tongans could go no farther, but the
Koro chiefs were free to come and go as they chose, though
few among them visited the Tongans save Vaitangi, who came
often to watch the shipwrights building canoes for his war
fleet. He held them fast to their agreement, nor did he fail in
his promise that no man of the Tongans should be taken for
sacrifice. Never did Puaka come with him on these visits. Téaro
and his chiefs well knew his ill will toward them, but as he
never displayed it openly their minds became easier as time
passed.

The story tells no more of those early years on Kurapo, but passes now to the time when Maui, son of Téaro, was in his tenth year. Some of the Tongans feared it would prove unlucky that Maui, as an infant, had been fed the milk of a Koro woman, the daughter-in-law of Vaitangi. Others believed this would mean long friendship between the clans, and so it had proved throughout the years of Maui's childhood. The lives of the Tongans were so little troubled that many of them thought no more of the quest for the Far Lands of Maui.

🐛 I I 🐛
The Coral Pebble

MAUI, NOW IN HIS TENTH year, was a lad of great promise, sturdy of body and showing early those qualities of mind and spirit expected of the son of the high chief. But he was a boy first of all, quick of temper and impatient of restraint, and the time had come when the freedom of childhood was to be curbed a little. With other sons of chiefs he was required to attend the priest's school to begin the long and tedious study required only of the sons of *ariki*.

The story tells of a day at the school when Maui was given the coral pebble to suck. He would have gone into the hills with two of his friends, Ru and Ma'o, to hunt for wild cocks, but when morning came he remembered that it was a day for school and Hapai, the master, gathered him in with the others. Maui told him of the plans he had made for the day and begged his freedom. Hapai would not consent, and Maui watched with a bitter heart as Ru and Ma'o set off for the hills without him.

The schoolhouse stood near the temple of Tané; it was a pleasant airy house open at the sides and surrounded by a balustrade of plaited bamboo. Hapai was the teacher of the small sons of the chiefs; the older ones were under Métua, the priest. They were taught to repeat the genealogies of the *ariki*, the chants and rituals connected with the building of ships, the gathering of food, fishing, and all the sacred cere- monies held at the *marae*. It was tedious heavy work for small boys, but this was the price they paid for being the sons of chiefs.

The lessons began and Maui was asked to recite one of the chants spoken at the temple after the birth of the son of a high chief. Maui knew this well, but in his anger at being compelled to go to school that day he purposely made mistake after mistake. Hapai halted him and called upon Pohi, the son of Rata. Pohi recited without fault and Maui was again called upon. The errors he made were even more than at first.

"You are not trying," the master said. "You will be given another chance later. When I call upon you again, see that you behave like the son of your father."

Hapai went on hearing the lessons of the other boys. It was his custom to sit with his eyes closed as he listened, for his full attention was required that he might detect the slightest error in these recitations. Maui kept his eyes fixed upon Hapai, and thinking he had a chance to escape he got slowly to his feet and was climbing over the balustrade when the master saw him.

"Maui!" he called.

The other boys grinned with delight as he motioned Maui to come forward. On the mat beside him was a carved wooden bowl filled with stones of various sizes. From it he took a smooth coral pebble, perfectly round and of a golden color. Maui knelt before him and opened his mouth. Hapai placed the pebble in it; then he said: "Confess your shame."

The pebble was so large that he could scarcely close his lips over it, but he was compelled to say as best he could: "I, Maui, son of Téaro, am deeply at fault and I willingly suck this pebble." The attempt to speak was so ludicrous that the other boys shouted with laughter. The master indulged them for a moment, then he sternly commanded: "Silence!" . . . "Return to your place," he said to Maui, and the lessons continued. Half an hour later the other boys were excused. "You will remain here," said Hapai; then he, too, left.

Maui was long in the schoolhouse. His jaws ached, and he was still angry because he had not been allowed to do as he pleased. Presently he saw Métua, priest of Tané, coming along the path from the *marae*.

The Tongans loved and venerated their priest. The power of his spirit was so great that it could be felt at once by those in his presence. He had the gift of foreknowledge and this increased the awe with which he was regarded by the people.

Métua entered the schoolhouse, but Maui dared not look up; he could see only the priest's feet and the hem of his mantle of tapa cloth. Métua sat facing him saying nothing. Presently he lifted the boy's chin so that he was compelled to look into his face. Maui was frightened by the stern expression he saw there. Métua held out his hand and Maui placed the pebble in it. It was a great relief to have it out of his mouth.

"Who are you?" the priest demanded.

The boy glanced up and quickly lowered his eyes again. "Maui," he said.

"Son of whom?"

"Téaro."

"Son of whom?" the priest repeated, sternly.

"Of Téaro-a-Ataranga, high chief of the Tongans."

"Named for whom?"

"The great hero, Maui-the-Peaceful."

Then Métua said: "Recite the chant of the *paia* who bathes the newborn child of a high chief in the presence of its father and the elder members of his family."

Maui began:

> *Te uhi-a-'iri o te tama o te aitu*
> *Te uhi-a-'iri i te vai ora o Tané . . .*

He repeated the chant from beginning to end without fault.

The story tells of the talk the priest then had with Maui, one which the boy never forgot. He was made to understand for the first time the sacredness of the knowledge handed on from generation to generation. The chiefs and the priests were the bearers of this knowledge, and the sons of chiefs must so train their memories that they could carry it on in turn to their own children. I say no more of this but tell of what followed.

Métua returned the coral pebble to Maui and the boy said: "What shall I do with it?"

"Make a little net for it of bark thread," said the priest, "and hang it around your neck for this day. Before evening comes hide it in a secret place."

"Why should I do this?" Maui asked.

"Because I wish you to," the priest replied.

Maui made the net and hung the pebble around his neck. The morning was then only half gone and he hurried up the valley hoping to find Ru and Ma'o and to catch a wild cock for himself. He went along the path by the river where some of the women were sitting in the shallows making tapa cloth. Resting upon stones lay the beam of *tou* wood upon which were laid the wide strips of bark, and the women were singing in chorus to the rhythmical beating of their mallets. Maui loved the songs they sang while at this work, but now he walked fast, hoping he would not be noticed; but as he passed, Vahiné, Taio's wife, called: "Maui! Where are you going? What is that you are wearing around your neck?" Maui hurried on without replying, but he heard the laughter of the women and Vahiné's scolding voice following him, for by this time all the village knew of his disgrace at school. He was both angry and ashamed, but as he climbed the path up the head wall of the valley he forgot the pebble and thought only of finding his friends.

He left the path and went into the forest lands where he flushed a cock so beautiful that he was bound to have it; but it was strong in flight and led him on and on for a great distance. At last he came out on the path once more where it bordered the cliffs along the northern side of the island. He had lost the cock but thought no more about it for a time. Never before had he gone so far in this direction, so he went on, gazing in awe over the brink of the cliffs, listening to the deep boom of the sea as it struck the walls of sheer rock far below. There was no barrier reef and no lagoons along this northern side.

He came to the highest part of the land, where the path began to descend toward the valleys of the Koros. At that spot was a tall tree standing alone. From a lower limb stretching across the path was hung a streamer of tapa cloth marked with a design sacred to the family of Vaitangi, high chief of the Koros: three broad lines of red, crossed diagonally by one of blue. It was the *tabu* placed there by Vaitangi's orders. People of the Tongan Clan could go no farther.

Maui stood looking at this sign. He had heard of it all through childhood and now he saw it for the first time. He glanced around hastily, then boldly walked past the *tabu* tree and stood on the forbidden land of the Koros. Their valleys were hidden below the hills, but he could see the lagoons along the western coast. He went back to walk a second time into the Koro lands, glancing defiantly at the *tabu* sign as he did so. When a dozen paces beyond it he looked quickly over his shoulder, but the streamer hung limp above the path, swaying gently in the light breeze. He returned and stood with his arms folded, gazing up at it.

"I am Maui, son of Téaro," he said. "I will come here whenever I please and do it again." Then he started homeward.

Well within the Tongan lands, on the eastern side of the central mountain, was a small lake, rarely visited, which lay directly below two high crags whose weathered pinnacles were nesting places for tropic birds and *itatae,* the small white ghost terns, most beautiful of seafowl. Maui passed that way in chase of another wild cock, which escaped him by flying across the lake. Determined to follow, the boy flung off his waistcloth and plunged into the lake, but as he swam toward the far side the cool water was so refreshing that he gave up the pursuit to lie at ease, on his back, watching the seafowl soaring high over the crags. Then he swam lazily, face down in the water, along the farther side where he could see the bases of the crags falling steeply toward the bottom of the lake.

While swimming slowly along he came to a place where a patch of deep shadow marked a break in the wall about two fathoms down. He would have passed on, but as he looked a misty radiance appeared at that spot, growing steadily brighter. It was sunlight; it could be nothing else. Glancing up he saw that the sun was now hidden by the crags above him; the light was coming through some opening on the western side. Breathing deeply for a moment the boy dived toward the place where this light emerged. The walls of a passageway were now clearly seen. Without pausing to reflect he entered it and was all but famished for breath when his head broke water in a cavern that appeared to be under the crag itself. The sunlight was streaming through an opening in the vaulted roof. A ledge of rock a little above the surface of the water bordered the far side. Maui drew himself up on it, his body trembling from the excitement of the risk he had taken. As he sat there recovering his breath the light slowly faded, for the sun had passed the opening. Presently he seemed to be in complete darkness, but as his eyes became accustomed to it he could see the passage through which he had come dimly outlined in the faint light that came from the lake. Thus assured that he could find his way out again, he tasted the happiness that comes to a boy who has discovered by chance, and at the risk of life, a secret place known only to himself. Of a sudden he remembered the coral pebble hanging around his neck. Métua had told him to hide it, and what better place could be found? Perhaps the priest had directed him. Taking the pebble in its bark net from around his neck the boy groped along the wall until he found a niche where he placed it. "Stay there," he said, "it is the wish of Métua, our priest." He was full of courage now, feeling that it was, indeed, Métua who had guided him to this place. Breathing slowly and deeply for a moment he dived toward the entrance to the cavern and came out once more on the surface of the lake.

The shadows of the mountains stretched far down the eastern slopes as he made his way across them toward the path leading to the Tongan valley. When halfway there he heard the startled clucking of a wild cock from somewhere below; then he saw the bird take to the air and fly directly toward him. Crouching in the fern he watched its flight which ended so near to him that he had it in his grasp the moment it touched the ground. It was a beautiful bird; he could scarcely believe in his luck. Far below he caught sight of Ru and Ma'o. Giving a shrill hail he started at a run through waist-high fern, but the land sloped steeply down and he leaped over the highest clumps. The two boys regarded him with wonder.

"*Au-é,* Maui!" said Ru. "You caught him, and we were chasing him for you!" Each of his friends had a cock of his own.

"He flew straight into my arms," said Maui. "I flushed two fine cocks but both got away. I searched for you everywhere."

"Where did you go?" Ma'o asked.

Maui told them of his visit to the lake but said nothing of the secret cavern.

* * *

At this period in Maui's boyhood his father had placed him in the care of Taio, a member of his household, that he might learn the lore of the sea. Taio's wife was Vahiné, first of the women servants, skilled in the preparing of food, the weaving of mats, the making of tapa cloth and all other tasks pertaining to women. She was quick of temper and sharp of tongue, and her scolding voice could be heard at all hours of the day; but she had a warm heart and was harsh in small things only. Maéva, Maui's mother, valued her highly.

None was more skilled to teach the lore of the sea than Taio. He could read all signs of the coming changes of weather. He could tell what wind would blow before it came; he knew in what seasons and in what places fish could be taken in the greatest numbers and could mark seafowl hovering over moving schools of fish as far distant as the horizon line. He was short, thick and powerful of body and could dive to great depths and swim for hours without tiring whether the sea were rough or smooth. None equaled him in catching the great sea turtles, which he took with his hands alone in such a way that they could neither dive nor shake him off but were compelled to swim in whatever direction he wished. Many a one he had brought to land from far out at sea.

Other young sons of chiefs were under his training, but Maui and Ma'o, son of Rangi, were oftenest with him at this time. Taio's youngest son, Ru, was their companion. Taio taught them to love the sea and to think of it, more than of the land, as home.

Taio's mind was stored with tales concerning the heroic deeds of Tongans as they sailed eastward, and he knew all the legends of the demigods. The most sacred of these was the story of the great hero Maui-the-Peaceful and his brothers.

One night, when they were returning home from fishing, Maui begged for the story, from beginning to end, of these brothers.

"Very well; you shall have it," said Taio. "You are now in your tenth year, and it is your father's wish that you should hear it from my lips." They were then a mile outside the reef. Taio slipped over the side of the canoe. "Go you there to the islet at the left of the passage. Haul the canoe up on the beach, and come to the seaward side. Wait there and listen."

The boys did as they were told. It was a windless night and the sea was calm, breaking so gently along the reef as to make scarcely a sound. They waited.... Presently they heard a clear high call that seemed to come from a great distance; it was as though some lonely wandering spirit of the sea had summoned them to follow.

Ru moved closer to Maui. "Was that my father's voice?" he said.

"He told us to listen," said Maui; then he and Ma'o began to doubt. They stared seaward, and at last they saw a dark spot moving steadily toward them, blurring the reflections of the stars. It was Taio. He caught the outer ledge of the reef, lifted himself over it, crossed the starlit pools amongst the coral and seated himself beside Maui. He took the boy by the shoulders, peering into his face.

"You heard?" he asked.

"Yes," said Maui. "It was your voice, Taio?"

"Of course; whose else?" said Taio. "But the call was that of your great namesake, Maui-the-Peaceful. Your father wished you to hear it for the first time in just this way, coming from seaward. Now you shall hear the story."

And Taio told the boys the ancient legend[1] of how the islands in the Great Sea of Kiwa had come to be. Ages ago, he said, in the time of the demigods, the great sea was empty of land, and one of the tasks set the demigods by the higher gods who gave them life was to fish up lands out of this sea. They obeyed first, but it was hard work. They were proud of their strength; they loved fighting for its own sake, and they taunted one another to battle. Work was forgotten and so great was the slaughter that the race of demigods slowly destroyed itself until only one family remained.

Now, when it was almost too late for the great task to be accomplished, the sons of this last surviving family went forth in their enormous canoes to make amends. Eldest of the sons was Mano-the-Strong; he had a line with four hooks and this he let down to the floor of the sea to grapple for mountainous lands buried there. There was Tumu-the-Witless, who was like a child in his love of destruction; he toppled mountains over, and wrenched off great crags with his hands and hurled them into the sea. There was Tavi-the-Jester, who from fragments of rainbows and the lights and shadows of the

[1] The complete legend of Maui-the-Peaceful and his brothers will be found on page 277.

early dawn created the phantom islands and anchored them on many a far horizon on the Great Sea of Kiwa. Their beauty filled him with deep content. They were to be there forever and at the same time *not* there. The smallest of the brothers was Maui-the-Peaceful, who hated war and who was told in a dream that by his voice alone — by the Call of Maui — he would lead the searchers of peace to the Far Lands, the islands hidden in the Great Sea of Kiwa.

Taio's canoe — he himself at the steering oar, the three boys at the paddles — crossed the lagoon and entered the river. The village was sleeping; no sound broke the stillness save the faint music of a *vivo*. Tamuri, the old flute player, was sitting in his dooryard playing softly to himself. They brought the canoe ashore by the assembly ground.

"Ru, you will stay with me," Taio said. "We have the fish to clean."

"Where is he now?" Maui asked.

"Who?"

"Maui-the-Peaceful."

Taio looked down the channel of the river flowing quietly in the deep shade of the trees overarching it. The space open to the sky where the stream entered the lagoon seemed to be at a great distance, and beyond was the moonlit sea.

"Out there, waiting for us," he said. "Who knows? He may be waiting till you are a man grown, able to lead us."

"But how shall we know when it's time to follow him?"

"When you hear his call, Maui. Only Métua, our priest, can say when that will be. He has the gift of foreknowledge."

III

Of Rata

ON THE EASTERN SIDE of Kurapo were three valleys. The one in the center was occupied by the village of the Tongans. The other two were unpeopled, and in the one to the north the Tongans built the war canoes required of them by Vaitangi as the price they must pay for permission to live on Kurapo. Téaro, Maui's father, was the first of the master builders; those next to him were the chiefs, Tuahu and Tavaké. After them came two of the *raatira,* Rangi and Manu. The skilled artisans worked under the direction of these men.

They took no pleasure in this work but built well because the love of ships was in their blood and they could not do otherwise. The boys of the clan who showed greatest promise served as apprentices. Maui, Faanui and Ma'o were among these. They were taught early to keep in mind that the time would come when the Tongans would again build great voyaging ships in which to sail on the quest for the Far Lands of Maui. Rangi, who was the father of Ma'o, was the principal instructor of the apprentices. Under his eye the boys made models of the migration ships, perfecting their knowledge and workmanship in this manner.

Rata was a younger brother of Téaro, Maui's father. He was a man of divided mind and no true worshiper of Tané. He had come to believe in the greater power of Koro, and his secret hope was that the Tongans might be led, little by little, to think no more of the quest for the Far Lands of Maui. Nevertheless, he was loyal to his own blood and had no desire to see the Tongans conquered and merged into the clan of the Koros.

He feared Puaka, the priest of Koro, and he knew as well as did the other Tongan *ariki* that the priest was the bitter enemy of their clan. Rata resented being second in authority to Téaro, but his feeling was carefully hidden. It was always in Rata's mind that, if the Tongans should one day be able to leave Kurapo, seek and find some other land eastward in the Sea of Kiwa, and if Téaro should die or be lost on the voyage, as had happened to many Tongan chiefs in the past — then would he, Rata, lead the Tongans away from the worship of Tané to that of Koro. He was intelligent, forceful and persuasive in speech, and fully trusted by Téaro; but Hotu, mother of Rata and Téaro, was disturbed by suspicion of her son's secret disloyalty. She kept her own counsel, for at this time she was not willing to admit even to herself that such a thing could be.

The story tells of a day when Rata came to the place where the war canoes for the Koros were building. Rangi and some of the artisans were resting there, sheltered from the midday sun; no others were working on that day. Two great canoes — one sixty, one eighty feet long — were shored up at the entrance to the valley. They were to replace others lost by the Koros on their last expedition against their enemies on the islands to the north. Rata walked slowly around these ships, examining their workmanship. He then came to where Rangi sat with Manu and their helpers. Paoto, one of the *ariki,* was there as well.

"You have never built better," said Rata. "These are noble ships."

"If we could work badly our shame would be less," said Rangi.

"Why should you feel shame?" asked Rata. "Building for the Koros is a small price to pay for living in this rich land of Kurapo."

"Are we never again to build for ourselves?" Manu said. "Eight years we have lived here, serving Tané with our hearts, but forced to give the skill of our brains and hands to Koro. It is a miserable fate for us Tongans."

Paoto spoke. He was a chief little respected by the Tongans for he was timid by nature and would take the easiest way in all things.

"Would Puaka, their priest of Koro, permit us to build for ourselves?" he asked. "Never! We were compelled to convert our own ships to war canoes for the Koros and no chance will be given us to build others. In these eight years Puaka's power has increased until we may well say that it will soon equal that of Vaitangi himself. We must have patience."

"Paoto is right," said Rata. "The service of Tané is no easy one; who should know that better than ourselves? Five hundred of our people were lost in the last great voyage. Unknown thousands of our ancestors have suffered the worst of deaths by starvation and thirst at sea; those swallowed up in great storms were to be envied beside them. It is because of his pity for these sufferings that Tané would have us rest long between voyages."

"On lands already peopled, where Koro is worshiped?" Rangi said.

"Tané is but one of the gods," Rata replied. "He takes what means he can to give us rest on the long and weary search for the lands he has promised."

"Why would Tané have the search so long?" one of the artisans asked. "It seems to me that his promised Homeland will never be found."

"How could it be otherwise?" said Rata. "Lovers of peace are few and their strength is small compared with that of the lovers of war. The Homeland promised by Tané must be so far, so lost in the Sea of Kiwa, that only those who never despair will be able to reach it. Generation after generation the search must go on — and thousands sacrificed for the good of those who may, some day, reach it."

Rangi glanced up quickly. " 'May'?" he said. "Do you doubt, Rata, that the Homeland will be reached?"

Rata was silent for a moment. "No . . . I do not doubt," he said; "but it is a weary way we Tongans have come. How many generations have passed since the quest began? But we must cling to hope. Generations are as days to the gods; Tané will bring us to the end of the quest in his own time."

"But . . . surely it cannot be Tané's wish that we stay here much longer."

"Our ancestors in other lands to the west have often waited for generations," said Paoto. "We live here untroubled. Say what we may of the Koros, they are a friendly people."

"Puaka, their priest of Koro, friendly?" Rangi said, grimly. "If he could have his way we would have been driven into the sea long since, with no means of escape. Vaitangi alone stands between us and that danger. If he should die we would soon know the bitter taste of the friendship of Puaka and his warriors."

"*Parau mau!* There is truth in that," said Manu. "All the younger chiefs of the Koros favor him."

No one spoke for a moment; then one of the artisans said: "Rata, tell me this. I am only a man of yeoman stock. I do not profess to know the deep purposes of our god, nor anything of his nature, but this is his most holy precept as taught us by Métua, our beloved priest: that all human life is sacred. Men shall not kill. That is true?"

"Métua says it is," Rata replied.

"Then we live here at a shameful cost," the other replied. "We Tongans are spared from sacrifice because the Koros find their victims among their enemies on the islands to the north."

"You object to that?" Rata asked. "You would prefer that men of our clan should be taken?"

"No; but it cannot be the design of Tané that we should rest content here. He teaches us to believe that *all* human life is sacred, even that of men who do not worship him."

Rata got to his feet, prepared to go. "Is it for you to fathom the designs of Tané?" he asked. "Only Métua, our priest, can do that, and perhaps not even he. The gods themselves must make exceptions to their laws." With that he left them, followed by Paoto, and the men resumed their work.

"Paoto believes as Rata does," said one of the men. "We must have patience."

"Who cares what Paoto believes?" said Manu. "Respect is due to his birth, but as a man he is as worthless as a rat-eaten coconut. He has no courage."

"But Rata is a man of intelligence," another replied. "He sees there is nothing we can do for ourselves at this time. We are few and powerless. He wishes us to be content and abide what the future may bring."

"And why should we not be content?" asked a third. "If matters go no worse for us than they do now, the Far Lands of Maui can wait. I have no wish to search for them."

"Rangi, what is your opinion?" Manu asked.

"It is not for me to judge Rata," Rangi replied. "He is the chief next in authority to Téaro himself; but never before have I heard him speak as he has today. My belief is that the less we listen to him in the future the better Tongans we shall be."

IV
The Coming of Vaitangi

WHEN MAUI was twelve the Koro war fleet sailed on a new expedition against their enemies on the islands to the north. Not long after they had gone, the Tongans prepared for the marriage of Tauhéré, Maui's sister, with Nihau, one of the younger chiefs, the son of Tavaké. Tauhéré was now a beautiful girl of eighteen; she was to be married at the same time with several other daughters of the Tongan *ariki* and great preparations were made for this event. An invitation to attend the ceremonies was sent to Vaitangi and whatever other Koro chiefs he might wish to bring with him.

Many pigs and fowls were killed; great quantities of fish were caught, and on the night before Vaitangi's arrival the lagoon was lighted far and wide by torches along the reef where women and children were gathering shellfish to be added to the feast to come. The earth ovens were prepared and the fires in them lighted to burn through the night so that the logs beneath the stones would be reduced to beds of coals and the stones white-hot and ready for the cooking of the food.

On the morning of that day Téaro with his *ariki* were on the beach surrounded by their people, awaiting the arrival of Vaitangi. He came in his pleasure ship built for him by the Tongans. It was double-hulled, the high prows and sterns decorated with banners and streamers. There was a platform across the hulls, forward of the mast, protected by a roof of pandanus leaf thatch supported on slender posts, beautifully carved, of *tou* wood. Beneath it sat Vaitangi; his son's wife, with Hina, her daughter; and Uri, who was the nephew of

Puaka, priest of Koro. Hina was a child of ten years at this time, and Uri was fourteen. Vaitangi also brought with him some of the older Koro chiefs who had not gone with Puaka and his warriors. With the household servants and the paddlers the ship carried sixty persons. It approached far out on the lagoon and when opposite the place where the Tongans waited a sweeping turn was made. The ship came seething in and the bows slid well up the beach where Téaro and his *ariki* stood to welcome their guests.

While the greetings of ceremony between Téaro and Vaitangi were taking place, Rata came to Maui who stood with a group of his friends near Vaitangi's ship.

"Maui," he said, "the young chief yonder is Uri, nephew of Puaka. Never before has he come to our valley. Go to him and greet him well in your father's name."

Maui had little liking for this task but did as directed. Uri stood apart, his arms folded, looking around him with an air of pride, of insolence, as though he considered the Tongans not worthy of his notice. Maui approached him and said: "I am Maui, son of Téaro. I have been asked to welcome you here in my father's name."

Uri looked him up and down without replying. He then turned his back and spoke to the boat-steerer of Vaitangi's ship who stood in front of it. The paddlers stood in the shallows on either side.

"Carry the ship up the beach into the shade," he commanded. "Quickly!"

Rollers had been placed nearby for that purpose and the boatmen sprang to obey. Maui waited for a moment, but as Uri paid him no further attention he turned and left him, hot with anger at this insult. He was joined by other young sons of the chiefs, who had witnessed it. Rata observed them walking away from Uri and halted them. "Maui, you dare behave in this manner to the nephew of Puaka and our guest?" he said.

"He would not speak to me," Maui replied.

"Let him be *your* guest, Rata," Faanui said. *"We* will have 'nothing to do with him after the shame he has put upon Maui!" — and the boys went on into the valley.

Near the river, on the opposite side of the assembly ground from Téaro's dwelling, was the house reserved for Vaitangi's use during his visits to the Tongan valley. The floor was deeply covered with sweet fern overlaid with mats. Vaitangi was now seated here with Téaro and Métua; he leaned back against a great roll of tapa cloth provided for his comfort. Servants brought refreshments: green drinking coconuts, fruits, and the greatest delicacies in the way of shellfish prepared in various ways, meant to stay the appetite; or, rather, to sharpen it in preparation for the feast to be held at midday. Vaitangi, whose huge body required a store of food, ate with keen relish, but at last he leaned back, shaking his head reluctantly as more food was urged upon him.

"*Paia vau*," he said. "Room must be left for what is to come. I shall be fit for nothing but sleep when the feast is ended." Servants then brought bowls of water and the napkins with which the chiefs rinsed and dried their lips and fingers. "Téaro, you make me feel at home here. I look forward to these visits, and to this occasion in particular."

"Why should you not feel at home in your own lands?" Téaro replied. "We repay as best we can a little of the hospitality bestowed upon us since the day when you gave us refuge here. It is beyond anything we had reason to expect."

Vaitangi smiled. "From the high chief of a Koro-worshiping clan?" he said. "Even one of these may have moments of forgetfulness and show humanity in spite of himself."

Métua said: "It is a long moment that extends itself to ten years."

"Métua, there has been no strangeness between us in all that time," Vaitangi replied. "How is this to be explained?"

"Because you remember the time long past when your own forefathers were lovers of peace," said the priest. "Because you are half Tongan at heart. Would that we might make you a whole one!"

"That you may do when Tané is able to change human nature," Vaitangi replied. "I have great respect for you, my friend, but none whatever for your belief. As for the Far Lands of Maui . . ." He shook his head. "How is it possible to hold such faith generation after generation in the face of endless disappointment, in view of all that has happened to your people? In proportion to your numbers, far more lives are lost on this quest for a Homeland than with us who are followers of Koro and lovers of war! Well, you must go to your doom, which is certain."

"Whether to our doom or not, we would go in peace," said Métua. He was silent for a moment and then added: "Vaitangi, both of our clans are fast increasing in numbers. The time may come within this generation when the valleys on this eastern side of Kurapo will be needed for your own people."

"That is more than likely," Vaitangi replied. "You may then go in peace insofar as I am concerned."

"We have no ships," said Téaro.

"But great skill in building them," Vaitangi replied.

"That would be permitted?" Métua asked.

Vaitangi gave him a steady glance. "Métua, neither of us are young men. Who can say when our time will come? When I am gone my son, Tomai, will reign in my stead . . ."

"He is a stranger to us, as you know," said Téaro. "We would gladly have welcomed him here but he has never come. What is his feeling toward us?"

"It is one of neither good will nor ill will," Vaitangi replied. "If I may say so without offense, it is, rather, one of surprise and contempt that you should be lovers of peace. His time and interest are wholly given to the training and leading of our young warriors now with Puaka. If I should die and my son be killed in battle . . ."

"A woeful day that would be for us Tongans," said Téaro, grimly.

"You say nothing but truth," Vaitangi replied; "so look to

yourselves in good times. Lay your plans well in advance
against the hazards of the future."

Métua gave him a searching glance. "Vaitangi, you are saying . . . ?"

"Have I not made myself clear?" Vaitangi interrupted, impatiently. "Is it for me to tell you Tongans what you must do?
Only this: your people have faithfully respected the *tabu* set
when you first came here. See that they continue to do so."

"That we shall," Téaro replied.

Vaitangi laid a hand on Téaro's knee. "What kind of talk
is this for a day of festival? Tell me now what sports and
games I am to see."

The midday feast was long in progress. Vaitangi and his
chiefs sat with the Tongan *ariki,* and at a little distance were
the sons of the chiefs, each with his food baskets arranged before him. Rata, knowing how matters stood between Maui
and Uri, had assigned his son, Pohi, to sit with the latter. Pohi,
in part because of the awe he felt in the presence of the nephew
of the dreaded priest of Koro, in part because of the commands of his father, treated Uri with great deference, which
added to Uri's self-esteem and the mean opinion he held of
the Tongans. He spoke loudly so that the others might hear,
boasting of the skill of the Koro youth in all games and sports;
of his own leadership in such games, and of the great strength
of his uncle, Puaka, whose war club was so huge that none but
himself could wield it. Pohi encouraged him in this talk, for
his father was watching from a distance.

Maui and his friends ate in silence for the most part; then
some of them, led by Faanui, began to speak in the allusive
manner common amongst the Tongans when they would not
be understood by strangers, a form of speech in which words
are given special meanings familiar only to themselves. Uri
guessed that he was being discussed in no complimentary
terms and it enraged him to be mocked to his face without his
being able to resent it. Despite Maui's frowns the others kept
it up at intervals until the feast was ended. As they watched

Uri going off with Pohi, Faanui said: "It was a poor revenge, Maui, but better than none. He deserved such treatment for his discourtesy to you and his boastful talk."

In Téaro's household there was an old man, Tamuri, the father of Vahiné, Taic's wife. He was very tall and so thin that when he walked he seemed to be all knees and elbows; and when he wished to be he was the greatest of clowns. Among our ancestors of centuries ago were to be found a few men known as *taata-mata-épiti,* men with two faces. One face was that of the clown; the other, that of a man deeply serious, of great dignity of speech and bearing. Tamuri was one of these men, deeply loved and respected by the Tongans. He was in charge of all festivals given by them. On the occasion of Tau-héré's wedding he had been busy for days in advance preparing the entertainment that was to follow the sacred ceremonies of the wedding itself.

Vaitangi had eaten so well at the feast that he spent the rest of the afternoon in sleep. At dusk his servants wakened him. He bathed and refreshed himself in the river and as night came on Téaro arrived to conduct him to the assembly ground. The people were already gathered there, waiting in the darkness. Upon the arrival of the chiefs, torches held by young men stationed around three sides of the assembly ground were set aflame, lighting the full extent of it and sending streamers of light through the gloom of the groves beyond. A pavilion beautifully decorated with ferns and flowers had been erected for the stately ceremonies connected with the marriage rites. When the chiefs were seated, these began.

Three young daughters of chiefs were to be married at the same time as Tauhéré, Téaro's daughter. They now appeared together, and, in the presence of the bridegrooms, performed the beautiful ritualistic dances connected with the rites of marriage. These occupied the early part of the evening. When they had ended, the brides retired to the House of Virgins to await the wedding solemnities which would take place the following morning.

When they had gone, all of the people — men, women and children — seated themselves before the pavilion to sing the ancient songs of the Tongans, telling of their history for generations past during the quest for the Far Lands of Maui. After this came boxing and wrestling contests which were favorite sports of the Tongan youth. Following these, when the children were sleeping, stretched out on the grass or with their heads on their mothers' laps, came the time for gaiety and abandonment.

Tamuri was now like a different man. He threw aside his dignity, and with his company of clowns, performed panto-mimes and dances that kept his audience shouting with laughter. Vaitangi's huge body shook with merriment, and seeing how well he was entertained, Tamuri and his clowns outdid themselves. The night was far advanced when he came forward with Fatéata, his wife, who was as bony and loose-jointed as himself, followed by a company of young men and women.

Tamuri halted before the high chief of the Koros and said:

"Vaitangi: here you see me and my old woman, a pair of dry forked sticks. There is no more sap left in us than in a dead *purau* tree. Nevertheless, we wish to honor you as best we can, and the drums will beat loudly so that you may not hear the creaking of our joints. If only you could have seen us years ago when our hearts were gay and our bodies filled with the warm blood of youth! But we have with us ten of our grand-children who are now as we were then. They will join us in this dance and make up for the poorness of our own per-formance."

Then the drums began to beat, and Tamuri and his old woman danced with such bone-stiff gestures and movements that Vaitangi laughed until the tears came into his eyes. Of a sudden, at a word of command from Tamuri, the supposed grandchildren stepped forward: five young men and five lovely girls dressed in kirtles of colored grasses reaching to their knees, with wreaths of flowers pressed down over their dark hair, and necklaces of fragrant blossoms half concealing their bare bosoms. As the drums beat in quickening tempo all the stiffness left the limbs of Tamuri and the old woman. They leaped to either side of the line of young men and women, dancing with a loose-jointed ease in the widest possible contrast to their movements of a moment before. The granddaughters, having advanced to within a few feet of Vaitangi, danced with all the abandon of youth, eyes alight, lips parted, with gestures so appealing, so gaily wanton and provocative that Vaitangi could not resist them. Ponderously he heaved himself to his feet and joined them, forgetting the dignity of his years and his position as high chief of the Koros, while the Tongans shouted their approval. The drums beat faster and faster and the girls who had formed a circle around him gave him no rest, vying with one another for the honor of dancing directly before him. At last Vaitangi, losing his balance, sat down with a heavy thud, breathing hard, his face and body streaming with sweat.

So ended the events of the evening. The people, Tongans and Koros together, dispersed reluctantly, as though they had been members of one clan.

As Téaro conducted his guest back to his dwelling, Vaitangi said: "Téaro, I have never been better entertained. I should come here oftener. You Tongans are a gay-spirited people."

"There has been sorrow enough in our lives, tragedy enough in our history," Téaro replied. "We gladly accept what opportunities may come for laughter."

On the following morning came the sacred ceremonies when Tauhéré and her husband, Nihau, were united in marriage, and the other young chiefs and their brides. In the afternoon there were spear-throwing and archery contests by the Tongan youth, and water sports and games in which both men and women took part. These I pass over to speak of Maui and the boys of his age, who were to match their skill at stone slinging. All the people were now gathered on the beach where the contest was to take place. A plantain stalk had been set up at a distance of sixty paces, and the people lined either side of the course. Téaro and Vaitangi stood near the boys who were to try their skill. Faanui was the first contestant; others followed until it came to Maui's turn. As he stepped into the circle marked in the sand, Uri came forward and, with a commanding gesture, held out his hand for Maui's sling. Maui glanced questioningly at Rata, who was judge of the contest, and his uncle said: "Maui, your father's guest and yours wishes to honor us by taking part in this match. Will you let him have your sling?" Maui did so, and stepped back among the other contestants.

With an air of insolence and pride Uri went to the pile of sling-stones and carefully selected three. Placing the first one in the sling he whirled it around his head and let go. He struck the target squarely. The second stone barely grazed the plantain stalk. The third was a miss.

Maui then took his turn. He saw his mother standing with Hina and her mother nearby. He saw Rangi, one of the shipwrights, teacher of the apprentices and father of his friend, Ma'o, regarding him with an air of confidence. Maui loved this man next to Taio himself. In his heart he made a little prayer to Tané that he might humble the pride of this nephew of the high priest of Koro. He made two direct hits; the third stone glanced from the plantain stalk but was nearer than Uri's grazing hit. As he gave the sling to Uri for his second try, he heard the loud murmur of pleasure that came from the throng of spectators. In the second throwing they were equal, with two hits and one miss each. Uri's face was sullen with anger that this son of a Tongan chief, two years younger than himself, should have the lead.

Vaitangi now spoke: "You will try again, Uri?" he said.

The boy nodded. "I misjudged the weight of the stones," he replied.

"Then see to it that you choose carefully this time lest you shame the Koros," Vaitangi said, with a grim smile.

There was deep silence as Uri stooped to select his stones. He threw many aside before making his choice, and the result of that throwing was again two hits and one miss. He scowled as he handed Maui the sling. Without hesitating in his choice Maui took up at random three of the stones that Uri had rejected, and he made three hits in the center of the target. The murmur of approval from the spectators was even louder than before, and Rangi could scarcely contain his joy. The crowd then moved farther along the beach where a tall coconut palm leaned out over the lagoon. A boy perched in the nest of fronds let down a new target: a log of dry wood attached to a long cord, which he set swinging in a wide arc.

"What is this — a further trial?" Vaitangi asked.

"It is the custom of our boys to end the contest in this manner," Rata replied; "but . . ."

"Then so it shall end," said Vaitangi, "unless Uri is willing to accept defeat."

The boy made no reply but took the sling once more and turned to face this last, more difficult target. The boy in the tree set it swinging at a level a little above the heads of the contestants. Uri waited long before each throw but failed in all. Maui failed in his first try, set the light wood to spinning at his second, and while it was thus spinning, struck it again.

Now the crowd cheered wildly, and Rangi's joy was so great that he ran to where Uri was standing and danced in derision before him, shouting, *"Aita faufaa, Uri! Aita faufaa, Uri!"* ("Worthless is Uri!") Rata stepped forward quickly, seized him by the arm and put his hand over Rangi's mouth. It was only then that Rangi realized what he had done. It was a serious matter for a man of common blood to mock one of the *ariki,* and to have publicly shamed the nephew of the high priest of Koro was an offense not to be forgiven. The crowd dispersed in silence, casting sober glances at the place where Téaro stood with Vaitangi.

"It shall be forgiven, by me, at least," Vaitangi said, with a grim smile. "No bonds of friendship unite me with the uncle of this boy, and Uri has only himself to blame. But . . . what is the name of the man who mocked him?"

"Rangi," Téaro replied. "He worships my son. No other excuse can be found for him."

"That is excuse enough," said Vaitangi. "But have a care for him! And let him have a care for himself; for what he has done will be known to Puaka as soon as he returns. *He* will never forgive it."

So great was Uri's shame and anger in his defeat that he would stay no longer in the Tongan valley. Without speaking to Vaitangi of his intention he returned home that same afternoon with two of his uncle's servants. Vaitangi's visit ended the following day, but at the request of Maui's parents, Hina and her mother were permitted to remain for a longer time. Maéva, Maui's mother, had never forgotten that she owed the life of her son to Hina's mother who had suckled him at her breast at the time when the Tongans first came to Kurapo. There had been warm friendship between the two women from that day.

V
Maui and Hina

Now HINA comes into the story, and it is told how those children, destined for one another, began their friendship. It was a vexing task Maui's mother had given her son: that of entertaining the small granddaughter of Vaitangi. Maui was at an age when all of his interests were centered in the sports and games of boys, and he protested strongly to his mother. Why should he be asked to amuse this child of ten years? Let that be done by a daughter of one of the chiefs, a girl of Hina's age. And his mother had said: "Maui, she is the granddaughter of Vaitangi, and she wishes to be with you. Say no more but do as I bid you."

Now the boy stood before his father's house, Hina waiting beside him. A score of his friends were engaged in a stilt battle on the assembly ground. Maui watched longingly the swift thrusts and parries as the boys of one side tried to overset those of the other. Presently, with an impatient sigh he turned to the child beside him.

"Would you like to see my tame frigate birds?" he asked. The child nodded and he led the way to the beach. He had a perch for the birds beneath one of the great trees there. Taking a small dip-net from a crotch of the tree, he said to Hina, "Wait here." He waded through the shallows of the lagoon to a mushroom of coral a little distance out. Mounting this, he dipped up some of the small fish that hovered around it. Beckoning to Hina he then returned to the beach. Scores of *kotaha* were soaring overhead, some of them so high in the air as to be scarcely visible. Maui called, and called again. Two of the birds dropped through the air like small black meteors; then, spreading their wings they checked their fall and swooped low to catch in their claws the small fish that Maui tossed up to them. A moment later they fluttered down to rest on his outstretched arm. He carried them to the perch under the tree and they hopped from his arm to the pole. Maui was a little annoyed that Hina was not more impressed by his mastery over the birds which he had reared and tamed himself.

"Do Koro boys have tame frigate birds?" he asked.

"Yes, several of them," she replied.

"The *kotaha* are the birds sacred to Koro, the god of your clan," said Maui; "but . . . you see? They obey me, a Tongan."

"Why should sea birds be sacred to any of the gods?" Hina asked.

"Because that is how it is," Maui said. "If you were the son instead of the daughter of a chief, you would know."

"What birds are sacred to Tané?" Hina asked.

"The *itatae,* ghost terns," Maui replied, proudly. "Ask the Koro boys if ever they have been able to tame them as I do the *kotaha.* Tané forbids it."

Hina made no reply but continued to regard him with a child's serious attention.

"Well, what would you like to do next?" Maui added, impatiently.

"Whatever you wish."

"But . . . don't you know what you want to do?"

"I am your guest. It is for you to tell me what there is to do."

Maui replaced the dip net in the crotch of the tree and looked at her with the same air of annoyance. "There is a lake I could show you but it is high in the mountains. It would be too far for you to walk."

Hina shook her head. "I should like to see it," she replied.

"Come, then," said the boy, curtly, and he set out at a fast pace along the path leading into the valley. When he reached the steep trail leading up the head wall of the valley he waited until Hina had caught up with him. "You still wish to see the lake?" he asked. "It is a long way."

"So you told me," Hina replied. "There was no need for you to say it a second time."

Without replying, Maui began climbing swiftly, never pausing to look back. When he had reached the flat-topped rock at the summit he saw Hina on the path far below. When at last she had reached the rock she sat nearby, her back toward him.

"You climbed well," Maui said.

She glanced toward him and there were tears of anger in her eyes. Presently she got to her feet. "I am ready to go on now."

"Hina, I was angry because you had not gone home with your grandfather. I left the anger on the path up the valley wall."

"I found it there," she said. "It is mine, now."

"You wish to keep it?"

She was long in replying; then, turning toward him she shook her head, smiling faintly. "But you should have shown more courtesy. You are a boy, stronger, and two years older. But I am here, as you see."

It was at this moment that the friendship between these children began. It came of itself, unquestioned, unexplained. They sat side by side on the rock, their feet swinging below the edge of it. All the eastern lands lay outspread beneath them, golden in the early-morning sunlight.

Hina said: "Maui, do you know about the time when you Tongans came to Kurapo — your father and mother and the others in the four ships?"

The boy nodded.

"My mother has told me," Hina went on. "I was just born and you were nothing but a little bundle of skin and bone. You would have died if my mother had not fed you at her breast, along with me. You sucked one nipple and I sucked the other. That makes you partly my brother."

"Who says so?"

"Doesn't it? My mother fed both of us. Puaka has never forgiven her for that. He wanted you to die, and you would have died without her milk. Your own mother says so."

"I know, Hina. She has told me. I'm sorry I was so rude to you this morning."

"You should be; and for the time when I was here before, a year ago. You didn't even notice me."

"Oh, yes I did. . . . Look, Hina." He turned to the mountain wall towering above them. "You see the great gap in the ridge on the north side? Do you know who made it?"

"Yes; it was Kamaloa, a great warrior in the time of the demigods. One of his enemies was hiding behind the ridge. Kamaloa hurled a huge stone. It struck the ridge and tore out the rocks there."

"Kamaloa! There was no demigod of that name," Maui replied. "It was Tumu-the-Witless. He tore the rock out with his hands, in one great piece. And when he threw it the rock hit the reef and made the fine passage to the sea."

Hina shook her head. "It couldn't have been. Don't you think my father knows? The Koros came here long before the Tongans."

"That has nothing to do with it," Maui replied, warmly. "Don't you think *my* father knows? And Taio? Taio lives with us. He knows the stories of all the demigods and all of their names. There is no Kamaloa among them."

They argued about this and at last Hina said: "Maui, what does it matter? I don't care *who* made the hole. I want to see the lake you were going to show me."

"But you ought to know the truth," Maui said. "It *was* Tumu, just after he and his brother, Mano-the-Strong, fished Kurapo out of the sea. And then . . ."

"All right; it was Tumu. Now will you take me to the lake?"

They followed the path which rose gently before them, along fern-covered ridges and through wide stretches of woodland until it turned seaward once more and came into the open along the high cliffs bordering the northern coast. They halted now and then to peer over the walls of rock that fell sheer to the sea, a thousand feet below. Hina showed no signs of weariness now. Though he said nothing Maui was impressed by her sturdiness, and she was as sure-footed as himself. As they were resting for a moment, Maui said: "I want to show you something else before we go to the lake. Have you seen the *tabu* tree? That is as far as we Tongans can go."

Hina shook her head. "I don't care to see it. I wish there was no *tabu* so that you could come to our valley whenever you wanted to."

"We're nearly there," Maui insisted, "and I want you to see it." He went on, Hina following, until they saw the tree clearly outlined against the sky. When they reached it they stood for a moment, gazing at the *tabu* sign fluttering in the breeze and directly over the path.

"We'll rest here," said Maui. "It's getting warm in the sun. I'll get some fern to make wreaths for our heads." He then walked with an air of proud indifference past the *tabu* sign, into the forbidden lands of the Koros, plucked an armful of fern, and returned.

"Is that why you brought me here, to show me how brave you are?" Hina said.

Maui felt a flush of shame. It was as though they had changed ages and he were a little boy, much younger than Hina. And he felt even more foolish when he replied, as though against his will: "I've walked past it several times, and I will do it whenever I please."

"Because you know I would never speak of it," said Hina.

"How could I know? You belong to the Koros."

"Why do you tell me that so often?" Hina said. "I don't think of your family or my family as Tongans or Koros. But be careful of Uri! He is a Koro and nothing else, like his uncle, Puaka."

Maui flushed at the mention of Uri's name. "You saw what he did when I spoke to him, the morning you came?"

"You paid him well for that," Hina said. "I was happy when you beat him in the stone-slinging match."

Maui gazed soberly at her. "You wanted me to?"

"Why not? I hate him and I hate his uncle! But remember, Maui! Uri will never forgive you for winning. He will wait for a chance to do you harm — real harm. . . . Let's not speak of him any more. Now I want to see the lake."

On their way inland Maui spied a jungle hen on her nest. Motioning Hina to wait he crept slowly through the underbrush and seized the bird. There was only one egg beneath her. He felt the legs and breast of the hen.

"She's fat," he said. "Are you hungry? . . . Then we'll cook it. There is a place a little farther along where we can get some *fei* to eat with it."

They came to a sunny glade where a pool of clear cold water was fed by a small stream from above. Here they halted and Maui removed a sharkskin wallet attached to the belt of his waist mat. In it were his fire stick, his sling, and a bamboo knife. He slit the fowl's throat and laid it in a clump of fern. "We'll have a fine meal," he said. "Now I'll get the *fei*." He returned presently with half a dozen mountain plantains and the dead limb of a *purau* tree. Seating himself on a boulder he broke off the butt end of the branch and placed it between his knees. "I'm ready," he said. "Get some leaves and twigs."

Hina gathered these and knelt beside him. Placing the sharp end of his fire stick against the soft bone-dry wood, Maui began slowly until he had it well grooved. He then worked with rapidly increasing strokes until a faint wisp of smoke appeared in the wood dust at the end of the groove. Hina bent down, breathing gently upon it, and when the spark of fire appeared she fed it with crumbled leaves, twigs, and larger sticks until a good fire was burning briskly. Maui singed off the feathers of the fowl, split it apart and cleaned it in the stream, while Hina laid the plantains on the coals to roast, turning them as Maui broiled the fowl. The juices sizzling down upon the glowing coals sent up a tantalizing fragrance. When the food was ready they let it cool for a time and then ate ravenously.

"Maui, what would our fathers say if they could see us here?"

"Eating together?"

Hina nodded. "This time we have both broken a *tabu.*"

"Tell me about your father," Maui said. "Why does he never come to our valley?"

"I don't know. It may be because Puaka doesn't want him to come. He's away now with the war fleet."

"Does he like Puaka?"

Hina shook her head. "But he honors him because he is so great a warrior."

"Do you see them when they come home?"

"The war fleet? Never."

"Why not?"

"No children see them. But the boys do when they are as old as you."

"I would like to," Maui said.

"No you wouldn't! Not the day they come. It's horrible!"

"How do you know if you haven't seen them?"

"I know what they do. On the evening of that day they kill the first of the prisoners they bring home. They take the bodies to the *marae* to sacrifice to Koro."

"Is your grandfather there?"

"Of course. He's the high chief. My father, too."

"I can't think of your grandfather being there," Maui said.

"He must be. Koro demands it. . . . Maui, don't speak of it any more! Let's go on now. I want to see the lake."

It was well past midday when they reached the borders of the lake. Forest land enclosed it on the eastern side, with a wide beach sloping down to the water. On the opposite side was a steep-walled terrace of rock, like a gigantic step from the central mountain whose peak, weathered by the winds and rains of ages, showed spires and pinnacles with patches of blue sky between. Others rose from the terrace below. High above them ghost terns and tropic birds sailed back and forth their reflections in the lake clear at one moment, blurred the next by flaws of wind sweeping across the water.

Hina gazed wonderingly about her. "What a beautiful place!"

"You see the holes high up on the crags?" Maui said. "That's where the ghost terns nest. They are just beginning now. In another month the baby terns will be hatching."

"Have you climbed up there?"

"Of course. Often."

"Of all sea birds I love the ghost terns best," Hina said.

"Better than *kotaha,* the birds of Koro?"

"Maui, they are not! Any more than ghost terns belong to Tané. They belong to themselves, and to the sky and the sea. Could you get me a pair of baby terns when they hatch?"

"They can't be tamed like the *kotaha.* When they're grown they'll fly away. But it's fun to raise them."

"Then I want to. Will you get me a pair of little ones?"

"How could I send them to you?"

Hina reflected for a moment. "I'll come for them. Bring them as far as the *tabu* tree, but stay on your side! I'll have to come with one of my mother's servants. How long will it be?"

"Ten days from now will be the first night of the new moon. Could you come on the first day of the moon to follow that? The terns will be hatching well by then."

"Yes," said Hina. "You won't forget?"

"Tongans don't forget their promises. I will be there early and wait till you come." Maui glanced at the sun. "There is something else I want to show you," he said, "but it isn't time yet. While we're waiting I'll make some little boats."

He gathered some small straight twigs, leaves from a *hotu* tree, and a length of smooth bark which he stripped down with his thumbnail for cordage. Hina watched, her hands clasped around her knees, as Maui shaped the bits of wood and smoothed them with a sharp-edged fragment of shell.

"How can you do it so fast?"

Maui gave her a quick glance as he worked. "Because I'm a Tongan," he said. "Can't the Koro boys make these little things?"

"Not as pretty as yours, and it takes them much longer."

"These are nothing. Wait till you see my voyaging ship. I was a long time making that."

"A voyaging ship?"

The boy nodded. "It's a model, exactly like the great ships we Tongans build for the voyages eastward."

"But . . . the Tongans don't make voyages. You stay here on Kurapo."

"You think so? We won't stay much longer."

"Why not?"

"Because we have to search for the Far Lands of Maui."

"Where are they?" Hina asked.

"I'll tell you about that some other time. . . . Look, Hina, they're ready. This one is for you. Be careful! Set it gently in the water. We'll see which one sails best."

The breeze was so light that it barely ruffled the surface of the water, but the tiny craft skimmed lightly over it until they were far out on the lake. Hina was delighted and Maui said: "Now I'll make another kind, so light that even this little breeze will make them skip out of the water."

"Where is the place you were going to show me? I'd like to see that first."

"It isn't time to go yet," Maui said.

"Why not?"

"Because I say it isn't."

"You don't want me to see it; that's why."

"Listen, Hina! It's a dangerous place to get into; the light must be just right when we start. Are you a good swimmer?"

"I can swim as well as any boy."

"And dive, too?"

"Of course."

"Show me," Maui said. "Swim across the lake, and when you come back dive as far as you can."

The lake was little more than three hundred paces wide. Hina threw off her mantle. Loosening the kirtle beneath she wrapped it more tightly, bringing one end up between her legs, tucking it securely at the waist; then she plunged into the water. Maui watched closely, with increasing assurance, seeing how thoroughly at home she was. The rocky wall fell sheer on the far side of the lake. When she reached it Hina turned, gave a strong push with her legs and started back, swimming easily. When about fifty paces from the beach she dived and broke water in the shallows where Maui was sitting.

"You're like a little porpoise," Maui said as she threw herself on the sand beside him. He glanced at the crags across the lake; the sun was now hidden behind them. "Soon we can go, but rest a little and get your breath."

A few moments later he led the way across the lake until they had nearly reached the western wall. Maui said: "Swim now with your face in the water. You will see a dark place below a ledge in the cliff. Keep watching it."

Presently Hina raised her head. "What is it, Maui? There's light coming through!"

"That's where we are going. Take some deep breaths. I'll dive first. Follow right after me."

As Maui's head broke water inside the cavern he turned quickly and saw Hina rising to the surface just behind him. The shaft of sunlight coming through the rocky vault was growing brighter; it fell directly on the ledge of rock along the far side of the cavern. They swam there and pulled themselves up on it.

"Were you frightened?" Maui asked.

The child nodded. "I couldn't have held my breath any longer."

"Now you know why I wanted you to wait. You can see the way to come in only when the light is coming through that hole. Have you ever heard Koro boys speak of this place?"

Hina shook her head. "I don't believe they ever come here."

"I have many times, with my friends, but none of them know

about this cave; I believe I was meant to find it. Métua, our priest . . ." He broke off, staring blankly at Hina.

"What is it, Maui?"

"I forgot. I shouldn't have brought you here."

"Why not?"

"I have disobeyed our priest. He gave me something to hide in a secret place. I brought it here. And now you know!"

Hina glanced around the great cavern where the dark water seemed to stretch away into limitless recesses. "But I *don't* know," she replied. "I don't know what it is or where it is. So you have done nothing wrong."

Maui got to his feet. "I'm going to show you what it is," he said. "Métua must have meant you to know. I couldn't have brought you here without his consent." Moving slowly along the ledge he searched along the wall until he found the coral pebble in its net of bark thread.

Hina examined it curiously. "What is it?" she asked. Maui told of his punishment at school; how he was made to suck the pebble. "And this is what I had to say when I first placed it in my mouth." Then, as at school, the pebble in his mouth, he mumbled: "I, Maui, son of Téaro, am deeply at fault, and I willingly suck this pebble."

Hina's laughter made the walls ring. "Did you have to suck it long?"

"It makes my jaws ache just to think of it."

"You must tell your priest," Hina said. "I don't believe he will mind your telling me, but if he does, then you can hide the pebble in some other place."

Maui returned the pebble to its niche in the wall. "I think he will tell me first. Our priest knows everything."

The sun had now passed the opening in the roof and the gloom was gradually deepening. "We'd better go now," Hina said, anxiously. . . . "Maui, we must hurry! We won't be able to find the way!"

"Don't be afraid. When it's dark enough you will see the opening by the light that comes from the lake." The gloom deepened until they could no longer see one another. A light much fainter than that by which they had entered now revealed the passage. "You see it, Hina?"

"Yes," the child replied. "I'm going, before I'm too scared to try it. Come right behind me!"

In the last faint light of day two weary children crossed the assembly ground to the house of Téaro.

"You were right, Maui," Hina said. "It *was* a long way."

⚡ VI ⚡
The Meeting at the Council House

ON THE MORNING of the day when those children had gone to the lake, Téaro gathered his chiefs at the council house. He paced the room until the last of them had come; then halted before them.

"I bring you such news as none of us could have hoped for," he said. "The decision we now have to make is of the greatest importance. When I have spoken, let each one of you give his opinion as to what our course of action should be." He then told them of the conversation that had taken place between himself, Métua and Vaitangi on the day of the latter's arrival at the Tongan village. "There is no deceit in Vaitangi's nature," he added. "His good will toward us is known to all of you. It was the desire to learn how far he might be willing to extend that good will that led Métua and me to speak as we did."

Téaro broke off, glancing from one to another of the *ariki* who were gazing at him as though they could not grasp the full meaning of his words; then Paoto spoke.

"But . . . what Vaitangi said was nothing, for well he knows there is nothing we can do."

Téaro glanced impatiently at this chief. "I will repeat for you, Paoto, those words of our talk. Métua said: 'But we have no ships.' Vaitangi replied: 'But great skill in building them.' You call it nothing that we may now make plans for the future with the consent of the high chief of the Koros? Needless to say, our preparations must be made in secret. Vaitangi wishes to know nothing about them; but what greater encouragement could he have given than the assurance that we shall not be hindered in them?"

Tuahu struck his broad knee with his fist. "The way is clear," he said. "It can be done and it shall be done!"

Marama said: "Téaro, let me understand this. You tell us that we may now, secretly, begin the building of ships for ourselves?"

"We may," Téaro replied. "Our preparations will take years to complete, which is the reason why no time should be lost in setting about them. We shall need seven ships — it may be, eight — to carry the numbers we shall have before the last of them is completed. You need not be reminded of the greatness of the task and of how slow our progress will be. We are not, of course, relieved of the work of repairing the war canoes of the Koros and building new ones as they may be required. But this is certain: we can keep from twenty to fifty men steadily at the work of building for ourselves, and the number can be increased from time to time as occasion offers."

Tavaké spoke: "No one could be more deeply content with the news you bring, but let us first consider the risks to be taken. How is the work to be done without Puaka's knowledge?"

"The risks are very great," Téaro replied; "but has there ever been a time in the long history of our people when we have not lived in the near presence of danger?"

"It has not been so here on Kurapo," Paoto said; "nor need it be so in the future if we are prudent."

"Prudence is a virtue that will not save us from the wrath of Puaka when he feels that he has the power to display it openly," said Téaro.

"But that time may not come," Paoto replied. "In the ten years that we have lived on Kurapo, Puaka has never once set foot in our valley. That he may despise us I am willing to admit, but . . ."

"Paoto, you are a man without sense," Tuahu broke in, impatiently. "The years are beginning to weigh heavily upon

Vaitangi. No one sees this more clearly than Puaka who will bide his time, gathering more and more authority into his own hands. Weighing, then, the dangers, where do we run the greater risk: in preparing now while we may; or, 'prudently,' as you say, shall we do nothing until the day comes when nothing can be done?"

"Paoto should know that Vaitangi himself recognizes our danger and is willing that we should escape it if we can," Métua remarked, quietly. "He believes us a foolish people, seeking a land where we may live in peace. But I can read his heart, and there, deeply hidden, unacknowledged, is the hope that we may find it."

"You believe that?" Rata asked.

"Of Vaitangi? I know it," the priest replied. "This is not to say that he is no true worshiper of Koro; but what would he not give for the faith that sustains us Tongans! That he cannot have; it is not in his nature. But his secret respect for those who do have it accounts for his willingness to help us." Métua then spoke of the increase in population on Kurapo, far more rapid among the Koros because of their greater numbers. There remained only one valley on the western side, which the Koros were then using to provide for their increase. "Their need for our lands will come, perhaps within this generation," he added; "but I give you this assurance — before half of that time has passed we Tongans will be sailing eastward once more. Our fate is hidden, like that of our ancestors for generations past. But, although some will perish, others of our blood, of our clan, will survive to carry on the quest. And who can say that we Tongans of this generation may not be the ones to reach the Homeland? Let that hope strengthen your hearts, if strength is needed, for it may well be Tané's purpose."

Métua's unshakable faith — his conviction that the Far Lands of Maui were there to the east, waiting to be found and certain to be found — never failed to inspire and lift up the hearts of the others; even Paoto's small and fearful soul knew, for the moment at least, the certitude of a great one. All felt a renewal of spirit as though the noblest of their ancestors were speaking through Métua's voice.

They now discussed in the greatest detail how and where they should begin their task. There was one place and only one where ships could be built with the chances of escaping detection in their favor. The valley to the south of that occupied by the Tongan village was farthest from the Koro settlements; and, owing to the nature of the country inland, it was inaccessible save from the seaward side. The head wall descended in three great steps of sheer rock, down which the river entered a narrow gorge which widened to the valley itself at a point two miles distant from the lagoon. This lower valley was a forest of great trees perfectly suited to be used as hulls for their ships. The trees selected were to be felled at intervals, the hulls to be hollowed and roughly shaped at the places where they fell, then floated down the river to the spot where sheds were to be erected to house the hulls of the vessels while the wood was drying and seasoning. The river for a distance of half a mile inland from the lagoon was wide and deep enough to float the ships when completed; they would have only to widen and deepen the channel at its mouth where it was obstructed by sand. Inland from the beach they would leave a wide strip of jungle intact, which would give perfect concealment from the seaward side. A narrow path, carefully hidden, would be made through this jungle to the building sheds.

"Good!" said Tuahu. "More than good! When shall this work begin?"

"Not a day shall be lost," Téaro replied. "With Puaka away with the war fleet we could not have a more favorable opportunity for a beginning. It may well be a month or longer before he returns. Until then we can give our full time to it, every man, every boy." He glanced at his younger brother, who had taken no part in this discussion but sat with his elbows on his knees, chin in hands, gazing at the mat before him. "Now we will hear from Rata," he said.

"The plan is well made," said Rata, "and Métua has promised that it will succeed. The task before us is one that cannot be finished in less than six years, it may well be eight years. I ask whether, through so long a time, it is possible to keep Puaka in ignorance of what we do?"

"Time alone can show us that," said Marama. "In any case, as our priest has said, it is a chance that must be taken."

"Through eight long years?" Paoto exclaimed, despairingly. "Rata is right: what hope can there be of guarding such a secret for so long a time!"

"Paoto, do you remember the night before we reached this land of Kurapo?" said Tuahu. "When the breeze fell away to a dead calm, and many were so near to death that they neither knew nor cared that the same empty sea lay before us? Téaro said: 'Take the paddles, those who can.' What hope had we then? Nevertheless, when dawn came, there was the land before us."

"Paoto has mistaken me," said Rata. "How could we fail to take such an opportunity offered by Vaitangi himself? But I would have us face the danger of discovery by Puaka so that, if it should come, we may be prepared to meet it."

"That we shall do," said Téaro, and then the meeting ended.

VII
Maui's Ship

Maui and hina, in Maui's small canoe, were far down the lagoon southward from the Tongan village. The canoe was floating above a coral shoal, half a mile from the beach, which rose steeply from the blue depths to within a few feet of the surface of the water. Hovering along the steeply sloping walls a few small fish could be dimly seen.

"This is the place," Maui said.

Hina peered down through sunlit water as clear as air. "There are not many here," she replied.

"Wait," Maui said. "I wanted you to see it this way at first."

He had brought some hermit crabs which were lying in the bottom of the canoe. He broke their shells, bit off the bodies from the claws, and chewed the meat which he then spat out in his hand, placing it on the thwart beside him. When he had finished he said: "Watch, Hina! It's magic. I must say a prayer first . . .

"Maui-Ataranga! Let the beautiful coral mountain below us here become alive. Let the coral become fish."

He then scattered the crabmeat chum over the surface of the water, and immediately thousands of tiny fish, invisible before, emerged from the caves and canyons in the walls of the shoal and rose to the surface of the water, darting here and there to seize the food Maui scattered for them. They were in such vast numbers as to hide the shoal, which seemed, indeed, to have been shattered into these small living forms: gold, gold and blue, deep azure, orange striped with black, pale yellow, crimson — as fantastically shaped and as brilliantly colored as the coral itself.

This was a sight the children of the islands scattered far and wide through the solitudes of the Sea of Kiwa have loved through the ages; and for those of the Tongan Clan the fish were called "the Promise of Tané." It was believed that these myriads of tiny finned creatures had been permitted to fall into the sea in curtains of rain, by the god of peace. They came from *Té Anuanua,* the Rainbow of Tané, that stretched from ages past into the future, the eastern end descending over the promised Homeland, the Far Lands of Maui.

So intent were the children in watching the beautiful sight that they were not aware of the approach of another canoe, now floating near their own, until a voice said: *"Maui-é!"* Glancing quickly up they saw that Métua was there.

Having eaten the food, the fish were descending again to enter the caves and crevices in the walls of the shoal. One small fish, of the color of sunlight, its body perfectly round, its fins like filaments of azure gossamer, still moved slowly here and there. The priest pointed to it.

"A hio!" he said. "Maui, is that your coral pebble?" Then turning to Hina: "My child, I told him to hide it in a safe place. Did he do so?"

The children stared at him, then at each other. There was a faint smile on Métua's face. "It is still safely there," he said, "in a place known only to himself; and that means to you as well, for you two belong to each other." Then he took up his paddle. *"Parahi, orua,"* he said, and continued on his way down the lagoon.

"He knows, Maui," Hina said; "and he's not angry because you showed me the cavern. We *do* belong to each other."

Maui continued to gaze after the departing canoe. "He knows everything, our priest," he said, in an awed voice. "But why did he want me to hide the pebble?"

"We must wait and see," Hina replied. "Shall we go on now? I want to see your voyaging ship."

They drew the canoe up on the beach and walked on, southward. There was not a breath of air and the heat of the sun was reflected fiercely from the coral sand. They were thirsty and halted to rest where a clump of coconut palms threw a cooling shade over the upper slope of the beach. Maui climbed one of the palms and threw down half a dozen green drinking nuts. With a small adz which he carried at his belt he opened two, cutting away the green husk at the end and the shell beneath. They drank greedily of the cool liquid, tilting back their heads as they drained the last drops.

"You want another?" Maui asked.

Hina shook her head. "That filled me full." Both children were bare to the waist, their bodies gleaming with sweat. "We'll cool off here before I show you the ship," Maui said. He sat with his hands clasped around his knees. "But I won't be able to sail it. There's not a breath of wind."

From her waist Hina brought forth a long loop of finely-woven cord, slipped it over her hands and began making string patterns. Maui watched with growing interest as the pattern began to take shape. Hina's small deft fingers worked more and more swiftly. It was an intricate design. When it was finished she stretched her hands apart. "Frigate birds flying," she said, moving her thumbs and forefingers to show the flapping of the wings.

"That's a beauty," Maui said. "I've never seen it before. Now I'll show you one."

He took the string carefully from Hina who studied the complicated pattern for a moment, plucking at a loop here and there; then taking the string she shook it gently and what appeared to be a hopeless tangle fell apart.

Maui made a design of a canoe with two men in it, their paddles moving. Hina more than matched this with another of a breadfruit tree, small triangles representing the fruit hanging from branches that moved, showing that a breeze was blowing.

Presently the surface of the lagoon was darkened by cat's-

paws of wind that came in gentle flaws down from the hills.
"I'll get my ship. Maybe I can sail it now," Maui said.

He returned a few moments later with a double-hulled
ship, three feet long, with high prows and sterns. The lower
part of the hulls had been hollowed out from single pieces of
wood, built up at the sides with others beautifully shaped and
fitted, laced to the lower parts with fine cords of sennit, the
seams calked with fiber and gum from the breadfruit tree.
There were two masts, with finely woven sails of pandanus
leaf. Maui set it gently down and stood gazing at it proudly,
pleased to see the expression of wonder and delight in Hina's
eyes.

"You built it, Maui?"

"Of course; who else? It's exactly like the great ships we
Tongans build for our voyages. You see how the crossbeams
are lashed to the hulls? That is one of the most important
things in shipbuilding. They have to be strong."

"What have you in the basket?"

Maui spilled the contents out on the sand. They were tiny
figures, representing people, carved of wood. Others repre-
sented pigs and dogs, and two little crates with crossbars
fashioned of the midribs of coconut-frond leaflets were to
contain fowls. Maui held them up. "You see them, inside?"

Hina regarded them with delight.

"This isn't one of the large ships," Maui explained. "Some
will carry one hundred people. Mine is for sixty. We have to
know how many each ship will carry. That is why Rangi has
us make the figures; they must be of just the right size in
proportion to the dimensions of the ship."

"They're wonderful!" Hina said. "And they look like people.
Who is Rangi?"

"One of our finest shipbuilders," Maui said, proudly. "He
teaches us, the apprentices. Now I'll load the ship. There's
a place for everyone and everything."

Hina knelt beside him as he placed the little figures inside.
The animals went forward in the bows, and a shelf above them

was for the crates of fowls. A low partition across the hulls kept the compartment for livestock separate from the space for the people. Maui set them in closely together.

"They haven't much room," Hina remarked.

"There never is, on the voyages," Maui explained. "The people have to be crowded together. Beside the animals there are young trees and plants to be carried, and all the food: bamboos for water, pandanus-nut flour, breadfruit and taro paste, coconuts and all the other things. You see? I've got everything: the paddles, bailing scoops, steering paddles, extra cordage — everything."

When he had finished loading the ship they squatted beside it, regarding it in silence for a moment.

"You haven't the food," Hina said.

"No, but I've saved the space where it has to go."

"You ought to have the food. How can they go without things to eat?"

Maui was pleased by Hina's interest. To the child it seemed as though the figures were real. "All right," he said; "you get it, then. We'll soon have a good breeze."

Hina ran to fetch leaves for wrappers and a length of bark which she stripped down for cordage. She made little packets of sand to represent the dry provisions, and pebbles were used for coconuts, taro root and yams. Maui placed them in the space reserved for food. "Now we're ready," he said.

He carried the ship down the beach and set it gently in the water, stepping back to examine her trim; then he raised the sails and made the lines fast. There was a mere ghost of a breeze near the shore. He gave the ship a light push and it moved slowly out; what wind there was was coming from directly aft. As it drew away from shore the speed increased. The lagoon was wide here; there was a break in the reef enclosing it wide enough to permit the passage of small canoes to and from the open sea. It was called the Little Passage.

"It's sailing for there," Hina remarked, anxiously.

"I want it to," Maui said. "It's a migration ship, on the way to the Far Lands of Maui." He stood watching it with keen interest until it was a mere speck in the distance. Hina said: "Don't you think we'd better go after it now?"

"You needn't worry. It won't take me long to catch up with it." Maui then remembered that his canoe was a quarter of a mile away down the beach. "Keep your eye on it, Hina!" he said, and ran to fetch the canoe. Hina watched with increasing concern. She had lost sight of the little ship by the time Maui was paddling swiftly back. She ran to the spot where they had rested and gathered up the green drinking nuts they had left there. She was again at the beach just as Maui reached her.

"I told you to watch it," the boy said, angrily.

"I did until I couldn't see it any longer, but it was going straight for the pass." She threw the coconuts into the canoe and stepped in.

"We won't need the coconuts," Maui said as he pushed the canoe out and headed for the passage.

"How do you know? Your little ship sails so fast we may have a long way to go."

"Stand on the thwart and keep watch," Maui said, paddling with hard strokes. Hina did so. As they neared the passage they looked anxiously about them but saw nothing. "It's gone through," Hina said. She stood on the thwart, bracing herself as the canoe met the swell of the open sea. The breeze blew more and more freshly as they left the shelter of the land.

"I see it!" Hina exclaimed. "Straight ahead!" The boy rose to his feet, following the direction of Hina's outstretched arm. Far in the distance he caught a glimpse of the little ship as it rose to the swell. "How she sails! It's a real exploring-ship! . . . But I don't want to lose it." He raised the small sail and seated himself again, the line in one hand and the haft of his steering paddle under his arm.

The canoe gathered speed and the children scanned the sea

with increasing concern. Maui steered in zigzags, keeping a general easterly direction, but no ship was to be seen. At last he dropped the sail. "We must have passed it," he remarked, glumly.

"If only you hadn't waited so long," Hina replied, in a heart-sick voice. "Paddle slowly. We've *got* to find it!"

The children's attention had been so fully engaged in scanning the sea that they failed to notice the sky to the west. It was being rapidly covered by a canopy of low-hanging storm clouds moving swiftly toward them. The wind was increasing from moment to moment, and the sea which had been so calm less than an hour before was covered with whitecaps. They were now several miles beyond the reef and the land was growing indistinct in the fading light.

"It's lost," Maui remarked, glumly. "I was a long time building it." He scanned the darkening sky with an air of indifference. "We'd better go home, now."

"We're a long way out," Hina said.

Maui pulled doggedly on; but he made little headway against the gathering force of wind and sea. "Come back here, Hina," he called, presently. Hina did so and he handed her the bailing scoop. "Hold on to that; we'll need it. You're not frightened, are you?" The child shook her head. "It's probably only a heavy squall, but we'd better run before it till it blows over." Watching his chance he brought the canoe about until they were headed east again, using his paddle only to keep them before the mounting sea. Glancing back, they saw the dim outlines of the land vanish in a curtain of blinding rain advancing swiftly toward them. "We'll be all right," Maui said. "It's a stout little canoe. If it fills we'll sit as we are till the storm blows over. But bail while you can."

And now the storm hit them full force, wind and driving rain together.

The story is told of how the children were waited for at the Tongan village as night came on and the storm increased.

Where they had gone was not known until a woman who had been fishing far down the lagoon to the south arrived with the news that she had seen Maui and Hina go out to sea through the Little Passage, late in the afternoon.

This news quickly spread through the village, and at the house of the chief the wailing voices of the women servants could be heard faintly above the roar of the wind. Téaro, his chiefs and many of the people were gathered on the beach gazing seaward into the blackness of the night, but there was nothing to be done until the night should pass. Two of the large fishing canoes were drawn up there, and the men stood by, ready to embark in the first light of dawn. Taio and Rangi were among them. Taio said, over and over again, speaking to the others, invisible in the darkness: "That boy is as safe as though he stood here with us, and Hina with him. A porpoise is not more at home in the sea than Maui." And Rangi would reply: "*Él Parau mau.*" But in their hearts was the fear they would not acknowledge: if the outrigger of Maui's canoe should break from the hull, the children would be helpless. A picture would cross their minds of two clinging to the hull somewhere far out at sea, and it seemed that the night would never end. . . .

When dawn came the sky was again cloudless; only the great swells moving eastward revealed what the force of the wind, now spent, had been. The last tremors of the breeze from the west died away, and there was Maui paddling wearily over broad-backed rollers that flashed like mirrors as the sun appeared. Far to the west the mountains of Kurapo stood out clearly against the sky, but the body of the land was hidden below the horizon. Hina was asleep in the bottom of the canoe, but as the sun rose higher the light shone full in her face. She opened her eyes and looked uncomprehendingly at Maui for a moment. Then she sat up and gazed around at the empty sea.

"Look forward," Maui said.

She turned and saw the distant land. "Is it Kurapo?"

"The tops of the mountains. We're a long way out."

"Maui, how can we ever reach it? I wish we had another paddle."

"We'll have the wind again, but not like the other. Only a breeze, and from the right direction this time."

He paddled steadily on, the canoe climbing the glassy slopes of the swells and sliding into the troughs between. The heat increased and the glare from the sea was blinding.

"You're not thirsty, are you?" Hina asked.

Maui smiled, faintly. "Not especially."

"We lost only one of the drinking nuts," Hina replied. "But, of course, as you said, it was useless to bring them."

Maui grinned as he leaned the paddle on the thwart beside him. "You should be a Tongan," he said. "You'd make a good voyager."

"I'd know enough never to go to sea without food and water."

Maui opened one of the nuts and they shared the cool liquid; then the nut was split apart and they ate the jelly-like film of just-forming meat inside. They looked longingly at the two remaining nuts, but decided to save them for later. A pair of ghost terns coming from the direction of the land circled over the canoe, turning their heads to look down at the children. "The birds of Tané," Maui said. "They're going to fetch a breeze for us." They watched as the birds flew on eastward, their forms seeming to melt into morning sunshine.

"Maui, you won't forget my baby terns?"

"Haven't I promised? I will have them at the *tabu* tree on the day of the new moon after the one that is coming. That will be a moon and a half from now. Don't *you* forget."

"I will be there waiting for you," Hina said.

Maui felt a faint breath of air on his neck and glanced back. "I told you, Hina! Tané sees us. It's coming, the breeze." He hoisted the sail which swayed idly for a moment or two but the sea was darkening with the first flaws of wind. The sail steadied and filled, and the canoe moved quietly on. Hina brought out her loop of the cord and began making string patterns. Maui watched her in silence for a time; then he said: "Would you like to hear the story of Maui-the-Peaceful and his brothers?"

Hina nodded. "Is he the one you were named for?"

"Yes. He was the last of all the demigods, and he's still living. It is Maui-the-Peaceful who leads the Tongans on their voyages, but we never see him."

"How does he lead them?"

"By his call. I'll tell you about that when I come to it in the story."

Maui then told the story as he had heard it from Taio, Hina putting in a question from time to time as he proceeded. She forgot her string figures and sat with her hands in her lap, listening with absorbed attention. When at last he had finished, she said, "Maui, it's a wonderful story! It's true, isn't it?"

"True? Every word!" the boy replied. "It happened just as I've told you."

"Have you heard it?"

"The call of Maui? Not yet. Not in his own voice. But I will."

"When?"

"When I become chief, in my father's place. The only Tongans who always hear it are the high chief and his son when he is a man, and Métua, the priest of Tané. But Tané will let others hear it if his priest wishes them to. That is what Métua says. It is at the times when the Tongans have been sailing for days and days, seeing no land except, perhaps, one of the phantom islands of Tavi-the-Jester; when the people in the ships are nearly dead and have no more hope. Then the priest prays to Tané, and he lets them hear the call."

"When I go with you will I hear it?" Hina asked.

Maui stared at her. "But . . . *you* can't go with us. You're a Koro."

Hina shook her head. "No, I'm not," she replied. "You remember what Métua, your priest, said? We belong to each other. He wouldn't have said it if it weren't true. Don't you wish me to come?"

"Yes . . . but . . ."

"Then I will," the child replied, quickly. "Maui, you can hardly keep your eyes open." She seated herself on the thwart beside him and gave him a nudge with her shoulder. *"Haéré! It's your turn to sleep."

"Well, for a little while," Maui said. The ridge to the north of the central mountain was only a little way above the horizon; the gap in it looked very small at that distance. "You see the hole in the ridge?"

Hina nodded. "It's the place where Tumu-the-Witless tore out the rocks."

"That's right," said Maui. "Steer for there."

It was mid-afternoon when Maui awoke. Hina was stirring him with her foot. The land was not more than three leagues distant.

"You let me sleep all this time?" the boy said.

"You needed it," Hina replied. "Look!"

Far to the south the peak of a sail showed clearly above the horizon. Maui studied it carefully. "It's the large fishing canoe. That will be Taio searching for us. . . . I don't want them to find us."

"Neither do I," said Hina. "Shall we try to hide?"

Maui grinned and nodded. He quickly unstepped the little mast, wrapped the sail around it and thrust them under the thwarts. Hina's eyes were shining with excitement. "Hurry, Maui! They can't have seen us yet but they're coming up fast!"

They sat together on the gunwale opposite the outrigger and bore down hard, lifting the latter, and the canoe filled until it lay in the sea, the gunwales flush with the water. The children lay in the sea alongside, peering over the edge of the submerged craft as they watched the approaching sail.

"Au-é! They're not going to see us!" Maui exclaimed, jubilantly.

The distant canoe was still hull-down when it bore away to

the southeast, and presently the tall sail vanished once more below the horizon. Then, Maui at one end of their canoe, Hina at the other, they jerked it back and forth, spilling out the water until it was no more than half full. Maui climbed in; and when he had bailed it dry, Hina followed. The mast was set in place, the sail unfurled, and they proceeded on their way.

They were discovered later by Taio's canoe, which bore swiftly down upon them — but at that time the children were less than a mile from the passage.

All the eastern lands lay in the deepening shadows from the mountains as Maui steered through and crossed the lagoon toward the crowd gathered on the beach. Maui saw his father standing apart, in front of the others, awaiting him. The canoe slid gently up the beach and, together, the children drew it out of the water. They walked slowly to where Téaro stood and halted before him. Maui looked up into his father's face with an anxious smile.

"I was searching for my little ship," he said.

VIII

The Return of the War Fleet

Now VAITANGI sent his pleasure canoe to the Tongan village to fetch home Hina and her mother and their servants. The Tongan *ariki* escorted them to the beach and all of the people gathered there to see them go, for Hina's mother was held in great honor by the Tongans. They had not forgotten that she saved Maui's life at the time when they came to Kurapo. Both she and her child had won the respect and affection of all, and the mothers of the children shed tears at parting as though they had, indeed, been members of one clan. While they were standing on the beach Hina once more reminded Maui of the young ghost terns he was to bring her, and Maui said that he would be waiting for her at the *tabu* tree at the time agreed upon.

When his guests had gone, Téaro gathered his people at the assembly ground and there told them what had been decided at the meeting of the *ariki*. After ten years of waiting, they were to begin building their ships, in which they would proceed once more on the quest for the Far Lands of Maui. He explained all that had taken place at the meeting of the council, and told them of the good will of Vaitangi which made these preparations possible, and of the secrecy with which the work must be done lest their plans should be discovered by Puaka.

The people listened in deep silence as Téaro spoke, and by the expressions upon their faces their thoughts could be read. There were some who remembered only that their lives had been untroubled during the years they had lived on Kurapo.

They dreaded the risks that must now be taken and the prospect of setting out once more into the measureless Sea of Kiwa; for, among the Tongans, as in all other clans of our race, were those who lived only from day to day, unwilling to look forward to and prepare for the hazards of the future. But these were few in numbers and they kept their fears to themselves. The others felt their hearts stirred and quickened by Téaro's words. A more fortunate moment, he told them, for beginning their preparations could not have been hoped for, with Puaka and his warriors absent from Kurapo. Two moons might pass before the return of the Koro war fleet and during this time the efforts of all could be given to the work. He then announced how the tasks would be divided, the leaders for each one and the men to be assigned to them.

Afterward, Métua spoke, calling one by one the great names of their ancestors, the heroic men who had led the Tongans from land to land, and it was as though the spirits of those leaders of generations past had assembled there as their names were called. Then Métua said: "I speak in the presence of our noble dead. Mine is the voice you hear, but the words are Tané's own, and this he wishes me to tell you: before ten years have passed we Tongans shall be far from this land, sailing eastward once more, lifting up the sky, horizon beyond horizon, as we approach the promised Homeland. And that promise shall not fail."

Now this meeting ended, and men were sent at once to make the path into the valley where the ships were to be built, and the path was finished before the evening of that day. It led through the jungle for a distance of half a mile, to the place where the land was to be cleared for building the great sheds to shelter the hulls of the ships.

The following morning Téaro and his chiefs gathered at the temple to perform the sacred rites which their worship demanded at such a time. Then, led by their priest, they came down into the valley, to the *marae* sacred to the shipbuilders. This was a small temple of terraced stone, fifteen paces long

by ten broad. Upon it stood the house where were kept the
tools that had long been in readiness for this day; none of
them had been used in building ships for the Koro war fleet.
Here were the great stone adzes and wedges for felling trees;
the smaller ones for shaping and hollowing the hulls of the
ships; the scrapers and polishers of shell and coral; the slender
sharp-pointed drills for piercing holes; the bone needles for
sewing plank to plank as the hulls were built up; tools for
carving the high prows and sterns; calking mallets and
wedges, and all of the other instruments used in the building
of ships. These were carried to the beach, where they were
dipped in sea water and the prayers said which made them
sacred to their uses in Tané's service, each in its kind.

These solemn rites occupied the whole of that day, and at
dawn the following morning all of the men, the youths and
boys of the clan, proceeded to the valley to the south, to remain there while the work was carried on. High on the central
mountain a lookout was stationed day and night, so that the
Tongans might know in advance of the return of the Koro
war fleet.

Now is told the manner in which the work progressed.
Fifty men were employed in clearing the land where the
sheds were to be raised, and in the building of these. Farther in
the valley fifteen of the great trees were marked for felling,
but only four were to be cut at this time. The bush around these
four was cleared and benches made for the workmen to stand
upon. Forty men, ten to each tree, were assigned to the felling.
First, a cutting was made three feet from the base of the tree
and three quarters of the distance around the trunk. The cutting was the length of a man's hand in width and the same in
depth. When this was done the hewers stood upon the benches
to make a similar cutting three feet above the other. Then, with
wedges and mallets, the wood was hewn out between the cuttings, and when the trunk had been thus reduced new cuttings
were made above and below as before, and so the task pro-

ceeded. Nearby sat the tool sharpeners, the apprentices and other boys skilled at this work. Maui was among these and it was a great honor to be so employed. The boys relieved one another as did the tree fellers. The sweat streamed down their bodies, for they worked without rest. The blades of adzes and wedges soon became blunted, and it was a matter of pride with the tool sharpeners not only to give the tools the finest of cutting edges but also to keep abreast of the demands made upon them by the workmen at the tree.

Day after day this work continued, from the first light of dawn until the dusk of evening. It is told how these Tongans, under Téaro's direction, in the space of one moon and twenty days, felled two great trees, and shaped and hollowed the twin hulls for one ship eighty feet long. And during this time another group of workmen had rough-hewn the planking needed to complete the hulls, together with the high bow and stern pieces.

Never before in the history of the Tongans had so great a work been completed in so brief a time. The twin hulls were shored up under the sheds ready to receive them, and the planking stored there for drying and seasoning. This heavy task had been no more than completed when a messenger came from the lookout to announce that the Koro war fleet had been sighted. The plan already made was then carried out. Thirty men under the direction of Tuahu were left here to continue the work, and the others returned to the village.

The story now returns to Maui.

The Koro war fleet returning home had been sighted on the day of the new moon. On the morning of this day, Maui had gone to the mountains to fetch the young ghost terns promised to Hina. With a small basket slung over his shoulder he climbed one of the crags on the opposite side of the lake. Hundreds of baby terns had now hatched and high above the crag the parent birds wheeled back and forth with faint protesting cries as the boy climbed to their nests. Having carefully selected two fledglings he descended to the lake, bathed and refreshed himself, and set out on the trail leading westward.

Upon arriving at the *tabu* tree he found no one there to meet him, but it was then early afternoon and he sat down to wait for Hina. He amused himself for a time by walking past the *tabu* sign as though half expecting it to show some evidence of anger at his bold action; but the streamer, frayed and discolored by wind and weather, hung limp in the still air, as though it were a symbol of the powerlessness of Koro to injure him, son of the high chief of the Tongans.

Having played the game of defying the Koros until he wearied of it, he sat in the shade of the tree and opened the basket to examine the young terns. He set them on the ground between his feet, and fed them with small fish he had brought with him. He stroked the little balls of white down, keeping his glance fixed upon the path winding down to the main village of the Koros, but there was no sign of Hina and the servant who was to come with her. He became drowsy in the still warm air. Returning the birds to the basket he curled up in the fern beside it and was soon asleep.

When he awoke a fresh breeze was blowing, and the fern-covered ridges and the glades of forest land were golden in the light of early evening. He sat up quickly, rubbing the sleep from his eyes. He could see the slender crescent of the new moon shining faintly in the cloudless sky.

It was the day of the second new moon that had shone since Hina had promised to meet him there. She couldn't have forgotten; Maui was certain of that. He again sat down to wait.

Chin in hands, he gazed out over the vast floor of the sea ruffled to the deepest blue by the northeast wind. Presently his attention was fixed upon something far to the north. It was the peak of a sail. Keeping his gaze steadily upon it he saw the ship emerge above the horizon. It was one of the war canoes of the Koros returning home. One by one, others appeared, until there were five in view, looking like toy ships against the great expanse of sea. Maui knew that six had sailed. Perhaps one had been lost; if not that, it might already have reached land while he was sleeping. With a strong breeze the others were coming on fast. He watched until they had disappeared behind a headland on the western side of the island.

What should he do now? He glanced at the basket resting at his feet. He had promised Hina to bring the birds and she had promised to meet him there. But she had failed to keep her promise. Well, then? How often his mother had told him, and his father as well, that he must never doubt the love of Tané for his children and his power to protect them from whatever dangers if their faith was strong and sure. His heart beat fast as he thought of the test of both his faith and his courage that he might now make. Surely, Tané had brought him there to put him to the proof, to learn whether this son of the high chief of the Tongans was worthy to be so. And when he returned safely home, what honor would be his! He could feel the pressure of Taio's strong fingers upon his shoulder and hear his voice saying: "Maui boy! What a leader you will be when the time comes for you to take your father's place!"

He glanced once more at the basket. There were Hina's terns. He had promised to bring them. "A Tongan never fails to keep his word" — Métua himself, the beloved priest of Tané, had taught him that.

The sun had just set and the sky was aflame with the splendor of the afterglow. With this to light him, the boy took up the basket and proceeded, half walking, half running, along the path descending toward the main valley of the Koros.

It was full night when he reached the head wall of the valley; the path here was only a little less steep than the one in the Tongan valley. He descended slowly but without hesitation and at length reached the gently sloping land of the valley floor. The darkness here was intense but he could follow the path by the occasional glimpses of starlit sky above it. Presently, he saw the flickering light from smoldering supper fires on the earthen floors of cookhouses behind the first dwellings.

All was silent there, which did not surprise him. The people would have gone to the beach to see the arrival of the war fleet.

He felt a growing confidence as he went on. In the darkness he could go where he would, even to the beach itself. There were so many of the Koros that no one would notice him. He would need only to keep in the shadows, away from the flares of torches and the fires lighted on the beach where the war fleet would now be at anchor. He felt a thrill of excitement mingled with dread as he thought of Puaka, the priest of Koro. No Tongan boy had even seen this formidable chief and warrior who showed his contempt for the Tongans by never coming to their valley; but Maui had heard often of his huge size; he towered head and shoulders even above Vaitangi, the high chief.

The boy went more cautiously as he came to the settled part of the valley, but here too the houses were deserted save for a few old people he saw here and there in doorways, too feeble to go with the others to the beach. No one saw him as he moved, as silently as a shadow, along the path. He halted when he reached the assembly ground, which was twice as large as that of the Tongans, covered with turf and bordered by great trees. Skirting the inner end of it he saw before him what could have been no other than the dwelling of Vaitangi, with the smaller houses of his many servants clustered in the groves behind it. A fire was burning in an open space nearby. By its light Maui saw many servants running amongst the houses in a distracted manner. All were women, and they were crying and wailing as they hurried in and out of the chief's house on various errands. Gathering his courage Maui moved closer, standing in the shadows where he had a clear view of the entrance. He searched in vain for a glimpse of Hina or her mother, but a moment later he saw one of their servants who had come with them to the Tongan valley. As she passed near, Maui ran out and seized her by the arm. The woman, who was wailing like the others, halted to stare at him; then seized him by the shoulders to peer into his face.

"Maui!" she exclaimed. "Maui! . . ."

"I've brought the baby terns for Hina," he explained, quickly, thrusting his basket into the woman's hands. "Why didn't she come?"

The woman continued to stare at him as though not believing in his presence.

"Hina? How could the child come when her father has been brought home, dead?"

"Dead!"

"Haven't I said it? Killed in battle! . . . Do you know what you have done, you son of Téaro? Run! . . . Hide!"

"Will you give the terns to Hina? I promised them."

The woman stared distractedly at him a moment longer; then she seized the basket and hurried away. But she turned to call back: "Go away from here, boy! *Run,* as I tell you! Keep clear of the path!"

Shocked by the news he had heard and not knowing what to do, Maui ran into the deep gloom of the trees bordering the assembly ground. The horror evident in the woman's voice and manner, as she recognized him, gave him a momentary feeling of panic; but despite her warning, and as though against his will, he proceeded along the path toward the beach. He had gone only a little way when he saw lights approaching. Hiding in a thicket where he had a clear view of the path, he waited. Soon he saw men with torches approaching, followed by eight others carrying a bier upon which lay a body tightly wrapped in white tapa cloth. Behind it came a procession of women, wailing and shrieking and naked to the waist, their hair hanging in disheveled masses over their shoulders. In the light of flares they appeared scarcely human. Their eyes gleamed wildly, their faces were distorted and covered with blood as they moved slowly on, savagely lashing their faces, heads, and their bare breasts and shoulders with goads set with sharks' teeth.

Maui went on, following the path around a rocky spur where the land widened again, and now for the first time he heard a confused clamor of many voices coming from the beach. Fires set widely apart sent their ruddy light far into the gloom of the groves and over the lagoon where the ships of the war fleet were anchored in line close to the beach.

Forgetting his fear in his eagerness to see what was taking place, Maui approached the canoe sheds which stood along the upper slope of the beach. Between two of them was a tree whose great trunk threw a deep shadow on the inland side. Concealing himself behind it, he peered out.

Warriors were crossing the shallows between the ships and the shore, carrying men bound hand and foot and throwing them on the beach like logs of wood. One of them was loosed and dragged to his feet. The crowd drew back, yelling with blood frenzy, as half a dozen warriors armed with short clubs formed a line along the beach, with intervals of ten or fifteen paces between them. The prisoner, a stalwart fellow, stared around him, his eyeballs shining in the firelight. He was to run the length of this line of men, dodging the blows aimed at him. If he succeeded in doing so his life would be spared. He flexed his arms and legs, numbed by long confinement, while the crowd yelled with impatience, urging him to start. Someone gave him a shove which threw him off balance. Leaping to his feet and running and dodging with great skill, he safely passed four young chiefs and was then brought down by a blow that crushed his skull. Now the frantic crowd rushed in, gathering so closely around the murdered man that Maui could not see what was happening. Presently the people drew back and he saw the chief who had killed the prisoner wearing the body as though it were a mantle, his head thrust through a great hole made in his chest. Drums began to beat and the chief leaped and danced and whirled with the bloody corpse until he stood before the war canoe in the center of the anchored line. Of a sudden the drumming stopped as a warrior of gigantic frame appeared on the forward fighting-platform of the ship, where he stood waiting as the frenzied yelling died away to silence.

It was Puaka; Maui knew it could be no one else. He was in full battle dress, and his evil face and towering figure looked even more formidable in the flickering light of the fires, his height increased by a war helmet adorned with brilliantly colored feathers. Maui gazed in terror at this priest of Koro whose hands rested upon the haft of a war club that reached to his waist. The warrior who stood facing the priest now lifted the murdered man from his shoulders, withdrawing his head which was drenched with the man's blood. The body, which was thrown to the ground before the prow of the canoe, was the first sacrificial victim killed to honor the return of the fleet.

In a harsh booming voice, Puaka addressed the people, telling them of the triumph of the Koro warriors in this last expedition against their enemies. Six ships had departed and six had returned. Maui heard without grasping the sense of what he heard. To the boy the priest seemed the human embodiment of Koro himself, and he was held to the spot where he stood as though Koro had willed it so. Presently the priest stepped down from the platform, the crowd surged toward him, and when the beach was again cleared Maui saw that rollers had been placed from the canoe sheds to the water's edge. To the ones nearest the water living prisoners had been bound, face up. Now the anchors were drawn up and the ships moved far out on the lagoon until they could scarcely be seen in the darkness. Then, from somewhere on the beach, a drum began to beat, first as a signal of readiness to the distant paddlers, then in a fast steady sequence to time the strokes of their paddles. As the ships emerged from the gloom the prows of each pointed directly to the doorway of its shed. They came seething in, abreast. As they neared the beach the paddlers leaped into the shallows and the bows came crashing down on the bodies of the living victims. Other men joined the paddlers, thronging along the sides of the ships which were rolled up the beach and into the sheds.

So quickly was this done that before he had time to escape

Maui found himself in the midst of the crowd, but no one heeded him. He was carried along in the direction of one of the fires.

Desperately he wormed his way out, and had just succeeded in getting clear when he found himself face to face with Uri. The latter halted to stare at him, an expression of amazement and unbelief on his face. He paused just long enough to give Maui a chance to run for his life toward the shelter of the groves. But turning his head, Maui saw that Uri was close behind.

Maui ran on, dodging in and out amongst the deserted dwellings until he came to a well-beaten path which led toward a pit of deepest shade. The wavering lights from the beach barely reached this path; Maui turned into it instinctively and sped toward the deepening gloom ahead. Halting there to glance back for an instant, he saw a shadowy form still following about fifty paces behind. He ran on, stumbling over roots and stones, until he came to a grove of trees whose branches blotted out the faint light of the stars. Feeling his way into it, his hand came in contact with a limb on the level of his head. Clasping it with both hands he swung himself into the tree and climbed on until he was twenty or thirty feet from the ground. There he rested, breathing hard, a hand over his mouth to subdue the sound of his breathing.

He could still hear, faintly, the shouts and cries from the beach, which seemed to deepen the silence around him. The sharp crack of a dead branch below warned him that Uri was somewhere there searching for him. The horror of what he had seen so numbed Maui's heart that he was unable to think, but gradually he became calmer. He realized that he was no longer in the main valley but in what appeared to be a narrow ravine leading off from it. He could stay there no longer. Whatever the risk he must make his way homeward through the Koro village before the people returned to their houses.

He was about to descend from the tree when he saw lights approaching along the path by which he had reached this place. They became brighter, throwing shafts of light into the tree where he hid. Swiftly and quietly he climbed higher, and as he did so the silence was broken by the deep booming of a drum. He could not tell from what direction it came. It echoed and re-echoed from the mountain walls until all the valley was filled with the sound. Maui climbed higher, and not until he had reached the topmost branches capable of bearing his weight did he realize where he was. The tree was one of the sacred grove surrounding the temple of Koro. Peering through the branches, he found himself looking down upon the flat-topped summit of the temple and not more than a dozen feet above it. Candlenut flares and stone lamps filled with coconut oil were burning there, and by their light he saw, at one end of the high platform, a huge stone image. It was Koro, god of war. In a recess near it stood the great Drum of Koro, so tall that its head was reached by a ladder to a small platform, where now a priest of the temple stood beating the Drum, whose deep throbbing seemed to fill all space.

A moment later the drumming ceased and as the reverberations died away Puaka appeared at the top of the stairway on the far side of the temple. He was no longer dressed as a warrior, but wore the ceremonial robes of the high priest of Koro. Behind him came the temple assistants, and following them, Vaitangi and the Koro *ariki*. Puaka halted, facing the image of the war god, and Vaitangi stood with him there; the lesser chiefs and priests were ranged on either side. No word was spoken. Then came a second procession: men, two by two, bearing on their shoulders the mangled bodies of the prisoners that had been crushed beneath the war canoes. Each body was bound to a carrying pole, and they were laid side by side before the altar of Koro.

Maui dared not move; he was barely concealed by the leaves and twigs and smaller branches growing from the limb that supported him which extended over the temple platform scarcely a dozen paces from where Puaka stood, his back toward him. The image of the war god, which faced him, tower-

ing above the company gathered there, filled the boy's heart
with terror. Koro seemed to be gazing directly at him and the
flickering lights and shadows, playing over his evil face, gave
it a hideous aspect of life. Moved by sheer animal terror — the
need to escape that awful scrutiny — and yet not losing the
realization of his danger, Maui moved slowly back and turned
to descend the tree. As he looked down he saw the upturned
face of Uri not three feet below, gazing at him with a smile of
ferocious joy. Scarcely knowing what he did, Maui leaped to
the temple platform. He fell forward on his hands and knees.
As he scrambled to his feet he gave one swift glance toward
the figure of Puaka. The priests were in the midst of a chant,
but hearing the noise behind them they turned their heads.
Maui caught a glimpse of Puaka's face as he ran to the stairway and disappeared.

At dawn the following morning Métua was sitting on a
bench outside his dwelling which stood near the Tongan
temple. Glancing up, he saw the figure of a boy half-running,
half-walking, along the path leading to his house. It was Maui.
His face, his bare chest and arms and legs, were scratched and
covered with bruises and his waistcloth was soiled and torn.
The boy ran to him, falling on his knees before him and bury-
ing his face in the priest's lap. Métua laid a hand gently on the
boy's head, waiting for him to speak.

⚔ IX ⚔
The Death of Rangi

THE TONGAN CHIEFS were gathered at the council house, and all had been said that could be said. Now they waited for Métua, who had been alone at the *marae* throughout the morning.

The people had been told what Maui had done. They came from their dwellings inland and seaward, drawn together by their common danger; even the very old had been helped or carried to the assembly ground. Many believed that their doom was certain and that they must prepare at once to defend themselves as best they could against the might of Puaka and his warriors.

Presently the tall spare figure of the priest was seen descending the path from the temple. He entered the council chamber, and a few moments later the *ariki* came from that place and stood in the open before it while the people gathered closely around them. Téaro said:

"Listen, now, to the words of our priest, and remember that it is Tané himself who speaks through his lips."

The eyes of all were turned upon Métua, searching his face, hoping to read at once the import of the news he brought, but they saw there only the expression of serenity they were accustomed to see when he addressed them.

Métua said: "We are not forbidden to defend our homes and our lives when no other course remains to us, but there can be only one interpretation of Tané's meaning as I prayed for guidance this morning. *We shall not be attacked.* For this, through the grace of Tané, we shall have Vaitangi to thank; his influence with the Koros is still above that of Puaka. Nevertheless, we shall have his open favor no longer, nor shall we be free from blood sacrifice as we have been in the past. Not only did Maui enter the lands forbidden to us, but he was found in the very temple of Koro. He went there unknowingly; he was innocent of any intent to break the *tabu* most sacred to the Koros, but so great an offense they will neither forget nor forgive. What vengeance they will take upon us we shall know when they come, but it will not be that we had reason to fear."

Téaro then said: "I make no excuses for my son save that of his youth, which is no excuse. What he has done cannot be undone. Remember what Métua has said: we shall not be attacked at this time; therefore, let all weapons remain hidden in your dwellings. But the blood of some of us here gathered will, certainly, be demanded. We must wait until we know who is to forfeit his life in punishment for what Maui has done."

Maui sat in his father's house, staring at the mat before him. His heart was numbed by the horror of what he had seen, by the horror of what he had done. He, the son of Téaro, had brought this greatest of dangers upon his people. His father neither spoke to him nor regarded him. He came and went, passing his son as though unaware of his presence; but the boy's mother and grandmother had pity in their hearts. They would have comforted him, but no comfort was to be found. The boy neither spoke nor moved. Hour after hour he remained as he was, staring at the mat.

Then Maéva, alarmed for her son, left the house and beckoned the others to follow. Maui gave no heed but remained as before, not knowing they had gone. His mother then spoke to Taio and Rangi, the two men the boy loved above all others, after his father: Taio who had taught him all the lore of the sea; who told him the tales of Maui-the-Peaceful and his brothers and of the heroic deeds of the Tongans of past generations as they sailed eastward; Rangi, teacher of the apprentices, under whose eye Maui had built his little migration ship. Maéva knew that these two, if it were possible, might be able

to arouse her son from his trance of horror. They entered the
house and seated themselves on either side of the boy, saying
nothing; giving him the comfort of their presence. Rangi laid
a hand on Maui's shoulder and for the first time he stirred.

"Maui boy," Taio said, quietly.

The boy raised his head, glancing first at Taio, then at Rangi.
He saw in their faces nothing but the assurance of their love.
Then a great weariness seized him. He leaned against Rangi's
shoulder and a moment later fell asleep. Rangi laid him gently
back on the mat. Taio went to the door and beckoned to the
boy's mother, who came in and took her place beside him.
"Good go with you for what you have done," Maéva said, and
the two men stole quietly out.

Now the story tells what happened in the village of the
Koros on the morning of this day. Vaitangi gathered his *ariki*
from both villages. All knew of the events of the night just
ended and they, too, awaited the coming of their priest.
Though little was said, Vaitangi could read their thoughts.
They remembered his kinship with Téaro which had led him
to favor the Tongans; to give them land and freedom from
blood sacrifice. All he had done for those worshipers of Tané
had been strongly opposed by Puaka. In his heart Vaitangi felt
a stern anger toward the Tongans. He had protected them all
these years; and now the son of Téaro, whether through
ignorance or the bravado of youth, had violated his friendship
toward his father's people. Nothing could have favored Puaka
more, or added more to his power at the expense of Vaitangi's,
than what had now happened.

Now came Puaka from the temple of Koro and took his seat
in the council chamber. Vaitangi rose and stood facing his
ariki.

"I have little to say to you," he began. "I have befriended
these Tongans, with the consent and approval of most of you
here gathered. You know, further, that Téaro's blood comes

from the same source as my own. Through the long history of our race, blood ties have been sacred. We have been taught by our ancestors to remember and respect them. So I have done here, although the Tongans are worshipers of Tané. What matters it to all-powerful Koro that, among the lesser gods, there is one, the least of them, who teaches his followers not to spill blood?

"But what has now happened is an offense against Koro himself. This boy, Maui, has defiled his temple. That it was done in ignorance matters nothing. Our priest will now speak in Koro's name. What he says must be done shall be done."

Now Puaka spoke, and both his words and manner were otherwise than had been expected by the *ariki,* most of all by Vaitangi himself. He made no attempt to lash them to fury and the lust for revenge, but spoke, rather, in a mocking manner, like one so confident of his power that he could bide his time before displaying it.

"You will remember," he said, "that when these Tongans came to our land I would have shown them no kindness, not even the courtesy granted at times when strangers come from the sea. The reason for this you know: the defiance of Téaro, their high chief, who refused to acknowledge that the power of Koro is greater than that of Tané. Vaitangi upheld them in that defiance, and some of you, the members of his council, upheld Vaitangi. And the Tongans, as though in reward for their defiance, were given lands upon which to live and freedom from any obligation to Koro whose power they defied.

"Vaitangi said that these Tongans would be useful to us. So they have been. I hated them. I still hate them. Would you expect me, high priest of Koro, to feel otherwise toward a clan that refuses to acknowledge his power? Vaitangi has befriended them, and that too is to be understood for, as he has told you, the ties of blood are not to be ignored. The blood in my own veins is less noble than that of Vaitangi. I acknowledge it. I am only the priest of Koro; but this — some of you, at least, will agree — is a position of importance since we live, not as the Tongans, in defiance of the laws of Koro, but in obedience to them.

"I am grateful that Vaitangi acknowledges my authority in the matter which now concerns us: the defilement of our sacred temple by the son of the chief who defied Koro himself. Before revealing Koro's will, I ask one question. Let each of you speak in turn, according to his rank. Bearing in mind the nature of the offense committed, what, think you, should the punishment be?"

Puaka turned first to Vaitangi, who said only: "What Koro has willed."

The older members of the council, though secretly blaming Vaitangi for his friendliness toward the Tongans, respected him and were fearful of the power Puaka was gathering to himself. They replied as Vaitangi had done. But the younger *ariki* who followed Puaka spoke hotly and eagerly. Some favored an immediate attack upon the Tongans which should not end until all had been killed. Others would have had Téaro, his son, and all members of his family sacrificed to Koro.

When all had spoken, Puaka said: "I now give you Koro's will, in one word, which was three times repeated as I knelt before his altar: *Wait . . . Wait . . . Wait.*

"The meaning of his command is plain," Puaka continued. "In his own good time Koro will make known to me the manner in which these Tongans are to meet their death at our hands, and not one of them shall live after the command is given."

"But what is to be done now?" one of the younger chiefs asked. "Are they to be spared lesser punishment while awaiting the full vengeance of Koro?"

A ferocious smile passed over the face of the priest.

"No," he replied. "Before speaking of that I have this further to say of the punishment to come. Koro said, *Wait!* What he left unsaid is this: Wait until the boy, Maui, is old enough to know what suffering means. Wait until he is chief in his father's place. Wait until his people have further increased in numbers, so that the blood to be spilled may, in some measure, cleanse my temple of the foul sacrilege he has committed there.

"As for the vengeance to be taken now" — Puaka turned to glance at Vaitangi — "our honored high chief will agree, I think, that the Tongans are no longer to be spared from blood sacrifice?"

Vaitangi nodded his head, grimly.

"The first blood spilled shall be that of a Tongan of my own choosing," said Puaka. "Tomorrow — with Vaitangi's permission? — I will myself go to fetch this man." His eyes gleamed in anticipation as he added: "For ten years these lovers of peace have thanked Tané for protecting them. It is time that Koro, and the priest of Koro, should show them that Tané can shed helpless tears of blood in their behalf."

It was the morning of the second day since Maui's return from the Koro valley. The shadows of the trees on the assembly ground moved imperceptibly westward, then slowly withdrew until they were pools of deep shade under the midday sun. And still the Tongans waited: in their dooryards, in scattered groups by the river and on the assembly ground. It was mid-afternoon when a messenger came from the lookout to the north. The Koros were coming by sea around that side of the island. Only one ship was approaching: Vaitangi's pleasure canoe.

Word was quickly passed to the people to clear the assembly ground, but they were to wait near it; then Téaro and his chiefs went to the beach to meet the Koro *ariki*. As the ship approached three figures only were seen beneath the roof that sheltered the platform reserved for the chiefs. They were Vaitangi, Puaka, and Puaka's nephew, Uri. In addition to the paddlers were thirty fighting men, the priest's bodyguard. They carried their weapons and were in full battle dress, but Puaka wore his robes of office as priest of Koro.

As they came ashore, Téaro and Métua stepped forward to

greet them. Puaka made no reply to the ceremonial words of welcome, but Vaitangi said: "Conduct us to your council house." No word was spoken on the way there. They entered the council chamber, and when all were seated servants brought refreshments; but Puaka waved them aside. He glanced at Téaro. "Bring your son to me," he said. Téaro gave the order to one of his men and a moment later Maui appeared. He looked at his father, who indicated that he was to stand before Puaka. The priest stared long at him, then turned to Téaro.

"It is strange that you, a worshiper of Tané, should have a son who so loves the sight of blood," he said. "He belongs to me. I should take him." He turned again to Maui. "You wish to come with me now? Or at a later time?"

The boy made no reply.

"You wish, perhaps, to give me some friend of yours; some older friend whom you love dearly, to honor us at this time? Will you name one to take your place at the altar of Koro?"

Puaka waited, but Maui remained silent.

"You have so many friends. You are thinking: 'Which one most deserves this favor?' I will help you to choose. You have a friend who is a craftsman among the shipwrights, a teacher of the sons of chiefs. He is also, I have been told, a dancer. My nephew, Uri, was honored by this man, who danced before him with great joy. His name is Rangi. Bring him to me."

Maui turned toward his father, a look of despair in his eyes. Téaro would have sent one of his servants to fetch Rangi, but Puaka said, "No!" With outstretched arm he pointed toward the door. "Go, you!" he said to Maui.

The assembly ground lay empty in the golden light of late afternoon. Maui crossed it to his father's house where many were gathered. His mother and grandmother were there, and the servants of the household; and Taio and his family; and Rangi, his wife, and their sons and daughters. Maui went to Rangi and halted before him, but he could not speak. Rangi's son, Ma'o, the most beloved of Maui's friends, said: "What is it,

Maui? They wish to see my father?" Still he made no reply until Rangi gently lifted the boy's chin and looked into his face. "*O vau?*" he said, and Maui nodded. The others watched numbly as they crossed the assembly ground, Rangi's arm around the boy's shoulders. As they approached the council house Puaka and the others there came out and stood before it. Puaka's bodyguard formed in line on either side, their spears and war clubs in their hands. The priest had his nephew, Uri, at his side. Maui and Rangi halted before them.

Puaka turned to his nephew. "This is the man who danced before you?" he asked.

"Yes," said Uri, glancing at Maui with a smile of triumph.

"I wish to see this dance," said Puaka. "You honored my nephew when he came here with Vaitangi to the feasts and games. Now you shall honor me. . . . Begin!"

Rangi looked steadily at the priest, showing no trace of fear.

"You refuse?" said Puaka.

Rangi made no reply.

The priest turned to Téaro. "Assemble your people here: all of them, men, women and children."

This was done. The people gathered silently, forming a wide circle facing the priest. When the last of them had come, he said: "I regret deeply my neglect of you Tongans during these past ten years. I have been guilty of disrespect to Tané, your all-powerful god, not having come before. But Métua, your priest, will intercede for me. I hope to be forgiven.

"This boy, son of your chief, became impatient. He said to himself: 'Why does Puaka, high priest of Koro, never visit my father's people? Surely, he has forgotten us. I myself will go to remind him that we long to see his face.' And so he came. Not finding me at my dwelling, he came to the temple of Koro. He is a Tongan — why should the altar of Koro be sacred to him? And there he found me.

"Then his boldness deserted him; he ran away without speaking to me. But I understood what he wished to tell me. It was this: 'Puaka, why do you neglect my father's people? Ten years we have lived in this land and you have left us in peace. No drop of our blood has ever been spilled in sacrifice. Surely, Koro is not pleased with you. Come, therefore. I, Maui, son of Téaro, remind you of your duties.' . . . And so I have come. It shall be as he wishes."

As Puaka gazed about him the mocking smile was replaced by an expression of pitiless ferocity.

"From this day forth, when the thunder of the great Drum of Koro is heard in our valleys, the summons shall be for one of you! It is Maui who requests it.

"When, at night, you gather in your houses, listening, waiting, not knowing which of your men shall next be chosen by Koro, give thanks to this son of Téaro for the terror in your hearts.

"You mothers, wives, sisters: when the food has been prepared for one who is to come, and you wait, and the hours pass, and he fails to come — then, or ever again, go to the dwelling of your chief and ask for Maui. And tell him this: 'Maui, our father (or brother, or husband) has not come home. His food has long been waiting. Go seek him for us. Surely, he is at the temple of Koro and has forgotten to return.'"

Puaka glanced at Rangi; then he said: "Now you shall know why they will forget to return. . . . Where is the family of this man, this renowned dancer? Let them step forth from amongst you."

A low murmur of voices was heard as the wife of Rangi and his children, two sons and three small daughters, came forward. They were ordered to stand at a little distance from their father.

Puaka glanced at the leader of his bodyguard. Immediately, three powerful warriors stepped from the line and seized Rangi from behind. With a cry of despair Maui rushed at them, but he was seized, dragged back and held by others of the guard. Rangi was a man of great strength and broke free from those struggling to hold him. Grasping one by the middle, he threw him over his shoulder and the man fell heavily, stunned for a moment. But others leaped upon Rangi before he could turn to meet them. One stood by, dodging this way and that, waiting his chance during this struggle. In his hand was a pointed, double-edged knife of bamboo. Now, as the others had Rangi helpless for a moment, he sprang in, thrusting the knife into his throat, severing the great artery. Rangi sank to the ground, the blood spurting from the wound.

Cries of grief and rage came from the people and they surged forward, but Métua ran toward them, holding out his arms. He knew, as did the people themselves, that an attack upon the priest of Koro would mean death for all. The others, brought to their senses, halted and fell back. The air was loud with the wails of the women and terrified sobs of the children; but some stood as though struck dumb with horror, watching Puaka's warriors as they bound Rangi's body to a carrying pole. At a command from the priest two of them lifted the body to their shoulders, and with the others surrounding Puaka, his nephew, and the murdered man they moved rapidly toward the beach.

Téaro and his chiefs remained where they were lest the people should yet follow and attack the guard. Vaitangi stood near them. When the others had vanished among the trees he glanced at Téaro, who went to him, and they walked to the far end of the assembly ground. Vaitangi halted and gazed sternly at Téaro.

"For what has happened you have only yourself to blame," he said. "From now on you shall see me here no more, nor any of my family."

He turned to go, but halted to add: "Build your ships! Build swiftly! You have no time to lose!" He then followed the others to the beach.

Now it was the night of the full moon and many were gathered in the doorway of Rangi's house. The period of mourning had passed, and the people listened in silence to the soft music of the *vivo* which old Tamuri played. None could equal him in playing the nose flute; he could make it speak as he wished, sadly or merrily; but now it was music to soothe the hearts of those worn out and emptied of feeling from mourning the death of Rangi. The light of the moon cast leaf shadows on the faces of the listeners and over their bare arms and legs. Nearby stood a clump of tall plantains, and the *hupé,* the breeze that flows gently seaward from the depths of the valleys at nightfall, set the broad leaves to rocking and swaying on their slender stems, as though it were the music of the flute that moved them.

Presently, some of the people began to sing in clear soft voices while Tamuri played. The songs came of themselves, at the moment; some were of earlier times, composed in the same fashion by men and women long ago: songs remembered because of some story in the lives of their ancestors worthy to be treasured and handed on. So the Tongans recorded fragments of the history of their daily lives. On this night was made a song of Rangi that quieted grief rather than stirring it afresh. It spoke of Rangi as no longer subject to the dangers and hardships the living must meet as they sailed on eastward in quest of the promised Homeland.

Peace, for him, had been attained — not in the east, but far to the west: in Hawaiki, the refuge eternal for the spirits of their dead.

The Building of the Ships

Now CAME the time long dreaded by the Tongans, when the hatred of the priest of Koro became active against them. They had lived so long under Vaitangi's protection that many had come to accept it as assured for the future; but after the death of Rangi they were fully awakened to a sense of the common danger and their best qualities came to the fore. Téaro had told them of Vaitangi's parting message of the day of Rangi's murder; and so, ever conscious of their danger but willingly accepting the risks involved, they proceeded with the building of their ships.

From this time on lookouts were kept on the headlands to the north and south of their valley, and a third inland, at a high and secret place overlooking the western side of the island, so that warnings could be sent of any movement of the Koros in their direction. Thus secure from surprise, Téaro kept half the men of the clan steadily at work felling trees and shaping the hulls for the eight ships that would be needed for carrying his people on their voyage eastward.

Maui was not permitted to resume his place among the shipwrights' apprentices. Téaro hardened his heart against his son and heavy was the punishment he was made to bear. He was kept at the lookout high in the mountains, having as companion one man only who was changed from week to week. From that place, the booming of the great Drum of Koro could be clearly heard announcing the times when important ceremonies which demanded a human sacrifice were to be held at the temple of Koro. It was then Maui's duty to make the long journey down to the Tongan valley, bringing word to his father. No one was permitted to speak with him: neither his mother, nor grandmother, nor his sister, Tauhéré, nor any member of the clan. They were ordered by Téaro to turn their backs upon Maui when they saw him coming, and those within the chief's house were compelled to do the same as he entered the dwelling. He could speak only to his father, and these were the words of the message he would bring:

"The great Drum of Koro has sounded again. I bring you warning so that our people may wait in their houses until they learn who next is to be taken, through my fault, as a sacrifice to the god of war."

Then his father would reply: "They shall wait. The blood of this man, whoever he may be, is upon your head. Get you back, now, to your post."

The weeks and the months passed, and before a year had gone by Maui had come eight times to bring this warning to his father, and among those taken for sacrifice were fathers, or uncles, or older brothers of friends whom he dearly loved. So heavy was this punishment that even those who had felt most bitterly toward Maui now had nothing but compassion for him. He had suffered enough; let his father forgive him as they had forgiven him. Maui's mother and grandmother pleaded in vain with Téaro. Not until a full year had passed was the punishment lifted.

His father then received him as though nothing had happened, saying no word of his punishment. His heart smote him at having put the boy to so cruel a trial and he watched closely for signs of its effect upon him. But, save that Maui now seemed older than his years, and rarely smiled, and said little, there was nothing to show that he had not borne himself with the patience and courage expected of the son of the high chief. He was then sent to live with Métua at the temple of Tané, for the time had come when he was to be under the instruction of the priest that he might fit himself for the high duties of later years. Téaro waited anxiously for what Métua would report, but two weeks passed before the priest came to see him. The two men met in the council house and talked until a late hour.

"Have no fears for him," the priest said. "He has borne his punishment with a strength beyond what might have been expected in a boy of his years."

"He feels no bitterness toward me?" Téaro asked.

"None," said Métua. "He believes that his punishment was fully deserved, but the sense of guilt has been planted deeply in his heart."

"That is something that time will cure," said Téaro. "What weakness do you see in him?"

"Fear," said Métua — "fear of Koro and dread of his power."

"He has told you of this?"

The priest shook his head. "He reveals it in his dreams. I have heard him cry out, in the night, not once — several times. In the dreams he is again in the temple of Koro, powerless to move or to turn his eyes from the face of the huge figure of the god who stands there. Koro is the mighty one, with a power of evil exceeding that of Tané for good."

Téaro was deeply concerned. He paced the council chamber for some time before again speaking to the priest.

"How is this to be conquered?" he asked. "What he fears in his dreams he will fear when awake."

"You trust me in this matter?" the priest asked.

"I do," said Téaro. "Who better than yourself is fitted to deal with it?"

"Then set your mind at rest," Métua replied. "Maui will conquer his fear, though the time may be long. Let him take his place once more with the other apprentices at work on the ships, for there his heart is."

"That he shall do," said Téaro.

And now there comes a silence in the story of Maui: the events between his fourteenth and nineteenth years are little known. Perhaps this portion of the tale was lost in transmitting it from generation to generation, or it may be that our ancestors passed briefly over it because of matters of greater importance to come. However this may be, I can tell you only what we, their descendants, know of what happened during those four years.

Each year Tongan men were taken by Puaka to be sacrificed on the altar to Koro. Although the Tongans were kept in complete ignorance of all happenings in the Koro valleys, they knew that Pauka was now in control of those people. Never again did Vaitangi return to their valley, nor any of his servants or members of his household. Puaka himself came but rarely. The common people were not even noticed by him, and he treated the *ariki* either with mocking contempt or with a kind of cold fury, letting them know unmistakably that he was now their master, whose commands were to be instantly obeyed. More often his orders were brought by one of the younger Koro chiefs. Neither Puaka nor any of his messengers ever went beyond the Tongan village, and they returned as they had come, either by sea, around the northern side of the island, or by the path leading inland across the plateaus and the mountains.

The Tongans were thus convinced that Puaka could have no suspicion of the building of the ships, but well they knew that his plans for taking full vengeance upon them were delayed only, not abandoned, and the dark threat of that vengeance hung over them constantly. Never did Téaro forget the words of Vaitangi's parting message: "Build your ships. Build swiftly! You have no time to lose!" Under his direction the Tongans worked as never before, and, when Maui was just nineteen seven ships were nearing completion. The prow and stern pieces and the planking for the eighth ship had already been shaped. The hewing down of the last tree needed was under way, and the Tongans knew that if their good fortune held, they would be ready for escape before another three months had passed. At this time Puaka had recently left

Kurapo with the war fleet on another expedition against his
enemies on the islands to the north. This gave the Tongans
an opportunity they could not have dreamed of, and Téaro
assured them that, if the war fleet should be absent for three
months, as often happened, the Tongans, before Puaka returned, would be far out at sea and safe from all pursuit.

It was on a night when the moon was full that Téaro and
Métua assembled the people on the wide beach fronting the
lagoon at the entrance to the Tongan valley. The Koro war
fleet had sailed from Kurapo only the week before, and it was
known that Puaka had gone with it, leaving his nephew, Uri,
now assistant priest of Koro, in his place. When the last ship
of the fleet was seen, vanishing over the northern horizon, to
the Tongans it was as though the shadow of evil had vanished
with it, for a time at least. Now they could breathe freely and
assemble freely — their lookouts always on guard — and talk
of the voyage to come, the prospect of early departure stirring
the hearts of all.

Every member of the clan save those on lookout gathered at
the beach, seating themselves in a wide half-circle facing eastward in the direction of their voyage, now so nearly at hand:
young mothers with infants at breast; the grandparents and
great-grandparents; the young men; the maidens; their fathers,
brothers, uncles, in the full vigor of maturity; and around the
borders of the crowd were the children, all of them born on
Kurapo, at their games and sports — happy, carefree, like
those of whatever clan during the period of childhood. Then
came the moon, floating serenely up, its glory increasing as the
last light of the afterglow faded from the sky beyond the
mountains to the west.

Then the Tongan *ariki,* each in his turn, addressed the
people. Some recited tales of the exploits of the great heroes
among their ancestors. Others spoke of the glory of the quest
before them; of the honor that was theirs to share in and carry
it forward, whether or not they themselves should reach the

promised Homeland. Others spoke of the dangers and hardships that lay before them, for it was never the practice of the Tongans to conceal or make light of these matters; they faced and reckoned with them in advance so that their courage might be equal to the greatest trials to be made upon it.

Métua, according to custom, was the last to speak, and he said:

"I wish to tell our young people, who do not remember the events of our voyage to this land of Kurapo, of one of the bitterest trials and disappointments that we may have to endure as we voyage on. You have been told by your parents or grandparents of the phantom lands of Tavi-the-Jester, brother of the great hero, Maui-the-Peaceful, whose call we follow as we sail eastward. Tavi was wrongly named Tavi-the-Jester by our ancestors, and yet that is to be understood, for the phantom lands that he created are beautiful beyond the reach of the imagination, and it is a bitter experience to us Tongans to see them in all their beauty, to watch them fade to empty air as we approach, and to see them take form again when we have passed through and beyond them. But Tavi is not to be blamed for this. There were no human beings upon the Earth when his phantom lands were fashioned, and he could not have known at that time that we were to come. Tavi was no jester, but a lover of peace, and beauty in ideal form; and so his lands, although never to be reached by us humans, are, nevertheless, eternal and will remain forever where he placed them in the measureless Sea of Kiwa. And remember this, you Tongans, both old and young: the Far Lands of Maui lie beyond them. Your hearts may grow sick, at times, but let you never despair; for I, the priest of Tané, tell you that our promised Homeland is as real as this land of Kurapo, and that our people will surely find it. We ourselves may be the ones to do so."

When all had spoken who wished to do so, they sang the voyaging songs of their ancestors, and among them was one which told of the alternating hope and despair of the Tongans as they sailed eastward on their quest. The voices of all, both men and women, were now heard in full chorus in this song, whose purpose was to prepare the younger people for the bitter disappointments to be met with on the measureless Sea of Kiwa:

> Lift up the sky, eastward!
> Lift on, horizon beyond horizon
> Toward the lands we seek:
> The Far Lands of Maui
> Hidden in golden light;
> The light of the rising sun.
>
> The sky is lifted up.
> The empty sea still lies before us.
>
> Lift on, sail on, horizon beyond horizon,
> While the moons wax and wane
> And the stars wheel in their courses.
> Before us lies the promised Homeland
> Hidden in golden light;
> The light of the rising sun.
> Numberless moons have waxed and waned.
> A weary way we have come.
> Still before us lies the empty sea.
>
> Lift on, sail on!
> We are the children of Tané;
> He has hidden us in the measureless Sea of Kiwa.
> Koro shall never find us here.
>
> We are lost in this great Sea.
> Our guide has forgotten us.
> No longer do we hear his call.
>
> Hearken! From horizons beyond horizons it comes!
> Lift on! Sail on!
> We are the children of Tané;
> Our Homeland is there before us
> Hidden in golden light;
> The light of the rising sun.

They sang until a late hour under the light of the moon; then all returned to their dwellings, happy in the thought that the last tree needed for the building of their ships would soon be felled.

Now the story tells of that day, and speaks of the valley to the south where the ships were building, as it was seen in the clear light of early morning. Excepting the very old, all of the clan were there, both men and women. Some of the women were collecting and preparing the thick, viscous sap of the breadfruit tree used for calking the ships; others, under the direction of the master craftsmen, were plaiting the double- and triple-ply sails of pandanus leaf, carefully rolling those to be used as spare sails and wrapping them in fold after fold of tapa cloth made waterproof, for stowage.

Within the long open-sided sheds stood the twin hulls for each ship, shored up at the exact distance to the fraction of an inch, one from the other, and men were at work fitting to the hulls, fore and aft, the great crossbeams that were to hold them securely together. Of all their tasks there was none of greater importance or requiring greater skill than this, for these crossbeams with their lashings must be so strong, so firmly bound to the hulls, as to be able to meet all the stresses of wind and sea when the ships, loaded with their human freight, were under way, the twin hulls straining and pulling one against the other. Here the strongest men were at work, under the direction of master shipwrights who watched each turn, cross-lacing and knot made in the ropes of sennit lashing beams to hulls. Sweat streamed from the faces and down the bare breasts and backs of the men engaged in this task.

At another shed men were building up from the hulls the thick, beveled-edge planking, each plank so perfectly shaped and smoothed that the seams between them could scarcely be detected, but as each one was set in place the beveled edges were calked with the sap from the breadfruit tree. The men lashing them to the hulls worked opposite one another, one row within the other outside the ships, chanting as they worked:

> Thread it from inside; it goes outside,
> Thread it from outside; it comes inside.
> Tie it firmly! Bind it fast!

Of all this busy throng, none were happier, or worked with greater zest, than the younger apprentices — boys of ten, twelve, and fourteen years. Some acted as tool sharpeners; others swarmed over the ships already completed or nearing completion, scraping, smoothing, oiling, polishing: the masts, the beautifully carved prows and sterns, thwarts, paddles, steering oars, bailing scoops, and the great hulls themselves, eager to bring to the last degree of perfection in workmanship the beautiful ships which their fathers and uncles and older brothers had built. They chattered amongst themselves as they worked, and when they saw Téaro or Maui or one of the other *ariki* watching them approvingly, their hearts swelled with pride.

But a woeful day was that for the Tongans before evening came. Téaro had spent the morning and the early afternoon supervising the work at the sheds. About midafternoon he went into the valley where men were felling the last tree needed for the eighth ship. He had not believed that the tree could be felled that day; but the men had worked without rest, hoping to bring him that happy news that it was down, the trunk trimmed and ready to be floated down the river to the sheds. Because of the thick undergrowth around it, Téaro could not see the tree as he approached, nor did the men suspect that he was near.

Of a sudden the hewers gave a shout of joy. The great trunk trembled, leaned, and came crashing to earth, with a shattering and splintering of limbs and branches. It was not until some time afterward that the men found the body of their chief crushed to death beneath it.

✿✿ X I ✿✿
Maui Hears the Call

SEVEN DAYS were spent in mourning the death of Téaro. The people were dazed, numbed in spirit. They sat in their door-yards, or in groups on the assembly ground, scarcely believing that they could have lost their high chief at the time when they were so near to the end of their preparations for escape, when his leadership was so urgently needed. Mauri was little seen during the period of mourning. He remained in his father's dwelling, apart from the other members of his family. But Paoto was abroad at all hours, mingling with the people. He was the chief least respected by them; nevertheless he was hearkened to at times when they were seized by doubt and despair concerning the future. Of all the *ariki* he alone was the prophet of misfortune and calamity, giving voice to the fears sometimes hidden in the hearts of even the bravest. Later they would feel shame at having listened to Paoto and would despise him more than ever.

On the evening of the final day of mourning Paoto joined a group of yeomen sitting on the grass at the inner border of the assembly ground. The sky was ablaze with stars and the faces of those seated there were hidden by the deep shade of the trees. With the customary greeting, *Ia ora na, outou,* Paoto seated himself amongst them. The others waited in silence to hear what he would say. Presently he spoke.

"We are at the end of our last day of mourning," he said; "a day that might have been foreseen from the time of our arrival at Kurapo. Have you others considered the cause of his death? Téaro was in the full vigor of life and health, all of his senses alert and active. How, then, could he have failed to see and hear, in time to save himself, the falling of the great tree that crushed him?" No one spoke, and he continued: "Because Koro, whose power no one can doubt, willed his death. No one could honor Téaro more than myself, but you older ones will remember how, when we first came to Kurapo, he refused to acknowledge the power of Koro. Could that be forgotten or forgiven by the war god, or Puaka, his priest? Never! Then came the day when Maui not only violated the *tabu* set by Vaitangi, who had befriended us for twelve years, but he entered the very temple of Koro himself. Why do I speak of what you all know? To warn you of what I am convinced is true: the time for Koro's full vengeance upon us is at hand. Unless we can escape from this land before the return of Puaka and his warriors, our doom is certain."

Silence followed; then a voice spoke in the darkness. "Paoto, of what worth is such talk? Do you seek to discourage us further? Do you think that Tané is powerless to aid us?"

"No," said Paoto; "but I would have us remember what Métua, our priest, himself acknowledges: the mightiness of Koro's power for evil, and the undying hatred toward us of Puaka. And now that we are without leadership . . ."

"Without leadership?" another voice broke in. "With Métua, our beloved priest, still with us, and with Maui to take his father's place?"

It was Taio who spoke; Paoto recognized his voice. He replied: "Taio, your love for Maui is known to all of us. It does credit to your heart, but not to your judgment. It blinds you to the fact of Maui's youth and inexperience. If he is to lead us in his father's stead, I see nothing but misfortune ahead, and perhaps death for all, granted that we can escape from Kurapo. If we are to succeed in this we must have as leader a man mature in both years and judgment. That man is Rata, Maui's uncle. It is my hope that he will be chosen when the council meets tomorrow."

Taio replied: "I am only a man of yeoman blood, but I have

had the honor of being Maui's teacher throughout the entire period of his boyhood. Putting aside the dignity of your position I will tell you this, Paoto: you are worthless as a judge of character if you would place Rata before Maui as the chief best qualified to lead us. All of his father's high qualities live again in Maui. Despite his youth, he has the maturity of a man ten years his senior. I predict that he will surpass even his father in seamanship, and that his name will be passed on to future generations of our people as one of the greatest chiefs who has ever led our people."

On this same evening, Maui had mounted the path to the temple, where he found Métua awaiting him; the priest was seated in the grassy court before the eastern side of the temple.

"I expected you, Maui," said Métua. "I know what you have come to tell me."

Maui glanced at the priest. "You know?" he said. "Métua, how is that possible? What I have to confess has been hidden in my heart since boyhood. I have scarcely dared to acknowledge it even to myself."

"Nevertheless, I know," said Métua, "but I would hear it from your own lips. Speak now, freely, openly, keeping nothing back."

Maui then unburdened his heart. Long was the telling. He began with the afternoon in boyhood when he had taken the two baby terns as far as the *tabu* tree where Hina was to have met him, and went on through the events of that evening when he had witnessed the killing of the prisoners brought home by the war fleet and had, later, unknowingly, entered the temple of Koro and had found himself facing the awful figure of the god himself. "Métua, I felt then, looking into that evil face, that we Tongans were doomed: my father, myself, and all of our people. It was as though Koro himself stood there, not an image made in his likeness. The fear of him and the sense of our powerlessness against him have been buried in my heart from that night to this. I have struggled in vain to conquer this fear. How, then, can I be worthy to take my father's place if I am chosen to do so? I am less fit for leadership than Paoto himself would be."

Métua did not reply for some time; then he said: "Maui, now that you have spoken freely and for the first time, do you not feel that a great burden has been lifted from your spirit?"

"Yes, I feel that," Maui replied.

"You have borne it alone too long, my son."

"How could it have been otherwise?" the young man replied. "Could I confess, even to you, that I, the son of Téaro, believed in Koro and his power for evil rather than the love of Tané as the greater force? I felt that I was lost, unworthy of my blood, unworthy of even the lowest place as a Tongan."

"And you believed that Tané himself had turned his face against you?"

"That above all, for when I prayed to him I received no reply. The fear in my heart was as great as before."

"You kept your secret hidden, as you thought, from me. Who should intercede for you if not the priest of Tané?"

"It was shame, Métua. How could I speak? Tell me this: was it Koro himself that I saw in that great image?"

"It seemed so to you?"

"Yes."

"You were then a child, my son; a boy of twelve years. Why do we Tongans have no image of Tané in our temple? Because nothing fashioned by human hands could truly represent the spirit of love. But the spirit of evil can be shown, for it comes from the evil in the hearts of men themselves."

"Then Koro has no reality save in the hearts of men?" Maui asked.

"No, Maui. The image made to represent him has no power save for those who worship it. But Koro, the spirit of evil, is as real as Tané himself, and he has great power to harm us. But with Tané's help men can conquer their fear that the power of evil is greater than the power of love. The time is at hand when you yourself will conquer it, once and for all."

"May Tané grant it!"

"Wait here," said Métua, rising to his feet. "Whether or no you are to be chosen to lead our people in your father's place is hidden even from the priest of Tané, but his will concerning you shall soon be known."

Métua vanished among the trees within the courtyard of the temple. An hour passed and still Maui waited. The waning moon was just rising as the priest returned. He took Maui's hand and they walked to the rocky promontory where lagoon and sea lay outspread below them. Métua stood in silence for a moment, looking far out over the lonely sea. Then, as though speaking in the very presence of Tané, he said: "Our loving Father, Thou seest us, Thy priest, and Maui, son of Téaro, whose ancestors for generations have led us eastward toward our distant Homeland. If this young man is worthy of leadership; if it be Thy will that he should take his father's place, I pray Thou wilt make it known to him."

They stood waiting, with bowed heads. Presently, in the profound stillness of the night, they heard, as though coming from an infinite distance, the clear call of Maui-the-Peaceful. Maui sank to his knees, his face hidden in his hands, his heart filled with joy and gratitude. A moment later the call was heard once more, the very ghost of sound, coming from horizons beyond horizons eastward, over the measureless Sea of Kiwa.

On the following morning the Tongan *ariki* assembled at the council house to decide who now should lead them; for, although the position of high chief was hereditary, passing from father to oldest son, Maui was not the first-born of Téaro's sons. An older brother had been lost with one of the ships that had become separated from the others on the voyage to Kurapo and never seen again, but what its fate was none could know. Therefore, since the vanished ship might have reached some land, and the older brother be still living, Maui could take his father's place only with the full consent of the council.

As they were crossing the assembly ground Métua said: "Maui, I shall not make known to the others that you have heard the call."

"That is well," said Maui.

"I would have them choose you for yourself alone. But should it be Rata, I would have you know what the others have not yet suspected: he is no true worshiper of Tané. Your father had great trust in him. Had he lived, it would have been my duty to warn him."

"Whether or no I am to take his place, your warning shall not be forgotten," said Maui.

It was Rata who, of right, presided at this meeting. The other chiefs sat on either side, and Maui at a little distance, facing them. Maui was a splendid figure of a young chief: well-proportioned, broad at the shoulders, slim-waisted, with his father's sturdy limbs and well-shaped head. And his features were so like his father's that it might have been Téaro himself, as a youth, who sat there, quietly waiting for them to speak. Rata was the first to do so.

"It will be understood," he said, "that I favor this young man above any other. In outward appearance he is his father over again. Nevertheless, my counsel is that he be not chosen. First, because of his youth. Granted that Tané's promise, revealed to us through our priest, is to be fulfilled and that we are able to escape from this land: are we to be led on our quest by a boy of nineteen years? But a greater reason is this: although, as I have said, he resembles his father outwardly, there the resemblance ends. I put aside considerations of blood relationship. I think only of our welfare as a clan. Therefore, I say openly, here in the presence of Maui himself, that he lacks those qualities for leadership that his father possessed. He is impulsive, headstrong, lacking in judgment. Young though he was when he violated the sacred Koro temple, even a boy of twelve, son of the high chief, should have reflected upon the misery such an action would bring upon his father's people. Maui says that he entered the temple unknowingly. That is as it may be; but he broke the *tabu*, only less sacred, established by Vaitangi who had been our friend and protector up to that time. My belief is that, when Maui entered the temple of Koro, there was planted in his heart a terror of the war god that he has never been able to overcome. Maui himself must acknowledge this. If he does, what more is there to be said?"

Then Métua spoke — these few words only:

"I have no wish to influence your decision, one way or the other, as to who our leader shall be. I ask only that you listen to what Maui has to say."

Then Maui rose and replied: "My uncle objects to my youth, but this is a fault that time will cure, and I am not, I hope, so lacking in my father's qualities as he would have you believe. My breaking of the *tabu* placed upon the Koro lands by Vaitangi was due, as my uncle says, to the impulsiveness of youth, but that I entered the temple of Koro knowingly as he, it seems, would have you believe, is not true. Nevertheless, the sense of guilt for having become responsible for the death of so many of our people is one that I shall carry to the day of my death. But it has, I believe, prepared rather than unfitted me for leadership. Rata says, further, that the fear of Koro was planted deeply in my heart as a boy, and that I acknowledge. Fear in itself is not a shameful thing; only if one is conquered by it does it become so. The noblest of our ancestors have known what it is to dread the power of Koro. But I ask you to consider well what Rata has said: that fear is at the basis of my nature. If you believe this, it is your sacred duty to choose someone else to take my father's place. I will now leave the council chamber, for I wish you to discuss this matter freely and openly. I have only this to add: if you decide against me I will, loyally and faithfully, serve under any member of this council whom you may appoint in my stead."

Maui then left the council chamber, and it soon became clear that all of the *ariki*, save only Rata, Vana, his son-in-law, and Paoto, strongly favored him. When these realized that the others would have Maui and no one else, they, too, gave him their suffrage, but Rata said: "Time alone can tell whether this young man is worthy of your trust, but I would remind you that you have chosen him whom Koro has the greatest reason to hate, on his father's account as well as his own."

Maui was then called in and informed by Rata himself that he had been chosen; and Rata said: "Maui, I opposed your selection because of my belief that you lack the qualities for leadership so necessary to us at a time when our very existence as a clan is at stake. But I have never doubted the nobility of your character and I know that it is not in your nature to harbor ill will against me."

"That I shall never do," Maui replied, "as long as you remain a Tongan." He then turned to the others and said: "I am deeply grateful for your trust in me and shall do my utmost to deserve it. I have this to suggest: that you do not confirm me in my father's place until we have escaped from this land and are far out at sea. I would first prove by my actions whether or not I deserve your confidence and your faith in me."

Tuahu said: "Maui, we have known you from childhood, and I, for one, need no proof of your qualities for leadership. I am as certain of them as that you stand here before us." The others, save the three mentioned, who were silent, spoke as Tuahu had done. They would have Maui confirmed at once as high chief in his father's place, and this was agreed upon.

Then they discussed what should be done with respect to the Koros, for it was necessary that they should be informed, not only of Téaro's death, but that Maui had been chosen in his father's place; and that Vaitangi and Uri — acting as priest during his uncle's absence — should be invited with the other Koro chiefs, to the ceremonies of Maui's inauguration. But the Tongans were forbidden to send a messenger to the Koro *ariki*, and so, while working steadily on their ships, they waited for the arrival of a Koro messenger who, customarily, had come once and, often, twice in every moon. But at this time none came, and the Tongans were both puzzled and anxious as to the reason why they failed to come. And so, when one moon had passed, it was decided that the services connected with Maui's confirmation as high chief should proceed nevertheless; but there were to be none of the feasts and games that would have followed under usual circumstances, for the Tongans knew that every day was precious to them.

At Maui's request, one day only was spent by the chiefs in the solemn service at the *marae* when he was invested with the sacred robes and the chaplet of red feathers which his father had worn.

On the evening of this day, when the ceremonies had been completed, Maui returned with Métua to his father's dwelling. As they approached it a man stepped out from the deep shade of the trees bordering the path.

"O Maui?" he said.

"I am," Maui replied.

The man then placed in Maui's hand a small packet wrapped in green leaves. "I was ordered to bring you this," he said. "The sender is known to you." He then vanished in the darkness along the path leading up the valley.

They entered the house, and Maui stood by a candlenut lamp, examining by its flickering light the parcel he held in his hand. With a glance at Métua he slowly removed the covering of leaves. Within lay a coral pebble, smooth, round, perfectly shaped, and of the color of sunlight. It was enclosed in a net of bark thread, but the meshes of the net were dry and withered and fell to pieces in his hand.

"You recognize it?" Métua asked.

Maui nodded, gazing at the pebble in silence, wonderingly, as though scarcely believing it the same that the priest had told him to hide in a secret place, so long ago.

When they were seated on the mats Métua said: "Maui, seventeen years ago, on the night when we Tongans reached Kurapo, you were at the point of death, and your mother as well. All of this you know; there is no need to repeat the tale. Vaitangi's daughter-in-law took you from your unconscious mother's arms and fed you at her breast with Hina, her own infant. It was then I knew that you children were destined for each other. Whether or not that destiny is to be fulfilled it is for you to decide."

"Hina has sent me this?" said Maui, still gazing at the pebble.

"Who else?" said the priest.

⚔ X I I ⚔
The Message

TOWARD NOON on the following day Maui was approaching the small lake hidden amongst the mountains. Seven years had passed since he had taken Hina there and guided her into his secret cavern. Never since that day had he returned, but there, he knew, he would find her. Why, he wondered, had she sent for him after so long a time? What message did she wish to bring him? He found it hard to remember that she would no longer be the child whom he had last seen. Never had he forgotten her, but after what had happened when he had broken the *tabu* set by Vaitangi, he had never expected to see her again. He hurried on, half walking, half running, but as he neared the lake he slackened his pace, halting within the shelter of the forest to look in either direction along the beach of white sand bordering the lake along the eastern side.

All was silent there, save for the faint cries of the seafowl wheeling above the crags on the far side. He drew in his breath sharply as he saw a pair of small footprints leading from the border of the forest across the beach to the placid level of the lake which was shimmering brightly as though someone had disturbed the surface of the water only a moment or two before. The sun had disappeared behind the tallest of the crags to the west. Quickly Maui threw off his waistcloth, trussed up the small garment beneath it and plunged into the lake. The light which, for so brief a time at that hour of the afternoon, revealed the entrance to the cavern, was beginning to fade. Maui dived, and a moment later his head broke water within the deepening gloom of the cavern itself.

For a moment he could see nothing; then as his eyes became accustomed to the semidarkness, he saw the figure of a girl seated on the low ledge of rock on the opposite side of the pool. The light which came through the opening in the roof, though fading now, fell like the ashes of gold upon her hair and her bare arms and shoulders. She sat with her arms clasped around her updrawn knees, and, in the dying light, her body seemed to be vanishing into darkness even as he looked at her. He drew himself up beside her, and as though to convince himself that she was real, he laid a hand on her cool wet shoulder.

"Hina . . . ?" he said.

After a moment of silence the girl replied: "I thought you would never come. I have waited since morning."

"And I have waited since we were children," Maui replied.

"Waited? . . . Where? In your father's house? Did you expect me to come to you there?"

"Hina . . ."

"Do you remember what you told me when we came here together, so long ago? You said: 'This is *my* cave. I shouldn't have brought you here; you're a Koro.'"

"I remember," Maui said.

"But it has been mine since that day."

"You tell me that you have come here since?"

"Didn't you know that I would, if only to thank you for the baby terns?"

"I never dreamed of it. How could I have, after what had happened? When your grandfather left our valley for the last time he told my father that we would never see him again, or any of his family."

"And you believed that he spoke for me as well? Does the daughter of a Tongan high chief have no mind of her own? Does your sister, Tauhéré, obey your father in all that she does?"

"Hina, you were only a child, then. How could I have guessed that you would ever come here again? I can scarcely.

believe in you even now, in this darkness. Let us go out, I want to see you."

"After this long time!" the girl replied bleakly. Maui could think of nothing to reply, and after another period of silence she asked: "Did you bring the pebble?"

It was now so dark in the cavern that she was only a voice to him. Taking the pebble from a fold in his *pareu* he groped for her hand and placed it there.

"I should go, now," she said, "leaving you here to suck it. What was it you were ordered to say by your schoolmaster on the day when he placed it in your mouth? 'I, Maui, son of Téaro, am deeply at fault, and I willingly suck this pebble.' I should make you say it again. . . . Maui! Maui! I came here six times in four years, hoping to find you; and then no more, until today. I saw that it was useless."

"Hina, you must believe me! I never thought of you trying to see me again. Why haven't you sent the pebble before? I would have come the moment I received it."

"Did you, today? I have been waiting for hours."

"There was a reason why I could not come earlier. Let us go out now. We can't talk in this darkness."

"Not yet. What I have to say is better told in the darkness. You know nothing of what has happened in our family?"

"Nothing," Maui replied. "The messengers Puaka sends us bring only his orders. They are as arrogant as Puaka himself and tell us nothing. We might be living in different lands for anything we have heard. Tell me, first, about your grandfather, and your mother. My mother longs to hear of her welfare."

"She is dead," Hina replied, in a desolate voice.

"Dead!" Maui groped for her hand and held it. "My little Hina! Your mother? Dead?"

After a silence the girl spoke again. In a lifeless voice, as though recalling events that had happened long ago, she told him how Puaka had steadily gained such power over the Koros that only a few of the older chiefs remained loyal to Vaitangi.

"Puaka hated my mother from the time when you Tongans came to Kurapo and she saved your life by feeding you at her breast. Later, when you were found in the temple of Koro, Puaka knew that he could do what he would against your family; that none of the chiefs would dare to stand up against him. But he worked secretly to destroy my mother. We have sorcerers in our clan who obey Puaka in everything — evil men who can kill even members of the high chief's family when he has lost his power to protect them. So it was in my mother's case. Puaka employed two of these men to destroy her slowly so that it would appear that she had died of some unknown and incurable illness. She wasted away until she was no more than a shadow of herself. When death came she was buried with great ceremony, and Puaka himself was one of the mourners. All knew that he was the cause of her death but none dared say a word against him."

"But . . . Vaitangi, your grandfather?"

"Maui, you would not know my grandfather could you see him now. He is dying of the same cause."

"You tell me that your grandfather, the high chief, is powerless to resist?"

"Yes. He believes it is Koro's will that he should die because of his kindness to your people and his long friendship with your father and your priest, Métua. He will do nothing to save himself, because he is convinced that nothing can be done. *Pifau*, it is called, this killing by sorcery. The men who practice it have power greater in this way than that of Puaka himself."

"But your grandfather still has friends among the chiefs. Can they do nothing to help him?"

"You know nothing of Koro sorcerers if you think that! And now there are only two or three of the older chiefs who remain loyal to my grandfather. Many love him, but fear of Puaka and of Koro rules their lives."

Neither spoke again for some time; then Maui said: "And I am to blame. Hina, do you realize that? For the death of so many of my own people; for the death of your mother . . ."

"No, Maui!" the girl replied, quickly. "My mother's death and my grandfather's would have happened in any case at a later time. Puaka is fifteen years younger than my grandfather, stronger in will, and with a heart filled with evil. With Koro's help he was bound to gather all the power into his hands, and so he has . . . Let us go out, now. I can stay only a little longer. First I will put our pebble back in its niche." Putting a hand on his shoulder, she got to her feet. They were now invisible to one another. A moment later she said: "Wait a little. I will go first. I am all but naked. You are not to see me so at this meeting, after so long a time."

She plunged into the pool, inky black in the darkness, but he saw her slim shadowy body as it passed through the area of dim light coming from the lake. He followed a moment later. Hina was awaiting him on the beach, dressed in a mantle of dyed bark cloth of a soft and beautiful texture, worn only by the daughters of chiefs, which was gathered over her breasts, leaving her arms and shoulders bare and reaching to her knees. Maui waded slowly toward her through the shallows and placed his hands on her shoulders, holding her at arm's length. She looked into his eyes, questioningly.

"Is it the Hina you remembered?"

Maui continued to gaze in wonder and adoration at the slim lovely girl, just blooming into womanhood, who stood before him. Slowly he shook his head. "Not the one I remembered. Not even the one I have dreamed of as she would be now. My little Hina! How could I have guessed that you would be so beautiful?"

"Didn't you think I was pretty when we were children?"

"Yes; but now . . . Hina, do you remember the day on the lagoon when I said the prayer to Maui-Ataranga, and the great coral shoal came alive with thousands of little fish? When we looked up, there was Métua, our priest. Do you remember what he said? He told us that we belonged to each other."

"And you remind me of this after seven years have passed," the girl replied, bleakly; "now when it is too late."

"Too late? . . . Why? . . . Hina, you are not married?"

She shook her head. "But I am to be, very soon."

"To whom?"

The girl made no reply. Maui seized her by the arms. "Answer me, Hina? Who is this man? Do you love him?"

"What right have you to ask me that?" she replied, proudly. "Whether I love him or not, how can it concern you who had all but forgotten me; who made not one effort to see me in all these long years?"

Maui stared at her for a moment; then got to his feet and walked down the beach. Presently he returned, slowly, and when he came to where she sat, stood looking down at her.

"Hina, I must know the truth."

"I have told you. I am to be married soon, when the war fleet returns."

"With your consent? . . . Answer me: do you love this man?"

"I am a Koro," the girl replied, "as you reminded me often when I came with my mother and grandfather to the Tongan valley. I am no longer a child, but a woman. I feel in me a great need and a great power for loving. Is there anything strange in that?"

"I am waiting," Maui replied grimly.

Hina sat with her eyes fixed upon the ground. At last, without looking up, she replied, in a low desolate voice: "You remember how, when we were children, you defeated Uri at stone throwing? He never forgave you for that. And now, in his turn, with his uncle's help, he has defeated you. Can you doubt that I love him when I have come to tell you this?"

She got to her feet, ran into the forest and sank down in the fern, her face buried in her arms. Maui quickly followed and knelt down beside her. "Hina! My darling! My little Hina! Forgive me! Forgive me!" She lay still, making no response as he pleaded with her. "Hina, I was mad, out of my senses for a moment."

Gently he drew her up to her knees and held her close, his cheek pressed against hers. Presently she took her hands from her face and gazed forlornly at him. As he lifted her to her feet she put her arms around him and clung to him so, her face pressed against his breast.

"Maui, I am lost! There is nothing I can do. Nothing."

"Uri! That man of mean lineage, whose uncle has murdered your mother! It is not possible!"

"But it is! I am betrothed to him."

"With your grandfather's consent?"

"Have you not understood? My grandfather is a broken old man: broken in spirit, broken in health, broken in will. He consented, if it may be called so. This will tell you more of his condition than any words of mine. He is like a child in Puaka's hands. Puaka knows that the one thing needed to give him complete control over the Koro Clan, and his nephew after him, is a marriage between Uri and myself."

"And, darling, that shall never be."

"Never!" Hina replied. "I will destroy myself first. The time will not be long when I must. . . . Maui! Maui! Destined children, Métua called us. And so we are: destined for death — both!"

"Never believe it . . ."

"Wait! Let me tell you what I know; it is why I sent for you. The time is near when you Tongans are to be destroyed. Not one of you will be spared. The attack will not come until Puaka returns; I am to be married then. My grandfather is to be kept alive until that time; but before he is destroyed you will be. You are to be taken as the sacrifice offered to Koro on the day of my marriage. Then will follow the attack on the Tongans."

"You are certain of this?" Maui asked.

"I was told by an old chief who is my grandfather's friend. He can do nothing to prevent it, but he wanted me to know."

"Hina, did your grandfather never tell you what he said to my father when he left our valley for the last time?"

The girl shook her head.

"He foresaw what was to come. He said to my father: 'Build your ships! Build swiftly! You have no time to lose!' That was six years ago. Can you believe that we Tongans have failed to heed that warning?"

Hina drew back and looked up at him as though trying to grasp the truth of his words. "Maui! You are telling me . . ."

"That we have been building our ships, by day and by night, from that day to this. The last ship will soon be completed. I was working upon it this morning, which is the reason I was late in meeting you. We have no time to lose."

The girl continued to gaze at him, an expression of mingled joy and unbelief upon her face. "If the war fleet is delayed beyond another moon," Maui added, "Puaka will find nothing but empty dwellings in our valley. Now, Hina, we must make our plans: when and how you are to join me."

"How can it be?" she said, woefully. "Maui, you must think of your people, not of me, lest all of your plans come to nothing."

"It can be and it shall be," he said. Hina was silent as he continued, eagerly and confidently, telling her of the preparations now so nearly at an end. "We are working day and night as I have said. Soon we shall be able to set the very night when we shall leave this land. I will let you know of this as soon as I myself know and we will then arrange where I am to meet you. It must be on the morning of the day itself so that the Koros will have no suspicion of what we do. I will come for you before dawn and lie hidden in the thickets just above the head wall of your valley . . ."

"No, Maui! Not there! Never again must you come within our lands! Promise that you will not!"

"Then by the *tabu* tree. I will wait there, hidden in the fern. Have you servants you can trust?"

"Yes; the man who brought you the pebble; he and his wife, both. They love me as they loved my mother. His wife is the woman to whom you gave the baby terns."

"Then you see how simple it will be? You will have only to give them an excuse for your absence during the day. When night comes and you fail to return, you will be with us, Hina — with me, looking back at Kurapo as it sinks into the sea behind us."

"If it could be now, this moment," Hina said, mournfully. She held his hand tightly between her own as though fearful to let it go.

"It will be at a moment not long to be waited for."

"And if it comes, what will your people say? What will they think when they see you bringing me, a Koro, amongst them?"

"You will be welcomed with joy, with deep affection. Can you doubt it?"

"By your mother and sister, of that I am sure. But the others . . ."

"My darling, do you think they have forgotten what we Tongans owe to your grandfather and to your own mother? Had it not been for your grandfather we would have been lost, waiting without hope for the return of Puaka. . . . Can you doubt what I say even for a moment? When Métua, our priest of Tané, knows that you belong to us; that we belong to each other?"

"He still believes it?"

"Last night when your servant brought me the pebble, Métua said: 'I have known since you and Hina were children that you were destined for each other. Whether or not that destiny is to be fulfilled it is for you to decide.' Hina, do you love me? You have not told me so in words. I want to hear you say it."

"I loved you when we were children," she replied, in a low voice. "I had for you then the deep affection of a small sister who had no brothers of her own. Now that I am a woman, can you even guess how I love you? . . . Maui, we have so little time."

"So little time? We have all the years of our lives to love each other."

"So little time that we can be sure of . . . and no more for today," she added mournfully. "I have been away since early morning and dare stay no longer."

"When can I see you again? Let it be soon, Hina. I may be able to tell you at the next meeting when we are to go."

She reflected for a moment. "Let it be twelve days from now. On that day there is to be a service to pray for the success of the war fleet. All of the chiefs will be at the temple during the day and the night as well."

He held her close, stroking her hair, her bare arms and shoulders, while she clung to him. At last she pushed him back. "Maui, my beloved one, I must go now."

They walked hand in hand to the border of the forest which enclosed the eastern side of the lake and parted there, for Hina would not permit him to go with her across the open lands beyond. In the golden light of late afternoon, Maui watched her descending the fern-covered slopes until she was lost to view behind a fold in the hills.

⚔ X I I I ⚔
The Fleet

THE STORY gives the names of the ships, their captains, and the number of people to be carried in each one.[1]

SHIP	PEOPLE
Tokérau (The Northwest Wind)	80

Nihau was captain of this ship. He was the husband of Tauhéré, Maui's sister, and a chief greatly beloved and respected by the Tongans.

Te-Ava-Roa (Long Passage)	75

Ma'o was her captain. He was the son of Rangi, the first of the Tongans taken for sacrifice after Maui had broken the *tabu*. He was strongly built and one of the best of seamen. Although Maui had been the innocent cause of the death of Ma'o's father, the friendship between the two had never been broken. They were like brothers.

Iriatai (The Horizon)	70

Her captain was Marama, the son of Tuahu, one of the four chiefs who had lived to reach Kurapo. He was thirty-five, and, like his father, a man of the noblest character.

Itatae (The Ghost Tern)	40

This was Maui's ship, the smallest of the fleet and the only one equipped with an outrigger. It was built for speed rather than carrying capacity. At times it would sail in advance of the other ships, act in keeping the fleet together in times of stormy weather, and assist any ship in trouble.

Anuanua (Rainbow)	80

Faanui was her captain. He was the grandson of Tamuri who was the father of Vahiné, Taio's wife. He was among

---

[1] For pronunciation of ships' names see Glossary.

the best of the Tongan deep-sea fishermen, and was held in
great honor by the Clan because he had sailed farther eastward from Kurapo than any other, including the Koros
themselves.

Kotaha (Frigate Bird)   85

Her captain was Vana. He was married to one of the
daughters of Rata, Maui's uncle, and greatly under the influence of his father-in-law.

Éata (The Cloud)   80

It was Taio, captain of *The Cloud,* who had taught Maui
all the lore of the sea, and had told him the tales of Maui-
the-Peaceful and his brothers.

Kiwa (Named for Te-Moana-Nui-a-Kiwa)   90

Tavaké, her captain, was an uncle of Nihau. Métua, the
priest of Tané, would sail in this ship, which would carry
the casket containing the four sacred stones from the ancestral *marae* of the Tongans.

The eight ships were to carry 600 people, not counting infants.
Kiwa, the largest, was 100 feet long, with a beam of 9 feet, and a
depth of 5½ feet. Maui's *Itatae* was 45 feet long; beam, 5 feet; depth,
4 feet. The measurements of the others varied between these two,
but none were less than 8 feet in beam and 5 in depth.

Five of the ships had been moved on rollers from the sheds
and were now shored up on the bank of the river while the
last work upon them was under way. Between the masts of
the twin-hulled ships, platforms of light *purau* were built,
reaching across the hulls, and upon these platforms, houses
that would shelter from twelve to fifteen people were erected.
These were to accommodate some of the older people and
the wives and small children of the *ariki.* The houses were low,
measuring no more than five feet between platform and
ridgepole. The roofs were of pandanus leaf thatch securely
lashed to the rafters, and over them was a net of tough bark
cordage so that the roofs could sustain all but the strongest
winds. The hulls, which provided shelter for all the others,

could be protected in stormy weather by stoutly woven mats drawn across them, having loops to be fastened over cleats fixed along the gunwales.

The women had long been at work preparing the provisions for the voyage. The approximate time when the ships would be ready to sail had been estimated well in advance, and gardens of yams and taro planted accordingly, so that these slowly growing root vegetables would reach maturity by the time when they would be needed. Pits in the ground, lined with leaves, were filled with breadfruit and covered, to allow the fruit to soften and ferment in the warm earth until it altered to *poi*, the thick white paste, so rich in nourishment. Breadfruit was prepared in yet another way: it was baked, then rolled thin and reduced to flour. This was packed in long rolls, wrapped in dried leaves, and placed within lengths of bamboo. The yams and taro, now fully matured, were being dug from the gardens, some to be baked and packed for sea stores during the early part of the voyage; some to be carried in baskets for use at a later time.

There were no idle women and children as this work went forward. Some were preparing the containers in which the food would be carried: baskets, calabashes, lengths of giant bamboo, and the like. Others were occupied with the food itself. Even the old and feeble did what they could to help, concealing from the others the heaviness in their hearts as they thought of the dangers and hardships of the voyage so near at hand.

Children were scattered in all parts of the valley and along the beaches, gathering pandanus nuts from which was made flour of another kind which formed so important an item of their sea stores. The ships would also carry as many fully matured coconuts as room could be found for. Protected by their dry hard husks, they would provide food of last resort — both the meat of the nuts, and the spongy yellow *utos*, so rich in nourishment, which form within the nuts at the time when they are ready to sprout. Also, the children were bringing in

the pigs and fowls, which wandered at will in ordinary times.
They were enclosed in pens and abundantly fed, that they
might be at their fattest when the time for departure came.
The dogs were left free, for they frequented the houses and
would follow the people when the time for departure came.

All of these preparations were in full progress when Maui
returned from his meeting with Hina at the lake. It was late
evening. He came home by way of the ridge enclosing the
southern side of the valley where the temple stood. He found
Métua seated on a mat under the stars. Maui took his place
beside him and told of his meeting with Hina and the news
she had brought: of the death of her mother, her betrothal to
Uri, and of the woeful condition of Vaitangi, now completely
under the will and the power of Puaka.

When he had finished, Métua said: "Let this be kept a secret
between us for the present. Say nothing even to your mother
until a later time, for it would only grieve her."

"I shall do as you say," Maui replied, "but the truth cannot
long be hidden."

"Nor need it be," said Métua; "only during these last days
until our people are safely at sea."

"And Hina with us?" Maui asked. . . . "Métua, you have
the gift of foreknowledge: this is known to all. Tell me, then,
what her fate is to be, and mine."

"Have I not told you, long since, that you were destined
children?" the priest replied. "The events of your destiny are
known only to Tané. You have heard the call of your great
namesake. Is it not enough to know that you are under divine
protection?"

"Forgive me," Maui said. "I spoke as I did because of the
deep anxiety in my mind. Never have I lost the affection for
Hina that came in our childhood days; but how was I to know
how swiftly this would change? How could I foresee that the
old affection would become deep love from the moment when
I next saw her? Métua, now that I stand in my father's place,
my first duty is to our people. And at the time when we are all

but ready to leave this land has come this love for Hina. Am I to think of that, and of our great need for each other? Am I to risk the safety of our people so that Hina may be saved, and thus, perhaps, bring ruin to all our plans?"

"Hina herself has spoken of this?" Métua asked.

"She has," Maui replied. "She fears the evil power of Koro . . ."

"And that is not to be doubted," Métua said, quietly.

"She has reminded me of how far his vengeance may carry. More than this: she believes that, if she could come with us, the result will be nothing but greater misery for our people; that there will be those who will lay to her charge all the dangers, misfortunes and evil chances that we shall have to meet during our voyage eastward."

"That is true," the priest replied, gravely.

"Then . . . I must give her up?"

"Have I said it? Could you believe it, after what you have already been told?"

Maui peered into his face, dimly revealed under the light of the stars.

"Métua, how am I to understand your words? Both your meaning and your purposes are dark to me."

"Not my purposes — they are Tané's," the priest replied. . . . "Maui, you know how long we Tongans have been searching for our Homeland."

"I do," said Maui: "for more than twenty generations."

"And always there have been those who doubt that it will ever be found; yet we have sailed on, generation after generation. The faint of heart have been left behind, or they have died during the voyages, often because of their lack of faith which deprived them of the will to survive. Others have abandoned us to join those who are worshipers of Koro and lovers of war."

"You tell me, Métua, what I already know."

"I have not finished. I speak of the purposes of Tané. He sees us, this remnant of the once great Clan of the Tongans.

He sees what a small band we are. He has nothing but pity for the lives that have been lost and the suffering endured on our search for the Homeland. But only those are to reach it who are men of serene courage and unshakable faith. That is Tané's will, and it must be so. The promise of Tané extends to them and to them alone. 'Holy is the human spirit; sacred the body, its dwelling-place.' Maui, when all Tongans, without exception, believe this from the depths of their hearts, the Homeland will be found. It may be within your own life-time."

"And in yours, Métua, for who is so worthy to reach it as yourself, our spiritual leader for more than sixty years?"

"I am an old man, now in my eighty-sixth year," Métua replied. "I feel no slackening in the will to live, but I may not have long to be with you."

"May Tané keep you safely for years to come," Maui replied, earnestly. "You have a greater power of life in you than men who might be your sons."

"Tané's purposes with respect to myself are hidden," the priest replied; "but I know them as they concern you and Hina. If her life is joined with yours, the union will prove to be the greatest of blessings, not only to yourselves and your children, but to the Tongan Clan for generations to come."

"Then so it shall be," Maui said, fervently. "I have no means to express the joy, the gratitude in my heart for what you have told me."

"It need not be expressed save by your actions as you lead our people on the voyage eastward," the priest replied. "Maui, the hope I have expressed is no idle one. But bear this in mind: the Far Lands of Maui will be reached only by those who are worthy of the quest."

"Never shall it be forgotten!" Maui replied.

⚡ XIV ⚡
The Wishing Marae

WHEN TWELVE DAYS had passed, four of the ships lay moored stem to stern in the river. The masts had been shipped and rigged, the sails were ready to be bent on, the paddles were in their racks, and the great steering oars lay aft beneath the thwarts, ready for use. Under the platforms where the steersmen would stand, was stored gear of all kinds that would be needed for the voyage: coils of extra line; fireboxes filled with sand; air- and watertight containers for fire sticks, bone-dry *purau* wood and tinder; lengths of bamboo filled with coconut oil; carved wooden chests of tools — adzes, shell scrapers, bone needles, calking hammers, and all other implements and accessories needed, whether at sea or on land. The master shipwrights were at work on the ships not yet completed, attaching the planks already shaped and fitted that built up the hulls; making the platforms and erecting the small houses to stand upon them, weaving the last of the matting spritsails, and rigging masts. Meanwhile the artisans and apprentices were shaping and polishing paddles, steering oars and bailing scoops, and preparing crates for fowls. In the sheds from which ships had been removed, provisions for the voyage were being stored, ready to be carried aboard.

Early on the morning of this day Maui set out along the path leading westward across the island. He walked rapidly and the sun was not yet two hours high when he reached the tree from which hung the *tabu* emblem. This was no longer the emblem of Vaitangi: three red lines crossed diagonally

with one of blue. The design on the streamer was now that
of the priest of Koro: a swastika, an ancient emblem amongst
the Koros and chosen by Puaka for that reason, for he would
have it believed that he was descended from a family of noble
origin, although it was known that he could trace his blood
back only four generations to an ancestor of no importance
among the Koro *ariki*.

As Maui stood looking at this emblem, he recalled with a
feeling of desolation all that had happened from the day in
boyhood when he had broken the *tabu* set by Vaitangi: the
horror of the scenes he had witnessed on the night of the return of the Koro war fleet; the terror in his heart when he
had found himself in the Koro temple, with the huge figure
of the war god facing him, holding him there, powerless to
move. He remembered the anguish of the year of his punishment when, by his father's order, he was shunned by his people, forbidden to speak even to his mother, and compelled to
carry to his father news of the sounding of the great Drum of
Koro, announcing the approaching death of another member
of the Tongan Clan for which he alone was responsible.

As he stood there, engaged in these somber reflections, he
heard a slight rustle in the fern and Hina was there beside him.
Her face was alight with happiness as he took her in his arms.

"Maui, how sad you look! Let us hurry away from this hateful place." She glanced at the sun. "The morning is not half
finished; we have all the rest of the day to be together. Come
quickly! We must not waste any of it!"

"Could you come without risk?" Maui asked.

The girl nodded. "I am safe for the day and most of the
night. Only the two old servants of my mother know that I
have gone, and even they do not know my reason for going.
You must promise one thing: we are not to speak, either of us,
of what is past or what is to come."

"But Hina . . ."

She put the palm of her hand across his lips. "For my sake;
for both our sakes! Do you promise?"

"Willingly, gladly, my little Hina, but I have news that you must be told . . ."

"Then tell me later, before we say good-by. This day is ours. We have so little time . . . that we can be sure of," she added quickly, as he was about to interrupt. "You remember what I told you? I feel in me a great need and a great power for loving . . ."

"Do you think it is greater than my own? But, darling, you are not to think that we have only this day. We have all the years to come . . ."

"I try to believe it, but this day is all I am sure of. Let us hurry on to the lake."

Hina followed him through an area of wooded land beyond which was a long ridge covered with bush and fern, rising in one place to a conical hill about three hundred feet high. The sides of the hill sloped gradually, and at the summit, which was flat and bare, stood a small stone structure. Maui halted there and turned to Hina.

"Do you think you could run all the way to the top of that hill?" he asked.

The girl regarded the long slope rising before them. "I might," she said, doubtfully. "Why?"

"The little platform at the top is the Tongan wishing *marae*. It is sacred to Rua, the god of wishes. If you can run to the top, never halting and not once falling, Rua will grant whatever wish you make when you reach his little temple."

"And if I should not succeed, what evil thing will happen?"

"No evil thing. Your wish will not be granted, that is all."

"Then I will try," she replied, eagerly. "You, too?"

"Of course, but look well before you decide. As you see, there is no path, and the hill is steep in places."

Her glance traveled slowly up the boulder-strewn slope.

"You want to risk it?" Maui asked.

Hina nodded, her lips pressed firmly together. "I can do it. I must! Darling, wish me up before I start, and keep wishing until I'm there."

"Rua doesn't permit it," Maui replied. "Remember, I'm coming, too, and we have, each of us, only one wish. Let me tell you this before you decide: only three Tongan girls have ever been able to do it."

"Then I can," Hina said. "Tell me when to start. Just the sound of your voice will help."

She glanced shyly at him. "I can't run in my *pareu*. May I take it off?"

"Darling, do you think I would object? Of course you must take it off."

Turning away from him she let it slip to the ground. Beneath she wore only a strip of soft tapa cloth around her loins. It was marked with a design of breadfruit leaves so beautifully printed that Maui could easily imagine that the girdle had been made of the leaves themselves, for the cloth, a delicate shade of brown, was so nearly the color of the girl's skin that it could scarcely be distinguished from her body. A faint flush mantled her cheeks as she turned toward him.

"I didn't want you to see me so until we reached the lake," she said.

"Darling, stand as you are only for a moment! How could I have guessed that you would be so beautiful?" He would have taken her in his arms but she eluded him. "No," she said. "When I have had my wish, not before." She plucked a fern, stripped off the leaves and gave him the stem to which they had been attached. With both hands she gathered her thick dark hair closely at the nape of her neck. "Tie it there, firmly, so that it won't come loose while I'm running." Maui did so; then she stood for a moment regarding the long slope above them, breathing deeply the while. She glanced back. "I'm ready."

"Hina, you can do it. I *know* you can! Breathe easily for a moment or two. . . . That's right. . . . Now then — ready? . . . *Haéré oé!*"

The slope was gentle for about fifty paces and the girl ran with the grace of a young gazelle, dodging in and out amongst the boulders and leaping over the higher clumps of fern that had impeded the way. Maui stood with his hands clenched, following every step of her progress. Now she had reached the steeper part, but she ran on at a pace that astonished him; it was as though, before starting, she had marked every bush and boulder that might cause her to fall. Maui felt his chest tightening and his breath coming in gasps as he watched, but on she went, her hair flying out behind her, and at last he saw her slim figure at the summit of the hill, clearly outlined against the sky, and scarcely larger than doll-size at that distance. She turned to wave and then sank to the ground.

Maui girded up his waistcloth, and, after breathing deeply for a moment or two, followed her. He had made this trial before, in his fifteenth year with a group of Tongan boys and girls, and had been one of two youths to succeed; all of the girls had failed. He remembered the agony of the earlier climb, but now, with Hina waiting for him at the summit, it seemed to him that he ran without effort. Nevertheless, when he reached the *marae* he sank down beside Hina, breathing so hard that he was unable to speak for a moment or two.

"Hina . . . You're . . . you're wonderful! You . . . you seemed to have wings on your feet."

"I *had* to do it, for both of us," she replied. "That is why I could. Do you remember the day when you left me so far behind, coming up the path from your valley?"

"You were a fine little climber even then," Maui said.

"I could have climbed faster, but I was so mad at the way you had treated me. . . . You remember?"

Maui nodded. "And that morning was the beginning of our friendship."

"No," Hina said. "Mine began the year before, when I came to your valley with my grandfather; and you didn't even notice me."

"Oh, yes I did; but you were such a little thing, then. Mine really began long before yours, when we Tongans came to

Kurapo and your mother fed both of us at her breast. But I was too young, then, to know it."

"But Métua did. He said we were destined for each other. Are you sure that he still believes it? Tell me once more."

"What did you ask me to promise? We were not to speak of what is past or what is to come."

"Only this once. I want to hear again what he believes about us."

"It is part of the news I brought. On the night twelve days ago, after we met at the lake, I told Métua all that you had told me — everything. I told him that you were betrothed to Uri, and that I am to be offered as a sacrifice on the day of your wedding . . ."

"Maui, that will never be! We will die together! If they take you I will go into the very temple of Koro, and that is death for a woman, even the daughter of a high chief."

"Darling, it will never be," Maui replied quietly. "Neither of us will die. I will tell you what Métua said. He said: 'Maui, I know Tané's purposes as they concern you and Hina. If her life is joined with yours, the union will prove to be the greatest of blessings, not only to yourselves, but to the Tongan Clan for generations to come.' . . . My little Hina, there is to be no *If* from this day. That is why we are here together. Now make your wish."

"What is the ritual? What must I say?" Hina asked.

"Nothing. Kneel on this stone and make your wish only in thought."

"You are not to know what it is?"

"Later we can tell one another, but not here, at Rua's *marae*."

She knelt on the low stone, crossed her hands over her bare breasts, bent her head reverently, and remained thus in silence for a moment or two. Maui then took her place and told Rua his wish. While this little ceremony was taking place a small land bird — an *omaomao*, perched on the topmost twig of a small tree near the *marae*, sang his sweet and varied song, as though it were the voice of that lonely place, making the sunny silence seem the deeper. As Maui rose from his knees the bird took flight. They watched him rising and falling as though over waves of air until he vanished in the glades below.

"He was wishing for us, with his song," Hina said.

"It is a happy sign when an *omaomao* sings when someone is wishing," Maui replied. "It means that neither of us has asked more than Rua can grant."

They descended the hill to the place where Hina had left her *pareu*. Before she could stoop to pick it up Maui took her in his arms and held her close. "Now, my little Hina . . ."

"Oh . . . !" Hina drew back a little and glanced up at him with a half-frightened look in her eyes. "Darling, you must give me a little time."

With his arms still around her he loosened the fern stem at the nape of her neck, and spread her hair so that it shadowed and half concealed her face. Then, clasping his hands around her slim waist he drew her closer still and held her so.

"Maui, have pity," she said in a low voice. "I have dreamed of you so long. Let me dream a little longer."

He released her, and she threw back her hair, glancing up at him in a shy pleading manner. He cupped her face gently with his hands.

"My little Hina, the dream is nothing . . ."

"But it is, to a girl . . . on the day when she knows the dream is to come true. Maui, do nothing more and say nothing more until we reach the lake. Let me have my thoughts to myself until then. . . . How can I believe in such happiness? Perhaps I only dream that it is coming true."

Maui led the way along the fern-covered ridges and the green glades between them until they reached the forest land enclosing the lake on the eastern side. Hina stopped from time to time to gather flowers and the low-hanging blossoms of flowering trees whose delicate fragrance filled the air. When they had reached the wooded lands she gathered sweet-smelling ferns that throve in the deep cool shade, making a green carpet for the forest floor and hanging in clusters from the mossy trunks of great trees. Her arms were filled with flowers and ferns by the time they reached the lake. Here she gathered armfuls more, and, choosing a place dappled with sunshine and shadow just at the border of the lake, she prepared a soft and fragrant couch.

Maui watched longingly as she worked. "Stay where you are," she said, when he would have come closer. "My servants should be doing this, but how happy I am that we have none. They would hide and watch us, afterward." She tossed up fern and flowers, mingling and spreading them. Filling both hands with flowers, she pressed them to her face, then spilled them slowly over her head and shoulders. "They smell of heaven," she said. She let her hands fall to her sides and an expression of deep sadness came over her face. "The heaven of now," she added, forlornly. "The heaven of today, and tonight, only." She rose and walked slowly to him.

"But . . . my darling, you made your wish. Was it for no more than that?"

"I didn't dare wish for more. And I was right. The *omaomao* sang while I wished."

"And he sang for me as well, which means that I asked no more than Rua could grant. I wished not for today alone, but for all the years of our lives. Try to remember that Métua said: 'If Hina's life is joined with yours . . .' "

"But *if*, Maui; *if*."

"You don't believe?" He strode to where she sat, seized her hands and drew her roughly up and into his arms. He flung her *pareu* aside and held her fiercely, kissing her lips, her throat. He ran his lips over her smooth shoulders and, bending her back over his arm he kissed her body, her breasts, again and again. She lay limp in his arms, an expression of ecstasy upon her face that fired every drop of his blood. Lifting her as though she had been a child he carried her toward the couch she had prepared. Hina, seeing what he would do, struggled so fiercely that she broke from his arms and slipped to the ground. She stepped away from him, throwing back her hair as she did so. She was breathing quickly and her eyes flashed with anger.

"Do you think you can handle me as you would a girl of common blood?" she demanded, proudly. "The daughter and granddaughter of high chiefs of the Koros is not to be won in that fashion."

"But Hina . . ."

"Have you no sense of the beauty of love? Would you devour it as a hungry man fills his stomach?"

"Yes, when the hunger is past bearing," Maui said. "I would relieve the agony a little, knowing that the beauty of love is yet to come."

The light of anger died out of her eyes.

"Maui, you must remember that I am still a child, in part. I am bold in thought, in my dreams — more so than you could guess; but the child is not yet the woman she longs to be. Your love will make me that, but you must give me time to prepare for it. I will tell you how I have dreamed it. You must meet me in the cavern where you first showed me the coral pebble." She glanced at the sun which was nearing the peaks of the lofty crags on the opposite side of the lake. "Soon we shall go there. Can you wait this little time?"

"My Hina, forgive me! I thought only of myself; of my need for you. It shall be as you have dreamed it. I see how well you have planned."

"Now I must fashion my wedding gown," she said. She had carefully put aside some of the most beautiful and fragrant of the flowers she had gathered. Breaking off a low hanging branch of a *purau* tree, she stripped off a long segment of the smooth bark and with her teeth reduced it to slender threads upon which the flowers were to be strung. She worked swiftly, deftly, choosing as though by instinct the various shapes and colors of flowers to be woven in beautiful and harmonious patterns. She fashioned only two: a charming wreath for her hair, and a necklace to fall over her bosom. The work was soon finished and she hung her ornaments from the branch of a tree,

in the deep shade. When she looked again toward the sun it
had just disappeared behind the mountain.

"I can go now," she said. "We shall remain in the cavern
only until the light begins to fade. You are to wait here until
I call. Turn your back. You are not to look toward the lake
until you hear my voice."

Maui did so. He heard the light splash as Hina entered the
water. He turned when she called. "Come now," she said, and
dived toward the entrance to the cavern. On the beach before
him lay the little girdle she had worn, decorated with the design of breadfruit leaves.

As Maui entered the cavern Hina was seated on the ledge as
before, her hands clasped around her knees, but now the shaft
of sunlight coming through the opening in the roof fell directly
upon her so that her body was clearly revealed in golden light.
As Maui swam toward her she rose and stood awaiting him
with her hands clasped behind her head. When he stood before
her she laid her hands lightly upon his shoulders.

"This is our wedding chamber," she said, "and now is the
moment of our marriage. . . . I, Hina, granddaughter of Vaitangi, take you, Maui, for my husband, for this day and this
night, and for the days and nights to come, if our lives are
spared. Now speak your turn."

Then Maui laid his hands upon her shoulders and said: "I,
Maui, son of Téaro, take you, Hina, for my beloved wife, for
this day and this night and for all the years of our lives, for it is
the purpose of Tané that this marriage shall be a blessing not
only to ourselves but to our descendants for generations to
come."

Maui would have slipped his arms around her but Hina pre-
vented him. "This is the place of our marriage, not of our
union," she said. "Get your coral pebble. We are to stay here no
longer."

Maui fetched it and placed it in her outstretched palm. She
held it in the shaft of sunlight and it glowed with a golden
radiance as though it were a small sun in itself.

"It is no common stone," Hina said, in an awestruck voice.

"It is a gift from Tané himself; it must be," Maui replied. "It is to be a symbol of our love and of our lives together."

"You must take it with you, Maui."

Maui gazed wonderingly at her. "How could you know that?" he said.

"I guessed it. Métua has asked you to bring it to him. For what reason?"

He shook his head. "But it concerns us. It is to play some important part in our lives. Métua has known this — he must have — from the day when he took it from my mouth at the schoolhouse."

"How are you to carry it from here? Not in your hand; you might lose it. Open your mouth." He did so and Hina placed it there, closing his lips firmly over it. Then she kissed him. "That is for the seal," she said. "You are not to take it out, even on the beach, until I tell you to."

She dived into the pool and passed through the entrance to the lake, Maui following. When they had reached the beach Hina took him by the shoulders and pushed him down. "Sit here until I am ready," she said. With the pebble in his mouth Maui watched as she went into the sun-flecked shade at the upper slope of the beach. Sunlight and shadow dappled her slim naked body, moving caressingly over it as she knelt by the couch she had made, smoothing it with her hands and giving it a few last touches. She sat back on her heels, regarding it for a moment; then rose and went to the tree where she had hung her ornaments of flowers. She pressed the wreath down over her hair, passed the necklace twice around her throat so that it hung just above her bosom. Having donned this simple wedding gown she came into the full sunlight and halted before her lover. In silence she held out her hand and Maui placed the pebble in it. Taking up his clothing she folded it neatly and carried it up the beach, laying the pebble upon it. Then she returned to him.

"Now you may take me," she said.

He lifted her eagerly and carried her up the beach.

"Oh, my Maui! My darling!" she said in a low voice as he placed her upon the couch. She opened her arms. "Now my dream has come true!"

As they crossed the shallows to the beach the lake shimmered with silver fire, the broken reflections of the stars; then the disturbed water slept again and the stars reappeared as though in a fragment of nether sky. Hina's waistcloth was lying on the beach where she had left it. She took it up and they dried each other. Maui brought the girl's *pareu* and his own and spread them on the smooth warm sand.

"You didn't forget about our pebble?" Hina asked.

"No; I put it in a safe place."

They stretched out on their backs, gazing into the sky.

"It was only a moment ago that we came here," Hina said, forlornly. "Just past midday. Now I open my eyes and it is night."

"It hasn't gone, the night; not all of it."

"But it's going, so fast!" She sat up and smoothed his damp tousled hair with her fingers; then, bending over him, she caressed his body. He took her hands in both of his. "Hina, we must talk now."

"Of tomorrow? Of what is to come? No, no, Maui! Not yet! The night will go slower, this part, if we stay out here."

"But we must plan . . ."

"Look, Maui! See how that faint little breeze scarcely blurs the reflections of the stars. This must be where the *hupé* is born. Let me tell you about the song I made to Hiro. He is our god of the *hupé*. He lives up here in the mountains where the valleys begin."

"Perhaps our lake is his home?"

"No, it would be higher," Hina said, "where he could look down all the valleys. He blows very gently down each one. He is a gentle god, the only one the Koros have. How Puaka must hate him! His breath flows down so sweetly — you know how it is, my darling — carrying with it the lovely fragrance from the high lands and from the depths of the valleys. He cools the lands below; and he soothes the bodies and the hearts of all but evil men, dreaming of the evil they still wish to do."

"Have you watched the *hupé* rocking some of the leaves of the banana trees while others on the same stalk are perfectly still?" Maui said.

"Yes; that is Hiro's magic. They dance in the moonlight for one another . . . Maui, is there anything so refreshing as the quiet sleep he brings?"

"To young people, like you and me, deeply in love and longing for love, dreaming about it as we toss and turn on our mats at night?"

"I was not speaking of people in love. It isn't coolness, but the promise of it, that he brings to lovers. Maui, when I lay awake, dreaming of you, and felt the *hupé* so gently caressing my cheeks and my hair, it seemed that Hiro was telling me: 'My child, I cannot soothe the fever that torments you now, but have patience. The day will come when, your dreaming past and your love fulfilled, you will feel, for a time, a sweet content as cool and welcome as my *hupé*.'"

" 'For a time,' " Maui said. "How wonderful it is that it's only for a time!"

"That is because Hiro understands us humans. He knows we have hot blood within us. . . . Darling, my content is passing even as we lie here; but wait! Now I will sing you my song." Then in a clear soft voice, as caressing as the *hupé* itself, she sang:

> Hiro — É,
> Please tell me what the night winds say . . .
> Will my dear love be mine some day?
> Youth will go . . .
> Tell him so . . .
> Let him know . . .

Hiro — É,
Like shadow where the palm trees sway
My life without my love will be.
Hear my plea . . .
Send him soon
Back to me!

Maui took her by the shoulders, gazing at her under the light of the stars. "My beautiful Hina! How could I have helped hearing that lovely song? But you must remember . . ."

"I haven't sung it all the seven years," she said. "I prayed to Hiro only the last two, when I knew how deeply I loved you. And . . . at last, he brought you."

They spoke without words, and presently Hina, drawing her lips away, said: "I am safe, now."

"For always, my little Hina."

"Whatever happens, I am safe."

"But can't you believe that it is for always?"

"When you are loving me I can."

She broke off as the waning moon appeared above the hills that cut off the view of the eastern horizon. "Maui, it is morning," she said, in a desolate voice.

"Not yet. Not for another hour."

"But I must go before day comes."

"Hina, it is the waning moon we see. On the last night of the moon to come we are to leave this land. You and I will see that moon rising when Kurapo has sunk into the sea behind us."

"If only we could be sure!"

"Darling, I will tell you now what I have been waiting all this time to say. I have heard the call of Maui-the-Peaceful. . . . *Now* can you believe?"

"You . . . you heard his voice?"

"As plainly as I hear yours, and a second time, from horizons beyond horizons to the east."

Hina drew him down to her. "Maui! Conquer my fear! You do when you are loving me. Conquer it once more, here, under the stars!"

X V

The Sacred Stones

SOMETIME LATER, the Tongan *ariki* were assembled at the *marae* for the most sacred ceremony ever held in that place. The stars in the eastern sky were beginning to pale, but it was still half an hour until dawn, and a single taper on its high stand stood near the altar to Tané, throwing flickering lights upon the faces of the men who stood there. Now that the time of departure was so nearly at hand, they were to dedicate themselves anew, as their ancestors had done before them, to the quest for the Far Lands of Maui. For the first time since the Tongans had come to Kurapo, the four small sacred stones were brought from the casket in which they had been carried from their ancestral *marae* all the long way over the Sea of Kiwa. They were placed at the corners of the altar which stood in the temple enclosure. In the center of the altar, upon a pedestal of carved wood fashioned to hold it securely, was a half coconut shell, black with age and polished to a dull luster.

The light of dawn slowly increased and the taper was extinguished. Métua stood at the altar facing east, Maui at his right hand, Rata on the left, with the other *ariki* grouped behind them. No one spoke. They were awaiting the arrival of one of the temple assistants, who had gone in a canoe beyond the lagoon to dip a calabash of water from the open sea. Presently he returned and passed the calabash to Métua.

A few scattered clouds in the eastern sky brightened to crimson and gold. The chiefs still waited in silence, broken only by the first songs of the birds in the groves surrounding the temple grounds. Now the sun appeared, its light transfiguring the face of the old priest as he began the most sacred of the Tongan chants. His voice and his countenance had in them the peace, the serenity of the sleeping sea far below them.

> Holy is the human spirit;
> Sacred the body, its dwelling place.
> Men shall not kill.

The others responded:

> This is the Law of Tané
> Obeyed by men of good will.

When the chant was ended, Métua offered a prayer. He spoke with deep reverence, simply, quietly, as though he felt the unseen presence of Tané listening to the words of his priest.

"Tané, our Father, lover of all mankind, followed by so few: trusting to Thy loving care and to the guidance of Thy servant, Maui-the-Peaceful, we prepare to sail eastward once more in the quest for our Homeland. Father, Thou seest what a small band we are. Thou knowest the weary way we have come over the Great Sea of Kiwa. We do not ask that we here gathered shall reach the Homeland. But this we know: Thou hast made us, under Thy guidance, shapers of our own destiny. We ask only that we may meet with courage the dangers that lie before us. If our faith is sure, our belief in Thy holy law unwavering, then shall the Homeland so long sought for be found, even by Thy children of this generation."

Métua then took from the altar the pedestal holding the coconut bowl and carried it to the eastern side of the altar where it was set upon a low square stone. From the calabash he filled the bowl until it brimmed to the edge. The others followed him. He then said:

"Mother of Oceans! Measureless Sea of Kiwa! In your solitudes, far to the east, lies our promised Homeland. The day is at hand when we are to proceed on our quest. We now look into Thy waters, searching our hearts and our faces mirrored there. For each man's heart is a secret place known only to himself. Let him search well, that he may know if he is worthy of this quest."

Then all turned their backs to the stone where the pedestal stood with the bowl of sea water, for each man submitted to this test unseen by the others, the result known only to himself. Métua was the first. He sank to his knees and gazed long at his mirrored reflection in the bowl; then he gave place to Maui, who did the same. The other *ariki* followed, each in his turn.

When all had finished, Métua lifted the bowl from its pedestal with his two hands. Still facing seaward, he said:

"Mother of Oceans! Measureless Sea of Kiwa! I drink of Thy majesty; of Thy peace and beauty. I drink of Thy bitterness, that I may have the courage to meet the hardships and dangers that lie before us. I drink of Thy waters that have washed the shores of our promised Homeland. May I be found worthy to see it."

He drank of the water and passed the bowl to Maui. When all had done so, this solemn service was ended. The chiefs left the temple in silence, not speaking to one another until they had descended the path to the valley. Then all but Rata, Tuahu, Paoto and Tavaké, who remained at the village in case of need, hurried on to the valley, where the ships were all but ready for the voyage to come. Only *Te-Ava-Roa,* the last ship to be built, was still unfinished.

*　　*　　*

It was near midday when one of the men on lookout at the high place in the mountains came running down the path to the assembly ground. The people working in the valley, seeing him, and guessing from his manner and the speed at which he ran that he brought unusual news, called out to him as he passed; but he gave no heed. He found Tuahu and Paoto sitting in the shade before the council house. The man halted before them, breathing hard.

"Where is Maui?" he asked.

"With the ships," Tuahu replied. "What has happened?"

"The war fleet! They are returning!"

Tuahu stared at him as though doubting his words. Paoto was the first to speak. He stood clenching his hands tightly. "I knew they would come!" he said in an anguished voice. "I have feared it from the beginning! Now we are lost!"

Tuahu paid no attention to this chief. He was thinking fast. "All the fleet?" he asked.

The man shook his head. "We have sighted three ships."

"How far distant?"

"Just above the horizon. I came at once. The others may be in sight by now."

Tavaké and Rata came, half-running across the assembly ground, and the people then in the valley gathered there. The word went round swiftly: "The war fleet! They are coming home!" But there was no panic amongst the people. The expressions upon their faces were grim as they crowded around the four chiefs, but they stood in silence, listening.

"Send for Maui at once!" Rata said.

Glancing inland, Tuahu saw another man from the lookout on the headland to the north running down the path which led to the valley. "Wait!" he said. The man soon reached them. "The war fleet . . ." "We know," Tuahu interrupted. "How many ships?" "Three," the man replied. "One — Puaka's great ship, has left the others and is headed this way."

"Now are we surely lost!" Paoto said, in a voice of despair. "Puaka will discover everything!"

Tavaké turned to him sternly. "Why do you say that? The jungle remains between the ships and the lagoon; nothing can be seen from the sea, and Puaka is coming from the opposite direction."

"Send at once for Maui," Rata repeated.

"No, Rata," Tuahu said. "We must send him word but beg him to stay where he is."

"With Puaka himself coming here?"

"For that reason," Tuahu replied. "We can make an excuse for Maui's absence."

"Remember this," Tavaké said. "Puaka doesn't know that Téaro is dead. He will ask for him, not Maui."

"We must decide at once what is to be done," Rata said. "There is not a moment to lose."

Nor was there. While the four chiefs were talking, Puaka's ship, the largest of the war fleet, appeared from behind a distant headland to the northeast, not more than eight miles distant. There was no wind that morning and the men were paddling. Even at that distance the rhythmical flashes of the paddles in the sunlight could be plainly seen. A man was immediately sent to inform Maui, and to urge that he remain there until later news could be sent.

Rata and the three chiefs with him were deeply concerned, for there were no more than one hundred people in the Tongan valley at that time, all others being with Maui. The chiefs made haste to put on their ceremonial robes, and the people were ordered to come near the entrance of the valley so that it would appear to have its customary number of inhabitants. And they were to retire gradually inland as far as the assembly ground if it appeared that Puaka would go to the council house. During Puaka's rare visits to the Tongan valley, he had scarcely glanced at any of the *ariki* save Téaro, Rata, Maui and Métua. It was therefore hastily and fearfully decided that some of the old men of the *raatira* class — the yeomen — still in the village, should don the robes of the missing chiefs, so that it might appear that the full council of the *ariki* were present to greet Puaka. This was a dangerous subterfuge but the risk had to be taken.

Rata standing in front, the others on either side, they waited the approach of Puaka's canoe. It was eighty feet long, with fighting platforms fore and aft and a smaller one amidships where Puaka himself stood in the midst of battle; it was also his honored place during the voyages; and when returning home from the expeditions against their enemies, a small house would be erected on this platform for his comfort. But now the platform was bare; the great fighting ship had been battered by wind and sea, and by enemies of the Koros as well. One mast was gone and the gunwales were splintered in places as though hacked by clubs and spears and damaged by stone missiles. Puaka's battle dress was torn and frayed, and the plumes of his great war helmet were in a sorry state. The ship lacked its full complement of one hundred and twenty fighting men; there were not more than eighty in the vessel, which was brought into the shallows broadside to the beach.

Rata stood at the water's edge, facing Puaka, who remained seated on his platform.

Rata was about to make a formal address of welcome. "Puaka, high priest of Koro," he began, but the priest interrupted him.

"*Haéré mai,*" he thundered in a harsh voice, making a beckoning gesture. "*Haéré mai, outou!*" (Come, all of you!) The little company of Tongan chiefs, real and supposed, waded into the water until they stood, shoulder-deep, a short distance from the ship; and Paoto, who was of short stature, was submerged to his neck. Then Puaka rose from his seat and stood regarding them with a hostile glare.

"Where is Téaro?" he demanded, and as no one replied, he repeated, in a voice of thunder, "Where is your high chief? Why has he not come to meet me?"

Then Rata said: "Our high chief has been killed . . . in an accident. He fell from a cliff."

Puaka's warriors looked from him to the Tongan chiefs, standing abjectly in the water. The priest's eyes gleamed balefully as Rata spoke.

"Dead? Good!" he replied, with an evil smile. "Do you know why he is dead, you worshipers of Tané? Because it was the will of Koro that he should die. He has been punished as you shall all be punished. Who now stands in his place?"

There was no reply, and, with a black scowl, Puaka said: "Will you answer me? Who is now the leader of your people?"

"Myself," Rata replied, in a low voice.

"You are now high chief of the Tongans?" Puaka asked. "You have been appointed in Téaro's room?"

Rata hesitated and then shook his head. "No; it is Téaro's son, Maui. I act for him only, in coming to greet you, and make you welcome."

"Maui?" replied Puaka, his eyes gleaming with pleasure. "Maui? . . . Then why has he not come to welcome me?"

"He is fishing, at sea," Rata replied. "He has been gone since early morning."

Puaka turned to scan the empty horizon, and the forbidding scowl deepened once more. "Where is your priest?" he then demanded. "Why is he not here?"

"At the temple," Rata replied. "He does not know that you have come. It was only a few moments ago that we ourselves saw your ship approaching."

Puaka said: "Fetch him to me." Rata glanced at Paoto who was about to wade ashore to send a messenger for Métua, when Puaka said, "No! Stand where you are!" Paoto gave him an awed glance and remained.

The priest reflected for a moment, elbows on his knees, looking at his two huge hands which he clasped and unclasped slowly; then he glanced at Rata.

"I shall stay here no longer," he said. "Tell this to your priest. Seven days from this day, Maui is to come to me. He is to come alone. If he fails to come, he shall be sent for; and a black day that will be for you worshipers of the god of peace." Puaka then ordered his paddlers to proceed. Looking back toward Rata, he said: "Stand where you are, you chiefs of the Tongans, until my ship is beyond the pass."

No greater humiliation could have been offered than that which Puaka had forced upon the chiefs: making them stand shoulder-deep in the lagoon before his ship and keeping them there after his departure. Never before had they suffered such an indignity, but they submitted to it knowing that their fortunes and their lives depended upon the events of the next few days. They watched the departing ship, deeply grateful that the only passage through the barrier reef, large enough for ships, on the east side of the island, was that opposite their valley. Had Puaka been able to follow the lagoon he might well have seen the prints of many feet on the beach where the ships were building, or have noted signs of activity there that could not have been completely concealed in the little time given the Tongans. Puaka's ship proceeded around the south side of the island, but it was well out at sea, two miles at least from the beach. Maui and the greater part of the clan with him watched from the jungle that concealed the mouth of the valley, until the ship had disappeared around a distant headland. Then Maui, having given instructions to the people who were to remain there, returned with the chiefs to the village where he called all of the *ariki* to the council house.

The meeting was brief, for little time could be spent in talk. Rata spoke first, telling of the meeting with Puaka; of the humiliation he made them suffer, and of the demand with respect to Maui. The faces of all were grim as they listened.

"This is the end," Paoto said, in his despairing manner. "We are caught, now, and helpless."

Vana, son-in-law of Rata, said: "We have seven days. Could we not do this? Could we not appear to submit to Puaka at once, even to the extent of destroying our temple . . ."

"You would be willing to do so?" Tuahu interrupted, gazing at him in horror.

"It could be done," Paoto broke in eagerly. "Tané is all-knowing; he would understand our desperate situation and permit us to pay lip-service to Koro. He would know that his own *marae* is established in our hearts until such time as we could again worship him openly, without fear."

"And you would have Maui carry this news to Puaka?" Marama said.

"It is Maui who must go," Paoto replied. "Puaka demands it."

Out of the silence that followed Maui said: "Rata, we should like your council as to what we must do."

Rata said: "My son-in-law's suggestion is a hateful one. Were we fully prepared for escape he would not have offered it, nor would we have needed to consider it. But *Te-Ava-Roa,* our last ship, cannot possibly be ready for sea until the time we had set for sailing: at the dark of this moon. This is the second day of the new moon. At whatever cost, we must gain the time yet needed. Therefore, we may consider what Vana has suggested without disloyalty to Tané or dishonor to ourselves. Our situation is, in truth, desperate. We must make what terms we can."

"If we make these terms, Puaka will be content, you think?" Tavaké asked.

"For the moment, at least," said Rata. "Before he is ready to proceed further against us, we shall be gone."

The others listened in silence, amazed and shocked at Vana's suggestion and that Rata should favor it. They strongly opposed it, but Métua said: "It could be done if there were no other way, and Tané himself would understand. For, sacred though his temple is, he would permit us to destroy it if we kept our faith in him and obeyed his holy law."

"Then should we not do so, to gain time?" Paoto asked.

Maui spoke: "That we will leave to the Koros," he said; "for they will destroy our temple. But it will not be until we have gone from this land, taking with us the four sacred stones which came from the first temple raised to Tané by our ancestors. Rata says that *Te-Ava-Roa,* our eighth ship, cannot possibly be made ready for sea until the time we have set for sailing. I say that it will be ready on the seventh day from this day. With Tané's help, you shall sail on the night of that day."

Maui's words, and the quiet manner in which he spoke, stirred them deeply; even Paoto felt a brief renewal of hope, but fear and despair soon conquered again, although he tried to conceal this, knowing that their only hope lay in Maui. For Paoto now realized that Maui had, despite his youth, his

father's high qualities of leadership. Paoto could boast of his
lineage and nothing more. He came of an ancient family and
among his ancestors there had been men whose memory was
held sacred by the Tongans. Paoto was tolerated by the people
for this reason, and many had a reluctant affection for him
because he was fully aware of the weakness of his own character. Secretly, he despised himself and believed that the
secret was known only to himself. His wife, Nanai-Vahiné, was
a woman strong in will and of unshakable faith; she never
doubted that the Homeland would be found. She was a
woman huge in size, and gay of spirit, loved by all the people.

The story tells how Maui, on the day of this meeting of the
ariki, made his plans for the little time that remained. Only
the people who were needed to finish the work yet to be done
were left in the valley of the ships. Twelve of the best shipwrights were set to work completing *Te-Ava-Roa*. This being
the last of the ships, there had not been time for the wood to
season, and work on it had been delayed for that reason, but
now not a moment was lost; the ships must be completed despite the fact that the wood was not properly dry. Another
group of men and boys were set to work deepening the channel at the mouth of the river where it was obstructed by sand-
banks. Half of the sea stores for the voyage were already lying
in the sheds from which the ships had been moved. The rest
was to be carried by night from the village where it was being
prepared. The people not needed for these tasks were to remain in the village ready for any emergency that might have
to be met with.

The greatest anxiety in the minds of the people was the fear
of pursuit, if they should succeed in escaping from Kurapo.
Six ships had left Kurapo in the war fleet, but only three had
been seen to return. The lookouts kept watch by night and by
day, but the three remaining ships might have returned by
night without being seen. But whether these were lost or not,
Puaka would set out in immediate pursuit the moment he

learned of the escape, and only three ships, filled with warriors, skilled in battle, might well destroy the Tongan fleet, crowded with women and children and with ships cumbered with supplies for the long voyage. The hearts of the people were heavy with dread as they thought of this possibility, but they kept their fears to themselves as their ancestors had done before them.

✤ XVI ✤
Maui's Humiliation

PUAKA RETURNED home with only three of the six ships that had sailed on the expedition against their enemies to the north. One had been lost during a storm on the voyage out. Two others had been overwhelmed by their enemies, and the men in them either taken or killed. Never before had the Koro warriors suffered defeat under Puaka's leadership. Not only had they returned with no prisoners, but twenty of their own men had been taken alive.

The Koros were shocked and stunned by the news and could scarcely believe that Puaka, their great warrior and priest of Koro, could have met with such a reverse in battle. Great was the mourning among the womenfolk for the husbands, fathers, sons and brothers who had not returned. Puaka realized the danger to himself in the loss of prestige which would, or might, result from his defeat. The following morning he called the Koro *ariki* together at the council house. He was in a black mood as he rose to address them.

"I have spent this past night alone in our temple," he began. "As I knelt before Koro I asked if the fault were mine that we had been defeated in battle; and that, if it were, he would strike me dead as I knelt before him. His reply was: 'Live on, my faithful servant. You have served me well.' I then said: 'Mighty god! How, then, am I to understand your anger against us, for we have suffered a bitter defeat at the hands of our enemies?' Koro then said: 'At the time when the boy, Maui, desecrated my temple, my command to you was to wait before destroying those worshipers of peace whose high chief refused to recognize my power. But you have waited beyond the time I would have had you wait.' 'Am I to be blamed for this?' I then asked. And Koro replied: 'My anger is directed against Vaitangi and those who have favored him, and opposed me, in showing forbearance toward the worshipers of Tané.' "

Puaka paused, and glared accusingly at some of the older chiefs who had remained loyal to Vaitangi. He went on to speak of the commands he had then received from Koro.

"These are — first: that the Tongans are to destroy their temple with their own hands while I and my army look on. Then this remnant of Tané's followers are to be slain, there, in the ruins of his temple."

One of the older chiefs, who despite the danger to himself had remained loyal to Vaitangi, asked: "Are all to be slain, without exception?"

Puaka replied: "This Koro leaves to my discretion, and I shall spare a few of their master shipwrights that they may continue to build our war canoes. Their wives and children shall be destroyed and they shall live amongst us as slaves."

"What of their women?" a young chief asked.

"Koro does not forget the rewards due to his warriors," Puaka replied. "When all the men have been slain except those few I have spoken of, Koro grants our fighting men a day and a night to take their pleasure of the Tongan women in the presence of the bodies of their dead. Then they, and their children, are to be killed.

"I will soon set the day when the attack is to be made," he continued. "I speak now of two who are to be slain upon Koro's altar: Métua, their priest, and Maui, who now stands as high chief, in his father's place. Maui shall be first. As you know, my nephew, Uri, is betrothed to Hina. This young girl is guiltless of the crimes of her grandfather who is now suffering punishment by the will of Koro. It is also Koro's will that her marriage with my nephew shall now take place, and that Maui shall be the sacrifice offered to him at that time. I have ordered him to come here six days from now. If he fails to come he will be fetched.

"I have one thing more to say: there is to be no mourning for the men we have lost. Instead of this, it is Koro's will that our people shall be entertained with feasts and games to be held throughout the day and the night of my nephew's wedding. See to it, you chiefs, that preparations are made at once for these festivities."

The story returns to the Tongans and tells of the grim and desperate efforts made for early departure, now that their danger was so great. It was agreed among the chiefs that the people should not be told that Maui was to go to the Koro valley on the seventh day, lest it increase the fear already in their hearts. As for Maui, he worked day and night upon *Te-Ava-Roa* with the others assigned to this task. One of the twin hulls had been only half shaped and hollowed, nor were the great crossbeams ready which were to bind the hulls together. The men worked in shifts; not a moment was lost; even so, Maui's hope, that they might sail on the night before he was ordered to meet Puaka, was not to be realized. Meanwhile, at night the beach was thronged with people, men, women, and children, carrying the last of their supplies from the village to the ships. They dared not work by day lest they should receive an unexpected visit from the Koros, nor did they use their canoes by night. All their sea stores were carried from the one valley to the other, the people keeping within the shadow of the trees along the upper slope of the beach. The pigs were led by the children, a tether to their legs and their snouts closed with strips of bark. But the greatest burden they carried in their hearts: fear of discovery before they could leave Kurapo; fear of pursuit if they should succeed in escaping.

Early on the evening of the sixth day Maui called his ships' captains together. Their faces were grim, for they knew that Maui had been commanded to meet Puaka in the Koro village on the following day.

Maui said: "You have worked harder and accomplished more than could have been expected; but *Te-Ava-Roa* is still unready for sea."

Ma'o, who was to captain *Te-Ava-Roa,* said: "Maui, let this be done! Sail, you others who are ready. As you know, there is a hidden cove not a mile from here to the south. I can move my ship there this night, with those who are to go in her. We can lie concealed and complete the work on *Te-Ava-Roa.* The Koros will have no suspicion that a ship has been left behind. When ready, we can await our chance, slip out in the darkness and follow you."

There was an immediate protest by the others at Ma'o's suggestion, and Maui said: "No, Ma'o, we go together and tomorrow night is the time of our going. This you can and must do, you others. Work the night through and the whole of tomorrow and *Te-Ava-Roa* can be at least fit for sailing. What remains to be done can be done at sea."

"What of yourself, Maui?" Faanui asked. "You will go to meet Puaka?"

"I must," Maui replied. "If I failed to go I would be sent for and everything would be lost."

"You will never return," Tavaké said in a heartsick voice.

"That is far from certain," Maui replied quietly; "but if it should happen so, it will not be the first time that a high chief of the Tongans has been lost. Say no more of this but think only of the safety of our people. In all of our history Tané has never failed to send a favoring wind at the time of our departure from whatever land, nor will he fail us now. Leave well before midnight, so that you may be far beyond the horizon before day comes."

"And you, Maui?" Marama asked.

"Ru has my instructions," Maui replied. "*Itatae* will be the last ship to leave. Ru will wait for me until midnight. If I have not returned by that time he will follow you."

Ru, Taio's youngest son, was the steersman and second in command of Maui's ship.

Then this brief meeting ended and the men returned to their work, most of them fearing that they had seen Maui for the last time. Ru remained with him, and they returned to the village and took the path to the temple of Tané. It was full night when they came back there. Ru remained at the priest's dwelling while Maui went with Métua into the temple grounds. The casket where the sacred stones were kept stood on the altar. The priest took from it the golden coral pebble which Maui had brought from the cavern at the lake. It was now enclosed in a net of strong fiber, the color of the stone itself. Métua hung it around Maui's neck.

"I am to wear it, yonder?" Maui asked.

The priest nodded. "It has lain in the casket with the sacred stones of Tané, which have been handled by our ancestors for more than twenty generations. Maui, the spirit — the *mana* — of the noblest Tongans has gone into the golden pebble which you wear. Be worthy of them. I know you will." The priest then embraced him. "Go, now," he said, "and may the grace of Tané go with you."

Maui set out with Ru along the path leading to the main Koro valley. The moon shone in a cloudless sky but it disappeared behind the mountains before they had gone far. Maui walked ahead, engaged in his own reflections, Ru following. When they reached the *tabu* tree they seated themselves beneath it.

"Ru," said Maui, "I will tell you now what I have told no one save our priest. It is to be kept secret from the others until a later time." Maui then told him of Hina, of the love that had grown up between them, of the news she had brought of the death of her mother and the woeful plight of her grandfather. He spoke of her betrothal to Uri and of her marriage to the nephew to the priest of Koro, now so nearly at hand.

"Whether it is set for the night to come or the night to follow, I do not know," Maui said; "but I will save her from it, if I can."

"Tané guard and keep you, Maui," Ru said, earnestly. "I will remind you of what you have often told me: that the destiny of us Tongans, under the guidance of Tané, is largely in our own hands. Surely, this applies to men as individuals as well as to the clan."

"So I believe," said Maui; "but a man may be mistaken in what he thinks he believes. There is but one way of learning the truth: he must be put to the test of action. That ordeal is now to be mine."

"May Tané give you the strength to meet it!" Ru said.

Maui was long silent. Then he spoke again. "Ru, it is not death that I fear. It is fear itself, the fear of Koro. When, as a boy, I entered his temple, and saw that huge figure with his evil face, his eyes staring into mine, holding me powerless to look away, I knew that I was in the very presence of evil. I have no words with which to express the horror and despair of that experience. I carried the fear in my heart until the death of my father. I then confessed it to our beloved priest, and with his help I believed that I had conquered it. But now that I am to stand once more in Koro's presence . . ."

"They will take you to his temple?" Ru asked, in an awed voice.

"It is certain," Maui replied. "Puaka will receive me there. Pray for me, Ru," he added, laying a hand on his friend's shoulder. "The mere thought that you are doing this will give me strength."

"That I shall," Ru replied. "I will be with you in spirit, and I would gladly be with you in the flesh, if that could be."

"Before we part, let me repeat what I have said. The other ships are to sail as soon as darkness falls, if that is possible. You are to wait for me no longer than midnight. If I have not come, proceed to sea at once. Steer southeast and lie, as nearly as you can, barely within view of the beach of Kurapo. *Itatae* can easily outsail, or, if it should fall calm, outpaddle any of Puaka's ships. If you sight them in pursuit, think no more of me, for I shall be dead. Lead them southeast, for they will believe that you follow the others. If we are not pursued, wait for me two days. My hope is to follow with Hina in a small canoe. At the end of two days you are to wait no longer, for we shall never come."

Now they took leave of one another. Ru stood in the path by the *tabu* tree staring westward long after the shadowy figure of his friend had disappeared toward the valleys of the Koros.

Dawn was at hand when Maui reached the place where the path began its steep descent to the valley. He waited there as the light increased, listening to the crowing of the cocks that came from all parts of the lowland. Now the people were stirring. He heard faintly the shouts and laughter of children at their morning baths in the river, and the clear, shrill *"Pé! Pé! Pé!"* of the women, calling their fowls together. Thin columns of smoke from breakfast fires rose in the still air, and spread in a milky canopy over the forests below. Nothing could have looked more beautiful, more peaceful in the morning light, and the sounds he heard were those he had been familiar with from babyhood. He gazed longingly back along the path he had come. As he turned to look into the valley once more he spied a group of women as they rounded a curve on the narrow trail that climbed the head wall. Maui concealed himself in the deep fern to wait until they had passed. He could hear their voices occasionally as they climbed, but they were silent for the most part owing to the steepness of the ascent. At the summit of the head wall there was a space of level ground, used as a resting place. Here the party he had seen halted to recover their breath. There were six of them, girls in their early and middle teens. Maui soon learned the nature of their errand: they were going into the forests for flowers and ferns with which to decorate the pavilion where Hina was to be married. Maui learned that the ceremony was to take place the following night, and that there were to be feasts and games for all the people both before and after the wedding. One old woman accompanied the girls who chattered freely of the coming events and the pleasures that were to be theirs.

One girl, stretched out on her back, her hands behind her head, spoke banteringly to the old woman.

"Mama Ruau, what would he be like — Uri? As a lover, I mean?"

"How should I know?" the old woman muttered, testily.

"What would it matter, what he is like?" another girl said. "I wish he would take me, just once. I would like to boast that I'd been loved by the nephew of Puaka!"

"I've had him," another girl said. The others protested loudly at this assertion, saying that Uri would not even glance at so homely a creature.

"He didn't care about my face; it was my body he wanted; anyway it was at night that he took me."

"Why haven't you told us before?" another asked.

"Because I knew you wouldn't believe me. But he did. Truly he did."

"I believe you, Vétia. What did he do?"

"He simply grabbed me, felt me over, and carried me into the bush."

"You knew it was Uri?"

"Yes; it was moonlight and I could see his face plainly."

"How was he? Tell us."

"I was so surprised and scared I can't remember. All I know is that he threw me down, took his pleasure, and walked away without even saying '*Maururu.*'"

"He didn't get you with child; that we know."

"If he had, it would have been killed at birth," Vétia replied. "I would have killed it myself. Who would want a child by such a brute?"

"Poor Hina! She can't love him, surely."

"Why should Uri care about that! But she'll have to bear his children. Puaka will see that she does. If she fails to, she'll be *pifaued,* as her mother was."

"Mama Ruau," one of the girls said, "tell us about your first lover. Did he please you?"

"Mamu!" the old woman replied. "Do you expect me to remember, after forty years?"

"I'll never forget mine," the girl said.

"You've never had one," a companion said, tauntingly, "and you fourteen!"

"I'm going to," the other said. "Tomorrow night."

"Who is it?" the others asked, eagerly.

"You're not to know," the girl said. "He is none of yours. He'll be loving me when Uri is loving Hina. I wouldn't change places with her, not for a thousand mats or the loveliest tapa cloth in all the chiefs' houses."

The old woman got to her feet. *"Haéré tatou!"* she said. "You've rested long enough." The girls, still chattering, followed her along the path toward the hills.

When Maui reached the valley he turned off the main path and followed one less frequented and farther from the river. He was not dressed in the robes of the high chief of the Tongans but in the simple costume of his daily wear, consisting of a mat and a small mantle of white tapa thrown across one shoulder. In stature and build, he might easily have been mistaken for one of Puaka's young warriors and was, evidently, so mistaken by some of those he passed who hailed him with the customary greeting from their dwellings. Maui hoped to reach the dwelling of Vaitangi before his presence in the valley was known, and he succeeded in this. As he crossed the open space before it he met the servant who was in Hina's trust, the one who had brought him the coral stone. The man stared without recognizing him at first. Quickly Maui made himself known and asked for Hina. Whether because of astonishment or fear, or both, the man replied only by a shake of the head. "Vaitangi is here?" Maui then asked. The man nodded. "Then take me to him at once," Maui said, and with an air of mingled terror and bewilderment, the servant led him into the large room that occupied the main part of the dwelling. Several women servants were there who stared as the other had done as Maui crossed to where Vaitangi sat, leaning upon a bolt of tapa cloth placed at his back to support him.

Maui was shocked at the change that had taken place in the old chief since last he had seen him. The flesh hung loosely on his huge frame, and on his face was the ashy pallor of death. His eyes, deeply sunk in their sockets, stared dully at the mat before him. He was not aware of Maui's presence until the latter said, "Vaitangi . . ." Maui repeated his name before Vaitangi raised his eyes, regarding him with a forlorn, puzzled expression; then his glance returned to the mat. Maui seated himself, facing the old chief. "Vaitangi, I have come to greet you. I am Maui, son of Téaro." The old man glanced up once more, and a barely perceptible frown wrinkled the withered skin of his brow, but he gave no sign of recognition. Seeing that the effort was hopeless, Maui rose and beckoned to the servant who had ushered him into the room. "Send word to Puaka that Maui, high chief of the Tongans, is awaiting him here," he said. The servant hesitated, gave him another frightened look, and departed. Maui vainly questioned the women servants who stood in a distant part of the room; they merely stared without replying. Two left the room, but one remained. Maui took this woman by the shoulder and demanded, sternly: "Will you tell me where Hina is? No one shall know that you have spoken." In a low voice, scarcely above a whisper, the woman replied: "At the House of the Virgins. She may come, presently"; then she too followed the others, leaving Maui alone with the old chief. He tried once more to speak with Vaitangi but it was plain that he was neither understood nor recognized. He went to the door and looked out upon the assembly ground, which was thronged with people, for the sports and games in honor of Uri's coming marriage were already in progress. The chiefs were seated in a pavilion on the opposite side of the ground, watching the contestants. A moment later Maui saw Puaka come from the place and stride toward Vaitangi's dwelling, the people making way before him. He was followed by his nephew.

Maui stood in the center of the room, looking toward the door. As Puaka entered he halted to gaze at Maui. A hideous smile came into his face, and as he approached he made a bow of mock courtesy.

"Welcome to the son of Téaro, high chief of the Tongans," he said. "You should have let me know when to expect you so that you might have been received with greater ceremony. I am happy that Vaitangi, high chief of the Koros and your father's old friend, was here to receive you."

Maui made no reply.

"My nephew has come to greet you as well," Puaka said. "He has not forgotten your old boyhood friendship."

Uri was now twenty-one. He was of about Maui's height, but heavier in build. He regarded his old enemy with the same look of insolent pride as that shown at the time of their first meeting. He turned to his uncle.

"Is he to stand before us as though in the presence of equals?" he asked.

"Kneel to my nephew!" Puaka commanded.

Maui stood with his arms folded, looking full into Uri's face.

"Did you hear me? Kneel!" the priest repeated, and, as Maui made no motion to obey, Puaka struck him a blow in the chest that sent him sprawling. He was no match in strength for the gigantic priest of Koro, but his spirit was unconquerable. He got to his feet, and, as he still refused to kneel, Puaka struck him a second time, on the head, a blow that knocked him senseless.

When he opened his eyes he found himself lying where he had fallen. Puaka and Uri were no longer there, but four of Puaka's warriors were standing at the doorways, apparently waiting for him to regain consciousness. Vaitangi sat at the farther end of the room, gazing at vacancy. As Maui rose to a sitting position Hina appeared at the doorway followed by two women servants. She gave an inward gasp of astonishment and dismay upon seeing Maui, but her face immediately assumed a blank expression and Maui himself gave no sign of recognition as he looked at her.

Hina turned to one of the soldiers. "Who is this man?" she asked.

"It is Maui, high chief of the Tongans," the man replied.

Hina went to her grandfather, kneeling beside him for a moment, speaking in a low voice and smoothing his hair as she did so. Vaitangi gave no sign that he recognized her. As she passed Maui again on her way to the door, she gave him another glance that seemed to express complete indifference; then she left the room, followed by her servants.

Maui got slowly to his feet, and two of the soldiers, taking him by the arms, escorted him to the assembly ground. He was surprised to find that it was now late afternoon. A throng of people was seated around the borders of the common watching a wrestling contest between women. A path was cleared through the crowd and Maui was escorted across the full width of the assembly ground to the pavilion where Puaka sat with his *ariki*. He stood at one side, with his guards, until the wrestling contest was finished; then he was brought to where the priest was seated and left standing there.

With a brusque gesture Puaka motioned Maui to turn toward the crowd. He got to his feet and stepped forward a few paces. As he stood there, the loud murmur of voices died away to silence. Puaka then spoke, his harsh and powerful voice carrying to the limits of the assembly ground.

"People of Koro," he began, in a mocking voice, "you see here, Maui, son of Téaro, and now high chief of the Tongan Clan. You will remember how this young man, in his boyhood, came to visit me at the temple of Koro. He has had reason, since, to repent of that visit, and his people with him. Now he has come again, to tell me that he wishes to renounce the worship of Tané. His people will destroy their temple with their own hands and place themselves at the mercy of Koro and his priest. How that mercy shall be expressed remains to be seen. But Koro commands me to tell you that he will accept this young man. He further commands me to provide him with a wife, for he is of marriageable age. I have, therefore, selected three beautiful virgins for him to choose from. Gather more closely while these maidens vie with one another in dancing before him, for the one he favors shall have the honor to be his bride."

Maui was then made to sit on a bench in full view of the people who formed a wide circle around him and the band of musicians with their drums who took places nearby. Now came the three dancers, their faces and their figures completely hidden by mantles that reached to the ground. As the drums sounded, the dancers threw aside the mantles, revealing three hideous old women who struck attitudes before Maui. They were naked save for kirtles of grass that concealed their middle parts. One, who was a monster of flesh, turned her back to Maui and bent over as far as she could, her hands behind her, flipped up her kirtle almost in his face, as a gesture of greeting. The second, a withered hag with pendant breasts hanging almost to her waist, took them in her hands and held them toward Maui with an air of appeal as though begging him to accept these, her greatest charms. The third was little more than a bundle of skin and bones with wisps of thin hair hanging over her face. She pretended to be having difficulty in keeping her grass mantle securely fastened over her bony hips, and she was so thin that there was little need for pretense. Of a sudden, the mantle slipped to her feet, leaving her naked. She turned her back to Maui, glancing coyly over her shoulder.

The crowd roared with laughter at this spectacle; then the drums beat and the dance began. The fat woman could scarcely move and did no more than stand in one place, her back toward Maui, swaying her huge backside in time to the drums, but the other two danced with gestures as coarse as they were laughable. The one with the pendant breasts whirled round and round, her breasts standing out at right angles, slowly approaching closer and closer to Maui until those withered remnants of womanhood could strike his face and shoulders. The laughter of the spectators increased; then the music came to a sudden halt, and the three women sank to their knees before him, puffing and blowing, and holding out their arms as though they would say: "Which do you choose?"

Among the great crowd that encircled the spot where this dance had taken place could be seen, here and there, sober faces — particularly those of older folk, who found no pleasure in seeing this young man of noble blood so mocked and humiliated by their priest; but for the most part, the people shouted with delight at seeing a performance so ludicrous. When the roar of applause had died away, Puaka spoke again:

"Among our people there is a virgin of the noblest lineage who has long been sick with love for this young high chief of the Tongans, and now that Koro has consented to accept him, she is to be granted a chance to win his favor, together with the maidens who have just danced before him."

Now a girl of about twenty appeared and a ripple of laughter went through the crowd as they recognized her. She had a bold coarse face, but a beautiful body which was concealed only by the customary short kirtle of dyed grasses so scantily made that her thighs were clearly revealed as she approached the place where Maui sat.

The drums struck into the slow stately tempo of the nuptial dance, and the girl, with an air of shyness and modesty, went through the movements of this dance with such grace and beauty that, except for her scant costume, she might indeed have been a virgin of noble blood dancing before her lover on the eve of marriage. Suddenly the tempo changed to that of one of the erotic dances, designed to arouse passion, in which little is left to the imagination insofar as gestures and postures are concerned. She kept her eyes fixed upon Maui's, with the air of a woman all but swooning for love. Then, as the drums ceased, she stepped forward and spat in his face.

✿ X V I I ✿
Escape

MAUI WAS again taken to the house of Vaitangi and left there, under guard, to await Puaka's pleasure. Vaitangi remained as before, staring at the mat, unaware of his surroundings and the few servants who passed through the room. As night came on two stone lamps filled with coconut oil were lighted, the small flames casting flickering shadows over the floor and along the walls, scarcely relieving the gloom of the great chamber. The assembly ground was now lighted with torches and Maui could hear the shouts, laughter and applause of the spectators as the sports and games continued. Before long a man whose figure was indistinct in the semidarkness entered the room and seated himself, cross-legged, facing the old chief and two or three paces distant from him. Maui could barely see his face, in profile, in the dim light, as he sat regarding Vaitangi in silence. The chief neither moved nor spoke but remained as before, unconscious of his surroundings. Presently the man took a pair of small clam shells from a receptacle which he carried, and, moving closer, he clipped a lock of hair from Vaitangi's forehead and placed it, with the shells, into the receptacle. He then rose, without seeing Maui in the shadows at the far end of the room, and left the dwelling. Maui could guess who this man was: one of the dreaded sorcerers of the Koro Clan who, by means of *pifau*, were slowly killing the old chief as they had killed Hina's mother; but Maui was amazed that they should come thus openly to fetch some small article personal to Vaitangi — a lock of hair, fingernail parings and the like — necessary to the sorcerer in his art of death. It was proof of the power in Puaka's hands, that he could employ these men with so small an attempt at secrecy.

The soldiers guarding him remained outside; there was no one in the room save Maui and Vaitangi. Noiselessly, a woman servant entered with some baked fish and breadfruit on a green leaf which she placed before Maui. As she did so she whispered: "Hina's canoe is hidden by the great *hotu* tree, a mile south from the sheds where the ships are. Tonight is your only chance. Try very late. She will come if she can."

The woman left him and returned a moment later with food for Vaitangi which she fed him with her fingers, as a mother feeds a small child. She then left the room without a glance in Maui's direction.

Slowly, with an effort, Maui ate the food that had been placed before him. It might well be his last meal; but if, with Tané's help, he should be able to escape, he would need all of his strength for the events to follow. When he had finished he prayed in silence, his hand clasped around the coral pebble which hung on his breast.

As time dragged by a great weariness came upon him. He lay back on the mat and fell into a troubled sleep in which he dreamed that he was a boy again, in the tree which overlooked the temple of Koro. He leaped to the temple platform, but instead of escaping he felt the huge hand of Puaka seize him by the shoulder. Awaking from this frightful dream he found that one of the guards had thus grasped him. "Come," the man said.

His guards closed around him, two walking in front, two behind. It was a late hour but the festivities were still in progress on the assembly ground and most of the houses were deserted. Presently they turned into the path that Maui remembered so well, leading to the temple of Koro. They halted at the foot of the staircase leading to the summit of the *marae* and a voice said "Go!" to Maui.

Slowly he mounted the staircase and upon reaching the summit he thought for a moment that the place was deserted save for the huge figure of Koro, lighted by tapers on either side. As before, the war god appeared to be staring directly toward him and Maui was conscious of the old feeling of horror and despair that had seized him in boyhood. He then saw two figures seated upon a stone bench to the left of the image. They were Puaka and his nephew, Uri. Slowly Maui crossed the platform and stood before them.

"Son of Téaro," the priest said, "let no word be spoken by you, for you stand in the very presence of Koro. When, as a boy you desecrated his temple by your presence, death would have been your punishment save that Koro willed otherwise. He was content to wait until you were a man grown and your people had increased in numbers so that his revenge might be more in keeping with the foulness of your crime. Well you know the power of Koro and the terror of that power, for it was planted in your heart in childhood. He now demands the blood of all your people, and yours is to be spilled first to honor the marriage of my nephew." Puaka rose from his seat. "You shall have this night to think of the doom of your people and this shall be the manner of it. Your priest, your *ariki* and all the men of your clan shall destroy the temple of Tané with their own hands; then they shall be slain there. My warriors, stirred to frenzy by blood lust, shall then be given a day and a night to take their pleasure of the Tongan women, your mother and sister among them. Then the women and children shall be slain, and their bodies left to rot in the sun with the others." The priest was silent for a moment and then added: "It is Koro's will that you be left here unguarded save by the terror of his presence, but my nephew is permitted to bear you company for the sake of your boyhood friendship. You shall stand where you are. If you speak, my nephew will slay you at once." The priest then crossed the temple platform and descended the staircase.

Maui stood about ten paces from the bench where Uri was seated. The latter was armed with a spear and a short war club. Unconsciously, Maui clasped his hands over his breast and his fingers touched the coral pebble. Of a sudden horror left him.

He felt a sense of peace as though he stood in Tané's temple, with Métua at his side. No longer was he compelled to look at the image of Koro. Courage filled his heart and a sense of power far beyond his own seemed to be flowing into his body as though from an inexhaustible source. He remembered Métua's words: "Maui, the *mana,* the spirit of the noblest of our ancestors, has gone into the golden pebble which you wear." He realized that it was their combined strength that he felt, and the assurance of it filled him with joy and sacred power. He turned quickly to Uri. "I defeated you in boyhood," he said. "I will defeat you again, here in the very presence of your god."

Uri stared, unable to believe for a moment that Maui had spoken; then he grasped his war club and rushed at him, aiming a blow at his head. Maui leaped aside, seized Uri's arm, and brought it down backward over his shoulder, breaking it at the elbow. The war club fell from Uri's grasp and before he could recover Maui seized him by the waist and threw him over his shoulder. Uri fell heavily, his head striking the stone floor. He rose dizzily to his knees, but before he could regain his feet Maui leaped upon him, and taking Uri's head between his hands he dashed it against the floor with such force that Uri lay unconscious.

Leaping to his feet, Maui glanced quickly around him. At one end of the *marae* was a house in which were kept the robes of the priests, and the sacred emblems pertaining to the worship of Koro and the lesser gods. The house was lightly built, with roof and walls of thatch. Putting his shoulder to one of the doorposts he pushed over this structure. Throwing aside the thatch he uncovered the carved wooden chests in which the most sacred articles pertaining to the worship of Koro were kept. Seizing Uri's war club he broke open the chests and tore their contents to bits, scattering and stamping upon them. Among these were the most prized possessions of the Koros: the banners flown from their war canoes when they went into battle. These, too, Maui tore to shreds, heaping the remains before the image of Koro which stood at the very edge of the upper platform. Maui stood for a moment, breathing fast, gazing unflinchingly into the face of the god. The last vestige of his fear was gone. Clasping his golden pebble in his hands he felt himself endowed with the *mana* of all his ancestors. He put his shoulder against the huge figure of Koro, and struggled with all his power to topple it from the temple platform. He tilted it slightly but it came back to its original position. Halting briefly to gather up his strength he tried again, and again moved it. Never relaxing his pressure he increased his advantage and a moment later the great image went crashing down the stone terraces of the temple to the broad walk that encircled it at the foot.

As he stood looking down from the upper platform he became aware that the sky to seaward was filled with a lurid glare becoming brighter even as he looked. He ran down the staircase and had no more than reached the bottom when Hina appeared around the corner of the temple. She rushed into his arms and clung to him for a moment unable to speak, and then she could do no more than gasp his name. Seizing his hand she ran with him around the walk encircling the *marae,* and they came upon the image of Koro lying there. The head had broken from the body and lay at a distance; but protruding from under the huge torso which blocked their path they saw the head and shoulders of Puaka lying on his back, his face hideous in death.

As they emerged from the small valley where the temple of Koro stood, Maui halted to look toward the beach, six hundred yards distant, where the great sheds for the war fleet had been. These were now a mass of flame revealing the beach far and wide and the throng of people gathered there. "I set them afire," Hina said. "Maui, come quickly!" she added in an anguished voice. She ran before him, keeping within the concealment of the groves. When they reached the place where her canoe was hidden the sheds were still burning fiercely. They carried the little canoe to the water's edge and a few mo-

nents later, both paddling hard, they had disappeared around
a point of land extending out into the lagoon.

The story tells what happened among the Tongans on this
same night. As soon as darkness fell they carried the last of
their supplies from the village. Such pigs and fowls as could
not be taken with them were loosed, to fend for themselves.
The old people were the last to leave the village; and a few of
them, too feeble to walk, were carried. The ships were moored,
in a single line in the shallows of the lagoon. Men, women and
children gathered by the ships in which they were to embark,
and the captains of the ships called their names in muffled
voices to be certain that all were present. Shadowy figures were
wading through the shallows, to and from the ships, carrying
baskets of provisions, clusters of ripe coconuts strung together,
pigs, crates of fowls, dogs, bunches of green plantains, handing
these to others who were stowing them within the ships. Some
of the old women squatting on the beach cried softly to themselves at the thought of leaving the safety of the land for the
dangers and hardships certain to be met with as they pushed
out into the unknown sea.

Now the people embarked, the women and children first, the
men afterward. When all were aboard, Tuahu, who was in
general charge of this work, called the ships' captains together.
"You have your instructions," he said. "You will leave the
lagoon in the order in which you are moored, *Anuanua* leading, *Itatae* last. Men at the paddles until you are well offshore
beyond the shelter of the land. . . . There is a fresh breeze
blowing from the northwest; hoist sails and take full advantage of it, through the rest of this night and, if the breeze holds,
until tomorrow at sunset; then sail is to be taken in, and you
are to drift, keeping well together, until *Itatae* joins us. Proceed, now, and good go with you all!"

The captains then boarded their ships and in deep silence
they moved across the lagoon, and through the passage to meet
the long swell of the open sea. As the ships left the beach not a

sound was to be heard save the faint tinkle of drops of water as they fell from the blades of the paddles. The little company that were to go in *Itatae* — forty in all — watched the ships in silence until the last one had entered the open sea. They were young men for the most part, with only five women amongst them, for whom there was no space in the other ships. One of them approached Ru who was standing apart, gazing seaward. She laid a hand on his arm. "Ru, it is past midnight," she said, anxiously. "Were we not to go then?"

"Get aboard," Ru replied, gruffly, "and you other women as well." He took aside one of his men and gave him some instructions in a low voice. "Proceed to the beach opposite the passage and wait there," he said. "I shall be back in little more than an hour." He then set out toward the village at a fast walk.

When he reached the path leading inland through the village, he broke into a trot and held that pace until he came to the place where the trail mounted steeply to the head wall of the valley which was like a pit of darkness only a little distance before him. He stood waiting, listening for some time, then, cupping his hands around his lips, he called, "Maui!" There was no response save the echo of his own voice, twice repeated. He waited and called again, but the response was the same as before, the last faint echo dying away to silence.

There was scarcely a gleam of starlight in this upper part of the valley, but Ru knew every foot of the path and he ran seaward again without once stumbling or halting until he reached the assembly ground, which lay open to the stars, the river bordering one side, the deserted houses on the opposite side scarcely to be seen in the deep shade of the trees that sheltered them. He crossed the assembly ground for one last look into his father's house. As he turned from the doorway, he saw one of the loosed pigs feeding greedily upon some remnants of food that had been left there. He stopped to scratch its ears but the pig fed on, not lifting its head.

"*Parahi*," Ru said. "The place is yours, old fellow. Yours and Puaka's," and he ran on to the beach.

❧❧ X V I I I ❧❧
Toward the Rising Sun

At dawn the following morning the seven ships were moving in line abreast, at intervals of about a quarter mile. The breeze was growing lighter and shortly after sunrise it fell calm. Kurapo was still in view and it now had the appearance of two islands, with a space of open sea between them. Before long even the cat's-paws of the dying breeze disappeared and the sea was like a mirror for the motionless ships and the scattered tufts of white fair-weather cloud floating above it.

A conch shell was blown from *Kiwa* in the center of the line, and the men in the other ships took their paddles and converged upon it. . . . Tuahu, in general charge of the fleet, was in this ship, with Métua. The other ships gathered closely around, and Tuahu said:

"We are now twenty leagues from the land, and whether this calm is one of good or ill fortune we shall soon know. We must prepare to defend ourselves as best we can, in case our escape has been discovered and Puaka is in pursuit. The women and children will shift into *Kiwa, Te-Ava-Roa, Iriatai,* and *Anuanua,* and the men from those ships come into the others. Make haste, for if the Koros are already at sea we shall soon be sighted."

Immediately the women and children sprang into the sea and swam to the ships indicated, the women carrying their infants on their backs, and the men took their places in the ships to be prepared for defense. When these changes had been made Tuahu said: "Now the women will paddle eastward to

a distance of two or three miles and rest there. Before this day
is ended, we will know what our fortunes are to be."

As the ships moved apart the men stood, grim-faced and
silent, watching them go; they then set to work preparing
Kotaha, Tokĕrau and *Éata* for defense. When all had been
done that could be done, the ships were moved into line, one
behind the other, facing west. The paddlers took their places
on the thwarts, their weapons at hand; the others occupied the
free space on the platforms where the houses were, on the
small platforms bow and stern and along the sides of the hulls.
Few words were spoken; the eyes of all were turned westward
where nothing could be seen save the seafowl coming out from
the distant land for their day's fishing: gannets, sooty terns,
ghost terns; singly, in pairs and small groups; some high up,
others flying over their reflections mirrored in the glassy water.
An hour passed, two hours, and still they waited.

At last a youth clinging to the top of the mast of the fore-
most ship called out: *"A hio! Téra!"* — his arm outstretched,
pointing southwest. Presently, an object so small as to be
scarcely discernible appeared against the horizon line. All eyes
were fixed upon it but no one spoke until the boy at the mast-
head gave a jubilant shout. *"Au-é!"* he cried. *"Itatae! Itatae!"*
He slid down the mast, his face radiant with joy. The others in
that ship crowded around him scarcely able to believe, and
another youth shinned up the mast to make sure. Clinging to
the mast with one hand and shading his eyes with the other he
gazed briefly at the distant ship and called out: *"Itatae! Parau
mau! Itatae!"* He was about to slide down when Taio called,
"Stay where you are! Keep watch!"

Soon all could see that the approaching ship was, indeed,
Maui's. The blades of the paddles flashed as one in the sunlight,
first on the side of the great outrigger, then on the opposite
side. The ship came on fast, and soon they could make out
Maui's figure standing on the platform in the bow. At this
signal, the men lifted their blades from the water and held
them upright on the thwarts where they sat. *Itatae* came on

under its own momentum and as it passed the others Maui called: "We are safe! Puaka's ships have been burned in their sheds! Not one remains." The men, their faces alight with joy and relief, sprang to their paddles to follow Maui to the four ships where the women waited.

One of the women in Maui's ship was his paternal grandmother, Hotu, a woman of great force of character, loved and respected by all the Tongans. The others saw seated beside her a beautiful girl unknown to them. She was not a Tongan, therefore she must be of the Koro Clan, or, perhaps, a young woman seized by the Koros from amongst their enemies on the islands to the north.

Taio said: "Do none of you recognize her? It is Hina, granddaughter of Vaitangi; it can be no other." Some believed and some doubted; when Métua was asked he replied, "Maui himself will tell you in his own good time. It is enough at the moment to know that Puaka's ships have been destroyed and that we are safe from pursuit." "Maui!" Taio exclaimed in a voice of wonder. "Destroyed, burned — Puaka's fleet! Who but Maui could have done it? Have I not told you others that he would be a greater leader even than his father?" He called to Paoto who was seated amidships: "Paoto! Tell us now what you think of Maui! Too young, do you say? Do you still see misfortune ahead?" Even the *raatira* felt free to speak as they would to Paoto who never resented the mock they made of him and his prophecies of disaster. He glanced back at Taio with an abashed smile. "I am well content to have been mistaken in my judgment," he replied. "*É,* Paoto," another said, laughing. "Your fortune is out, today. You have nothing to worry about."

And now the Tongans were like another people. The heavy burden of uncertainty and dread they had carried for so long was lifted from their hearts, and old and young were like children together. Maui's own heart was filled with joy and gratitude to Tané. All of his people were there: not one had been lost. There flashed through his mind a picture of the huge headless image of Koro and the crushed body of Puaka protruding from beneath it.

In the need for haste in leaving Kurapo, time had been lacking for the proper distribution of the sea stores; and now, knowing that they were safe, this matter was attended to. The women and children leaped into the sea to make room, while the men redistributed the supplies so that each ship would have the proper amount of food and water for the number of people carried. The squealing of pigs, the crowing of cocks, the happy shouts of the children in the water, the orders passed back and forth from ship to ship and the hum of talk sounded strangely in the wide air of the lonely sea. As the sun climbed toward the zenith the heat became intense and some of the younger children began calling for water. Their mothers quieted them as best they could. What would Maui think of them, begging for water so soon? They were no longer free to drink all they pleased. Hush, now! When the rains came they would have all they wanted.

By late afternoon the task of getting the ships in order had been completed. The most important task of all had been the careful examination of the lashings of the crossbeams holding the twin hulls of each ship together, for their greatest danger was that these lashings might work loose in heavy seas certain to be met with as they proceeded on the voyage. Men worked throughout the day on *Te-Ava-Roa,* and at last it was ready to embark its people once more.

In assigning the people to be carried in each ship they followed the practice of their ancestors. None knew better than themselves the dangers of the sea and the risk of separation in the storms likely to be met with. Families were divided as much as possible for a double purpose: in the event of a ship being lost, all the members of a family would not perish with it, and if land were discovered by a ship separated from the others, those who survived to reach it would not be too closely related in blood. Husbands and wives, with their infants, were kept together, but their blood relatives and their older children were in the other vessels.

Now, as evening drew on, the ships gathered closely around *Itatae,* rising and falling gently as the long glassy swells passed beneath them. This was the time the people had been waiting for. They were eager to hear of their deliverance. They knew nothing of what had happened in the Koro village the day before, and only the chiefs were aware that Maui had gone there in answer to Puaka's summons. They listened with deep attention while Maui told them, first, of all that pertained to Hina: of their meetings at the lake, of the news she had brought of the death of her mother, of the approaching death of Vaitangi, and of her betrothal to Uri. He went on to speak of what they all knew, of the childhood friendship between Hina and himself, how it had ended at the time when he had broken the *tabu* of Vaitangi, and how friendship had become deep love from the day when he had met Hina again.

"I appeal now to you, Tané's people, my people," he then said. "I ask you to take Hina to your hearts as you did when she was a child, for she is a Koro in name only and by the chance of birth. She belongs to us, and she belongs to me, now your leader in my father's place. I have only this, more, to tell you. It was Hina who, at the risk of her life, and at a moment when she believed me dead, set fire to the sheds housing the Koro ships, destroying them all that you others might escape from Puaka and his warriors."

There was a moment of silence, followed by a deep murmur of approval which passed from ship to ship. Hina's eyes filled with tears as she saw the friendly glances directed toward her from all sides.

Tuahu said: "Maui, I speak for all when I say that Hina is welcome — more than welcome — among us. She will find here none but loving hearts."

Then Métua spoke, reminding the people how, when the Tongans reached Kurapo — so many at the point of death by thirst and starvation — Vaitangi had welcomed them, and Hina's mother had saved Maui's life by suckling him at her breast with Hina, her infant daughter. "I knew, then," he said, "that those children were destined for each other; that, when the time came, it was Tané's will that their lives should be joined together. So it has come to pass. I will say this, further: the union of Maui and Hina will be a blessing, not only to themselves and their children, but to the Tongan Clan for generations to come."

Rata said: "Maui, we Tongans know, as our ancestors before us have known, the mighty power of Koro. How, then, were you able to escape from his temple?"

"I have told you," Maui replied. "I was left unguarded there save by Puaka's nephew, Uri. I fought with and defeated Uri, and left him lying senseless before the great image of Koro."

"And Koro himself lacked the power to hold you there?"

"You see me, Rata. I am no ghost, but flesh and blood. It must have been so."

Nihau said: "Rata, it is strange that you should ask such a question. Do you believe that the power of Koro is greater than that of Tané?"

"No," said Rata; "but never before in our history has a Tongan escaped alive from the temple of Koro."

"There is always a first time for every happening," Marama said. "Why should you wonder that Maui has been spared? It may be Tané's purpose that, under Maui's leadership, we shall reach the Homeland. Could you believe that?"

"Our ancestors have been seeking it for twenty generations," Rata replied; "but it could be" — and he said no more.

One thing only Maui kept secret from all but Métua: his desecration of the temple of Koro and his destruction of the image of Koro which had crushed Puaka to death in falling. Métua had counseled him to keep this matter private until a later time.

Now was held the most sacred of all ceremonies connected with their worship, which would have taken place on the beach at Kurapo when they were ready to embark, had circumstances permitted. The ships were brought closely together so that the chiefs in each one could cross to *Kiwa* where Métua, their priest, stood with one of his temple assistants, holding in his hands the casket containing the four sacred stones from their ancestral *marae*. Again there was deep silence, no one speaking save the priest himself, the chiefs gathered around him. Métua raised the lid of the casket and took from it the sacred stones, one by one, passing them first to Maui, who passed them on until each of the chiefs had handled the stones that had been touched by their ancestors since the time when the quest for the Far Lands of Maui had begun. The *mana* of the noblest Tongans through all the centuries past had thus gone into the stones, to be added to by those who took up the quest in their turn. As each stone was received again by Métua, he placed it in a strong, closely woven mesh bag. The top was drawn together, securely fashioned, and Métua leaned over the side of the ship to dip it in the sea, saying as he did so:

"Measureless Sea of Kiwa that has carried us so far in the direction of the rising sun: may it be that we Tongans of this generation shall reach the Homeland hidden in Thy solitudes." When the four stones had been thus dipped, Métua took each of them in turn and held it toward the sky, saying: "Eternal heaven of Tané: I name the four stars that guide us toward the Far Lands of Maui." As he returned the stones to the casket, he named the four guiding stars the Tongans followed.

And now the story tells of the thing that happened always as our people, the Tongans, of whatever generation, set out to continue the quest for the Far Lands of Maui. It was Tané's will that all of his people: the chiefs, the *raatira* and the commoners alike, should hear the call of Maui-the-Peaceful so that their hearts might be filled with hope and courage and faith in his promise that their Homeland was there to the east and would, surely, be found. Even the doubters and the faint of heart were permitted to hear it at such times; but, thereafter, only the noblest among them — men and women of unshakable faith — would hear. So, now, when the solemn service of the dipping of the sacred stones and the naming of the four guiding stars was ended and the stones returned to the casket, the moment had come. Of the six hundred people there waiting, only the older ones who had survived to reach Kurapo on the previous voyage, had heard the call. All of the younger folk, some too small to remember the earlier time, and those born on Kurapo, had accepted the word of their elders, or doubted it, according to their natures. But now, as they saw Métua making his way forward amongst the people in *Kiwa* to the small platform in the bow of the ship, their hearts were filled with awe and wonder, for they knew his purpose in going there. The hush that fell upon the voyagers was like that over the great sea in which they floated.

As Métua mounted to the platform he looked to the west where the sun had just set behind the peaks of the two highest mountains of Kurapo clearly outlined against the horizon. Then he turned to the east and said, quietly, in a voice that all could hear:

"Tané, our Loving Father — we await now the summons of Thy servant and our guide, Maui-the-Peaceful."

The afterglow died away in the west and twilight deepened. No sound was heard save the voice of a fretful child whose mother immediately hushed it by giving it her breast. To the east the sky was lightening with the coming of the moon. Still they waited. The upper rim appeared above the horizon line, sending a faint path of light across the sea, growing in splendor until the full orb rose clear, and the glory of its light fell upon the ships and the people gazing toward it. Then, as though coming with the light itself, from beyond the horizon, they heard the call; and a moment later it came again, but starryfaint the second time, as though from lands infinitely remote, hidden in the farthermost solitudes of the Great Sea of Kiwa.

The hearts of all were so filled with awe, and reverence, and wonder that, at first, none could speak. They stood or sat, their attitudes the same, gazing eastward along the path of light made by the moon — waiting, hoping to hear the call once more; but it was not repeated. Then the spell was broken and they stared at one another. There were faces radiant with joy and assurance; others looked at them for confirmation, as though not daring to believe what they had heard. As they found their voices once more the hum of talk increased, and presently was heard a shout: *"Matai! Matai!"* (The wind!) The attention of all was drawn westward as they felt upon their cheeks the first faint tremors of the breeze. The glassy sea was darkening with cat's-paws of wind moving toward them.

"Get sail on the ships!" Maui called. "Here comes the favoring wind of Tané!"

Immediately all was activity. The great spritsails were hoisted. The steersmen sprang to their places and ran out the steering sweeps. Jubilant shouts were exchanged from ship to ship as the sails flapped idly and then steadied to the gently increasing pressure of the breeze. A current of joy, of common feeling passed swiftly from ship to ship. With the mountain peaks of Kurapo still visible above the horizon they had felt that their voyage had not yet begun, but now as the ships began to move, the spirit of generations of seafaring ancestors stirred deeply in their hearts. The yearning to sail on in the direction of the rising sun was instinctive with them like the migrating instinct of bids. They were fulfilling their destiny. Somewhere in the vast sea stretching away before them were the Far Lands of Maui — the promised Homeland where they would never again be disturbed by the threat, or even the thought of war and bloodshed. Although there had always been doubters and fainthearts amongst them, their numbers were few compared with the clan as a whole, whose faith was sure, whose belief in the Homeland had been passed on from generation to generation. And, in the hearts of each generation the hope was renewed that they might be the ones destined by Tané to end the quest; to see with their own eyes the Far

Lands of Maui in all their beauty, rising above the eastern
horizon.

The captains of the ships had received their instructions
from Maui in advance. The sea to the east of Kurapo had already been explored for a distance of six days' sailing and no
land found; nor did the Tongans wish to find land, even for a
temporary resting place, so near to Kurapo. Therefore the ships
were to sail well together, by day as well as by night, until they
had sailed beyond the limits explored by the Koros. Maui's
ship, *Itatae,* sailed a little in advance of the others which followed in line abreast and about a quarter of a mile distant,
one from the other. As they were taking this formation the
people in *Kiwa* took up the song that had been handed on to
them by their ancestors: a song to stir their hearts, and to steel
them as well, expressing the hopes and fears of the Tongans
for centuries past.

> The Far Lands of Maui,
> Hidden in golden light,
> The light of the rising sun.
> Lift up the sky, horizon beyond horizon
> Toward the lands we seek.

Came the response from *Tokérau,* the ship to the left of *Kiwa:*

> The sky is lifted up.
> The empty sea still lies before us . . .

But while they sang they were thinking, rather, of the sea behind. They looked back, watching the mountain peaks of
Kurapo sink lower and lower until they had vanished below
the western horizon. The sky had closed behind them, and the
empty sea to the west filled their hearts with peace and deep
content.

⚔ XIX ⚔
The Fair Wind of Tané

THE BREEZE held steadily through the night and at dawn it increased from gentle to fresh. *Itatae* was far ahead, the other ships still below the horizon to the west. Maui stood on the small platform used as a lookout in the bow. The sharp prow cut swiftly through the waves throwing spray high in air, drenching and half concealing him at times. Now and then as the wind veered a little the outrigger would rise from the water and the men stationed at the outrigger runways would shift quickly toward it to bring it smacking down to the sea. The only others awake at the time were the men attending the sail and Ru at the steering sweep, swaying gently upon it as he kept the ship before the wind.

Maui turned to look aft. "Ru, she's all but flying!" he called. "É," Ru called back; "she flies better on one wing than the others with two. Can you see them?"

Maui shook his head. Mats were drawn across the hull from the bow as far back as amidships to protect the sleepers from the flying spray. Maui climbed down from the platform and stooped to unfasten two of the loops holding them to the cleats along the gunwales. He looked down to see Hotu, his grandmother, and Hina sleeping side by side, the old woman's arm thrown lightly across the girl's breast. Maui watched them for a time still scarcely able to believe that Hina was there with him, safe and sound. He refastened the loops over their cleats and stood on the gunwale, steadying himself with a hand clasping one of the stays of the mast. Watching his chance he ran quickly along the gunwales to the steering platform. Ru grinned understandingly. "*É*, Maui, she's safe now. I prayed as you asked me to, with all my heart and soul. Maybe that helped."

"I know it did," Maui replied. "I thought of you, Ru, as they were taking me to the Koro temple to meet Puaka."

"Maui, what a ship! With a little more wind she'd leap from the water like the *titiraina,* the little boats with the leaf sails we made when we were children. Remember?"

"Do I not!" said Maui. "Those were happy days."

"Happier than this one?"

"Ru, I'm dreaming; I must be."

"Then dream that we take in sail," Ru replied, with a grin. "We're far ahead."

Maui gave his orders, the sail was lowered and the ship lost way until she was lying idle, Ru keeping her before the wind. Half an hour passed before the other ships were sighted. They appeared over the horizon almost at the same moment and a little to the south of *Itatae.* As soon as Maui's ship was seen they altered direction slightly to come into position on either side of her. They approached swiftly, with intervals of four or five hundred yards between the ships, and went seething by, *Kiwa* not more than twenty yards distant from Maui's ship. Taio stood at one of the steering sweeps. "Maui!" he shouted. "*Parahi oé! Haéré vau!*" "*Haéré noa!*" Maui called back, with a wave of his hand eastward where the sun had just appeared.

Maui waited until the ships were mere specks far ahead; then the sail was raised and *Itatae* flew on, rapidly lessening the distance between them. When they were nearly abreast, Maui turned to Ru. "Come alongside *Te-Ava-Roa,*" he said. Ru brought the hull side of *Itatae* to within half a dozen yards of *Te-Ava-Roa,* and at the same time the sail was shifted to slacken speed. Ma'o was at one of the steering sweeps.

"*Maui!*" he called. "*Au-é, té matai-é!*"

"Is all well with you, Ma'o?" Maui asked.

"*É, méa maitai-roa!*" Ma'o replied.

"You're heavily loaded. The crossbeam lashings are not working?"

"Holding firm and fast."

"You're certain?"

"Come aboard and see for yourself."

Maui motioned Ru to draw closer in, and leaped across to the steering platform of *Te-Ava-Roa*. Ma'o called one of his men to take his place and went with Maui to examine the crossbeam lashings, so hard and firm and tightly seized that they seemed as solid as the great beams themselves.

"*É*, they're holding well," Maui said. "You have nothing to worry about for the present, but keep watch!"

"Never fear," said Ma'o.

"What a pity that we lacked time to let the timber for *Te-Ava-Roa* season properly!"

"She'll do as she is," Ma'o replied, proudly. "I love her already, she handles so beautifully. I wouldn't trade ships even with yourself."

"Remember — yours is the post of danger. At the least sign of slack, signal us, Ma'o."

"I will; depend upon it," the other replied.

Maui had no sooner returned to his ship than a signal was heard from *Anuanua* at the northern end of the line, four sharp blasts of a conch shell. All knew what it meant: birds, fishing, had been sighted. There was an immediate stir in all the ships; heads appeared above the gunwales, all were looking north into the sky beyond *Anuanua,* where a great flock of sea fowl had appeared as though from empty air. Arms were pointing and eager voices were heard:

"*Éi'a! Éi'a! Au-é, te, éi'a-é!*"

"*Haéré tatou! Vitiviti!*"

"*Méarahi te ma'a!*"

The ships changed direction, sailing with the wind abeam toward the birds, but as they drew near they saw that *Anuanua* was already in the midst of the school. They followed closely,

keeping a sharp lookout in case the school should widen out or
suddenly change direction. The men in *Anuanua* were heaving
in the fish as fast as they could cast their lures into the water.
Hundreds of birds circled overhead, plunging to gobble up the
small fry driven to the surface by the ravenous tuna pursuing
them. The fish were swung inboard so fast that soon *Anuanua*
with her load of human freight could take no more. She drew
off, giving place to *Itatae,* which was nearest. Before the school
sounded Maui's ship was loaded to within a foot of her gunwales.

The ships then resumed their course, sailing closely together
while the fish were passed from ship to ship, each one receiv-
ing a share in proportion to the number of people carried.
Enough had been caught to provide a day's feast of fresh fish
for all the six hundred. When the distribution had been made
they drew apart as before, with Tané's favoring wind carrying
them on in the direction they would go.

Day after day good fortune followed them. Although the
wind slackened somewhat, it never failed them by day or by
night: the lightest of whitecaps were always to be seen on the
wind-wrinkled sea as though *Te-Moana-Nui-a-Kiwa* were, indeed, the gentlest of mothers assuring her children, the
Tongans, that they had nothing to fear from her.

After the third day they no longer saw the sea birds of
Kurapo flying from and returning to the land now so far behind them; they had sailed beyond their customary range of
flight. Only an occasional gannet, that far wanderer among
seafowl, would appear, skimming along the wide hollows between the swells. With the curiosity native to the gannet he
would approach the ships and soar closely overhead, tilting his
head from side to side for better views of the people crowded
into them. Taking advantage of this failing, common to gannets, the people would wave him down and seize him as he
sailed by within reach. Several were caught in this way, played
with, stroked and petted and loosed again; for all sea birds

were loved by the Tongans, and at this time none were suffering from the pangs of hunger.

Their food was measured out twice daily, at mid-morning and late in the afternoon. At first they ate the yams and taro root that had been cooked on Kurapo, and each person had a portion of plantain. No distinction was made between children and adults; all received the same portions, but the older people ate sparingly so that the children might have more. Each person had a small bamboo drinking-cup, of the same size, and the ration of water was three cups daily, but mothers with infants at breast received an extra cup. The livestock fared even better than the people themselves, for the Tongans fully realized the value of their fowls and pigs and dogs. A great sow heavy with young had been embarked in *Anuanua*. She took up room sorely needed, and was generously fed and watered, the older people often saving a part of their own food for her. The weather being fine and the sea smooth, the fowls were taken from their crates in the daytime and perched along the gunwales with tethers of bark attached to their legs and fastened to the cleats just below the gunwales.

Despite the crowded conditions and the discomfort these entailed there was no muttering or complaining. All shared them equally. The wives and small children of the *ariki* quartered in the little houses exchanged places with those in the hulls so that all might share in the cooler, better conditions which the houses provided.

During the long uneventful days the people never lacked for diversion and entertainment. To them, the descendants of seafaring ancestors, there was nothing monotonous about the sea. They were alert to every slight change in the aspect of sea and sky. They took delight in watching cloud formations, pointing out to one another what they saw there: shapes of birds, fishes, men, and the fabulous monsters of the deep. They invented tales of what they saw, while the children listened with wide-eyed wonder and begged for more.

And their elders told them the tales of Maui-the-Peaceful and his brothers: how Mano-the-Strong and Tumu-the-Witless were sent out by their father to fish for lands; of Tumu's love of destruction, and how Mano gave him the mighty kick which sent him flying through the air, horizons beyond horizons; of the splash he made when he fell into the sea, causing a wave so huge that it destroyed some of the islands that had already been fished up from *Te-Moana-Nui-a-Kiwa*. Above all, they loved the tales of Maui-the-Peaceful's childhood and of how his brother, Tavi-the-Jester, created his phantom islands. The children watched for them as they sailed on, each one hoping to be the first to sight one of Tavi's phantom lands, so beautiful and yet so impossible to reach.

Most of the people slept during the heat of the day. In their narrow quarters they lay closely crowded together, arms thrown across one another, heads pillowed on the laps or the legs of their neighbors, mothers protecting their small children within the crook of their arms. The dogs mingled with them, finding what room they could for themselves, and an occasional plaintive yelp was heard as they were buffeted from place to place. The greatest discomfort came from the pigs, which were kept forward; the strong odors of dung and urine were hard to bear for people who loved cleanliness and clean sweet air. But they comforted themselves, knowing that a day of calm would come when they could bathe in the sea while the ships were thoroughly scrubbed and cleaned. During the hours of sleep there was little talk or movement save when someone tried to ease his cramped position by turning from one side to the other, and, finding it impossible, relaxed again with a weary sigh. Strips and squares of sunlight moved over the sleepers as the ships rose to the long swells or rolled slowly from side to side.

The crowding was, of course, hardest upon the elderly folk. Three old grandmothers were lying side by side in *Iriatai* after the midday siesta when most of the others were astir again.

"Oh, my little house by the river!" one said. "I keep dreaming of it. I think I am sleeping on my cool clean mat over the soft layer of sweet grass; and then I think that someone has played a joke on me and placed rocks and pebbles and dead branches under the mats. I wake up, and how my old bones ache!"

"*É*, it is hard upon us *Mama Ruaus*," another said. "When I hear one of the cocks crowing up forward I think we are back at Kurapo and that it's just getting on for daylight. I wait to hear the other cocks answering from all around the valley. Then I remember where we are."

"What spirit they have, the cocks," the third remarked. "They can scarce move in the crates, but they try to flap their wings, and they crow as blithe and cheery as if they were about to flutter down from the breadfruit trees."

"*É*, there's no creatures with stouter hearts," the first one said. "We may well take a lesson from them."

"You'd say they know where we're bound and were trying to cheer us up. . . . Well, who would want to change places with the softest-bedded old woman left on Kurapo?"

Except for the middle hours of the day there was always a stirring-about amongst the people. With cords of sinnet the fathers made harnesses for the small children. With these securely fastened upon them they dipped the children into the sea, letting them ride there, heads just above the surface, while the cool water laved their naked bodies. And they would lift them high, to let them splash again. The parents tired of this pastime long before the children did.

Young and old amused themselves for hours at a time making string patterns. This was an art with them, handed down and perfected from generation to generation. Many of the patterns were of beautiful and intricate designs, requiring a full half-hour to complete. Others were made to move when completed, showing figures representing birds in flight, waves rising and falling, men fishing, and the like; and always they were inventing new ones.

On the morning of the fifth day Maui believed that they had sailed beyond the farthest point eastward ever reached by the Koros. Now the practice of their ancestors was followed that they might cover as wide an area of sea as possible. The ships moved apart to form an arc of from fifteen to twenty miles, the distance depending upon the clearness of the air and the condition of the weather. So they would sail through the daylight hours until late afternoon when they closed in for the night. On moonlight nights, with a calm sea, they sailed at intervals of a mile; on starry nights, of half a mile. In cloudy weather they were no more than two or three hundred yards apart. It was the duty of the steersmen to keep at the proper distance from the ship on the left. Throughout the night signals by conch shell were sent from ship to ship, from left to right, and back again from right to left. So they kept in touch.

Rata, the father of Pohi, was one of the chiefs in *Kotaha,* whose captain was his son-in-law, Vana. *Kotaha* carried eighty souls. The breeze from the west blew sweetly day after day, and the people, like those in the other ships, could scarcely believe in such good fortune.

Manu said: "When I wake of a morning I expect to find that the wind has veered round to the east; but no; still it comes from the west. How is this to be explained at a season when we should have none but easterly winds?"

"What is there strange in that?" Téma replied. "It is the fair wind of Tané, as our priest has said. Tané never fails to send it when the Tongans sail from whatever land."

"That is true, Téma," another remarked; "but I have never heard Métua say that the fair wind of Tané continues to blow day after day, as it has been with us, long after the land departed from has been left behind."

"It is, truly, a matter for wonder," Manu said. "When the westerlies blow it is the season for storms — dark days and black nights, with blinding rain and heavy seas, but we have had nothing but the smoothest of seas and the bluest of skies."

Vaiho, a white-haired *raatira,* now spoke. "That is because, as we know, it is not yet the season for the true westerlies. Manu, never wonder at good fortune, or speak of it. We should accept it in silence, with grateful hearts."

There were murmurs of approval from the others at this remark, but Rata said:

"If, as some of you believe, Tané has command over the weather, remember that the power is not his alone. Koro can do the same."

"Then why has he not used it?" Vaiho asked.

"How do you know that our fair wind is not Koro's rather than Tané's?" Rata replied. "I am not saying this is true, but we know the mighty power of Koro; Métua, our priest, acknowledges it."

"Would he send us a fair wind to carry us farther from his power?" Téma asked.

"Can you believe that Koro has power only on Kurapo, when our ancestors have found that he is worshiped everywhere, on islands they have reached in former generations?" Rata replied.

"You think, Rata, that Koro sends this wind to blow us eastward, where we will find lands peopled with others who worship him?"

"So it has been with our ancestors; so it could be with us," Rata replied.

"And they escaped from him everywhere," Vaiho said, proudly, "just as we ourselves have escaped."

"At a fearful cost," Rata replied, grimly. "Ten generations ago we Tongans numbered eight thousand souls. Now we are six hundred."

"It was not the power of Koro that so reduced us," Vaiho said. "This is strange talk, Rata, coming from you, Maui's uncle."

"It is well that you others should be prepared for what may come, so that you may steel your hearts to meet it," Rata said.

"But tell us what it is that you fear," Téma said. "We are

neither cowards nor weaklings, and it is well, as you say, to be prepared."

"It concerns my nephew, Maui," Rata went on, speaking as though he would far rather keep silence but was forced to open his mind to them. "He has courage and strength of will, and there are no qualities more necessary in the character of a high chief. But, like his father before him, he carries courage to the point of recklessness. His stealing Hina from Puaka's nephew almost at the moment when she was to be married to him — this having happened, who could measure, now, the depth of Puaka's hatred?"

"Let him hate as he will," Manu said. "Thanks to Hina — may Tané bless and guard her! — we are forever beyond his reach."

"Of Puaka — yes. Of Koro — no. Remember that Puaka is the priest of Koro."

Rata broke off as they heard the faint sound of the conch shell blown from *Kiwa,* the ship on the left of *Kotaha* and about three miles distant: it was the signal for the ships to close in for the night. Vana replied with the same signal to show that the summons had been heard.

Rata's manner suddenly changed. He smiled as he glanced at the faces of those gathered around him. "My fears are mere shadows," he said. "Let none of you take them to heart."

At sunset the ships were moving in a compact line, following *Itatae,* two miles ahead.

🐾 X X 🐾
Children of the Sea

EARLY IN THE AFTERNOON the breeze became lighter. The ships were extended in an arc so wide that those at the southern end of the line were below the horizon from those at the northern end. *Itatae* was sailing near to *Kiwa* at the time. Maui ordered the steersman to draw alongside.

"What do you think, Taio?" he called.

"It will be calm by nightfall," Taio replied.

"So I believe," Maui said. "We will close in while the breeze holds. Signal *Anuanua.*"

Anuanua was next to *Kiwa* but at such a distance that only the upper part of the hull could be seen as she rose to the swells. Taio blew a long clear summons on his conch shell, and after waiting a little repeated the call. Presently they heard, faintly, *Anuanua* sending the signal on to the ship beyond. Maui then sailed on northeast ahead of the others to come near the center of the twenty-mile arc so that *Itatae* could be seen by the ships at either end as they drew in toward him.

The sun was near to setting when the breeze died away. The ships were still far scattered but all were now within view. Sails were lowered, the paddles gotten out, and they moved toward *Itatae*. Masses of white cumulus cloud floated motionless above their reflections in the calm sea, and as the sun vanished below the horizon line they caught the colors of the afterglow, growing in splendor from moment to moment. The light from the clouds and their reflections cast upon the sea transformed with an effect of magic the moving ships and the faces of the people in them. Ripples at the bows moved out in widening arcs of crimson and gold to meet with others, the light and color mingling and changing in an element that appeared to be neither sea nor air nor cloud but a fusion of all three.

All the people were sensible of the glory, the peculiar grandeur of that end of day. Maui stood with Hina in the bow of his ship as the others drew near. Marama waved to them but gave no hail, as though reluctant to break the spell that seemed to have descended upon them at the moment, but as the ships closed to within speaking distance, he said, in an awed voice: "Maui, never before have I seen such a sky, and the sea is no common sea. Surely, we are now in the far solitudes of the Sea of Kiwa, and with this beauty she tells us."

The spell of silence was broken as the ships came to rest. The children leaped into the water with shouts of joy. Their parents quickly followed, and soon all of the clan save a few of the old folk were in the sea that shimmered with mingled light and color as though the great Rainbow of Tané had been shattered upon its surface. The merry shouts of the children and the happy talk of their elders in the water, reunited once more after the long passage from Kurapo, gave evidence of the peace in the hearts of these children of the sea, and their unspoken gratitude to Tané who had brought them so far and so happily in the wished-for direction.

There were no laments at the failing of the wind. This pause in their voyage after many days of serene and uneventful sailing was, surely, a destined pause, to give them rest and refreshment, a chance for briefly reuniting families, for giving thanks to Tané for his watchful care. Thus far they had but one cause for anxiety: the water supply. No rain had fallen since they left Kurapo. But they were not greatly troubled. The wind from the west that had carried them so far was Tané's wind, not the true westerly. That would soon come, for the Austral summer was at hand; the scattered masses of piled-up cloud were a promise of it. Soon there would be rain in abundance.

After the long-wished-for bath they returned to their respective ships, and as night came on they were brought closely around *Itatae,* and the talk passed back and forth as easily as though the clan were gathered for one of its meetings on the beach at Kurapo.

There had been one occurrence only to sadden their hearts. Hoani, an old man beloved by all, one of the people in *Tokérau,* had died three days before and was buried on the evening of that day.

"Oh, the great pity!" an old woman remarked. "Hoani buried in the sea, so far from home!"

"Grandma, there is no cause for sorrow in that," a voice replied. "The sea is the home of us Tongans, even more than the land. It has always been so."

"True it is," another said. "How many of our people have been buried in the sea. Thousands, in the great voyages of the past."

"Hoani himself wished it so," another voice said. "He fell asleep as peacefully as a child. There can be no deep sorrow for so quiet a death when a long life has been fulfilled."

There was a murmur of assent from the others.

"*É,* Hoani lived long and well."

"And long may his children and grandchildren survive him!"

"It is an honor to die at sea when our time comes."

Faanui now spoke of the great sow, heavy with young, they carried in *Anuanua.* She had farrowed four days ago, and what a time *that* was! Nanai Vahiné had acted as midwife. Eleven pigs, and all living: two boars and nine sows.

"Maui, what am I to do with so many new passengers?" Faanui asked. "Even before they came we were so crowded we could scarcely move."

Maui laughed. "You *would* bring the sow, Faanui, and you will have to keep her children while they're sucking. We will distribute them later."

But all agreed that the sow was too huge to be carried much

longer. When her little ones had been given a start in life she would have to be butchered.

Others related incidents that had happened in the various ships, omitting nothing that gave cause for laughter. Drifting in the darkness, on the unknown sea, aware of the dangers ahead and knowing how faint was the hope that all would survive them, they welcomed every occasion that gave them moments of forgetfulness and relief from the natural fears hidden in the hearts even of the bravest.

Métua, Maui, and the other chiefs encouraged the people in this lighthearted talk and themselves joined in. But, presently, the silence of mid-ocean held at bay for a little time came flooding back, and with it returned an awareness of their loneliness, of the wastes of ocean stretching away before and around them.

Then Métua spoke, and, as always, when they listened to the words of their priest, the people felt uplifted, their hearts filled with his own deep faith in the sacredness of their quest and the promise of Tané that the Homeland would, surely, be found.

He said: "There may be — indeed, there must be — other clans or fragments of clans, people of our own blood, sailing eastward over the Sea of Kiwa; but it may well be that we alone are worshipers of Tané and lovers of peace. Certain it is that our ancestors found none but worshipers of Koro in the lands they reached. If it is true that we alone follow Tané, what words could tell of the grandeur of our quest, and the hope for future races of men that lies within ourselves? When we have reached the Homeland — and we surely will — few though we are in numbers, the memory of the great voyage of the Tongans, carried on generation after generation, will never be forgotten by those who come after us. And the faith that inspired us will be as a living flame, not to be quenched when we are gone from the Earth but to kindle the hearts of all men. Koro will be overthrown forever, and the races of men, wherever they may be, will live as we do by the sacred law of Tané."

Maui then spoke of the grandeur of the quest itself.

"From the beginning," he said, "we Tongans have been explorers, discoverers, pathfinders. Love of the unknown is in our blood. When our ancestors first came to the western borders of the Sea of Kiwa they were not a seafaring folk. Nevertheless, they became one. At first they voyaged on rafts, logs of wood bound clumsily together; then in the crudest of boats in which they clung to the shores of lands, never venturing beyond sight of them. As the generations passed they learned the art of building such ships as we now have. With these, they could no more resist the desire to sail on in the direction of the rising sun than we ourselves can do so."

"Would they have come, Maui, had there been no Homeland to search for?" a voice asked.

"We know that they have," Maui replied. "I speak, not only of the Tongans, but of other clans of our once-united people now scattered over the Sea of Kiwa. As Métua has said, our ancestors have found none but lovers of war on the lands they reached; nevertheless, they are people of the same blood as ourselves."

Another voice spoke in the darkness. "Maui, can the distance be measured, or even guessed at, that the Tongans have sailed since our ancestors left the western borders of Kiwa?"

"Let Métua reply," Maui said.

"In time — yes," the priest answered, "but not in space. Twenty generations is the measurement in time, but we know that our ancestors remained long in various lands they reached. Even so, the fact that they have continued to sail eastward through so long a period clearly shows that we have come a vast distance from the western borders of Kiwa."

"And the eastern borders?" someone asked.

"There are no borders to the east," Métua replied. "In the direction of the rising sun the Sea of Kiwa is measureless."

Manu spoke: "Rata has told us that we will find worshipers of Koro on lands to the east, however far we may go."

"My uncle said that?" Maui asked.

"Manu has misunderstood me," Rata put in, quickly. "I said, merely, that, as we had found them before us in the past, it was reasonable to expect that some of the lands — if they exist — still to the east might be peopled by lovers of war."

"I will speak of a dream I have had since we left Kurapo," Maui said. "In the dream I found myself on an island, a green circle of land with a lagoon within it, like those our fathers have seen. There was a passage into the lagoon, and no one, anywhere, upon the land. I heard a voice that said: 'Maui, it is Tavi who speaks. You stand upon the ringed island that I fished from the sea, from the shoulders of a drowned mountain. Rest and refresh your people here. You are now in the solitudes of the Sea of Kiwa, never before beheld by the eyes of men. Sail on, following the call of my brother, your great namesake, Maui-the-Peaceful.' Then came silence; I heard the voice no more. Several nights later the dream was repeated exactly as before. . . . Métua, so real was this dream that it must have a meaning, surely?"

"It was no idle dream," the priest replied quietly. "The voice you heard could have been no other than that of Tavi who fashioned the phantom islands."

"He said nothing of his phantom lands?" Marama asked.

"Nothing," said Maui. "In the dream I was conscious only of a feeling of deep joy that we Tongans had sailed into the great solitudes of the Sea of Kiwa never before seen by the eyes of men. This dream, then, answers the fears of my Uncle Rata that lands ruled by Koros may still be before us. Now in truth are we discoverers, pathfinders. Does not that stir your hearts? We shall see lands never before viewed by human beings."

"And Tavi-the-Jester's phantom lands as well," Paoto said. "Perhaps we will approach one when many of us are at the point of death, only to see it fade to empty air and empty sea."

"It is to be expected that we shall view some of those lands," said Maui, "but there is no reason to believe that we shall be at the point of death when we do so."

"It is well to be prepared for the worst," Paoto replied, "and the suffering of our people in past generations gives us reason to expect it."

"Paoto is a lover of misery," Nihau said. "How great his disappointment will be if it fails to come!"

Now the ships drew apart and the people composed themselves for rest. The sound of voices gradually died away. Maui and Hina sat on the steering platform of *Itatae*, their arms around each other, speaking in whispers. There was no place where they could stretch out at ease. When drowsiness came they curled up side by side as best they could and were soon asleep. From *Iriatai* came soft music from the flute of old Tamuri, as though some gentle spirit of mid-ocean were giving voice to the peace and beauty of the night.

XXI

The Great Calm

WHEN MORNING CAME the ships were lying in nearly the same positions they had taken for the night, and the masses of cloud floating above them appeared to be those they had seen the evening before. Once again they glowed and flamed in the increasing light, but as the sun rose the splendor faded to the pure white of cloud masses having in them no promise of rain.

No sooner had day come than all was bustle and activity in the fleet. The ships were brought closely together. Most of the people were again in the sea to make room for the cleaning and scouring of the vessels. The supplies and provisions in one were moved to another while this work was in progress. The dogs were thrown into the sea to swim about with the children and bathe themselves. The pigs were lowered over the sides of the ships and thoroughly scrubbed while the ships themselves were being cleaned. Masts, rigging, sails and crossbeam lashings were carefully examined and such repairs made as were necessary, but, with the exception of *Te-Ava-Roa,* there was little to be done. In the latter ship the seams along the upper part of the hulls were recalked and the work of relashing the crossbeams was done over again. Two days were spent in cleaning and repairing the ships under the best possible conditions for such work, for the sea was dead calm, but there was growing anxiety over the diminishing water supply, and still no promise of rain.

Families were reunited at this time, during the daylight hours, and Maéva, Maui's mother, and his married sister, Tauhéré, joined him in his ship. They had seen nothing of

Hina during the voyage; now they made the most of their opportunity to be with her and to show her the deep affection in their warm and loving hearts. Maéva urged upon her son that the opportunity offered be taken to solemnize his marriage with Hina. "Never have I forgotten my debt to Hina's mother," she said. "I long to take Hina to my heart, in her dead mother's place, and make her my daughter."

"I had thought to wait," Maui said, "until we reach some land where our marriage could be celebrated in a fitting manner."

"My son," Maéva said, "what could be more fitting than that the high chief of the Tongans should be married at sea? That you are already married in truth, I know, for Hina has told me, and that she now carries your child in her body; but I long to welcome her as my daughter, and your wife in very truth, and that cannot be until the sacred rites have been performed by Métua, in the presence of our people."

"It shall be as you wish," Maui replied.

"You see the wisdom of my counsel?" his mother asked. "Let nothing be left to chance. If anything should happen to you — which Tané forbid! — before the marriage takes place, Hina would not and could not be recognized by our people. Her standing would be that only of a girl of noble blood whom you had gotten with child."

"I see it," Maui said, "and thank you, Mother, for being so thoughtful and wise in Hina's behalf."

And so, on the afternoon of this day, the marriage took place on *Kiwa,* the other ships gathered closely around and their people looking on. Maui and Hina sat facing each other, and between them Métua placed the casket containing the sacred stones. Upon the lid of the casket was spread a small square of white tapa cloth, and when the chants had been sung and the prayers said, Métua drew a few drops of blood from Maui's forefinger and then from Hina's and the blood was mingled on the cloth to indicate the sacredness of their union. Then Hina went with Maui, his mother, and his sister, Tau-

héré, to the various ships — where she was welcomed with
deep respect and affection by all of the Tongans save Rata,
who greeted her with scant courtesy. He was ill-pleased because he had not been consulted, and his counsel asked for,
before the marriage. But in their happiness Maui and Hina
scarcely noticed his coolness of manner. When they had gone
to all of the ships, they returned to *Itatae*.

Now everything was in readiness for continuing the voyage,
but the calm held, and on the following day the sky was again
cloudless. Faint breaths of air darkened the surface of the sea
at moments and then died away. As the sun climbed toward
the zenith the people lay in the ships, gasping for air, protecting themselves as well as they could with mats from the
intense glare of the sun and its reflection upon the glassy
water.

So five days passed. The ration of water was reduced from
three cups daily to two, and then to one, and real suffering
began. The voices of small children could be heard begging
for water, and the older people denied themselves a part of
their own scant ration to lessen a little the torment during
the heat of the day of their small sons and daughters. The
older ones had been schooled to endure thirst with fortitude.
On Kurapo, as on other lands where the Tongans had lived,
boys and girls, as soon as they entered their teens, were taught
to accustom themselves to thirst for periods of from two to
three days, so that suffering from this cause might not be
wholly strange to them; nor was there danger of any of them
being tempted to drink sea water, for they knew that death
would surely follow. They bathed in the sea four or five times
daily, to take what little water they could through the pores
of their skin, but soon the older people were too weak to do
more than lie in the water alongside the ships for a few moments, and were then lifted in.

Nightly, Métua offered prayers for rain, and on the morning of the sixth calm day the sky was again partly covered

with heaped-up masses of cloud, widely scattered, some with dark cores at the centers, giving at least the promise of rain. Maui now ordered the ships to separate, each of them to follow a cloud in the hope that showers would fall. The strongest men took the paddles and pulled wearily toward the cloud masses drifting slowly overhead, some of them far distant. Soon the ships were widely separated. The people in each watched, with mingled hope and despair, the cloud they themselves were trying to reach and those followed by the other ships. Light curtains of rain were seen to fall here and there, but the ships were now so far apart that the people in one could not know whether the ships nearest to the showers had succeeded in reaching them or not.

Kotaha was approaching such a cloud, still about three miles distant — one that seemed to have materialized out of blue sky and empty air. It was growing darker, heavier with rain from moment to moment. The men at the paddles were putting all their strength into their work, and Vana at one of the steering sweeps was urging them on to greater effort.

"*Hoé! . . . Hoé!*" he called. "Make the hafts of your paddles bend! We're nearly there!"

"*Au-é te ua-é!*" Manu exclaimed. "There is enough rain in that cloud to fill all our containers, and more too!"

"*Tané!* Don't let it fall until we are under it!" Téma exclaimed in an anxious voice.

"Change over, the paddlers!" Vana said.

Fresh men now relieved the weary ones, taking their places so quickly and skillfully that there was not the slightest loss of speed, but, rather, an immediate increase of it; but *Kotaha* was the second largest ship of the fleet, containing eighty people, and it was weary work for the paddlers. Their lips, like those of all others in the ship, were cracked with drought and their mouths as dry as dust.

"*Hoé! . . . Hoé!*" Vana called. "We will have all the water we can drink in another quarter of an hour."

Vana had scarcely spoken when the rain began to fall in a

darkening curtain with clear-cut edges on either side. They could faintly hear the sound of cool sweet water, a miniature deluge falling into the sea, blotting out the view of the horizon beyond. The men pulled desperately, but were still a quarter of a mile distant when the downpour slackened, and by the time they had reached the place only a mist was falling, shot through with rainbow lights. The people tried to breathe it in and succeeded in barely moistening their lips. The ship lost momentum and floated motionless. No sound was to be heard save the heavy breathing of the weary paddlers.

"The Rainbow of Tané!" Vana remarked, savagely. "Thus he answers the prayers of our priest!" No one replied. Presently one of the paddlers said: "Rata, how much water have we left?"

Rata said: "Enough for two days, following this, with one half cup of water daily for each person."

Again there was silence. The glances of the stronger ones who had best endured the torment of thirst were turned upon those lying in the hulls, old people, their eyes glazed with suffering, their parched lips open, gasping feebly. Many pointed in silence to a woman lying in the hull on his side of the ship, with a small child sucking at her dry breast.

Another of the paddlers, dipping his finger in the sea that he might moisten his dry lips, said: "There are some here who will not survive the night without relief."

"They must have it. There is no choice," another said.

"If one is to have it, all shall have it," Rata said. He motioned to a man who was seated nearest the place where the bamboo containers for water were stored. The man passed him one of these, and a cup. A swallow of water was poured into the cup, and this was given to the woman who had tried to relieve the torment of her child. When the cup was placed to her lips she shook her head, feebly. "The child," she said, nor would she swallow the meager taste of water until her little son had been served. It was at such times that the finest qualities of the Tongans came to the fore. The old were served first, and the women and small children. The young men and women and the older boys and girls showed the greatest compassion and self-restraint in ministering to the others and care was taken in pouring out the water so that each person had exactly the same amount. Although some of the young people, when their turn came, drank their portion, many of them, having rinsed their mouths, spit it back into the cup so that others might have it. Rata did the like, as well as many of the paddlers, although these latter were in all but desperate need of the little refreshment they might well have claimed for their own.

During this time the attention of all was engaged in the passing out of the water. One bamboo container holding no more than two quarts had served eighty people. Now Vana, who had helped in distributing the water, returned to his steering platform. He glanced quickly around the horizon and pointed westward, the direction from which they had come. "Yonder is a cloud that has formed while we were pursuing this one, but whether or not we can reach it in time . . . Paddlers, change over!"

The men were now so weary that they were slow in making the change; meanwhile the two steersmen brought the ship around until it was headed toward the cloud, nearly as far distant as the one they had failed to reach. *"Hoé! . . . Hoé!"* Vana urged, but the ship was scarcely under way again when rain started to fall from the distant cloud. Vana saw that the attempt to reach it was hopeless and ordered the paddlers to rest; nevertheless they pulled on until the rain slackened to mist and vanished as the other had.

"You have spent your strength and increased your thirst for nothing," Vana remarked, bitterly. "Now we see that it is not Tavi-the-Jester who is tricking us, but *Tané*-the-Jester!"

Vaiho spoke. "Rata," he said, "can you keep silent while your son-in-law makes a mock of our god?"

"Is he not making a mock of us?" Vana replied fiercely. "If

he cared for us would he let rain fall into the sea when he knows that we are but perishing of thirst?"

"There is some excuse for Vana," Rata said. "A man is not wholly accountable for what he says after the bitter disappointments we have suffered."

"No others have spoken so," Manu said. "Do you believe that Tané mocks us?"

"I do not," Rata replied; "but remember what I have said: Tané is but one of the gods, and who are we to say that his power equals that of Koro? You have heard what Métua has said: In this measureless Sea of Kiwa we few Tongans may be the only clan who are seekers for peace. Is it likely, then, that Tané's power to help us can equal Koro's will to harm us?"

"If he is so great a god, why should he be concerned about our small band who have done him no harm and offer no threat to his power?" Téma asked.

"No harm?" said Vana. "When Maui has stolen Hina who was to have been the bride of Uri, nephew of the priest of Koro?"

"My son-in-law is right," Rata said with an air of reluctance. "It is to be understood that Koro listens to the prayers of his priests even as Tané does, and who can doubt the strength of Puaka's hatred toward us?"

"Do you believe that Koro is now taking revenge upon us at the request of his priest?" Vaiho asked.

"It may well be so," Rata replied. "How can we be sure that the Fair Wind of Tané may not have been the Evil Wind of Koro blowing us into this desert of the sea where no winds blow and showers of rain fall only to mock us because they cannot be reached? The story of our ancestors shows clearly that such deserts exist. Scores, hundreds of our people have perished of thirst in such places."

Now this talk ended, among those few who still retained the will to talk. The others lay inert, some asleep, some in a stupor, half-conscious, moaning and muttering in their misery. The sun was high overhead, beating fiercely down upon the glassy sea and the forlorn little company in each of the ships lying at distances of from three to five miles from one another. No more clouds promising rain were to be seen within the entire circle of the horizon. There was nothing more to be done. In *Kotaha* the mats were spread across the hulls to shield the people from the sun. Vaiho, who had volunteered to keep watch, was now alone, seated on one of the steering platforms, elbows propped on his knees, his face in his hands to shield it from the glare of light reflected from the water.

Maui's ship was slowly approaching *Éata*, whose captain was Taio. As they drew near Maui saw that Taio was distributing water to his people. "You caught rain, Taio?" he called.

Taio shook his head. "We shall have rain and to spare before nightfall," he replied. "I am serving what little we have left to those in greatest need. Do you the same, Maui."

Maui stared overhead, around the circle of the horizon, and again at Taio. "Are you mad?" he called. "What promise of rain do you see in this sky?" Maui knew that of all the Tongans there was no one so weather-wise as Taio, but now he feared that the torment of thirst had unhinged his judgment.

"You trust me, Maui?" Taio replied. "If you do, call the ships together. Before the farthest of them can reach us the sky will be black with cloud. Waste no time for there will be wind behind."

Scarcely daring to believe, Maui nevertheless signaled the ships again and again until all had heard and were slowly moving toward *Itatae* and *Éata*. And now, as though Tané were, indeed, answering the prayers of Métua, clouds that grew denser and blacker from moment to moment formed in a sky that had been all but cloudless only a little time before. As the ships drew in, the people who were able to stir got to their feet and clung to the gunwales, staring at the darkening sky as though not able to believe what their eyes beheld. In *Kotaha* the paddlers, their eyes alight with joy, were pulling with vigorous strokes. "*Hoé!*" Vana called, cheerfully. "Let us all be together when the rain comes."

"*É*, Vana," Vaiho said, "and no thanks to you that it *is* coming. Tané-the-Jester, you called our god. Despite your blasphemy he has heard the prayers of Métua."

"Tané can forgive what a man says in bitterness of heart," Vana replied.

"For the sake of the others, who never lose their trust in him," another remarked. . . . "Rata, what do you say now? Does Koro thus take revenge upon us by sending rain?"

Rata remained silent.

As the ships were drawing together the little water they had left was quickly served out to the greatest sufferers, and a few of the older people were, indeed, almost at the point of death. Clouds were fast covering the sky but a few shafts of late afternoon sunshine pierced through widely-scattered rifts amongst them and fell upon the gray sea in pools of silver. Soon these vanished, and by the time that all the ships had reached *Itatae,* the canopy of blackening cloud was unbroken from horizon to horizon.

There was no need for orders from Maui. In every ship mats had been rigged for catching water and the empty containers stacked beside them. There was little talk, for the torment of thirst was still with them. The helpless ones had been placed in the huts on the platforms. The faces of all the others were turned toward the sky as they waited eagerly, forlornly, for the rain to fall. Moments were like hours to the people so desperately in need of relief. A man in *Tokérau* stood on one of the thwarts and raised his arms in a gesture of pathetic appeal. "*Haéré mai, te ua! Haéré mai!*" he said, and a moment later, rain began to fall.

Harder it came, and harder. Although the ships lay closely together, at moments they were all but hidden from view, one from the other. Faces upturned, their mouths open, their bodies streaming with rain, the people drank the cool sweet water from the air itself. The older folk were lifted to their feet; mothers held their small children aloft in their arms that they might catch the full effect of the downpour. Men and boys could be dimly glimpsed filling the bamboo water containers at the broad streams that poured from the mats. Harder still it came, an awe-inspiring deluge that blotted the ships from view, but, above the roar and hiss of this horizon-wide cataract falling into the sea, faint joyous shouts were heard. After a little time these were changed to cries of warning and alarm. Rain, so desperately longed for and prayed for, was now falling at such an appalling rate that it became, for the moment at least, their enemy. The hulls of the ships were filling with it faster than they could be bailed out. As they sank deeper and deeper with the weight of it, women and children and many of the men leaped into the sea to lighten the ships and give room to the bailers, who worked with desperate haste lest their fowls and pigs be drowned. They bailed with their scoops, with their cupped hands, but the mats were of the greatest use. Four men to each, they dipped and tilted them, pouring water over the side gallons at a time.

Gradually the downpour slackened; the outlines of the ships began to emerge, and presently the rain ceased. A strange sight came to view in the clear rain-washed air. All the clan were in the sea save the men bailing out the hulls of the vessels and the boys who had remained aboard to save the livestock. Old women clung to the gunwales; the smallest children were on their mothers' backs, clinging to their hair or with arms around their necks. Bedraggled crates of fowls were stacked on the cross-hull platforms. The pigs, brought up from below, were festooned along the sides of the ships with their front legs over the gunwales as though hung up to dry, with a small boy steadying each one. Even the great sow that had farrowed in *Anuanua* had been heaved up in time to save her from drowning. Other small boys were perched wherever they could find room, out of the way of the bailers, holding puppies and baby pigs.

Male and female alike, children and adults, they were Te-Moana-Nui-a-Kiwa's foster children. The experience of their ancestors through many generations had taught them how to meet the hazards of the sea, and now that they had survived without loss the most dreaded of them all — for the time, at least — their hearts were again filled with hope and courage. As their food was in water-tight containers they suffered no loss in this respect, and all of their vessels for water were again full, with the promise of more rain in abundance, so they might not need to use any of their precious supply for days to come. Now, with the ships bailed dry once more, they began to re-embark. They were in a gay mood, and even those who had suffered the most from thirst were fast recovering. Nanai-Vahiné, the wife of Paoto, huge in size, was being heaved aboard, but her weight was that of two ordinary women. She slipped from the grasp of those who were trying to pull her in and fell into the sea again with a great splash. The scant garment of tapa cloth that partially covered her had been reduced to a sodden pulp that clung to her body in wisps and shreds. When at last she had been pulled up the side she held the last vestige of her garment over her middle and did an impromptu dance on one of the thwarts that made them all shout with laughter; then she ducked down out of sight. The other women were in no better plight insofar as garments were concerned, and some were stark naked. As the last of them climbed into the ships a cock in one of the crates, after a futile attempt to flap his wings, crowed lustily. All cheered him. "Hear him!" one man shouted. "He has the true spirit of a Tongan cock! He loves the sea." "É, he has webs between his toes!" another said.

In the midst of the merriment not a moment was wasted in preparing for what they knew would come — wind. All knew that this sudden change in the weather was the prelude to the expected change of seasons, when there would be no lack of rainfall, with the strong westerly winds that marked the beginning of the Austral summer; and when rain fell so abundantly in a calm sea, wind would not be far behind.

Members of families who had been reunited during this period of calm were distributed as before among the various ships. Tauhéré, Maui's sister, returned to her husband, Nihau, in *Tokérau*. She wished to have Hina with her, but Maui's mother begged to have Hina with her in *Kiwa*.

"Only for this next part of the voyage, Maui?" she asked, pleadingly. "Métua is there, and *Kiwa* carries the sacred stones. Never has the ship been lost which carried them."

"So it shall be, if Hina is willing," Maui replied.

"I shall do as you wish," the girl replied.

"Then go with my mother, my darling. I shall feel certain of your safety in *Kiwa*."

Hotu, his grandmother, was also taken into *Kiwa*, and the five other women in Maui's ship were distributed among the others; for with stormy weather coming Maui wished none but men in *Itatae* that they might be freer in the task of keeping the ships together and assisting a ship in trouble, if that should come.

Now Maui gave his captains their orders for the night. There would be no stars to guide them and they were to keep closely together, blowing their conch shells frequently.

"We have bent on our small sail so that you others will be able to keep pace with us," he said. "If the wind veers to the north or south, blowing up a heavy sea, I will signal you by torchlight whether we are to sail into the seas or with them. Above all, keep well together, no more than two hundred paces apart. Let a small fire be kept smoldering in your fireboxes, so that you may signal one another by flares if that should be necessary."

The ships were drawn into line while they were waiting for the wind. In the fading light the people waved to one another and parting messages were shouted from ship to ship. *Itatae* took her place in the center of the line, about fifty paces in advance of the others. The last gray light was fading to darkness when the wind came. It blew gently at first but with increasing strength from moment to moment, and it came, as had the Fair Wind of Tané, directly from the west. Soon the ships were seething along at their proper distances, their masts bending slightly to the wind. Then came full darkness; and with it, another deluge of rain.

Disaster

Te-Ava-Roa LOST CONTACT with the other ships on the second night after the westerly winds had come. On the third night she was alone and lying helpless. During the succession of heavy squalls of wind and rain she had lost both her sails. Now, although the wind had slackened, it was still blowing strongly under a sky of intense, unrelieved blackness. The men had taken the paddles to help the steersmen bring the ship around to head into the following seas. In doing this, the ship, so heavily loaded, fell into the trough of the seas and before she could be brought to meet them, the lashings of the forward crossbeam, already dangerously loosened, had given way, so that the bows of the twin hulls had been pushed almost together and were leaning toward each other. Men had succeeded for the moment in lashing them in that position, while the people crowded aft in the already crowded ship to lighten the bows, so that there might be a chance to push them apart to the U-shaped notches that fitted over the gunwales. By daylight, in a calm sea, this might have been done without great difficulty, and the lashings renewed that held them so; but with foam-crested swells moving under them in endless procession beneath a sky as black as the sea, the attempt was all but hopeless.

Yet they did not abandon hope. They succeeded in getting the ship headed into the seas, and the paddlers worked desperately to keep her there. Nothing more could be done without light, and rain and flying spray had extinguished the coals in their firebox. Ma'o was now crouched in the bottom of one of the hulls, aft, with boys protecting him with mats from wind and spray while he made fire again.

In the darkness the people waited in numbed silence, not daring to move, knowing that death stared them in the face. The only sounds to be heard were the washing and slapping of the combers passing under the ship, the terrified sobbing of some of the small children who had been trampled upon in the darkness, and the forlorn blowing of the conch-shell trumpet; three calls in succession, announcing disaster and the need for immediate help.

Presently a tiny spark of fire appeared in the blackness, faintly revealing the face of the boy who knelt at Ma'o's feet, breathing gently upon the pinch of glowing wood-dust. With the greatest care he fed tinder upon it, adding bits of wood and bamboo splinters. An increasing flame appeared, lighting up the face of Ma'o and those around him. Meanwhile, torches had been prepared: rags of tapa cloth soaked in coconut oil, bound loosely together and impaled upon the prongs of fishing spears.

As these were lighted, a terrifying sight appeared out of the darkness. The people stared in awestruck silence at the ship and at one another. What they saw appalled them, but at least they could see. Two sturdy lads, one aft, one forward, held the torches, renewed from time to time with balls of oil-soaked rags handed up to them. There was no sign of panic upon the faces of these boys. The expression was, rather, one of grim pride that they were able to control and conceal the terror hidden in their hearts. Meanwhile, the man with the conch shell continued to send out the appeal for help over the measureless Sea of Kiwa.

The steersmen kept the ship headed into the seas while the others worked to strengthen the lashing of the crossbeam aft. Those at the forward beam prepared for the attempt to push the bows apart. Having plaited three of their strongest coils of line, men lowered themselves into the sea and, with the help of those above, the line was carried twice around one of the bows, and the free line was passed to men in the other so that when the moment came for making the attempt they could prevent the hulls from yawing widely apart. At last all was in readiness. The men were like parts of one body, functioning by instinct, each one knowing what must be done and how it must be done in this struggle for life in which human strength was to be pitted against the strength of the sea.

Ma'o took his place on the bow platform where he could overlook the ship. He peered into the darkness ahead, but in the flickering light of the flares he could scarcely see a dozen yards in that direction. He glanced aft, over the grim set faces of the people crowded there. "Hold steady!" he called to the steersmen. The strongest men in the ship were standing by the forward crossbeam, awaiting Ma'o's order. If the beam could be fitted in place and held so, while being lashed, they would have a chance for life.

"Ready!" Ma'o warned. He glanced once more at the steersmen whose eyes were fixed upon him; then he peered ahead, his arm raised, motioning them to bring the stern around slightly.

"Cut!" he shouted.

Two men standing by with adzes cut the lines holding the bows together. Men pushed with all their strength, but the might of the sea was against them and the bows were thrown together again with a sickening thud. Those holding the line kept them so until Ma'o called, "Now! Quickly! Push hard! Hard!"

This time, the sea helping a little at first, the bows were separating so that men could get the purchase of their bodies between them, their hands grasping the gunwales of one, their feet braced against the other; but again the sea defeated them. The hulls crashed together once more and two men, unable to save themselves, fell into the sea and were crushed between them. Now cries of terror were heard from some of the women. *"Mamu!"* Ma'o called, sternly. "Stop your screaming! Stop, I

say!" But the women lost control of themselves and their terror
was communicated to the others.

The third attempt was the last. The beam was all but fixed
in place when a heavy sea, foaming in from the darkness,
threw the bows widely apart and tore the line from the hands
of the men trying to hold it. Another sea carried the bows
aft, tearing loose the lashings of the rear crossbeam. A few
strands held momentarily, so that the ship lay in the form of
a V, the stern toward the seas. Another great comber crested
with wind-whipped spray lifted the stern high, and as it was
lifted the hulls broke apart and capsized, spilling the people
into the sea. The boy holding one of the torches was thrown
clear of the ship, but as he fell into the sea he held his torch
high above his head so that the people struggling in the water
could see to reach the capsized hulls which were drifting
apart. But a moment later came black darkness, and from the
midst of it the anguished cries of those clinging to the hulls
trying to direct those who failed to reach them.

When it was discovered that *Te-Ava-Roa* was missing, Maui
brought his ship alongside *Kotaha* and turned over the command of the fleet to his uncle, Rata. The ships were to lower
their sails and merely keep before the wind while he went in
search of *Te-Ava-Roa*.

"You are to wait for two days," Maui called to his uncle. "If
I have not returned by the morning of the third day, hoist
sails and proceed on your way."

It was a solemn moment for all when *Itatae* turned to head
westward. None knew better than themselves the danger of
eternal separation on the Great Sea of Kiwa; this had often
happened during the voyages of their people. Faces were
grim as they watched *Itatae* growing smaller and smaller until
the tip of the sail had vanished below the horizon.

The sky was still overcast but the wind died away in the
afternoon. *Itatae* made long boards to the west but nothing
had been sighted. Maui stood on the bow platform scanning

the empty sea. He had had no sleep during two days and nights. His men waited anxiously for his orders, hoping that he would abandon the search. Presently he said: "Take the paddles and proceed westward until nightfall. Ru, you will take charge while I rest a little. Send young Miko up the mast to keep watch." Then, while Maui slept, the men paddled on in silence, feeling the loneliness of the great empty seas, their hearts heavy at the thought of the increasing distance they were putting between themselves and the other ships.

"Will he turn back tonight?" one of the men asked, in a low voice.

Ru shook his head. "It is Ma'o's ship, remember, that we're searching for. Maui loves him like a brother. He will not give up hope of finding him for another two days at least."

"It is a great risk," another said.

"But one that must be taken," Ru replied. "So it has always been with us Tongans. Come, now! Quicken the stroke! We're no more than crawling. Tané sees us. We are in his care. . . ."

He broke off as there came a hail from the boy at the mast-head: *"Ieru!"* (Wait!)

"What is is, Miko?" Ru called.

"Something floating out there," the boy replied, pointing to the north. "I can't be sure. . . . A coconut perhaps."

Ru brought the ship around to head in that direction. "Keep your eye on it, Miko. . . . Now where away?"

"Wait! I've lost it," the boy replied. . . . "Now I have it again. Straight ahead!"

The men paddled steadily, Ru keeping the ship in the direction indicated by the boy's outstretched arm.

"Au-é! It's . . . it's not a coconut!"

"What, then? . . . A turtle?"

The boy continued to stare ahead. "I can't be sure, yet. . . . *Haéré noa!"* He dropped his arm and stared at Ru in a strange manner.

"What is it, Miko? What do you see?"

"Haéré noa! Haéré noa!" the boy replied, and turned to gaze

ahead once more. "It's moving!" A moment later he slid down the mast and stood looking at Ru, unable to speak, an expression of fear and bewilderment on his face.

"What is it, Miko?" Ru repeated. "Can't you speak? What have you seen?"

"A man!" the boy replied in an awed voice. "He's swimming toward us!"

"A man! What are you saying? Get back to your post. If it is a coconut there may be land hereabout."

"I'm afraid, Ru," the boy said. "It may be a sea monster; but the head is like a man's, and I could see its arms moving!"

Maui was awakened and mounted the platform in the bow. *"Hoé! Hoé!"* he called to the paddlers, "but gently! If it's a turtle we'll have a fine feed of fresh meat."

It was a man, not a turtle, that Miko saw, swimming alone through the measureless wastes of the Sea of Kiwa, and the man was Ma'o. Even when they had reached him and lifted him into the ship they could scarcely believe in his reality. Although he was very weary he was not exhausted, and when he had been given water and a little food he told Maui and his men what had happened to *Te-Ava-Roa*.

"When the ship was torn apart," he said, "I was thrown into the sea with the rest, but I found one of the hulls and helped others to reach it. There were thirty of us, perhaps more, clinging to it, but it was tossed and rolled by the sea and many were drowned as it rolled. I tried to help the others to hold fast, but in the darkness there was little one could do. When morning came, I alone was left. I saw the other hull floating not more than a mile away; but there was no one on it, Maui: I am certain of that. The sea was going down. A little after dawn I saw sea birds flying from the north. Two ghost terns lighted on the hull, which was floating on its side at the time. I had prayed to Tané in the night, and I believed that he had sent the birds to tell me that he had heard my prayer. It must have been so. It was as though I heard his voice saying: 'Ma'o, you are not alone in this great sea. Have courage! Swim to the north, for there is land in the direction from which these birds have come.' And so I did. And . . . and you found me, Maui."

No one spoke for a moment. Maui sat with his arm around Ma'o's shoulders. Ru said: "And you have been swimming for a day and a night?"

"I was not swimming all of the time," Ma'o replied. "I rested, lying on my back. Twice rain fell heavily. I lifted myself as far as I could and drank it from the air. It was a little salty from the spray mixed with it as it struck the sea, but it saved me."

"You did not lose hope, Ma'o?"

"I still had strength to swim. I could not lose hope while that remained. . . . Now I will rest, for I am very weary."

A moment later he was fast asleep.

Maui said: "If any of you doubt that we shall reach our Homeland, think of Ma'o. Never shall his name be forgotten as long as there are Tongans living to honor his memory." He turned to Ru. "We will continue northward," he added, "for land may lie in that direction. If we find it by tomorrow, we will proceed immediately in search of the others."

✥ XXIII ✥
Refuge

THE STORY RETURNS to the other ships left by Maui under Rata's command. On the night of Maui's departure high wind and blinding rain struck them again, extinguishing the small fires they had kept burning for the purpose of signaling from ship to ship: nevertheless, with no sails hoisted and merely keeping before wind and sea, with signals by conch shell exchanged frequently throughout the night, they had not lost touch. The ships labored heavily and the people were in miserable plight, perpetually drenched by wind and spray and compelled to bail constantly. This weather continued throughout the following day and night, but on the morning of the third day watery gleams of sunlight pierced the clouds; the rain ceased, and the wind died away. The ships were widely scattered but all were within view and by midday they had assembled on *Kotaha*. The house on the platform of *Iriatai* had been blown flat, and those on two other ships were all but down. The crossbeam lashings on *Kiwa* and *Anuanua* had become dangerously loosened; had wind and sea not fallen when they did those ships would, inevitably, have been lost. Most of the people in them crowded into the other ships to make room for the men at work on repairs. By early afternoon the sky was cloudless, and the breeze, again from the southeast, was so light that it barely wrinkled the surface of the sea.

While the repairs were being made, Hina, with Maui's mother, moved into Rata's ship. Rata's manner toward Hina was one of cold courtesy. He spoke as though convinced that

Te-Ava-Roa was lost, giving as his reason for believing so that Ma'o, her captain, was the son of Rangi who had mocked Puaka's nephew and had lost his life for that reason.

"And now Koro, in answer to the prayers of his priest, has taken a further revenge by destroying the son, and all those with him."

Maéva was deeply hurt and indignant at hearing her brother-in-law speak in this way, and well understood his purpose in doing so. It was, by indirection, to cast blame upon Hina. It was as though he were saying: "And what of Maui and Hina? What must be Koro's hatred of them who have so brazenly defied him? And we others shall suffer with them, and because of them." But Maéva remained silent, not wishing to expose Rata's purpose before the others.

The people on *Kotaha* listened soberly to what Rata had said. Then Vaiho spoke: "Rata, we are waiting here for Maui. Before nightfall we may see both *Itatae* and *Te-Ava-Roa* appear above the horizon. Is it not better to hope while we may than to despair before hope is gone?"

"My orders from Maui were that, if he failed to appear on the morning of the third day, we were to proceed without him," Rata replied. "This is the day, but we shall wait until morning." Rata was seated beside Hina. With an air of assumed compassion he took one of Hina's hands and held it between his own. The girl gave an involuntary shudder of fear as he did so. "Cling to hope, my child, but you must be prepared to lose Maui. Although you belong to the Koros by birth and blood we know that, in your heart, you belong to us. And Koro knows it."

The girl made no reply.

Now came evening, and by that time the damaged huts had been raised, the ships bailed dry, and the crossbeam lashings made strong again so that all of the ships were ready to proceed on the voyage. But they waited through the night with flares burning on *Éata,* and, at intervals, four men on *Anuanua* blew their conch shells in unison, the sound moving mournfully out over the great solitude of waters. But no answering call came back.

After their long buffeting by wind and sea, the people were very weary, and before the night was half-spent most of them were sleeping. Hina sat in the high bow platform of *Kiwa* looking westward over the sea — now so calm that the blurred reflections of the brightest stars could be seen there. Presently a shadowy figure climbed to that place and seated himself beside her. It was Métua. Although he did not speak, the girl felt the deep comfort of his presence and the feeling of loneliness and dread that had oppressed her spirit throughout the day left her. When he rose to go he laid a hand on the girl's head.

"My child, you must not lose hope," he said.

"You think there is reason for hope?"

"In some of the voyages of our ancestors, ships that had been separated for weeks, even months, have found one another again when all hope had been abandoned."

"You yourself have hope, Métua?" Hina asked.

"When you and Maui were children I knew that you were destined for each other," the priest replied. "I believe that now as firmly as I did then."

Under the same clear skies, with a gentle breeze from the southeast, the ships proceeded on their way. Once again they were sailing in a wide arc with intervals of about three miles between them. In the late afternoon the signal for closing in for the night was given from Rata's ship. When they had done so it was learned that a floating coconut palm frond had been seen from Taio's ship and several birds flying north had been sighted from *Anuanua* at the northern end of the line. This caused great excitement amongst the people, for a palm frond still afloat was an indication that land must be near. Sails were taken in and the ships lay-to through the night. Shortly after dawn the following morning birds were again seen flying from the north. Rata gave orders that they should sail for three days in that direction and if no land were found they would turn eastward once more. The ships now spread to the widest possible intervals until they were barely within view of one another, and, early in the afternoon came the signal from *Éata,* at the western end of the line, that land had been sighted. As the signal was passed from ship to ship they closed in toward *Éata,* and from each in succession the land was raised, a faint irregularity against the horizon, appearing and disappearing as they rose to the swells and slid into the troughs between them. Tears of joy and relief flowed unchecked down the faces of many of the older folk. They scarcely dared to believe, even when the whole of the island was in sight, but there it lay in the golden light of late afternoon — scattered green islets threaded at wide intervals along a coral reef enclosing a lagoon seven or eight miles long by four or five in width. Only a few of the older people had ever before seen a lagoon island, but all knew that such lands existed. As they drew near and coasted along the shore the place was like paradise itself. On the larger islets the fronds of coconut palms were swaying gently in the breeze, and they saw clumps of screw pine, *hotu* and *tamanu* trees and broad green forests of *purau*. Across wide stretches of reef awash they looked across the lagoon to the islets on the far side, their outlines blurred by distance and looking scarcely real against the background of open sea. There were six of these in all: two on the north side, two on the south, a small islet at the western end, and one, the largest, following the curve of the reef from the eastern end for the distance of a mile or more toward the south.

As they sailed slowly along, the people searched the shore-line eagerly, anxiously, fearing there was no entrance to the lagoon, but as they rounded the eastern end they discovered a fine passage through the reef. Now they had nothing more to ask. They could enter and moor their ships in that peaceful mid-ocean lake, where they could lie in safety, protected from all danger.

The sea, so long their enemy, was now their friend, as

though to reward these weary voyagers for all the misery they had suffered. Taio's ship was the first to enter. The current was running gently into the lagoon. Taio stood in the bow of *Éata* scanning the passage, but there was good depth of from five to six fathoms. Ship after ship, they came in from the sea, the people gazing in silence at the caves and forests of coral so beautiful in the sunlight of late afternoon streaming down upon them through water as clear as air. Scarcely a word was spoken. The quietness of the ships as they passed from the open sea into the sheltered lagoon seemed to enter the hearts and the bodies of the people, making them incapable of either speech or movement. They anchored in a little cove midway along the largest islet, bordered with coconut palms which leaned out over the lagoon as though entranced by their reflections in the still water.

When the ships were moored the people gazed at the land still almost doubtful of its reality; then the children began to pour out with shouts of joy. The dogs followed them; then came the others. The limbs of some of the older folk were so cramped and helpless after their long confinement that they had to be carried ashore, where they sat in deep content watching those wading back and forth across the shallows as they unloaded the ships. The pigs were carried ashore, and the crates of fowls, but even when the crates were open the fowls still lay inert within them. The people gathered round as they were being released. Marama pulled out a cock and stood him on his legs. His attitude, finding himself at liberty and upon land, once more was so expressive of wonder and unbelief that the people looked on with pity, taking pleasure in his pleasure. He staggered as he flapped his wings and crowed.

"Look!" said Marama. "He can't believe. You would think he was saying: 'I'm dreaming. This must be one of Tavi-the-Jester's phantom islands.' " The other fowls were quickly released and tottered about feebly for a few moments, but they soon recovered the use of their legs and scattered in all directions. So it was with the pigs. At first they lay where they had been dropped, not even trying to walk; but one by one they got to their feet and scampered off into the bush.

The people gathered strength with every step they took. Everything was brought ashore from the ships: the provisions, fishing spears, bundles of mats and spare sails, the boxes of tools, the precious plants and young trees in bamboo pots which had been tended with the greatest care throughout the voyage. Some were dead and others in a sickly condition. The moment they were brought ashore they were carried into the thickest bush, where they would be protected from full sunlight, and planted in the best soil, mixed with humus, that could be found.

While some unloaded the ships, others scattered over the land in the search for food. Men and older boys speared fish in the shallows of the lagoon; women and children gathered *maoas, pahuas* and other shellfish along the reefs on the seaward side of the island; boys climbed the palms for green drinking coconuts; children gathered dry wood along the beaches, bringing it to the place where fires had been lighted. Soon a great store of food had been collected, and more was brought in from moment to moment as the people returned from their quest. Fish and shellfish had been caught in great abundance. Boys who had gone to the far end of the islet returned with scores of seafowl and baskets filled with their eggs. While the fish and the birds were being cleaned and roasted over the coals, Taio came staggering in with a great sea turtle which he carried on his back, followed by Vahiné, his wife, with two baskets filled with its eggs.

Night had fallen by the time the food was ready. Green palm fronds with the butts cut off were spread on the beach and the food placed upon them. The people gathered around the fires, the men in one place, the women in another, their hearts filled with gratitude, not only for the food, but also for the relief from the discomfort and misery of the crowded ships. They ate in silence for the most part, so intent upon filling their bellies that they had little time for talk. Although a great store of food had been prepared, by the time the meal ended nothing was left.

It was a tradition among the Tongans, handed down from generation to generation, that when, during their voyages, certain ships reached land while others were still missing, nothing should be said of the absent ones until two days and nights had passed. So, now, when Métua had offered the prayers of thanksgiving to Tané for their safe arrival, they stretched out on the warm sand, gazing in silence over the quiet waters of the lagoon or into the depths of the starlit sky. Deep were their forebodings concerning the missing ones, but all were very weary and soon their fears vanished in the blessedness of sleep.

XXIV
The Vengeance of Koro

RATA'S HOPE that chance might one day place him in the position of highest authority in the Tongan Clan was now realized. He had become convinced that Tané's promised Homeland had no more reality than the phantom lands of Tavi-the-Jester, and that unless he could persuade the Tongans to renounce their worship of Tané for that of Koro, their doom was certain. The time was near, he felt, when he could speak openly of this to the people. If Maui were, indeed, lost — and he had little doubt of it — the position of high chief would fall to him by right of birth. He would keep his purpose secret as long as Métua lived, but the priest was now in his eighty-seventh year and it was not in the course of nature that he could live much longer. He displayed no lack of concern as to the fate of *Itatae* and *Te-Ava-Roa*. Boys were stationed on three of the islets to keep watch during the daylight hours from the tops of the highest coconut palms, and during the first two weeks ships were sent out to search the sea in all directions. At the end of this time, as no sign of the missing vessels had been found, the search was abandoned.

Meanwhile, the people had established themselves on the islet where they had come ashore. Their dwellings followed the curve of the lagoon beach. Canoes were built for fishing within the lagoon and for visiting the various islets. A temple of squared coral slabs for the worship of Tané was erected at the eastern end of the village islet bordering the passage. As it was only for temporary use it was a small structure with two terraces. Métua's dwelling was near the temple.

Maui's mother and Hina had been given permission by Rata to live on the islet at the western end of the lagoon. Both were certain that Maui still lived, and they chose this islet because it gave a clear view to the west. Taio and his family lived with them at this place. At night a fire was kept burning on the outer beach so that Maui would see it if he approached during the hours of darkness.

Taio's family were a great comfort to Maéva and Hina. Whatever their fears, they kept them hidden and spoke of Maui cheerfully and with confidence as though they expected to sight his ship at any moment.

When the temple to Tané had been completed the chiefs met there for its dedication and to place within it the casket containing the sacred stones. This service occupied the greater part of the afternoon. The sun was near to setting when the last of the chants was sung:

> Holy is the human spirit;
> Sacred the body, its dwelling-place.
> Men shall not kill . . .

The face of the old priest seemed transfigured in the golden light as he repeated the words of Tané. Then the casket containing the stones was placed in the aperture made to receive it, and the service ended.

Métua asked the chiefs to go with him to his home. When they had refreshed themselves with drinking nuts he paced the room for some time while the others waited for him to speak.

"I have asked you to come here at Maui's request," he said. "Were he here, he himself would tell you what I now have to say, for he planned to do this at the first land we reached. It was his wish that, if *Itatae* should become separated from the other ships, I should do this in his place."

The chiefs waited for him to proceed. Presently he added:

"On the night when we left Kurapo, Puaka, the priest of Koro, was killed. Maui was the unconscious cause of his death."

His listeners stared at him as though unable to grasp the meaning of his words.

"Dead! Puaka dead?" Rata exclaimed.

"It is true," Métua replied, quietly.

He then told them what had happened at the Koro temple on the night when Maui was taken there to be sacrificed. He spoke of the golden coral pebble which Maui wore and how it had been placed in the casket with the sacred stones carried all the long way over the Sea of Kiwa. "The *mana* of our ancestors through twenty generations is contained in the stones," Métua said, "and this, through the grace of Tané, was passed into the coral pebble to protect him against the priest of Koro. By means of the strength thus given him he was able not only to save his life, but to topple the great stone image of Koro from its pedestal and send it crashing from the high platform to the ground below. Unknown to Maui, Puaka was passing along the walk below the temple. He was crushed beneath the image. Maui himself saw this as he escaped from the temple grounds; and Hina as well, for she went there at the risk of her life in search of him."

The chiefs were so stunned by the news that none could speak for a moment; then Rata said: "Métua, there is no doubt of this?"

"None," the priest replied.

"Then we shall never see him again," said Vana. "Who can doubt that he and all of those with him have been destroyed by Koro?"

"I can doubt it," Tuahu replied. "The power of Koro is great; that we know, but — blesséd be Tané! — we are not helpless against him. Does it not stir your hearts to know that a high chief of the Tongans could defy Koro in his own temple and escape unharmed? For I believe that he still lives and that we shall see him again."

"He is dead," said Paoto in a woeful voice. "I am as certain of it as that Téaro, his father, was killed by Koro before we left the land of Kurapo."

"Métua, did you know beforehand what Maui would do?" Rata asked.

"I knew that, through the *mana* of our ancestors, he would escape with his life, but I did not know that he would, or could, destroy the great image of Koro," the priest replied. "But this could not have been done against the will of Tané and I am at peace with respect to it."

Rata now spoke with a bitterness he had never before displayed toward the priest. "You may well be at peace," he said. "You are an old man and have not long to suffer the consequences of the revenge Koro will now take upon us. But we others will feel the weight of his power until the last one of us has been destroyed."

"It shall not be so," the priest replied, quietly. "Rata, you are a man of little faith and will not believe what I say. I am, indeed, old, and nearing the end of my days, but this I will tell you others while I may: Maui still lives and those of you who remain true to your faith in Tané will see him again. This more I will tell you, for it is the will of Tané that it should now be known lest you despair of the power of his love to protect you. The quest for the Far Lands of Maui will end within the lifetimes of some of you now living. May this strengthen your hearts through the dangers and disappointments yet to be endured."

Métua would say no more, and requested them to leave him — for he was very weary. The import of what their priest had told them was beyond the power of the chiefs to grasp.

"Within our lifetimes," Tavaké said, repeating the phrase again and again. "After twenty generations the quest is to end. Within our lifetimes . . . we are to see the Far Lands of Maui. Blesséd be Tané! Within our lifetimes . . ."

"The priest made no promise that any of us would see the Far Lands of Maui," Rata replied. "What he said was that the quest would end within the lifetimes of some of us now living.

And so it will, perhaps in this small poor land where we now are."

"Shame to you, Rata!" Marama said. "Can you believe that Métua, our beloved priest for more than sixty years, would deceive us?"

"He is an old man, as I have said," Rata replied, "and his faculties are not what they were. He would not, knowingly, deceive us, but he deceives himself. It is my opinion that he has believed, through all these years, that he would see the Far Lands of Maui. Knowing now that this cannot be, it is necessary for him to believe that Maui and some of the Tongans now living will reach it. Maui is dead through the consequences of his own act, and Hina and her unborn child will not long survive him."

The other chiefs, save Vana and Pohi, were appalled at what Rata said. They had long had reason to suspect that he was no true Tongan, but never before had he spoken in this manner.

"Rata," said Nihau, "you have said in my own hearing that you honor Hina."

"And if I did, what weight will this have with Koro?" Rata replied. "Not only did she destroy the war canoes of her own people, but she entered the sacred ground of the Koro temple. This no woman has ever done or could do and escape Koro's vengeance. We shall suffer with her and because of her. I speak as I do because it is my duty to warn you others. Mark me well! The time will soon come when we shall feel the full weight of Koro's anger."

"We are glad that, for once, you have spoken from your heart," Tavaké said, "for now we know you, Rata. May Maui soon come! For you are no more fit to lead us than Uri, the nephew of Puaka, would be." Then they left him.

The weeks passed, and the day came when Hina's child — a son — was born. Maéva, Hotu and Vahiné were with her at this time. Hina's labor was light, and now, with her child in her

arms, she was happy for the first time since she had parted
from Maui. Having been born and reared in the Koro Clan, she
had feared that Koro would take vengeance upon her by killing the child in her body — and she could not but doubt that
Tané's love could protect her from the evil designs of the war
god. But now came the feeling, the assurance, that she was so
protected; and her heart filled with happiness that grew from
the confidence that Métua's prophecy concerning Maui and
herself would be fulfilled and that she would see Maui again.
She would sit hour after hour, her child in her arms, looking
to the west over the lonely sea, singing songs about his father
to her little son, inventing the airs and the words as she sang.
Day after day she watched and waited, and night after night
she prayed for Maui's safety; but at dawn when she hurried
to the outer beach to scan the sea, she found it, as always,
empty to the far horizon. Nevertheless, her child was the living
proof that Maui would find them; and believing this, she
became the stay and comfort of Maéva, who had all but abandoned hope.

When the boy was two months old Maéva decided that they
could no longer postpone the service at which he would be
named and dedicated, as the first-born son of the high chief, to
the service of his people. Maéva and Hina knew what his name
was to be, for it had been Maui's choice in case he should have
a son. He was to be called Tavi, in honor of the builder of the
phantom islands, for Maui had never thought of Tavi as a
jester but as a creator of beauty in ideal form. On the morning
of the day set for the service Taio set out for the village with
Maéva, Hina and her child, his family following in another
canoe.

It was a day of oppressive heat; no faintest tremor of a breeze
flawed the glassy surface of the lagoon. The sun shone with a
brassy glare through a veil of saffron-colored cloud that
covered the sky from horizon to horizon. There was a high surf
along the reefs. Great swells, gathering height as they ap-

proached the land, crashed in a chaos of foam and broken water that swept across the reefs and spent their force in waves that slid far up the beaches, almost to the trees that bordered them. Taio's face was grave as he noted these signs of an approaching storm.

"It is well that the naming ceremony is set for today," he said. "I doubt that it could take place tomorrow."

"We are to have a storm, you think?" Maéva asked.

Taio nodded. "And it will be no common storm. Blesséd be Tané that we are on land! There is wind and sea to come such as no ship could survive."

"How can you be sure, Taio?" Hina asked.

He smiled. "I am always boasting of my skill in reading signs of coming weather," he replied, "but I am not always right. I hope I have guessed wrong what is now on the way to us."

When they reached the village, Maéva and Hina went to Rata's house. He was the only male relative of the family and it was necessary for him to act in Maui's place at the naming service. This was an odious task to Rata, the more so because after Maui's son had been christened he would become, by the law of the Tongans, high chief in his father's place, to assume his duties when he reached the age of manhood. Rata would be only his regent until that time. Nevertheless, much as Rata hated his duty on this occasion, inflexible custom demanded that he should fulfill it.

Taio crossed the island to the outer beach, where he found Marama and Tavaké seated with others at the upper slope of the beach, watching the great seas thundering across the reef, the spent waves reaching almost to the place where they sat. The people had great respect for Taio's knowledge of the weather; rarely was he mistaken in forecasting it. As Tavaké and Marama questioned him the others gathered around to listen.

"A great storm is coming, I am certain of it," Taio was saying. "We may not have the full force of it until tomorrow, but that is to be seen. We have no time to lose in preparing for it."

"You think, Taio, that it may be the *metangi hurifenua?*" (the wind that overturns the land), Marama asked.

"It may well be," Taio replied. "Tané be thanked that our village is on the highest of the islets! The center part is at least twenty feet above the sea, and large enough to give refuge to us all. Even so we may have little height to spare."

Taio went with Tavaké and Marama to Rata's house, where the other chiefs had gathered. Rata was dressing himself in Maui's ceremonial robes in preparation for the service at the *marae*. When Marama had given them Taio's opinion of the nature of the storm to come, Rata accepted it eagerly as a reason for postponing the naming ceremony, but Tuahu said: "No; it must be carried through as planned. The naming of Maui's son has already been delayed two months, and there is no indication that the storm will break before tomorrow." The other chiefs agreed with Tuahu, and Rata was forced to bend to their opinion. They then discussed the preparations to be made while they were at the *marae*. Their first thought was for the safety of the ships. If they should be lost, the people would be doomed to remain on this island, for the trees upon it were not of a kind to furnish material for building new ones. They knew that in times past some of their ancestors had met with great storms on low islands and had saved their ships by sinking them in the lagoon. It was decided that they must do the same.

They went out to where the men waited for instructions as to what they must do. Rata explained that the ships were to be sunk off the lagoon beach in depths of between eight and ten fathoms.

"Should we not leave one to ride out the storm?" Nihau asked. "If it proves to be what we expect, wind and sea and rain will be of such force that some of the older people may not survive it. The ship would give them some protection."

This was agreed to, and *Iriatai* was the ship chosen for this purpose. It was a risk to be taken but a necessary one.

"Taio, I put you and Manu in charge of this work while we are at the *marae*," Rata said. "Set about it at once."

Four of the ships were shored up on the beach beneath sheds that had been built for them; two were still at anchor in the lagoon. Those in the sheds were quickly put into the water and brought as close to the beach as possible while they were being partly filled with sand: then they were moved out to the required depth for sinking. While this was being done, other men brought heavy coral fragments from the outer beach which were carried in canoes to the ships. One by one five of them were sunk to the floor of the lagoon. Lines were carried from the bows of the ships and made fast to the trunks of the largest trees growing on the beach so that they might not be moved from where they lay. Even with all the men of the clan engaged upon it, this work required the whole of the morning.

Meanwhile, the service at the *marae* was not yet over. It was no brief ceremony, for there were many chants to be sung and prayers to be said at the ceremony for the son of a high chief, and none could be omitted. Tavi, the name now given to Hina's little son, was bathed first in sea water, then in fresh, in a large Tridacna shell sacred to that particular purpose. Then he was well wrapped in soft tapa cloth by one of Métua's assistants and carried to his mother, who stood with Maéva outside the wall that enclosed the temple grounds. They remained there with the child while the rest of the ceremony continued. Many women and children were gathered there, looking on from a distance: they could faintly hear the voices of the chiefs and the temple assistants as the chants were sung. Tears had come into Hina's eyes as she heard fragments of the chant sung while her child was being bathed. She had first heard this in childhood when Maui took her to the lake and showed her the coral pebble that he was made to suck by Hapai, the schoolmaster, because he willfully refused to remember the words

of it. And now — where was he? On some other island that
he had discovered far from this one? At sea? He might be
nearing them at this moment with a great storm approaching.
She tried to drive these fears from her mind. She shut her eyes
and prayed in silence: "Tané, loving Father! Save my dear
husband! Save him for his people. Save him for the little son
whose life is now being dedicated to Thy service! Save him
for me!" She took great comfort in remembering that Maui
wore the coral pebble into which had gone the *mana* of his
ancestors. Surely that would protect him and carry him safely
through whatever dangers he might have to meet.

And now, as the service was nearing its end, came the wind.
It blew only freshly at first but increased in strength from moment to moment. The coconut palms swayed in wider and
wider arcs as the force of it grew, their fronds threshing and
turning; the dry ones clinging to the trees were torn from
them and fell to the ground in great numbers. Hina had prepared a basket of plaited palm fronds in which to carry her
son. She had lined it with closely woven matting as a further
protection from wind and rain. Now she placed the sleeping
child in it and with a strip of tough *purau* bark she lightly
closed the opening at the top. Taking up the basket, she was
returning with Maéva to Rata's house when they were overtaken by the chiefs.

The service at the *marae* had ended. Rata's face was grim as
he passed them — half-running, half-walking to the place
where *Iriatai* was being moored to the low gnarled trunks of
two *hotu* trees growing near the beach. All the people were
gathered there, waiting for the chiefs. Men were standing in
the shallows on either side of the ship, holding her there for
those who were to go into her. Several had already done so;
others hesitated, torn between the desire for shelter from wind
and rain and their fear as to the safety of the ship in the height
of the storm. Decisions were made for some of them by their
sons or grandsons who picked them up and carried them

through the shallows, passing them to Marama and three of his men who were to remain in the ship.

Rata came to where the priest was standing with Maéva and Hina.

"Métua, get you into the ship," he commanded brusquely. "Others will then follow, knowing they will be safe where you are. Maéva, you and Hina shall go with him."

"I will go but they shall not," Métua replied, quietly. He smiled faintly as he laid a hand on the girl's shoulder. "My child, the ship is only for us ancient ones who can no longer endure hardship." He kissed the girl lightly on both cheeks and as he did so he said, in a low voice that Hina alone could hear: *"He will come."* Then, having embraced Maéva in like manner, he went to the ship. Twenty others followed him, making the number of people in *Iriatai* thirty-five. The ship was then let out to the extent of her moorings, and two great anchors of coral rock were thrown out from the stern.

Scarcely had this been done when the storm struck them with all its appalling force, and the gray light faded until the gloom was almost that of night. Most of the people had already gone to the high land in the center of the islet, but some were still in their houses and others had returned to the outer beach as though compelled to stand there, facing their common danger. None were prepared for this sudden, incredible assault of wind and rain and sea. Their houses vanished in a moment. The coconut palms bent far over and the air was filled with flying fronds and nuts and the limbs and branches of other trees. Waves of from six to ten inches deep came licking across the land and were swept up by the wind and carried on in sheets of blinding spray. The people, feeling the water beneath their feet, stared at the ground scarcely believing that such a thing could be. They could be dimly glimpsed making their way toward the higher land. Some were on hands and knees, unable to stand against the mighty torrent of air; others sheltered themselves momentarily behind the trunks of trees, clinging to them while gasping for breath.

Hina and Maéva, with Taio's family, were near the place of refuge when the full force of the wind struck them. The basket containing her child was nearly torn from Hina's arms, and might have been had not Taio seized her. He took the basket. "Hold fast to me!" he shouted. With both hands she grasped the broad belt of his waist mat and took what shelter she could behind him as they pushed slowly forward, leaning forward into the wind which supported them in that position. Maéva and Vahiné clung to Marama. At last they reached the place where the others were, and they lay prone behind a slanting ledge of coral that protruded from the soil, giving them a little protection from the wind. Their mats were nearly jerked from their hands as the people wrapped themselves in them. With Taio's help, Hina and Maéva succeeded in getting themselves rolled in one mat with the child between them. All the livestock had been brought to this place, and pigs and dogs and humans lay packed closely together getting what little warmth they could from one another's bodies. In their common misery, the people were like one body, too numbed in spirit either to hope or to fear. But to Rata, at least, the mighty voice of the Great Sea of Kiwa was that of Koro himself.

✥ XXV ✥
Maui's Return

ON AN AFTERNOON three weeks later five of the ships again lay at anchor near the beach of what remained of the village island. It was now two islets, the eastern end separated from the land to the west by a stretch of bare reef fifty paces wide which had been swept clean by the sea. Where the *marae* to Tané had stood nothing remained but sand and heaps of coral fragments. With the temple had gone the casket of sacred stones from their ancestral *marae* carried for twenty generations all the long way over the Sea of Kiwa. The islets on the northern reef had vanished. The one at the western end remained, but it was now only the ghost of an islet that stood, of an evening, in forlorn silhouette against the disc of the setting sun. *Iriatai* was lost during the storm; and twenty of the people on land had been drowned or killed by flying debris during the height of the storm.

The Tongans, their numbers reduced to four hundred and thirty, were appalled when they learned the full extent of the disaster that had overtaken them. Most of the coconut palms had been destroyed and the land could no longer support them. They had saved their canoes by carrying them to the high land before the storm broke. Knowing they could not remain long on the island they built small lean-to shelters to replace their houses. They searched the reefs and what remained of the islets and salvaged thousands of both coconuts and pandanus nuts, which were saved for sea stores on the voyage to come.

Fish were still abundant and great quantities were caught,

the surplus cleaned and dried on racks in the sun to provide food for them at sea. Meanwhile the ships sunk in the lagoon were emptied and raised to the surface. None had been damaged and they were again made ready for sea. New houses were built on the cross-hull platforms and cordage made from the fiber of coconut husks.

During this time the people worked grimly, doggedly, as their ancestors before them had done in times of disaster. Most of them were convinced that Maui and all those with him were dead. They accepted Rata's leadership not only because Maui had placed him in command but also because, with Maui dead, Rata became high chief by right of birth.

Now came the time when Rata resolved to speak openly to the people of the plan he had long cherished to draw them away from their worship of Tané and persuade them to abandon the quest for the Far Lands of Maui. In view of what had happened, he had no doubt of his success with the greater part of the clan. Some of the chiefs — Tuahu, Tavaké and Nihau, for example — he knew he could never persuade, nor did he wish to do so. They would strongly oppose him — and a few of the people would as well. They could go their way, but he was convinced that the greater part of the clan would follow him.

On an evening when the ships were all but ready to sail, Rata called the people together. When the clan had assembled he stood before them and said:

"Tomorrow, if the wind favors, we shall leave this wrecked and ruined land. We shall sail on eastward . . . but not in quest of the Far Lands of Maui." He paused, but as no one spoke he continued: "I am now your high chief in my dead nephew's place. I speak of him as dead, for that is as certain as that you hear the sound of my voice. You know — all of you, now — what Maui did on the evening when we left Kurapo. He destroyed the great image of Koro, and Puaka, priest of Koro, was crushed to death by its fall. Dearly have we paid for this. *Te-Ava-Roa* is lost; Maui's ship is lost; *Iriatai* is lost, with Métua, priest of Tané, and all who were in that ship. Tané's *marae,* and the casket containing the stones carried for so many generations over the Sea of Kiwa, have been swept away by the sea. Twenty others were drowned, here on land, during the great storm. Can any of you believe that this is the result of chance and not by the design of Koro? Would you tempt him to give you further proof of his power?"

He broke off, and Tuahu replied, quietly: "Rata, are you speaking in Koro's name? You are now his priest?"

"I am a Tongan," Rata replied, "and those who follow me will still be Tongans. But we know that we are powerless to resist Koro or to escape from him. The experience of twenty generations of our ancestors has proven it."

"In what manner do you propose that we should acknowledge this?" Tuahu asked.

"By renouncing our worship of Tané."

"Then, if we succeed in reaching new lands, are we to build a *marae* for the worship of Koro? Teach our young men the glory of war and the joy of killing? Whom are they to kill, one another?"

"What our worship is to be remains to be seen," said Rata, "but we are to seek no longer for Tané's promised Homeland, for it has no more reality than the phantom lands of Tavi-the-Jester."

Then Tavaké spoke. "Rata, in all the history of the Tongan Clan, never before has a blood relative of the high chief renounced his faith in Tané. Think what you do! Think of the everlasting shame you will bring, not only upon yourself, but upon your children and your children's children for generations to come! Think of the guilt that will give your heart no peace, if you divide this remnant of the Tongan Clan now so few in numbers."

"And *why* are we so few?" Rata said. "Because we have worshiped a god in whose service thousands of our people have perished. 'Life is sacred to Tané.' Can you still believe it when he has led us, generation after generation, on a quest that will end only when the last one of us has perished in the sea? Tané is either powerless to protect us or indifferent to our fate. Koro is full of compassion compared with this god of peace who gives us only the peace of death."

This meeting lasted far into the night and all spoke who had the desire to do so. None of the chiefs had Rata's eloquence, his gift of persuasion, but their unshakable faith in Tané gave to their words the deeper eloquence which faith inspires. The hearts of many of the people were torn with uncertainty as to the decision they were now required to make, for Rata had said he would sail on the following day and only those were to go with him who would renounce their faith in Tané. If only Métua, their beloved priest, could be with them to reply to Rata! But he was dead, a victim of Koro's vengeance. If Tané were powerless to protect his own priest, what of themselves?

Tuahu and the chiefs loyal to Tané were sorely tempted to tell the people of the prophecy made by Métua, that within the lifetimes of some of the people then living the Homeland would be reached, but they refrained, thinking the people should be tested by the strength of their faith. Those who renounced it to follow Rata would prove themselves unworthy of continuing the quest for the Far Lands of Maui.

Long was that night. When the meeting ended many remained on the beach arguing, pleading with one another as to the irrevocable step now to be taken. Never had they foreseen that a time might come when they would be a divided clan, and the shadow of impending separation cast its gloom deep into their hearts. To some it seemed inevitable that they should follow Rata. It was traditional with the Tongans to accept the counsel of their chiefs, in particular their high chiefs, and Rata now stood in that position. They honored their chief and believed he was gifted with superior wisdom, the ability to make right decisions for the people. But many had long suspected that Rata was no true Tongan; and now that he had openly denounced their worship of Tané, they were unspeakably shocked. Nevertheless, there remained the traditional sense of loyalty due him, the more so because Maui himself had delegated his authority to Rata. Some of them, worn out by the attempt to decide what they must do, fell asleep, hoping that, somehow, the events of the day to come would reveal to them where their duty lay.

Early the following afternoon they gathered once more on the beach before the anchored ships. Tuahu and the loyal chiefs stood in one place; Rata in another, with his son, Pohi, Vana, his son-in-law, and Paoto — the only chiefs who had elected to go with him. The people stood together in one group facing the chiefs. Rata spoke first.

"Now you are to decide whom you are to follow: myself, or the chiefs yonder. It is my belief that we shall find rich high lands in this part of the Sea of Kiwa. They may lie only a little distance before us, beyond the horizon. When such a land is found, we shall establish ourselves there and think no more, forever, of the Far Lands of Maui. I have said that we may find lands eastward already peopled, but I think it unlikely. It is much more likely that, having renounced the worship of Tané, we shall be helped, not persecuted, by Koro, who will guide us to a land never before seen by human eyes. A land of rich valleys, like those of Kurapo, and quiet rivers and lagoons teeming with fish. Such lands have been found by our ancestors and abandoned because they were lured on by the call of Maui-the-Peaceful. . . . The Peaceful! He should, rather, be called the Jester, like his brother Tavi, for he has sickened the hearts of us Tongans for centuries past.

"Choose, then, whom you will follow. If you go with Tuahu and the chiefs yonder, which of our bands, think you, will Koro pursue with the awful power of his vengeance? I have no more to say."

Then Tuahu said: "I will not plead with you. I will not tempt you with false hopes and false promises. I remind you only of the glory of our quest, never abandoned by us Tongans, nor will it be until we reach the Far Lands of Maui. You must decide for yourselves whom you are to follow, Tané or Koro. Let it be done quickly. Those who choose Koro stand by Rata, his priest to be. Let those who remain true to their faith in Tané come this way."

Three hundred of the people moved to where Tuahu stood, while fifty or more moved to Rata's side — but it was clear that those who went to Rata were moved, not like the others by the power of faith, but by that of fear. So great was their dread of Koro that their only thought was to escape his further vengeance. There was no separation of families; all went together, either to the Tané side or to the Koro side. A deep silence fell upon them while the choice was being made, but their faces revealed the anguish in their hearts. Seventy remained where they were — as though unable to grasp the bitter truth that they must decide, once and for all, whom they should follow; but one by one, or in groups of two and three, they went to one side or the other until Nanai-Vahiné, the wife of Paoto, alone remained to make her choice. Only in this one case had there been a division within a family. Nanai, her broad homely face clearly revealing the misery in her heart, gazed with an air of forlorn appeal first toward the Tongans with Tuahu, then at those standing with Rata. "Paoto!" she called in a woeful voice. Paoto made no reply but looked toward his wife, an expression half-defiant, half-pleading upon his face. He was like a small boy conscious of guilt in having disobeyed his mother but resolved to brazen it out. There was something so humanly touching and at the same time so comic in the little scene enacted between the two that, for a moment, the awful tension was relaxed and the tragedy of the situation forgotten. One of the men on Tuahu's side called, "Fetch him, Nanai! We need our prophet of doom!" The woeful expression on the woman's face changed to one of indignation. She strode to where her husband stood, seized his arm, and, despite Paoto's half-hearted protests, dragged him into the midst of the loyal Tongans.

Only seventy people had now chosen to go with Rata. His face was grim as he looked from this small group to those who stood with Tuahu; he had believed that the greater number would go with him. Turning to those with Tuahu, he said: "I appeal to you for the last time. I offer you a chance for life. I offer you the only means for escape from the wrath of Koro. If you go with Tuahu, Koro's vengeance will follow until the last one of you has perished." He waited, but no others moved to his side. Tuahu said: "Go your way, Rata, and we will go ours. But, go quickly. You have torn our people apart and the pain of this separation is more than some of us can well bear."

Kotaha was Rata's ship, and his son-in-law, Vana, was her captain. She was already loaded with her share of the scant sea stores the people had been able to prepare. It remained only to take aboard her share of the livestock — pigs and fowls and dogs, most of which had been saved from the hurricane, having been brought to the high land where the people themselves took refuge. While Vana and his men were performing this final task those who were to go and those who were to stay looked on in numbed silence, unable to grasp the fact that the moment of separation had come. Then, as though suddenly awakened to the woeful truth, they rushed together and clung to one another, tears streaming down the faces of both men and women. The children wept because their parents did, although some of them were too small to grasp the truth of what was happening. The older folk pleaded with one another either to go or to stay, according to the choice they had made; and Rata, fearing that some of his people might repent of their choice, urged and then commanded them to go into the ship.

A fresh westerly breeze was blowing; the sails were quickly hoisted and *Kotaha* moved away from the beach and headed for the passage to the open sea, the people following her course, going along the shore to the desolate bit of land, strewn with wreckage from the storm, where their *marae* had stood.

There they remained, their hearts wrung with grief, watching the ship growing smaller and smaller — until, at last, the tips of her sails had vanished below the eastern horizon.

The other ships were all but ready to sail; but the chiefs decided to delay their departure a full two weeks, lest they should meet with *Kotaha* and have the grief of separation to endure all over again. With the wrecked and ruined land reminding them of the sufferings they had endured and the bitter losses they had sustained, a feeling of loneliness, forsakenness, had settled upon the people. They knew that their ancestors had suffered as bitterly as themselves in times past, but never before had the casket containing the sacred stones been lost. It was their firm belief, passed on from generation to generation, that as long as they had these stones they need never despair of reaching their Homeland. But now, having lost them, what were they to do? To some it seemed that their last hope was gone. They had searched every foot of the land remaining where the temple had stood. In their canoes they had searched the shallows of the lagoon to the point where the clear waters fell to the blue depths. But the casket had not been found.

On an evening a week after the sailing of Rata's ship, the chiefs gathered the people at the place where the village had been. The debris left by the storm had been cleared away so they might have the illusion, at least, of living in a purposeful, orderly manner. The chiefs wished to dispel, if possible, the feelings of gloom and despair that had brought them to a state of settled melancholy. A great fire was built on the beach and the people seated themselves around it to sing some of the songs of their ancestors which never failed to stir them. As the singing continued the look of hopelessness upon their faces vanished. The sufferings of their ancestors, the heroic courage with which they had faced and conquered the dangers that surrounded them gave the little band renewed conviction of the nobility of their quest, the grandeur of their destiny and reawakened faith in the fostering love of Tané. Never would he abandon them as long as they remained worthy of his care.

> Lift up the sky eastward!
> Lift on, horizon beyond horizon
> Toward the lands we seek!
> The Far Lands of Maui
> Hidden in golden light;
> The light of the rising sun . . .

Never had the deep faith, the unconquerable spirit expressed in the words and music of these ancient songs served them to better purpose. They felt the unseen presence of Métua, their beloved priest; indeed, they could almost believe he was there in the flesh; for Tuahu, now eighty years old, one of the four chiefs who had survived with Maui's father to reach the land of Kurapo, closely resembled their priest, in spirit as well as in body.

Their greatest need was for a new spiritual leader, and when the singing ended Tavaké proposed that Tuahu be chosen. "It was, I know, Métua's wish that, in case of his death, Tuahu should be our priest," he said. "Who could be more worthy to take his place?" In the tradition of the Tongans the priest of Tané was chosen not by the chiefs alone but by the voice of all the people. All were deeply in favor of Tuahu and he became their priest from that moment.

Then Tuahu arose to thank them. "No one could take the place of Métua," he said, "but with Tané's help I shall do what I can to be worthy of your trust in me. My first act shall be one that Métua himself would approve were he here in my place . . . Our little temple has been destroyed, and I well know the grief in your hearts at the loss of our most precious possession: the four stones from the first temple built by our ancestors before ever the quest for the Far Lands of Maui was begun. But, think you our loving Father will refuse to hear our prayers on that account? The temples we have built in His honor and for His worship were symbols only of His unseen temple in our hearts."

Tuahu walked to the beach where lay heaps of broken corals left there by the storm. He picked up four of these at random, pieces no larger than his fist. Returning to where the others sat, flickering lights and shadows from the fire moving across their faces, he stood before them, his hands outstretched that all might see what they contained. "I bring you four sacred stones to replace those we have lost," he said. "With them I rebuild our temple, as sacred in Tané's sight as any that we have raised to him in times past."

He then placed them on the ground to represent the four corners of a square. Stepping within this he faced eastward, and after a moment of silence he said:

"Our loving Father: Thou seest us, here in Thy temple in this ruined land lost in the Great Sea of Kiwa. We have been woefully tried, and some, woefully tempted, have abandoned us, believing that we are indeed lost. But we, firm in our faith, feeling Thy unseen presence and the spirit of Thy boundless love, prepare to continue our voyage. Father, strengthen our hearts to meet the danger still before us; and if it be Thy will, let us hear once more the call of Thy servant, Maui, that has led us all the long way over the Sea of Kiwa."

Tuahu stood as still as stone, still gazing eastward. A moment later the call was heard, not as though coming from horizons beyond horizons, but from somewhere on the dark expanse of sea that lay between them and the horizon at hand where the first ghostly light announced the coming of the moon. The people gazed at one another in awed silence, half-doubting that they had heard the call. Nihau sprang to his feet, staring intently in the direction from which it had come. "It was a human voice!" he exclaimed. Then he himself called, and a moment later an answering call came back. Nihau's face lighted up with joy. "You heard it?" he cried. "It is the voice of Maui — our Maui!"

He ran toward the point of land bordering the passage, all of the others following. Taio snatched up a blazing brand from the fire and with it he lit torches of dried palm fronds which he passed to others who held them high above their heads so that the passage from the sea and the area for a quarter of a mile on either side stood out clearly in the ruddy light. The moon was just on the point of rising and as it appeared above the horizon they saw a ship scarcely a mile distant, in clear silhouette against it. They saw the furled sail, the clear outline of the hull and the outrigger booms, the blades of the paddles, a dozen on each side, flashing in the moonlight. It was Maui's ship.

"*Itatae! Itatae!*" Faanui called.

"*Parau mau! Itatae! Au-é! Au-é!*"

"*Maui! Haéré mai! Haéré mai!*"

The people went wild with joy. Boys ran across the fringing reef and plunged into the sea to swim out to her. Some of the people were shouting incoherently, embracing one another in their excess of emotion; others too deeply moved for speech kept their eyes fixed upon the ship as though fearing it might vanish if they looked away even for an instant.

Now the ship headed for the passage, appeared within the circle of light made by the flares. Maui was on the platform in the bow, Ru at the steering sweep, but they looked neither to right nor left until they were safely through the passage. The light of the fire on the beach guided them to the anchorage in the cove. Hina stood at the water's edge, her little son in her arms, the light of heaven in her eyes. With her stood Maéva, and Taraka, Ru's wife, with their two small children, and Moétua, a beautiful girl of sixteen, a sister of Ma'o. When she saw her brother she gave a cry of joy that seemed to give voice to the pent-up emotions of all. Maui waded through the shallows, his men following. All were there; not one had been lost. Hina could not speak when he came to where she stood. She held out her little son and Maui enclosed them both in his arms, his cheek resting on her head.

The Island of Fire

ON THE MORNING AFTER the return of *Itatae* the people gathered on the beach to hear Maui's story. They could scarcely believe in the events of the night before, but there was Maui's ship riding safely at anchor, and there was Maui himself with Hina beside him, and Tavi, his son, on his lap. He stroked the child's hair, felt of his sturdy arms and legs and shoulders, looking from the lad to Hina and back again as though still trying to convince himself of their reality.

Maui told them first of the fate of *Te-Ava-Roa* and how they had found Ma'o swimming in the sea a night and a day after the ship had been lost. He told them of the island they had later discovered far to the north. There was no passage through the reef and they were obliged to risk their ship by bringing it across the reef, through a heavy surf. The hull was not damaged but the great outrigger had been broken and they found only a few small trees on the island, none large enough to furnish material for another one. Having repaired the outrigger as well as they could, they put to sea again and, after a hazardous voyage of five days, discovered another lagoon island with a fine passage through the reef.

"And to this island we will go," he said. "It is far richer than the island where we now are, and from forty to fifty feet above the sea. We found cool sweet water at a depth of no more than ten feet."

He then told them how, having fitted *Itatae* with a new outrigger, they sailed again in search of the other ships. "We covered a great area of sea, west, and north and east and found nothing. We had no food left and only a little water. We decided to return to the island we had left, if it could be found, and by the grace of Tané we were able to reach it. We did not despair of finding you others. We believed that you must be somewhere far to the east, and so we set to work preparing sea stores, all that *Itatae* could carry. And then — blesséd be Tané! — one night while we were in the midst of this work I had a dream. I know now that it was the night when the great storm struck this island and Métua was lost. We had strong winds and heavy seas at that time but no more than that. In the dream I saw Métua standing before me. 'Maui,' he said; 'sail south, not east. Follow the ghost terns,' and then he vanished. There were *kotaha* and gannets and black terns on our island, but no ghost terns: not one had we seen. We could not leave until we had finished preparing our sea stores. On the night before we were to sail I had the dream a second time, and when morning came two ghost terns were hovering over the ship. As soon as we were outside the passage the terns left us, flying south. We followed, and on the third night we saw a spark of light far to the west; it was the fire you had made on the beach here. At first we thought it was a star very low in the sky, but its light increased and dimmed as we watched, and we knew it could be no star. We turned west to bring it in closer view, and so we found you."

The people needed no other proof of Tané's watchful care than the safe return of *Itatae*. Had Koro possessed the power would he not have destroyed Maui and Hina, and their child? Now that he was with them again it was as though a cool clean invigorating wind had swept across the island carrying away the stagnant air filled with doubts and fears and forebodings that Rata had left behind. They were Tongans again, worthy of their heroic ancestors who had never failed to rise above themselves in their darkest moments.

Maui felt no sorrow because of Rata's departure; he had long known that his uncle was no true Tongan; but he grieved because Rata had been able to persuade seventy of the people to go with him. He could well understand how, after the storm, by working upon their natural fears of Koro, Rata had succeeded in convincing them of Tané's powerlessness.

No time was lost in preparing for departure from the island which held such bitter memories for them. The sea stores in the ships were more than sufficient for the short way they had to sail; and so, three days after Maui's arrival, the other ships followed *Itatae* out through the passage and headed north, bound for the island from which Maui had come.

Although Maui had described it they were not prepared for the contrast between the poor bare land they had left and that which now enclosed them as they sailed into the lagoon. Instead of great stretches of bare reef with a few sandy inlets scattered along it they found themselves surrounded by a belt of land from four to five hundred paces across, from inner beach to outer beach, and extending nearly the entire distance around the lagoon. There was one small islet at the eastern end separate from the main body of land. The island was beautifully green from end to end. Groves of coconut palms and pandanus trees were scattered over it, with cool fern-covered glades in miniature valleys made by the rains of centuries. Enchanting vistas could be seen on all sides with glimpses of sky and sea beyond. The beaches around the lagoon were broad and firm; fine hard-packed coral sand, carpeted with shadow-patterns from the ironwood, *tamanu* and *hotu* trees that bordered them.

Now followed a happy time for the Tongans. The island Maui had found seemed to have been designed by Nature as a place for rest, relaxation and enjoyment. They had sailed far from Kurapo and had suffered many hardships. They had been cooped up in the crowded ships for days and weeks together, and the one poor island they had found had been destroyed by wind and sea before they had got the first weariness out of their bodies. It was decided to remain on the island they

had now reached, through the remainder of the Austral summer and during the six months to follow, when the prevailing
winds would be easterly. There were women big with child
who needed rest and comfort and ample food that their babies
might come into the world strong and healthy. There were
young men and women at the mating age who needed leisure
and beautiful surroundings for their love-making. There were
young sons of the chiefs whose schooling to fit them to take
their fathers' places in later years had been interrupted during
the voyage, and, although the boys were not concerned, their
fathers felt differently about it.

And there was need for the older people to resume their
immemorial pursuits and pleasures: to beget children to replace those lost at sea; to fish; to make gardens; to catch sea
turtle; to enjoy in comfort their midday siestas; to gossip; to
talk of the great Tongan heros of former times; to gather on
the beaches under the light of the moon to sing the songs
handed down to them by their ancestors; to enjoy the simple
pleasures of common folk which have always been and will
never not be. And now they were free, their own masters,
breathing the pure invigorating air of the solitudes of the Sea
of Kiwa, with no hideous shadow of Koro hanging over them
to darken their hearts and their lives.

Our ancestors were, by nature, a gay-spirited people. Laughter bubbled up from the depths of their being like spring
water. Because they were lovers of peace and seekers for it,
their lives were overshadowed by tragedy, and this was all the
more reason why they missed no occasion when they might
put aside their cares and sorrows and be their gay, natural
selves.

Maui and Hina had had no opportunity to be alone together
since the time when they had met at the lake on Kurapo. Now,
leaving their son in the care of Maui's mother, they took one of
the small canoes they had brought with them and proceeded to
the islet at the far eastern end of the lagoon. Hina was so gay,

so brimming over with happiness, it seemed to Maui that he was seeing her for the first time.

"Hina, are you my wife?" he asked.

"Your wife?" she replied. "How could that be? I'm a young girl, a virgin, dreaming of love."

"I can easily believe it, but . . . didn't we leave a child in the care of my mother?"

"A child? Did we? Then it was a dream child."

"Whose could it be?"

"I remember, ages ago, dreaming of someone. . . . There was such a hungry look in his eyes and I pretended not to notice it. He took me in his arms, but I was shy and frightened and fought him off. He must have seen, or felt, how badly I wanted him, but he could not read the heart of a young girl. He was so sorry that I was angry with him, and then I felt sorry for him. I said: 'Let me dream a little longer,' and he did. Maui! Don't tell me . . . You . . . you didn't take advantage of me in my dream?"

"Can you blame me that I was compelled to? Hina, you are so beautiful . . ."

"Then I am no longer a virgin! I will make you pay dearly for that! There is no woman more dangerous than one who has been ravished in a dream."

The islet was a delightful place, even more beautiful, Hina said, than Tavi-the-Jester's phantom islands. "Maui, perhaps it *is* a phantom island. How can I believe that I have you here? Perhaps we're ghosts? Maybe we were both caught and killed when I came to look for you at the temple of Koro?"

He held her close for a moment, stroking her dark hair.

"Darling, I will tell you a strange thing," he said. "This *is* one of Tavi's islands. I'm certain of it. You remember, he fished one real island from the sea?"

"I remember," Hina said. "It was after he left his brothers, Mano-the-Strong and Tumu-the-Witless. When his little brother, Maui, was still a baby."

"Yes. And do you remember the dream I had at sea? I was alone on an island, and I heard Tavi-the-Jester's voice. He said: 'Maui, it is Tavi who speaks. You stand upon the ringed island that I fished from the sea, from the shoulders of a drowned mountain. Rest and refresh your people here. You are now in the solitudes of the Sea of Kiwa never before beheld by the eyes of men.' "

"And Métua said it was true, that dream," Hina replied; "that it was the voice of Tavi himself that you heard."

"Hina, it was this very island that I saw in the dream. I knew it the moment I first saw it. And the islet where we now stand is where I heard his voice."

"Then we were destined to come here," Hina replied, in an awe-stricken voice.

"We were destined for each other, from childhood," Maui replied. "Métua knew it, perhaps from the day when your mother suckled us both at her breast."

"And we were destined to love each other here. Your dream proves that. . . . Maui, I am no longer the child I was at the lake. I am neither shy nor frightened, if you wish to put me to the proof?"

Late in the night they were lying on the beach looking eastward over the dark sea.

"You remember when we were lying, like this, on the beach at the little lake," Hina said; "and the old moon rose and we knew it was nearly morning? I was frightened and desperate. You remember what I said? I believed we were seeing each other for the last time."

"Sing me the little song you made to Hiro."

Hina did so, and when she had finished she said: "I sang it often after Tavi came, and Hiro heard me. He brought you the second time. I knew he would. . . . Maui, will there be mountains and deep valleys on the Far Lands?"

"I'm sure of it," Maui replied.

"Then Hiro will follow us there to be our god of the *hupé*.

He doesn't belong with the Koros." Presently she laughed, a
clear merry laugh that was music in Maui's ears.

"My little Hina, how good it is to hear you laugh."

"I was thinking of the night at the lake," she said, "when
I told you what Hiro said to me: 'My child, I cannot soothe the
fever that torments you now, but the day will come when, your
dreaming past and your love fulfilled, you will feel, for a time,
a sweet content as cool and welcome as my *hupé.*' And you
said: 'How wonderful it is that it's only for a time!' "

*   *   *

During the week that followed, Maui and Hina thought only
of each other. Maui built a little hut of plaited palm fronds
which Hina prepared, to shelter them at night. They fished;
they swam in the sea; they gathered shellfish along the reefs;
they took long mid-day siestas, the sea breeze humming softly
through the branches of the ironwood trees. They were like
children, grown-up children, as carefree and happy as birds
at mating time.

One morning Maéva sent for them. Hotu, Maui's grandmother and the mother of Rata, was dying. Maui and Hina
could scarcely believe this. Death seemed an incredible thing
to the two young lovers.

Hotu had been an active vigorous old woman until the day
when Rata renounced his faith in Tané and persuaded seventy
of the Tongans to follow him. Never before in the history of
the Tongans had a blood relative of the high chief renounced
his faith, and the shame, the humiliation, this brought his
mother robbed her of the desire for life. No one blamed
Hotu; she was held in the highest respect by the Tongans and
it grieved them to see the old woman willing her own death,
for this could be done by our ancestors as it can still be done
by some of our people to this day. When all desire for life has
been lost, men and women of strong will can bring about
their deaths by the force of will, and often they can foretell the

day when death will come. Hotu had done this and asked that
Maui be sent for.

The people were in the midst of building their houses and
the one for Maui's mother and grandmother had already been
finished. Many were gathered there when Maui returned. He
found his grandmother lying on a mat, his mother seated beside her with Tavi in her arms. Hotu had not failed in body
and her mind was as clear as it had always been. Only the
somber expression upon her face and the look of death in her
eyes convinced Maui of the truth. He seated himself beside her
and took her hand. "Grandmother?" he said. Tears came into
the old woman's eyes as she stroked his hand. "That I should
have to break into your happiness, Maui — yours and Hina's,
when you have waited so long! But I had no choice. I shall be
dead tomorrow. It was necessary for me to see you."

"Mama Ruau, what are you saying! You shall live . . ."

"When I have no longer the wish to live?" she interrupted.
"When my own son has brought me to the depths of shame?
No, Maui. . . . Hear what I have to say. . . . You will see him
again."

"I will see Rata, my uncle?"

"Believe what I tell you for so it will be. It is not of my son I
am thinking but of some of those with him. You will not deny
any who may wish to go on with you the chance to do so?" She
looked anxiously into his face while waiting for him to speak.
"For my sake, Maui? They were sorely tempted. Rata took
advantage of them at a moment of weakness; when so many
of our people had been lost and it seemed to them that all hope
was gone. Rata has great eloquence, and remember that he
stood in your place. He had convinced them that you were
dead. They believed it their duty to listen to him and follow his
counsel."

"If we find them, would you have me plead with them?"
Maui asked.

"There will be no need," his grandmother replied. "When

they see you the loyal hearts will follow you willingly, gladly. As for the others, let them remain with Rata."

"I shall do as you wish," Maui said.

"Now I can die in peace. May the grace of Tané be with you always."

She embraced him, and he left her with no sense of her impending death, but she died on the following day. Maui told the others of his grandmother's prophecy, that they would again see Rata and those who went with him. Some doubted that this could be, but most of them believed; for, among the Tongans as in other clans of our race, in every generation were born a few people who had the gift of foreknowledge. Métua had been one; Hotu was another.

It was decided that another ship should be built to replace *Iriatae,* lost in the great storm, so that the people could travel in greater comfort when the time came for them to continue their voyage. They set about this work as soon as their houses were built. They found trees suitable for building a ship sixty feet long, capable of carrying forty people and additional livestock which they knew would increase rapidly during their stay on this island.

The days, the weeks and the months passed and the people lived in happiness and content such as their ancestors had not known since they set out in quest of the Far Lands of Maui. For always in the past the lands reached had been peopled by worshipers of Koro. Now for the first time they were alone. No booming of the great Drum of Koro troubled their rest or filled their hearts with dread while they waited to learn who next would be taken to meet his insatiable thirst for blood.

Now the Austral summer again approached when the westerly winds would blow. They had spent nine months on the island by now and their sea stores were prepared for the voyage to come. During this time eleven children were born and many more conceived. Several women were at the point of childbirth and departure was delayed a little until these should be delivered. Hina was among them; she wished her second child to be born on the islet where she and Maui had been so happy together, and when her time was near Maui took her there with his mother and Vahiné, Taio's wife. He then returned to the village to supervise the work of getting the new ship ready for sea.

All preparations for departure had been completed when Hina's child — another son — was born. The westerly winds had come and the ships were to put to sea as soon as the child had been named. He was to be called Maui, in honor of his father and his father's great namesake, Maui-the-Peaceful.

Never, Maui thought, had Hina looked so beautiful as on the day when he came to tell her they would sail at dusk. He found her seated on the beach, the child at her breast. Her face was radiant with happiness as she looked up at him.

"Maui, how he sucks!" she said. "He looked so small and red at his birth, but see him now. I feel as my mother must have felt when she suckled you and me together and you grew so strong and sturdy, fed with her milk."

"Hina, the mystery, the wonder of it," Maui replied, as he seated himself beside her.

"That you should have given me another son?" Hina said. "What is there wonderful about that, except for the mystery of birth? I want half a dozen more sons, and daughters as well."

"Not that, but the place of his birth," Maui replied. "Here where we are Tavi sat, ages ago, on just such an afternoon as this, perhaps. It was the day when Maui-the-Peaceful set out to search for the Far Lands he was to guide us toward in after-times. From this beach Tavi watched the sail of his brother's canoe dwindling and blurring until it was lost to view. Could he have known, then, do you think, that we were to come?"

"It could be," Hina replied. "The demigods had powers second only to those of the gods. A few of our own people have the gift of foreknowledge. The demigods must have had it to a far greater extent."

"We will again hear Maui's call before we sail."

"That is certain. And *this* little Maui, his namesake and yours, will hear it, not knowing that he hears," Hina replied, looking down at the child.

"How are we to understand so strange a thing?"

"We are not required to understand, my husband," Hina replied, quietly. "Tané asks only that we hold fast to our faith in him. We are in his hands, under his care. That is all we need to know."

The sky, the sea, and the quiet waters of the lagoon were aflame with the full splendor of the afterglow as the six ships with all their people in them approached the islet and came to anchor. Tuahu waded ashore bearing the Tridacna shell in which the child was to be bathed, the others following. By the time the service was completed the last light of day was gone and the sky was ablaze with stars. Then, while the people waited in silence, Tuahu stood facing eastward, as countless priests of Tané had done before his time.

"Our loving Father, on this, the most sacred ground ever trod by the feet of our people, we have named this child, honored as his father was with the name of Thy servant and our Guide, Maui-the-Peaceful. We know that the distance he has led us is as nothing to that we yet must go. But our faith is strong and sure. We are ready to continue our quest. If it be Thy will, may we again hear the call of Maui."

And the call was heard — not from the east, as always before, but far to the north of east; and a second time it came, and a third, each time from the same direction. Some were amazed, bewildered, as though the sun and moon had changed their courses in the heavens, but Maui understood.

"Now I see that my grandmother's prophecy is to be fulfilled," he said. "Our Guide will lead us, for a time, not toward the Far Lands of Maui but to those who followed Rata. They can no longer hear his voice, and have lost their way. Rata and some who followed him have lost it forever; but there must be a few who would return to us. So my grandmother believed, and her dying request was that we search for them. It is Tané's will that we do so; otherwise we would have heard Maui's call as before, coming directly from the east. It is not to be wondered at that, in moments of deep despair, faith may burn dimly in the hearts of us Tongans. So it has been with some of our noblest ancestors; but, by the grace of Tané, despair has always been conquered and hope and faith renewed."

"You see, all of you, how nobly we are led," said Tuahu: "by our Guide, Maui-the-Peaceful, and by his great namesake, Maui, the son of Téaro. He knows through his own experience the temptations that beset mankind, and his heart is filled with sympathy and forbearance toward those weaker than himself."

The people again embarked, and when the new day had come the ships were sailing in an arc fifteen miles wide from tip to tip, with nothing but the empty sea around them.

Their first view of the land was not the land itself, but of the fiery glow reflected upon the clouds hanging above its highest mountain peak. Through the night they steered toward it, and when day came the cone-shaped summit was well above the horizon, the plume of smoke rising high above it bent toward the southwest by the wind. Late in the afternoon the wind failed, and as darkness came on they lay within the deep shadow of a land that stretched away as far as the eye could reach in either direction.

Never before had the Tongans seen an Island of Fire — but they knew such lands existed. In legends handed down from the times of their earliest ancestors fire and blood were spoken of as though they were parts of the same element. Deep were the forebodings in the hearts of the people as the ships lay closely together for the night. The light from the great burning mountain cast a lurid glare on the desolate slopes below where gulfs and what appeared to be winding rivers of blackness marked ravines and abysses filled with shadow.

"Maui," said Paoto, "how are we to know that this land is not the very home of Koro and the burning mountain his temple?"

"It could be," Maui said; "but in that case he has prepared for worshipers yet to come. We shall find no one there save Rata and those who followed him."

"And how are they to be found, in so great a land?" another asked. "We might search the coasts for years without discovering their ship."

"That we shall see when we reach the land," Maui said, "but Maui would not have led us here if the search were hopeless. However this may be, we will not leave the land until *Kotaha* is found."

The following morning they proceeded and the people were awestruck at the size of the land. They had believed it close at hand, but all that day as they sailed it rose higher and higher above the horizon as though the great mass of it were still to appear. It was not until early evening that they caught the first glimpse of the surf beating along the rocky coast. They could find no cove or inlet in which to shelter before darkness came, but toward noon of the following day they came to a bay bordered by a beach of white sand, and there, in a shed on the foreshore, they found *Kotaha*. Although the beach was marked by the prints of many feet, no one was to be seen around the whole extent of the bay. There was only a fringe of land at the level of the bay. A little beyond a line of low black cliffs contained the land that lay above. The hush of midday had fallen upon the place. The silence was so profound that the footprints crossing and crisscrossing the beach gave the people the feeling that they could not be real; that, somehow they remained there after the people had long since vanished.

"What are we to do now?" Nihau said.

"We shall remain here no longer than is necessary," Maui replied. "Their village must be above the cliffs yonder. Tuahu and I will search for the path leading up to it. Remain in the ships, you others."

Itatae was brought close to the beach and Maui and Tuahu waded ashore. The footprints directed them to the path which mounted through an opening in the line of cliffs. Above, they found themselves on level land that extended inland for the distance of a mile or more to a wall of rock rising high above the trees, a mountain stream falling sheer over the ledge above. The path led through a thicket of trees and low bush to an open common, formed by nature, and covered with lush grass. Among the trees on the farther side they saw the dwellings of Rata and his people. It was the hour of the siesta and all were sleeping. Having crossed the open space, Maui and Tuahu halted and Maui gave the call common amongst the Tongans to announce the arrival of visitors.

Pohi, the son of Rata, was the first to appear. He stared at the two men with an air of such complete unbelief that Maui said: "We are no ghosts, Pohi. Call your father and waken the others, for we have not long to stay here."

Rata came, and Vana, and in less than a moment all were there looking into his face, unable to speak. Maui knew immediately those who would go with him and those who would stay with Rata. Then he said:

"You have found a great land here. I had not believed that Mano-the-Strong and Tumu-the-Witless had fished for lands so far to the east in the Great Sea of Kiwa, but the land is here to prove it. They are dead, the demigods; no longer are they to be seen upon the Earth, but their spirits are immortal. Tumu was a lover of destruction, and he loved fire above everything else as a means for destruction. Rata will say that it is the spirit of Koro that rules here, and that may well be — for Tumu has never been more than the servant of Koro.

"I have little more to say. Only this: our ships are in the bay, below the cliffs yonder. We are sailing on to the Far Lands of Maui. It may be that, in the voyage to come, we shall meet with suffering, hardship and danger beyond anything we have known up to this time. Many of us may die of hunger or thirst, or be lost in storms certain to be met with in the Great Sea of Kiwa. Bearing in mind the suffering of our ancestors through twenty generations, and which we share, if any of you wish to share them with us, you have only to follow me to the ships."

Without giving Rata or any of the others a chance to reply, Maui and Tuahu then returned to the beach nor did they look back until they had reached it. Thirty people had followed them without a moment's hesitation. Others were seen approaching at a distance, but several halted and turned back. Maui signaled *Itatae* to come in. While the people were going aboard, those who remained with Rata gathered at the edge of the cliff overlooking the bay. Maui turned for a moment looking toward them; then waded slowly through the shallows to his ship. His men took their paddles and *Itatae* was slowly moving out to where the others lay when they heard a faint cry of appeal from among the little group looking down from the top of the cliff:

"Maui! . . . *Iéru! Iéru!*" (Wait!)

Maui ordered his men to rest on their paddles; they were about fifty yards from the beach. A moment later a man with a small boy in his arms was seen coming down the path in desperate haste, followed by his wife carrying another child. They did not wait for the ship to return to them, but taking their children on their backs they plunged into the water and swam out to her.

Kiwa leading, the ships moved out of the bay to the open sea. *Itatae* went last. Ru was at the steering sweep. Maui stood beside him, his gaze fixed upon the forlorn little group gathered at the edge of the cliff. A few moments later they disappeared behind the headland at the entrance to the bay.

⚹⚹ X X V I I ⚹⚹
The Far Lands of Maui

I HAVE TOLD at the beginning of this story how our ancestors of the Tongan Clan reached the Land of Kurapo. I now tell how they came to the end of their quest and saw before them the Far Lands of Maui. What distance they sailed from the beginning to the end of their voyage cannot be definitely known, but this is certain: it was the greatest voyage ever made over the Sea of Kiwa by any clan of our race since the time when we became a scattered people at the western borders of that sea. There are some who say that Kurapo was the ancient name of the Island of Truk; others believe it was Ponape, but neither of these lands answers the description of Kurapo handed down by our ancestors. The length of the voyage, in time, is definitely known: it covered a period of fifty-one years. Maui was nineteen when the Tongans left Kurapo, and seventy when the Homeland was reached.

The story says that seven more of Tavi's phantom lands were seen after the Tongans left the Island of Fire. That many real lands were found where they halted to rest and to build up their strength and their numbers once more cannot be doubted; but the names of those lands have been lost to us, nor is anything known of the time spent upon each one. None of them had ever before been seen by the eyes of men, and some were so rich and beautiful that the people half believed that they had reached the Homeland so long sought for. But always, sooner or later, Maui would hear the call of his great namesake, coming from beyond the horizons to the east, and they would prepare to follow. Only those who wished to go on did so. Some who despaired of the quest remained behind on various lands that were found, but the greater part sailed on with Maui.

There were times when all went well with them for days and weeks together. At other times when their sea stores were exhausted and no fish were caught they were compelled to sacrifice most of their livestock. But no matter what their suffering they kept two pairs each of pigs and dogs and fowls in the hope of reaching lands, and always they had done so before coming to the last extremity. Thirst was an ever-present torment, and sometimes an agony. But at times when many had died of thirst and it seemed that all would do so, rain would fall. It was during the latter part of the voyage that rain was first called "the Tears of Tané," weeping in pity for his children who never lost faith in him. It is known by that name to this day among the remaining descendants of the Tongan Clan.

After the birth of Tavi on the lagoon island at the time of the great storm, Hina had borne Maui five more sons and three daughters. The third son was lost at sea, but the other children survived. As the years passed, and they grew to manhood and womanhood, all married; and Maui and Hina had the joy of seeing an increasing number of grandchildren growing up around them. Hina was still a woman of great beauty, honored and loved by the Tongans and all but worshiped by her children and grandchildren. Her hair was now snow white, and although she was frail in body, her unconquerable spirit carried her through all the dangers and hardships met with during the course of fifty years.

The ships which had left Kurapo had long since been replaced by others bearing the same names. There were now only five: *Kiwa, Itatae, Anuanua, Tokérau* and *Te-Ava-Roa,* carrying four hundred and five people, fifteen less than the number of Tongans who had survived to reach Kurapo. Few remained who had sailed from Kurapo. Of the *ariki* there were only Maui, Nihau and Paoto; of the *raatira* — the class of yeomen — Ma'o, Téma and Manu. Ma'o, now in his seventy-first year, had been made priest of Tané after the death of Tuahu, and no one could have been more worthy to take his place. In all the history of the Tongans, as far back as memory went, no other Tongan had ever been known to commit himself to the Great Sea of Kiwa, swimming alone in that sea for a day and a night, upheld by his faith in Tané. Many were the songs made in aftertime to honor Ma'o. One, sung by Tongan children to this day, begins:

> His ship was his body;
> The paddles were his hands and his feet;
> The sail, his valiant heart
> Filled with his faith in Tané.
>
> Alone he voyaged in the empty sea
> Toward the Far Lands of Maui.
> Alone, alone, alone;
> Alone in the Great Sea of Kiwa.

Of the children of Taio and Vahiné, only Ru was left. With Ma'o he was the most dearly loved of Maui's boyhood friends. Ru's wife, Taraka, a daughter of Tavaké, still lived. They, too, had a family of grown sons and daughters and many grandchildren.

And now the story tells of the death of Paoto on the evening before the Far Lands of Maui were sighted. Paoto was the oldest member of the clan, the only one left who had reached Kurapo with Maui's father. All the years of his life he had despaired that the quest of the Tongans would ever come to an end. In earlier years the Tongans had had little respect for him; they called him their "prophet of doom." But as time passed they came to regard him with affection and with deep compassion. He could never conquer his fear that the power of Koro for evil was far greater than the power of Tané for good. Nevertheless, only once, when he had been tempted to follow

Rata, had his allegiance to Tané wavered, and the Tongans had long since forgiven him for that. His dread of Koro was faced daily and succumbed to daily. The people realized that, through no fault of his own, he lacked the faith that sustained them through all the suffering and hardship and danger met with. He longed to possess it and attributed his complete lack of it to some defeat in his nature impossible to overcome. He fully believed in the Far Lands of Maui but could not believe that any of the Tongans would survive to reach them. And yet, for all his unbelief — much as he dreaded Koro and convinced though he was that those who followed Maui were doomed — when, at various lands the Tongans reached, the time came for moving on and some who despaired of the quest remained behind, Paoto never — save on that one occasion mentioned — wavered in his own decision: to sail on with Maui.

Throughout the day the ships had been sailing in a wide arc, with a beam wind, under a sky lightly veiled with cloud. As they closed in for the night the wind failed and rain began to fall. Tavi's son, Hiro, was now in command of *Itatae*. Maui and Hina were in *Kiwa* with Ma'o, and Paoto was with them. His little strength had been slowly ebbing during the week past, and on this evening it was evident to all the people in *Kiwa* that his end was near. He lay in the house on the cross-hull platform, his head resting on Hina's lap: Maui and Ma'o sat on either side. His small body was so wasted away that he resembled an aged child. Opening his eyes he looked into Maui's face appealingly. Maui bent over him, his ear close to Paoto's lips. The old man spoke in a voice scarcely above a whisper.

" 'The Far Lands' . . . Will you ask the people to sing it? . . . I would hear it once more, for the last time."

Maui gave them word. Paoto lay with his eyes closed, scarcely seeming to breathe as he listened to that most ancient

of the Tongan songs, so filled with mingled hope and courage,
disappointment and despair.

> Lift on, sail on, horizon beyond horizon,
> While the moons wax and wane
> And the stars wheel in their courses . . .
> We are the children of Tané:
> Before us lies the promised Homeland
> Hidden in golden light;
> The light of the rising sun . . .
>
> Numberless moons have waxed and waned.
> A weary way we have come.
> Still before us lies the empty sea.

The singing ended, and in the silence that followed nothing
was heard but the sound of rain falling gently into the sea.
Paoto opened his eyes once more and groped for Maui's hand;
he could no longer see him in the fading light.

"Maui . . . cling to hope, if you can, but . . . the Tears of
Tané . . . How long he has shed them! . . . For more than
twenty generations . . ."

Then, with a little sigh, he was gone.

When the prayers had been said and the chants sung, Paoto's
frail body was committed to the sea, the last resting place of
so many thousands of Tongans before his time.

Paoto's death added to the sadness, to the feeling of dis-
couragement and depression that had settled upon the spirits
of the people. For weeks they had sailed eastward, the empty
sea always before them, with never the sight of a bird to give
them a momentary hope that land might be near. They had
not suffered save from the weariness and discomfort of long
confinement in the crowded ships. There had been no lack of
rain, and both fish and sea turtle had been caught in quantities
that nearly sufficed their need for food. But the loneliness, the
emptiness of the sea, day after day, day after day, weighed
heavily upon them. Never since leaving Kurapo had they
sailed so great a distance without a sight of land.

To relieve them from the burden of their thoughts, Maui ordered the paddles to be used, and they moved slowly on in the direction they would go. The paddlers relieved one another every hour, but it was weary work and in the early hours of the morning the signal for rest was sent out from *Kiwa*. The ships, having drawn closely together, lay idle on the calm sea, and soon all were sleeping save for the men on watch.

As the first gray light of dawn appeared the rain slackened and the blurred outlines of the ships could be seen as they rose to the long swells and vanished momentarily into the troughs between them. Hiro was seated on the steering platform of *Itatae*, a mat over his head to protect him from the rain. Presently he threw it aside and sat with his hands clasped around his knees looking eastward toward the false horizon, scarcely a mile distant. The rain had all but ceased and overhead patches of clearing sky could be seen in the slowly increasing light. As Hiro gazed idly ahead his figure suddenly became rigid. He sprang to his feet, rubbed his eyes, and continued to gaze eastward, but for a moment or two he saw only the curtains of gray mist brightening slowly with the coming day. Presently a faint outline appeared and as quickly vanished again. It was land! It could be nothing but that; but although Hiro had seen it he could not yet believe. Then the clouds of thinning vapor parted again; and behind them, high up, like an airy pinnacle floating free from Earth, the peak of a great mountain appeared.

"*Te Fenua!*" Hiro called. (The Land!) "*Te Fenua! Te Fenua!*"

The men on watch in the other ships sprang to their feet, staring incredulously toward Hiro, then eastward in the direction of his pointing arm. A moment later they, too, saw, and the jubilant cry was carried from ship to ship. Heads appeared above the gunwales, and more and more until all the four hundred weary voyagers were gazing eastward with expressions of incredulous joy upon their faces. At first, some, staring straight ahead, saw nothing but the gray sea, but soon all were gazing into the sky where the lofty peak was seen — now dimly, now clearly — through the shifting cloud that clung to its sides. Then, as though Tané had willed it so, the mists were shot through with shafts of golden light, growing in splendor from moment to moment. Veils of transparent vapor that hung in the air were transformed into a mist of golden rain falling upon the land and into the sea, and as the first direct rays of the sun appeared, the great Rainbow of Tané was seen stretching from horizon to horizon, the eastern end falling upon the land itself.

A hush fell upon the people as they gazed. In silence the men took their paddles, and, with *Kiwa* leading, they moved slowly toward the land, many fearing that it would dissolve before their eyes and they would find the empty sea before them. But it grew more distinct as they approached, and what at first had appeared to be one island was seen to be three, lying at distances of two or three leagues apart. The largest, whose lofty mountain had first been seen, lay to east of the others. They steered for this one.

As they drew near they saw that the western coast was bordered by cliffs falling to the sea from heights of six hundred to a thousand feet, but above and beyond the cliffs forests and broad savannas could be seen, sloping gently upward toward the base of the great mountain that rose from the center of the land. As the ships moved slowly around the coast the people gazed in wonder and delight at the varied landscape passing before their eyes. There were no lagoons as at Kurapo, but the shoreline was indented with open bays and landlocked coves, each of them tempting the weary voyagers to enter; but it was not until late afternoon when they had reached the eastern side of the land that they entered a deep bay sheltered from the sea, backed by a broad rich valley extending far inland where a fine river could be seen winding quietly seaward. The inner end of the bay was bordered by a beach of white sand. Here the ships came to anchor.

Standing in waist-deep water Maui took Hina in his arms

and carried her ashore, the others following, scarcely daring to believe that they had the solid earth under their feet. They gathered around Maui waiting for him to speak, as though unable to believe that their quest was ended until he should tell them so.

"My children," he said, "for twenty-two generations we Tongans have sailed eastward in search of lands where we may live in peace. At last we have found them. Tané, our loving Father, has fulfilled His promise. Our last voyage is ended. We have reached the Far Lands of Maui.

"You are silent, and that I can understand. You hear my words and they are nothing but words. How are you to believe them? The measureless Sea of Kiwa still stretches away eastward, horizons beyond horizons. Surely, you think, this land is but another of those where we have halted to rest before sailing on in the direction of the rising sun.

> Numberless moons have waxed and waned;
> A weary way we have come.
> Still before us lies the empty sea . . .

"And so it does, yonder; but we go no farther. No more shall we hear the call of our Guide, Maui-the-Peaceful, leading us on. His task is ended. He has brought us safely to the end of our wanderings. Let the glorious truth come home to you little by little, as it must and will. And now let us give thanks to Tané that we have lived to see this day."

And, little by little, the realization that they had fulfilled their destiny was, indeed, brought home to the Tongans. No lands found during their voyage all the long way eastward over the Sea of Kiwa could compare with the Far Lands of Maui. Before deciding where their home should be, they sailed around the two smaller lands, putting in at every bay and inlet, exploring the valleys and the high lands beyond, examining the soil, taking note of the food-bearing plants and trees, so many of which were new to them. The three islands offered them room and to spare for growth in population for generations to come; and they found no living creatures upon any of them save the sea birds, and many beautiful varieties of land birds, all strange to them, that filled the air with their songs. They found so many sites perfectly suited to their needs that they were hard put to decide where they should make their home. At last, having visited them all and considered them all, they chose the deep bay where they had first gone ashore, for it was instinctive with the Tongans to build their villages in valleys looking eastward toward the rising sun. Their dwellings were scattered along the full curve of the bay, and their temple was built midway, by the river. Two of their ships were kept at anchor in the bay, for use in going from island to island. Sheds were built on the foreshore to house the others. Often, in passing, the people would halt to look at them, recalling their hopes and fears and despairs as they had sailed eastward; the misery suffered in them; the days and nights of mountainous seas, heavy gales and blinding rain, when they feared that all the ships would be lost; other days when they lay becalmed, under a burning sun, tormented by hunger, or thirst, or both. And their hearts filled with gratitude to Tané who had brought them safely to the end of their quest.

Epilogue

It was at night that Captain Winnie had begun his tale, and it was at night that he reached the end of it. The sky was cloudless and the air so clear that the great luminous path of the Milky Way was faintly reflected on the mirrorlike surface of the lagoon. As Winnie fell silent I waited, expecting to hear more. A moment later he said: *"Tirara.* The story is finished."

"But . . . where *were* the Far Lands of Maui?" I asked. "You haven't told me that."

"I thought you might guess it," he replied. "One lone mountain peak, Rano Raraku, is all that remains of them: the island of Rapa Nui — Easter Island, to give it its modern name."

"The island of the mysterious stone images?"

"Some believe there is no mystery with respect to the images," Winnie replied. "Rapa Nui was the farthest outpost to the east reached by Polynesians, and the Tongans were the clan who found it. At that time there were three islands: the Homeland promised them by Tané. And there they lived in peace, untroubled, unmolested, for many generations."

"Do you think it possible that Koro may have overtaken them, in the end?"

Winnie was silent for a moment; then his deck chair creaked as he turned to peer toward me in the starlight.

"What do you think?" he asked. "Which power has triumphed down the ages? Tané, the god of Peace, or Koro, the god of War?"

"It may not have been the power of Koro, in the case of the Tongans," I replied.

"You are entitled to hold to that opinion," said Winnie, "for the truth can never be known. But the scores of stone images still to be found on Easter Island must, somehow, be accounted for. Some Polynesians of these days believe them to be exact replicas of the one that Maui sent crashing down from Koro's temple on Kurapo. Puaka's boast of the power of Koro was no idle one. We see ample proof of this in our own day."

I said nothing to Winnie, but I was thinking of images more enduring than stone: of the Phantom Lands of Tavi, miscalled "the Jester." He was a lover of beauty and a lover of Peace, a creator for the future. An idealist — yes; but I have enough faith in humankind to believe that a time may well come when his Phantom Lands will no longer fade to empty sea and empty sky before the eyes of men.

THE END

THE LEGEND

The Legend of Maui-the-Peaceful and His Brothers as Told by Taio to Young Maui and His Friends

Ages ago, *in the time of the demigods, the Great Sea of Kiwa was empty of lands. One of the tasks set the demigods by the higher gods who gave them life was to fish up lands in this sea. They obeyed at first but soon neglected this work. They loved fighting for its own sake and were seldom at peace. They were proud of their strength and taunted one another to battle. They were divided into families, not clans, and the parents took the greatest joy in matching their sons against those of other families; even the parents and grandparents joined in these battles. They were huge in size. Their weapons were clubs fashioned from the trunks of the greatest trees, and the stones for their slings were boulders that scores of men of later times working together could not have moved. Now and then they would remember their appointed task and all the families would join in fishing up lands; but while doing this they would boast of their strength and taunt one another until, stirred to eagerness for battle, they would fight on lands just raised from the depths of ocean, or from their ships, until the sea was strewn with wreckage and dead bodies. Others would sail homeward to fight on the mainland where there was more room.*

So great was the slaughter in these many battles that the race of demigods slowly vanished until but one family remained. The parents were Atéa-Ragi, and Haka-Hotu. The sons were Mano-the-Strong, and Tumu-the-Witless.

"What shall we do now?" Mano asked his father. "There are no more battles to win. Shall Tumu and I fight until one or the other of us is killed?"

"No, you are brothers," Atéa-Ragi said. "Now I see that we demigods have brought doom upon ourselves. We were ordered to fish up lands in the Great Sea of Kiwa. Little have I done in this way and you two nothing at all."

"The blame is yours and mine," Haka-Hotu said. "We egged on our sons to fight."

"They needed no urging," said Atéa-Ragi. "I am to die, that I know, for my neglect of this task, but our sons have their full strength. They may be permitted to live long if they fish for lands."

"I will go first," said Tumu.

"You are not called 'the Witless' for nothing," his father said. "Mano shall go first and learn the way of it; then he shall teach you."

So Mano built a great canoe with an outrigger and went out on the sea to fish for lands. He had a line with four hooks and this he let down to the floor of the sea to grapple for mountainous lands buried there. As he drew them up huge holes were left in the bottom of the sea, and these remain. He towed the lands behind his canoe to places where the depths were not so great and there he would let them sink, but large parts would remain above the surface. Mano took pride in this fishing but it was heavy work. He was long on the voyage and when he returned home his mother had given birth to another son. He was first called Tavi-the-Lazy, but later, Tavi-the-Jester.

Mano wished to rest, but his father would not consent. "There is no time for rest," he said. "It falls to you and Tumu to fish for lands that might have been raised long since. If time permits, your mother and I will provide more sons to help you, though the one just born shows no promise of great strength."

Then Mano took Tumu-the-Witless with him. They sailed far beyond the lands Mano had raised before; these were now green and pleasant places with forests growing in the valleys.

The peaks of the high mountains gathered clouds around them and there was no lack of rain.

"What war clubs those great trees would make" — Tumu said, longingly — "if there were others of our race to use them on!"

"We are to think no more of that," said Mano. "We have work to do, as our father says."

He grappled a drowned land to show Tumu the way of it, and as it rose from the depths Tumu leaped upon it, delighted to see it sink again under his weight.

"If you are to fish with me you will not do that again," said Mano. "You must wait until the land is anchored in its proper place before setting foot upon it."

They sailed on eastward, and the next land they grappled was so huge that it needed all the strength of both to bring it up. Tumu was of great service for he was nearly as strong as his brother. He needed direction but could pull well when told. They rested long after this fishing, their canoe anchored to the land; many moons waxed and waned while they slept. Mano was the more weary, for he had been long at this work. When he awoke, he saw his brother ashore kicking over the high mountains for the delight he took in watching them topple and crash into the sea. Mano rushed ashore and gave his brother a blow that knocked him from his feet. "Do you think we are raising these lands only to destroy them?" he said. "Save your strength for the work to come."

They sailed on, raising other lands in that part of the sea, but Tumu was like a child in his love of destruction. Often while his brother slept he would go ashore and rush here and there toppling mountains over, wrenching off great crags with his hands and hurling them into the sea: masses of rock, still to be seen near the shores of lands in the Sea of Kiwa. At last in his rage Mano's strength became that of a score of demigods. He gave Tumu so mighty a kick that he was sent flying through the air far beyond the horizon to the west. When he fell into the sea the splash was so great that the wave caused by it flooded and half-destroyed some of the lands Mano had raised long before.

On the voyage home he found Tumu swimming westward. He had gone a weary way, and begged his brother to take him into the canoe. "Will you promise to kick over no more mountains?" said Mano. "Yes," said Tumu. After that he did as he was told and became a great help to his brother. He soon found that he had no strength to waste in foolishness, for their father gave them little time for rest. Even demigods were not equal to the heavy tasks Atéa-Ragi set for his sons, and when they returned from their fifth voyage they had aged greatly and were very weary. But Atéa-Ragi had no pity on them. "You must go out again," he said. Tavi, the third son, was now grown, but he had neither the size nor the strength of his older brothers, and his parents called him Tavi-the-Lazy because he was useless even in household tasks. Nevertheless, Atéa-Ragi said that he, too, must fish for lands. "Then let him fish from his own canoe," said Mano, "for he would only be a hindrance to us."

Their mother had given birth to a fourth son, not yet named, and still an infant. But he was so small compared to what Mano and Tumu had been in their infancy that his mother had nothing but contempt for him. "You have lost your strength," she said to her husband. "It is now clear that our family will soon perish. Let this infant perish first for it shames me to look at so puny a thing."

She then fashioned a wicker basket and put the child in it. "Take him with you," she said to Mano, "and when you are far out on the Sea of Kiwa cast him adrift, for little as he pleases me I would not see him die."

Then Mano and Tumu set out in their canoe and Tavi in his smaller one. There was no wind at the time and the older brothers paddled their ship, towing that of Tavi-the-Lazy. When at last the breeze came Mano gave Tavi a line with hooks for grappling drowned lands. "You have little strength," he said, "but do what you can." He sat for a time looking at the basket in which their small brother had been placed. He

*then passed it to Tavi. "You shall set him adrift as our mother
ordered," he said. "Tumu and I have work to do here. Sail on
eastward."*

*Tavi took the basket and sailed on. He sailed a great dis-
tance. Now and then he looked into the basket where the
small brother lay asleep, and the oftener he looked the less he
wanted to drown the child. "There is no hurry," he thought.
"First I will fish for an island."*

*He let down his line with the grappling hooks and caught a
land far out on the Sea of Kiwa. He pulled hard and long, to
no purpose. Having rested, he pulled again. Now the line
came in with something not beyond his strength to lift. Peering into the water as he hauled, he saw a wide circle of land
with nothing in the center rising toward him. When it broke
the surface his canoe was floating within this circle. His
brothers had told him of such rings of land, of a reddish color,
which came from the shoulders of drowned mountains. They
needed no anchoring but floated of themselves until in some
way they became attached on the surface to the mountain
peaks in the depths which thrust up walls of rock to catch and
hold them.*

*There was a gap in this circle of land wide enough to per-
mit the passage of Tavi's canoe. He paddled through it and
then rested. Small though the land was, it had wearied him to
bring it up. He found no pleasure in this fishing so he threw
his line into the sea, and that was the end of such work for
Tavi.*

*But he loved sailing over the great Sea of Kiwa. He shifted
his sail as the wind changed, letting it carry him where it
would — north, east, or south, taking no thought of distance or
direction. He loved watching the stars by night and the patterns of the clouds by day. Nothing troubled his mind but the
thought of returning home. What of the small brother still
with him, resting so quietly in his basket? And what could he
say of his fishing?*

"The child must be hungry," he thought, so he took him

from the basket and held him on his knee while he fed him. The little brother laughed, bouncing himself up and down on Tavi's knee. With his small firm hands he seized Tavi's nose and pulled his ears. Thinking of his mother's command, Tavi knew he must act at once or not at all; so, hardening his heart, he stood up and threw the child into the sea. The small brother thought this was nothing but play. He laughed with delight at being in the water and swam after the canoe, which was sailing under a light breeze. Tavi sailed on for a great distance; then his heart smote him. He sprang to the sail, quickly lowered it, and paddled back, putting all his strength into every stroke. The child was still swimming strongly. Tavi took him up. He wanted more of this sport, but seeing that Tavi would not let him go he then lay quietly and was soon asleep.

His heart now at peace, Tavi sailed on. But some day he would have to go home. What then? He fell into a deep reverie, and, while sitting thus half awake, half dreaming, he thought of a way of making lands of a new kind. Immediately his mind became alert, and his heart filled with happiness. He felt power flowing into him, but it was of the spirit, not the body. He was a lover of beauty as his brother, Tumu, was a lover of destruction. Like all the demigods, he had the gift of magic; but it was only now that he realized the nature of his gift.

With cloud vapor and the skin of the sea he began shaping a phantom island: the lowlands, the hills, then the high mountains with valleys and deep gorges winding amongst them. There was no laziness in him now. He slept little at night for thinking of the work of the following day. When the first of his phantom islands was completed and made fast to the horizon line, he sailed off to a distance that he might view the whole of it. From the first glimmer of dawn until the sky was filled with stars he sat in his canoe, his small brother on his knee, watching the changing lights and shadows passing over the island. Its beauty filled him with content, but the test was yet to come. The island was to be there, and, at the same time, not *there.*

The following morning he sailed toward it. The peaks of the mountains were golden in the early light, the slopes descending from them pale green tinged with gold, and the steep-walled gorges of the deepest purple changing to blue. As he approached, the colors slowly faded and the outlines of the lofty peaks and ridges became fainter and fainter until they melted into the blue of the sky. Tavi sailed on, passing through his phantom island, now vanished, but as he looked back it began to take shape once more against the empty sea, and as the distance increased he again saw it in all its lonely beauty until the highest peaks had vanished below the horizon.

Now Tavi was content, knowing that phantom islands, as he could make them, were eternal. They would remain forever on the horizons where he had placed them, and yet never be there. He sailed on as the wind would have it, dreaming his lands before creating them on many a far horizon over the Sea of Kiwa. The time spent in fashioning each one was far greater than that needed by his brothers to fish up lands of earth and stone. But he felt no weariness, and often he built by night as well as by day. The dreams for some of his islands required that he work only by the light of the full moon, which was mingled with them; and they were among the most beautiful, equal perhaps to those built of rainbow fragments which he gathered in and used as fancy directed.

During this time his little brother had grown from infancy, through childhood and on to his fourteenth year. This was long as time is now counted, for a year in the life of the demigods was equal to four generations in the lives of men. Glad was Tavi that he had not drowned this brother for they became the greatest of friends and companions. He had to have a name, so Tavi called him "Maui," and, later, "Maui-the-Peaceful," because from babyhood on he was never fretful or quarrelsome, and he loved the peace and beauty and loneliness of the sea as Tavi himself did. During Maui's childhood Tavi told him of their parents and brothers; of the last battles of the demigods, and of the land where they lived, far to the west. Thereafter, these matters were no more spoken of. To Maui the sea was home, and to Tavi the memories of his youth became dim. All of his time and interest was given to the building of his phantom islands. Maui longed to help, but the gift for such creation was Tavi's alone; try as he would, he could not pass it on to Maui. "Am I good for nothing but to sit and watch?" Maui would say, sadly, but Tavi told him to be patient. "You are young," he said, "and time will reveal what you can do best." But, although he could not build, Maui was of great service to his brother. Never having seen real lands — for he was an infant when they had passed those fished up by Mano and Tumu — the suggestions he gave Tavi as to outlines, shapes and colors, gained by his study of clouds and sky, fired and quickened his brother's fancy so that the phantom islands became more and more beautiful as time went on.

One afternoon, as they were sailing quietly eastward, Maui standing in the bow of the canoe, Tavi at the steering-paddle, Maui gave a call so filled with the beauty of that time and place that Tavi was deeply stirred by it.

"What was that you sang?" he asked.

Maui glanced back. "I don't know," he said. "It came of itself."

"Sing it again."

Maui did so, and the Great Sea of Kiwa seemed to widen beyond the reach of thought, and the peace of it to deepen. Tavi was long silent; then he said: "Such a call could not have come of itself. You were chosen to hear it, but who knows whence it came and what it means?"

"Why should it have meaning?" Maui asked.

Tavi pondered the question; then he said: "I am an old fool, Maui. Perhaps only because I want it to have meaning, and I can't even guess what that should be." But the beauty of the call haunted him. Often thereafter, when he had worked with-

*out rest to complete a phantom island and they were lying
near it gazing up at its lofty walls and pinnacles, he would ask
Maui to repeat the call. Maui would stand in the canoe, his
hands cupped around his lips, and send it toward the island.
Then they would hear it echoed and re-echoed more and more
faintly, in phantom-like music as beautiful as the island itself.*

*Two score and five of these islands Tavi built; then, sud-
denly, he felt a draining of his strength, a slackening of the
wish and the will to create. He was puzzled by this change.
Joy left him, and he sat in the canoe gazing dully before him,
taking interest in nothing. Maui tried to arouse and hearten
him. At last Tavi said:* "Maui, it is useless. My work is done.
We will now sail westward to the home you cannot remember
and that I have all but forgotten. Who knows what we shall
find there, or whether the land can be found?"

"I can find it," *said Maui.*

"How could that be?" *Tavi asked.* "We have sailed. so far
over the Sea of Kiwa that I myself know only that it lies somewhere to the west. You were an infant when we left it and can
have no recollection of the way."

"Nevertheless, I can sail to the very cove from which we
came," *Maui replied.*

"You know this?" *Tavi asked, staring at him in wonder.*

"Yes," *said Maui.*

*So Tavi, who was very weary, lay in the bottom of the canoe
while Maui steered, both day and night. Tavi slept much of
the time. When he woke he would sit with his head propped
against Maui's knees. He had so lost himself in the wastes of
the sea that he could have found none of his phantom islands,
but Maui knew where each of them lay and when Tavi wished
to see one Maui would take him there. Tavi was astonished at
his never-failing sense of direction.*

"Maui," *he said,* "you have now discovered your own gift —
which is that you can never be lost, even on the measureless Sea
of Kiwa." *They then had in view one of the phantom islands.
As they passed through and beyond it Tavi looked back,*

watching the airy shapes take form and color once more against the background of sea and sky.

"What a fool I have been!" he said. "I have spent my life and my strength building these islands, and of what use are they?"

"They are very beautiful," said Maui.

"I know, but beauty alone is not enough." He smiled, wearily, "I am being well repaid for my foolishness. What would I not give for a day ashore in a fair green land, and here are none but phantom islands of my own creation to mock my need of rest."

"You fished up no real ones as our brothers did?"

"One," said Tavi; "a small circle of land lifted from the shoulders of a drowned mountain, but where it lies . . ."

"I will take you there," said Maui.

The land was found as promised, no longer a circle of reddish rock but so green and pleasant that Tavi felt refreshment flowing into him from the mere sight of it. There was the passage inviting them to enter and tall coconut palms loaded with nuts, swaying in the breeze. The canoe was anchored in the lagoon and Maui helped his brother ashore. After a few days of rest on solid land Tavi felt greatly strengthened and they sailed on westward. Tavi could not cease to wonder at Maui's unerring course. They began to pass lands their brothers had raised, but halted at none of them for Tavi was eager to reach the mainland where their home was. He gave no word of direction nor was any needed. Maui sailed into the very cove from which they had set out so long before. There was a sandy beach below the cliffs that hemmed in the cove. They found the canoe of Mano and Tumu but it was falling to pieces. The seams gaped, the planking was rotting away and the mast lay where it had fallen, cracked, seamed and whitened by the sun. They looked about them but there were no footprints in the sand, and the once broad, well-beaten path was overgrown with bush.

"Wait here," Tavi said. "When you see me appear at the edge of the cliff yonder, come and join me."

He made his way to the high land above the cliff. He found his mother sitting near their dwelling, so changed and wasted by the years that he scarcely knew her. He seated himself beside her.

"Well, Mother, home at last," he said.

"It is more than time," Haka-Hotu replied. "You have fished up lands?"

"After my fashion."

"How many?"

"Forty and five . . . No, forty and six."

His mother glanced at him. "I little thought to hear it, lazy as you were in your youth. Where are these lands?"

"Yonder," said Tavi, pointing eastward, "but a great distance beyond those of Mano's and Tumu's fishing. They have returned?"

"Long since. Even their strength was not equal to the tasks your father set them. To give you such news as there is to tell, they are dead, and your father as well."

"You have been alone here, since?"

"How else, with you away?"

"No more sons?"

Haka-Hotu made no reply, but stared seaward. Then she said: "It is plain that you, too, are near the end of your days."

"I feel that," said Tavi, "and so I came home. After we are gone, what then?"

"The age of the demigods is ended."

"That seems clear enough."

"A great change is coming over the Earth," his mother went on. "It has been long on the way. Living things are growing smaller. I remember my great-grandfather telling of the birds and beasts common in his youth. There were birds of great size with fanged teeth as well as claws. They would seize and carry away half-grown children who were in constant dread of them. And there were beasts so huge and fierce that half a dozen demigods were needed to kill one. All these have vanished. Why?"

"Who knows?" said Tavi. "Perhaps it was time for them to go, and ourselves with them. The Earth may not be large enough for creatures of such size. Think of Tumu, kicking over mountains!"

"You are nothing so big," said his mother; "not half the size of your brothers. And the last son . . ."

Tavi glanced at her. "Mano told you, perhaps. He could not drown the child, small as he was; for that reason it may be. So he asked me to do it. I, too, was reluctant; he was a handsome little fellow, quiet and good-natured. But your command was not to be disobeyed so I threw him into the sea."

Haka-Hotu sat, chin in hands, a look of desolation on her face. Tavi rose, strode to the edge of the cliff, stood there for a moment, and returned.

"Bitterly I repented," his mother said, "but then it was too late. You had gone."

"Why should you have repented? The child was small and puny, as you said. He showed even less promise of great strength than myself."

"We were proud, your father and I. Like all parents we rejoiced in the huge stature and strength of our sons. Then you came to your small growth, and the son who followed . . ."

"I have often wondered that you did not have me drowned as well," said Tavi. "Did you care for me at all, Mother?"

"Why not?"

"Little you showed it. My earliest recollections are of being slapped and cuffed from one place to another."

"It did you no harm. If the truth must be told, it was myself I punished for being fond of you."

"A strange way was that of taking punishment, and so my small drowned brother would say if he could know."

"He suffered but a moment. I have suffered since the day when I last saw you and Mano and Tumu far out at sea. You could not hear my voice calling you back."

"You would have saved the child?"

"I had long known what pride is," Haka-Hotu replied, "but

only from that day did I slowly learn what love is. I hated myself for giving way to it, for what has a mother of our race to
do with love? But he was so little . . ."

Haka-Hotu's voice faltered. With a huge thumb she
squashed a tear that was about to fall.

"And you loved him because of that or in spite of that?"

"Because of that, which is a shameful thing for a mother of
demigods to admit. What has happened to me? Is it old age
that has given me this tenderness of heart?"

"Perhaps it is part of the change you have spoken of," Tavi
said. "It may be that pride is to give place to love."

"How can there be either when we are gone? No living creatures will be left save these smaller forms of birds and beasts.
But that youngest son might have comforted my last days.
Often I have dreamed of him as he would be now: as much
smaller than yourself as you are smaller than your older
brothers."

"Tell me of those dreams," said Tavi.

His mother began. Presently she broke off, sensing another
presence. Slowly turning her head, she saw Maui standing
there.

*   *   *

Taio halted in his story, stretching his arms and giving a
great yawn.

"And there was Haka-Hotu," he said, "staring at her son,
Maui-the-Peaceful. She knew him because he looked just as she
had seen him in her dreams. And that's all for tonight. I will
tell you the rest some other time."

"Taio!" young Maui exclaimed. "You promised the story
from beginning to end!"

"You're not sleepy?"

All three boys said "No!" with one voice, and Ma'o said,
"You can rest a little while we ask some questions. You haven't
explained things."

"Éaha!" Taio said, gruffly. "What haven't I explained?"

"What is the skin of the sea?" Maui asked.

"That doesn't need explaining. What is the skin of your body? The outside layer, of course."

"But you can feel that," Ma'o said. "You can't feel the skin of the sea."

"You can if you touch it lightly; but only Tavi could lift it with all the colors in it. It is so thin that it can be seen only in certain kinds of light. That is why Tavi used it for the phantom islands."

"How could the one real island he fished up float?" Ru asked.

"By magic, of course," said Taio. "I have spoken of that."

"Is it true that the phantom islands are still where Tavi placed them?" Ma'o asked.

"Yes, that is certain," Taio replied, soberly. "Our ancestors have seen a few, but most of them are supposed to be far out there to the east."

"It was a cruel thing to build islands that are not real," said Maui. "Why did he want to mock our people?"

"He didn't," said Taio. "You must remember that there were no people at that time; only the demigods, and Tavi's family the last of them."

"Who fished up Kurapo?" Ru asked.

"Maui, tell this ignorant son of mine."

"Was it Mano, and Tumu-the-Witless?"

"Of course. What happened then?"

"I don't know," said Maui.

"What! You, the son of Téaro, our high chief?"

"My father has never told me."

"But I have, now, at your father's request. Use your eyes! Learn things for yourself! . . . Ma'o, tell this ignorant son of the high chief. He knows no more than Ru."

Ma'o sat, shamefaced and silent. The waning moon had just risen, silvering the surface of the calm sea and throwing its ghostly light against the sheer eastern wall of the central mountain whose jagged summit stood out clearly against the sky.

"It was here on Kurapo that Mano gave Tumu-the-Witless the mighty kick," said Taio. "The mountain here had twice the height when the island was fished from the sea. Tumu kicked off the peak. You see the dark gap in the ridge to the left? He tore that out with his hands. Where do you suppose that mass of rock is now?"

The boys were silent.

"It was one good thing Tumu did without knowing it. When Kurapo was fished up, the reef that now encloses the lagoon had no break in it. The rock Tumu hurled fell directly on the reef, making the fine passage we have now. It split apart when it struck the reef. The islet where we're sitting and the other across the passage were built up on those parts. . . . Now I will tell you the rest of the story."

*   *   *

Haka-Hotu lived but a short time, as time was then measured, after the return of Tavi and Maui-the-Peaceful. Her mind wandered often and her temper was uncertain. On some days she was gentleness itself; on others, peering down at her sons not half her stature, she became so enraged because of their small size that she would have killed them had she been able to catch them. She would imagine that she was living in times long past when the great battles were taking place. Then so much of her old strength returned that Tavi and Maui were obliged to keep clear of her. She would take up huge rocks to hurl at the ghostly parents whose sons, she imagined, were fighting Mano and Tumu. For the most part she slept, groaning and muttering in her sleep. One day she awakened, her mind clear, but she was very weak.

"I have had a strange dream," she told her sons, "but no idle one. I saw what is to come. The Earth is to be peopled again."

"With demigods?" Tavi asked.

"No," said his mother. "With creatures shaped like ourselves but far smaller even than Maui. And they will love battles as we did, but fight in a different manner."

"*Then they are doomed even before they appear upon the Earth,*" *said Tavi.*

"*Amongst them there will be a few who are lovers of peace,*" *said Haka-Hotu.* "*In the dream I saw these banded together because they hated killing. They fought bravely but only when attacked, to protect themselves and their families. But they were few against many. I saw them being driven to the borders of the sea where we now are, then going out upon it in their little boats, some from the cove below here. It was for them, perhaps, that we demigods were ordered to fish up lands.*"

They waited to hear more, but Haka-Hotu's mind clouded again, and so she remained until her death.

The sons buried her there; then Tavi took his brother on a journey far inland to show him the country where the demigods had lived. It was nothing but ruin and desolation. The forests had been destroyed and the once fertile valleys were strewn with great rocks hurled in the battles of former ages, and with the bones of the demigods who had perished in them. Tavi was greatly wearied by this journey. "Maui," he said. "I would not die in this wrecked and ruined land. Could you repair our canoe and make it strong and seaworthy again?"

Maui did this, and once more they sailed eastward, Tavi lying in the bottom of the canoe as before, and Maui steering. They passed the islands their brothers had raised, becoming more and more scattered until the last of them had been left behind.

"Where shall we sail now?" said Maui.

"Take me to my ringed island with the lagoon inside," said Tavi. They sailed there, and Maui helped his brother ashore. Tavi drew in the pure air with deep enjoyment. "What could be better," he said, "than this clean cool air of the solitudes of the Sea of Kiwa. If I had breathed it from babyhood as you have I think I should never die."

They remained there for some time; then Maui said: "Shall

we sail on now?" Tavi wished to, but his strength was not
equal to a longer voyage. Both knew that he was dying but
neither spoke of it. As always, they took great pleasure in being together. Tavi's manner of speech was one of quiet drollery
but by nature he was deeply serious. There was wistfulness in
his voice when they talked of his phantom islands.

"I love them, Maui, fool that I am," he said.

"They are more beautiful than the sea itself," his brother
replied.

"I am not so modest as to deny it, but what are they good
for? Speak the truth: do you love them as I do?"

"Yes," said Maui, "and for the same reason: because they will
remain as they are forever. No one can ever set foot on them."

"That is what I hoped you would say."

One day when Tavi had slept long, Maui returned to find
him just awakened, and with a strange expression upon his
face.

"Maui, I have dreamed out our mother's dream of what is to
come," he said. "It is true: there is to be another peopling of
the Earth, and a small number amongst those to come will
search this great sea for lands where they may live in peace."

"There are those fished up by our brothers," Maui said.

"The lovers of war will drive them from each one."

Maui smiled faintly. "Then let the peaceful ones sail on until
they find your phantom islands."

"You have been too long in my company," Tavi replied,
soberly. "You have acquired unconsciously something of my
surface nature. May you never be called Maui-the-Jester! That
is how I am to be known in the future: as a jester who built
phantom islands to sicken the hearts of the peaceful searchers
for real lands. I was told this in my dream."

"Told? By whom?" Maui asked.

"By Tané, the god of peace, who will be worshiped by these
voyagers."

"What more did he tell you?"

"Of the honor that is to be yours," Tavi replied, earnestly. "Of the immortality to be granted you if you obey him and guide these courageous wanderers."

"In their search for what?"

"The Far Lands of Maui. They are Tané's own but are to be called by your name. These lands have existed as long as the Great Sea of Kiwa in which they are hidden."

"In that case I can find them," said Maui.

"That is certain. You accept this service of Tané?"

"Willingly," said Maui.

"When you have found these lands sail westward again and you will then meet the first of the people you are to guide—already in the Sea of Kiwa, living on some of the islands raised by Mano and Tumu."

"How shall I lead them?" Maui asked.

"By your voice alone," said Tavi, "for they shall never see you. By the call that came of itself, as you thought. I was right in believing that it must have meaning, that call. Then, in the dream I was told something scarcely to be believed. I was told that even Tané's own lands, to be called by your name, are not so beautiful as some of my phantom ones."

"That I can understand," said Maui. "It is because Tané's lands are real and must be lived on by creatures of flesh and blood."

"Furthermore, I was told that, in guiding the searchers to come you are not to avoid my phantom islands. Surely this was wrongly dreamed. I misunderstood Tané's words."

"No," said Maui. "Tané wishes to prove the courage and the faith of the searchers for peace. He would have them conquer not only the dangers of the sea but also the bitter disappointment of hope deferred. And so they must if they are to be worthy of this quest."

"You believe that?"

"I am sure of it." He took his brother's hand. "Good-by. Wait for me here."

"I shall," Tavi replied, "but it is to be doubted that you will find me when you return. Your voyage eastward is far greater than any we have made together."

Maui went to his canoe, raised the sail and took the steering oar. As he crossed the lagoon toward the passage he waved his hand.

Tavi walked slowly to the seaward beach and seated himself there, watching the canoe growing smaller until the tip of the sail was lost to view. As the first stars were beginning to appear, he heard his brother's last farewell from horizons beyond horizons: the clear high call that had "come of itself" so long before.

Glossary

Ariki	a chief, or chiefs
A hio!	Look!
Au-é!	an expression of joy, sorrow, wonder, alarm, etc.
Au-é te matai-é!	Oh, the good wind!
Au-é, te ua-é!	Oh, the rain!
Ei'a!	Fish!
Haéré	Go
Haéré noa	Continue, or Keep going
Haéré tatou	Let us go
Haéré mai, te ua!	Come, the rain!
É	Yes
Hoé!	Paddle!
Ia ora na	An expression of greeting
Marae	A temple
Méarahi te ma'a!	Food, plenty of it!
Mamu!	Hush! Keep quiet!
Méa maitai-roa	Very good, or All is well
Maururu	An expression of thanks
O	It is (As in O Maui! — It is Maui!)
O vau?	It is I? (whom they want?)
Paia vau	I am not hungry, or I have enough
Parahi orua	An expression of farewell
Parau mau	It is true, or You are right
Pareu	A waistcloth
Tirara!	Enough! or It is ended
Vitiviti!	Hurry!

PHONETIC SPELLING FOR PRONUNCIATION OF NAMES

CHARACTERS

TONGAN CLAN

Téaro	(Tay-ah-ro)	High Chief
Maéva	(Mah-ay-vah)	His wife
MAUI	(Mow-ee)	Their son
Rata	(Rah-tah)	Brother of Téaro
Tauhéré	(Tow-hay-ray)	Maui's sister
Hotu	(Ho-too)	Mother of Téaro and Rata
Métua	(May-too-ah)	Priest of Tané (Tah-nay)
Tuahu	(Too-ah-hoo)	A chief
Tavaké	(Tah-vah-kay)	A chief
Paoto	(Pah-o-to)	A chief
Marama	(Mah-rah-mah)	A chief
Vana	(Vah-nah)	A chief — Rata's son-in-law
Nihau	(Nee-how)	A chief — Maui's brother-in-law
Pohi	(Po-hee)	A chief — son of Rata

LESSER CHARACTERS OF TONGAN CLAN

Taio	(Tie-oh)	Of Téaro's household
Vahiné	(Vah-hee-nay)	Taio's wife
Ru	(Roo)	Their son
Tamuri	(Tah-moo-ree)	Father of Vahiné
Rangi	(Rahn-gee)	A shipbuilder
Téma	(Tay-mah)	A shipbuilder
Manu	(Mah-noo)	A shipbuilder
Vaiho	(Vai-ho)	A shipbuilder
Ma'o	(Mah-oh)	Son of Rangi

KORO CLAN

Vaitangi	(Vai-tahng-ee)	High chief
HINA	(Hee-nah)	His granddaughter
Puréa	(Poo-ray-ah)	Hina's mother
Puaka	(Poo-ah-kah)	Priest of Koro
Uri	(Oo-ree)	Nephew of Puaka

(Note: In the pronunciation of the above names the stress is, in most cases, equal on all syllables.)

SHIPS

Tokèrau	(The Northwest Wind)	To-kay-rau
Te-Ava-Roa	(Long Passage)	Tay-Ahvah-Rooah
Iriatai	(The Horizon)	Ear-ee-ah-tie
Itatae	(The Ghost Tern)	Ee-tah-tie
Anuanua	(Rainbow)	Ah-nooah-nooah
Kotaha	(Frigate Bird)	Ko-tah-ha
Éata	(The Cloud)	Ay-ah-tah
Kiwa	(Te-Moana-Nui-a-Kiwa)	Tay-mo-ahnah-nooee-ah-keewah. Referred to as Kee-wah